ELIZABETH FORREST

RETRIBUTION

DAW BOOKS, INC.
DONALD A. WOLLHEIM, FOUNDER
375 Hudson Street, New York, NY 10014

ELIZABETH R. WOLLHEIM
SHEILA E. GILBERT
PUBLISHERS

First Printing, May 1998

1 2 3 4 5 6 7 8 9

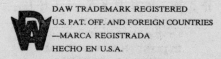

DAW TRADEMARK REGISTERED
U.S. PAT. OFF. AND FOREIGN COUNTRIES
—MARCA REGISTRADA
HECHO EN U.S.A.

PRINTED IN THE U.S.A.

Dedicated to those who suffered and we lost, and to those who suffered and we still are able to cherish . . .

Ryck Kirby, gone too soon, and

Gary Lee Sutton, for his sharing his love of tennis and teaching as long as he was able . . .

Jim Klohs, with our continued prayers . . .

Marj and Marty Azarow and Teren Guyan for sharing their experiences with me.

To my beloved Furr People:
Mason, Tyger, Princess Stinky . . . Rex, Willow, Sylvester, Junior, Melody, Pogo, Solo, Goliath, Star, Peggy, Hoppy, Mac, Jeannie, Buffy, Blaze, Raffles, Banjo and Dandy.

I gratefully acknowledge the following
for their help, friendship and expertise:

Dr. Dick Salsitz and his wife Tanya
Kirk Miller and the Open Door Gallery of Tustin
The colony of Laguna Beach
And, especially, Canine Companions for
Independence

Chapter One

"**M**ommy!"

She heard the cry through the thickness of her dreams and though it woke her, she lay for a moment, eyes still shut, wondering whether she had really heard something or not. Her skin felt more awake than the rest of her—warm, soft and yet raw, and she became aware that she nestled spooned against another body under the sheets, their naked forms intimately close. The realization jolted through her, waking her more quickly than even the thin sound of her daughter's voice as she called again.

"Mommy?"

She rolled out of the nest they had made, quickly and surely reaching for the worn robe she had tossed on the foot of the bed, taking care not to wake the man she left behind. As she belted the robe, she could smell him on her flushed skin, the perfume of their lovemaking surrounding her, and as she worried about her daughter, she also gloried in the rareness of the visitor, of the sensuality, of what they had shared. Mary took care to tuck the blankets in and about him, reluctant to let the bed cool while she went to see what troubled Charlie.

They had left most of the windows open, and a brisk sea-salt scented wind had chilled the small house down considerably. Mary pulled her robe a little tighter, and made a mental note to shut most of them before she returned to bed. If she returned to bed.

Charlie, who had always had a precocious ability to see in the dark, stirred the moment she reached the doorway of the tiny bedroom. She gave a little sigh.

"I'm sorry, Mommy."

Mary found the edge of the bed and sat on it, reaching out to search for her daughter's face, but Charlie caught up her hand immediately and held onto it. "It's all right, honey," she soothed. Her daughter's hand felt cool in hers. She could feel the rasp of whisker burn across her cheeks from Quentin's ardor, and she flushed at the thought that her daughter might see it on her face. She curled her fingers tightly about Charlie. "Did you have a bad dream?"

"Awful." Charlie shuddered and though her slender, wiry body scarcely filled the day bed, it trembled with her movement. "Is it midnight yet?"

"I'm sorry, honey. Not quite." Mary bent low over

her as she murmured, "It'll be fine." She tried not to let worry seep into her voice as she stroked Charlie's tangled hair away from her face with her free hand. So many bad dreams . . . and other things . . . happening to Charlie. She had precious little coverage in health insurance since Reynold had died, and their main doctor had seemed unconcerned. But Mary felt a wrongness in Charlie that seemed to cut through her, and worry bled right after it. "Can you tell me about it?"

"No," whispered Charlie hoarsely, tightly.

Her fingers felt like ice in Mary's. She rubbed them slightly, then pulled the blankets up higher and more firmly around her daughter's wiry, ten-year-old frame. "Sometimes it helps if you talk about it."

"No words," returned Charlie, and then panted a little as if even that had taken effort to say.

"Do you want me to turn on the light?"

Charlie shook her head. Mary felt it rather than saw it. "All right, hon. I can tell you a story."

Another quiet pant. Then, "Sing."

Mary hesitated, then pitched her voice quietly and began to sing "This Old Man," one of Charlie's favorites. "This old man, he had none, he played knick-knack on his thumb . . ." her voice went spinning into the night air.

When she had finished, there was a long silence. Her daughter still lay awake, barely warming to her touch. Mary was tired, and felt guilty that she wanted nothing more than to crawl back into bed, her shared bed, this night. She sighed in spite of herself, and Charlie flinched at the sound.

"Is he still here?"

Mary hesitated a moment, then answered, "Yes, honey, Quentin is still here."

"Good." Charlie squeezed her hand, some warmth finally seeming to return to her. "He'll keep us safe."

"Do you think so?"

"Oh, yes! Like Daddy did." Charlie scooted closer to her, curling her body about Mary's hip. "Is he going to stay a lot?"

"Maybe." Quentin had talked softly to her about marriage while they had made love, but she discounted that for the passion they shared. Morning would tell her if he meant it or not. "Would you like that?" She moved a long, wispy strand of Charlie's hair behind her ear. She wanted to be in bed with Quentin in the morning.

"I think so."

There was a slightly dubious note to her answer, no less than the doubt in her heart, but it had been years since Reynold died. She wondered how Charlie could even remember her father, as her own memories of her husband faded. Mary put the back of her hand to Charlie's forehead, felt it still clammy.

"Are you feeling better, honey?"

"Yes." Charlie took a deep breath. "Can you get

me a new canvas tomorrow? And paint, I need more paint."

Charlie, who never asked for anything, did not hesitate to ask for this. Mary stared across the dim view of the small Laguna bungalow, mentally drumming up a picture of her checkbook. She could get it if Charlie did not want too many tubes. She would have to budget their grocery money very carefully till the monthly death benefit check came in, but she thought she could manage even though her own paychecks were meager. "All right, love," she whispered toward Charlie's delicate, shell-like ear. "In the morning."

"I don't know what colors . . . I need to see the brochure again. When I see them, I'll know."

The art store they shopped at had given her brochures for each paint manufacturer, their color palettes spread across glossy pages in a near rainbow infinity of availability. Charlie, who had never had art lessons, and who painted with an intensity of genius, did not know the names of many of the colors until she seized upon their likeness in the brochure. And when Mary took her to the art store tomorrow, as Mary knew she would do, Charlie would often wander off and ask questions about the paints, the undercoats, the preparations, the combinations, and sometimes come back with a request for another tube or two. But she never asked for anything she did not use.

Mary found herself smiling in the night. "I know you'll know," she answered. She leaned forward still more until her lips brushed Charlie's face, and she kissed her daughter. Charlie's breathing had already begun to slow and deepen, as she fell back into sleep. She wondered what Charlie would paint, knowing that this was how her daughter coped with the overwhelming feelings of loss and fear they had both been plunged into . . . the dreams that brought both terrible nightmares and soaring hope to her child . . . and once she committed them to canvas, Charlie would sleep well again for days, sometimes weeks. Her daughter's breathing grew even more regular. *So quickly*, Mary thought, *so deeply*. Did children ever realize how wonderful it was to sleep so easily?

She would not leave till her daughter's fingers went limp in hers, and the breathing became a gentle purr.

In the morning, Quentin would wake, and ask Mary again, his proposal heartfelt, and her answer even more so.

And Charlie would miss the first half of a school day while she pondered her choices from the brochure and again at the art supply shop, finally selecting a handful of vivid paints: yellows, oranges, violets, and whites.

And all that week she would work with fever pitch on a painting that took Mary's breath away, and she decided finally that she had to show someone else her daughter's paintings, that even in a colony of the talented like Laguna Beach she had to know and understand what Charlie was doing.

The art supply shop manager would gasp when he saw what Charlie had finished, and chide Mary for carrying it about when the paint was still drying and the surface could be marred, and he'd place a call to a local, well-known gallery owner who would drive over immediately in his BMW and pale when he saw what Charlie had painted. Charlie would stand in quiet ten-year-old shyness and say little until the owner asked her what paints she had used, and then she would rattle them off.

"Do you have any more like this?" the gallery owner would ask keenly.

Charlie would hesitate a moment and then answer, "Not like that."

Her mother would say quickly, "She has filled my screened porch with paintings."

And Charlie would look at her intently, then flush slightly with embarrassment or firmness, as she disagreed, saying, "Not like that. It is the first of three."

"Three?" the gallery owner would prompt.

"There will be three of them," Charlie would answer forthrightly.

"A trilogy!" the gallery owner would respond in delight.

Charlie would only shrug. "I need three to do it right," she would insist politely.

And the gallery owner would look avidly at Mary, saying, "I would like to do a show for her, if the other paintings are as good. This is talent, a bit raw, but talent that most of us would give our left arm for."

And Mary, strangely unsurprised at his response, would agree to show him the other paintings and to a public viewing.

And from that moment, Mary and Charlie would never look back. She would gasp when the gallery owner priced the paintings first at ten, then twenty, then fifty thousand dollars. Charlie would begin to show a polish in the public eye as she attended shows and interviews and talked with prospective buyers of her art from around the world. Quentin loved them all fiercely, and put Charlie's money aside for her, and there would never be a doubt in anybody's mind that this was a family, knit together by love, and holding strong.

Then Charlie would begin work on what she called the second painting, after a month of troubled dreams and fitful nightmares, and the finished canvas would be almost as much a subject of controversy as her young genius had been in the first place. The second painting would be as dark and horrifying as the first had been full of light and buoyancy.

But they would take it all in stride until the evening when Charlie would be interviewed on global news unveiling the painting, and she would go into seizure and collapse in front of God and everyone, and Mary would wonder if her own heart would stop forever.

Chapter Two

"Clarkson!"

Wade turned around in the tiny, dingy locker room, tossed his scrubs into a nearby barrel for cleaning, and elbowed his locker shut. He wanted not to hear the bellow, but it thrust its way behind gummy eyes and a head that pounded with an ever thickening need to rest and sleep. With a sigh, he put his hand behind his neck to rub muscles that felt lumpier than the sagging mattress he was heading for, and tried to knead them looser as he stumbled toward the door.

"In here, Dr. Phelmans."

The locker room door pushed open. A beacon of yellow light from the main hospital corridor came streaking across the old, brown glazed linoleum as the immense doctor entered.

"Not good, Clarkson, not good at all." Phelmans waved a clipboard full of performance evaluation sheets in his beefy hand.

Wade stared at him, fatigue seeping through every pore of his body, and wondered if Phelmans could ever have worked the kind of shift he just had. If he had once, he couldn't do it now . . . the sheer bulk of the doctor's body would drop him in his tracks, just as it wearied Wade even to look at him.

Phelmans peered at him as though hoping for a response. Wade knew better. A response opened argument. He did not want to argue. He just wanted to be allowed to get in his car, drive back to his crummy apartment and lumpy bed, and crawl into oblivion. He looked down at his chief and inhaled deeply, as though fresh air alone could revive him. He did not take drugs to keep going, as some of his fellow residents did, nor did he rely heavily on caffeine. It was sheer willpower, and the love of what he did, and the adrenaline from doing it right that kept him going through shifts as long as seventy-two hours without more than a few hours sleep caught on the fly.

"Your reports, Clarkson, are late."

"I handed in my reports through the computer, Dr. Phelmans."

The doctor's heavy face flushed pinkly, and his piglike eyes glittered in hard triumph. "If there is one thing I have tried to pound into your minds again and again, it is not to depend on the computer system. The computer is down, Clarkson, and your reports are late."

A surge of irritation carrying a spark of energy not unlike a rush buoyed Wade up for a moment. Phelmans hated the computer system. He could not use it well himself, and Wade knew that the hatred covered the doctor's fear and inadequacies.

"What the frigging use is it if it never functions! I did my work."

"That is beside the point. You use an unreliable system for your reports, and expect the hospital to suffer the consequences? I hope you do not intend to leave until those reports are ready to hand in." A dark vindictiveness glittered at the back of Phelmans' eyes.

Wade took a deep breath. He would not win this fight . . . he had never won any of them yet and did not expect to until the day he logged his last minute of work.

He reached for his locker and yanked it open, grabbed a sheaf of papers in a folder, searched through it, pulled out ten wrinkled forms, and replaced the folder. "Here's the originals . . . handwritten. It's the best I can do." He shoved the forms at the doctor.

Phelmans sputtered a moment as he took the papers, shuffled through them, the crimson in his face settling toward purple. He muttered to himself as he sorted the papers, then attached them to his clipboard. "Bear in mind, Clarkson, that paperwork does not make a good surgeon. I shall be evaluating your reports carefully. Already I see an unnecessary CBC you ordered." He cleared his throat. "Not everyone has what it takes to be a doctor."

With years behind him and spare months stretching before him, Wade kept his mouth shut. His jaw ached with the tension, he could feel it arcing into his neck. He made no attempt to keep the contempt he felt from creeping across his face.

Phelmans looked at him, and he knew the other saw it, and read it clearly. "And, Clarkson. . . . I want you back here in twelve hours to start the next shift."

"Twelve! I'm up for twenty-four hours off." During which time he had planned to sleep like the dead.

"I know what your schedule is, and I have changed it. When you become a real doctor, Clarkson, you will discover that sickness and pain do not keep a schedule. Your patients will need you when they need you, not when you need them. Is that understood?"

"If it wasn't, you have made it so." He slammed the locker door shut with a resounding clang. "I'll be here."

The fat doctor's mouth worked a moment, uttered nothing, tightened. With a speed Wade would not have guessed possible, the doctor turned on his heel and left. Wade swallowed in an effort to ease his throat and followed him, the brightness of the outer corridors, the newly painted walls, the outer face of the hospital stunning with promise, cheer, and competence. The contrast was stark to the inner rooms he had just left.

Phelmans disappeared ahead of him into another corridor, leading to the staff doctors' offices. Wade rolled his shoulders, exhaled, and headed to the parking lot.

After the illumination of the hospital, he found himself dazed for a moment as he stepped into total darkness, clouds shunting across the sky, glowering, black, and the pavement rain-darkened. Even as he stepped out, the rain began again, pelting heavily, and he broke into a trot to his car. Puddles sprayed as he hit them, and the cuffs of his trousers immediately became sodden. The lock on the car door stubbornly refused to accept the key smoothly, and water slicked his hair down and chilled the back of his neck before he finally got the door open and slid into his battered sedan.

The cars he drove past all resembled his: worn, old, dinged, with rust-eaten edges. As he got ready to pull out of the main lot, he cast a look back in his rearview mirror to the doctors' lot . . . gleaming, new, expensive cars in a sheltered garage lot, their metallic forms barely visibly in the driving rain and glare of his vehicle's headlights. There were days when that view cheered him. Tonight was not one of them.

Despite the storm, he put the driver's side window down halfway, letting the rush of cold air hit his face, keeping him awake, if chilled and damp. His eyelids burned as he watched the road, winding into the countryside, the trees bent and curving, their leaves lashing blackly in the night. This was not a night he wanted to be out in. He prayed that the worn tires of the car would hold the asphalt, that he could ride the thinning beams of the headlights all the way home, to sleep, to rest.

And he fought the rough burning of discouragement inside him. They wanted him to quit, just like all the others, would ride him unmercifully and he had to get through, he had to . . . but if someone were to give him two cents right now, he would turn around, find Phelmans, and tell him to shove the residency up his fat ass. What kind of hospital worried about a blood panel when they'd just spent over half a mil overhauling the doctors' dining room? Was that the kind of medicine he wanted to be bogged down in the rest of his life? The brutal workload facing him if he decided to specialize further would bury him if he let it. Pigs like Phelmans cared nothing about talent or compassion. They were in medicine to support their appetites for old ex-wives, new trophy wives, fancy cars, and big country clubs. Wade had seen enough of them to fill his craw for a lifetime. He could transfer his surgery residency to another hospital; he'd had interest, he could do it. Or he could quit altogether. He had options.

He took a deep breath, letting the icy raindrops the speed of the car carried in brace him against the curtain of sleep, the overwhelming need to rest, that kept threatening to descend on him. He must have drifted, for the wheel suddenly jerked under his hands, and the car swayed as another car passed him, horn angrily bleating. Wade shook himself and held steady as the vehicle whooshed on ahead, wavering back and forth across the lanes.

The car faded to a pair of red taillights, and his eyes narrowed to watch them, the driver uncaring or unable to hold a smooth passage over the road. The son of a bitch had to be drunk. He was lucky he hadn't been run into a ditch. The car skidded sideways over an especially damp patch, then accelerated so rapidly Wade lost all sight of it on the curving road.

The rain had stopped, but the lane stayed glistening black, tires spraying through the layer of water left behind. Wade settled his hands about the wheel more firmly. He found himself thinking of Southern California with its vast freeways, sunshine, and newer hospitals. He inhaled to clear his mind.

Afterward, he was not able to say if he heard it first or saw it. Seeing would have been impossible, of course, because the trees and bends hid it. So he heard it . . . the screeching of brakes, the high piercing sound of desperation, and the tumultuous crash of metal and chrome and plastic and impact. Beams pierced the night hanging over the treetops, like lightning, sweeping in first one direction, then another. He did not understand what he saw although he feared what he would discover after the next bend.

Even his fear did not prepare him for the carnage. On the rain-slicked road bodies lay strewn as though tossed there like dice. One vehicle, crumpled and torn nearly in two, had come to a rest canted upward in a ditch, its headlights beginning to yellow. Body damage was so gross, it was no wonder its occupants had been thrown out. Bits of clothing and shoes knocked off by the impact lay in sodden puddles. The other car, the one he recognized, lay on its roof, the driver crawling out a nearly nonexistent door. Dear God, it was not enough to kill himself, but he had to take others with him. . . .

He pulled over, tires crunching on debris, his heart in his throat, no doubt in him that he should stop, a thought niggling in the back of his mind that this was disaster, what could he do, and he could get sued if he could not help the helpless. Phelmans would not stop. He would slow, shout that he was going for help, and would drive on down the road to the country club two miles ahead, where phones existed.

Wade did not think that anyone lying on the asphalt would live till EMTs could arrive.

He turned the key and the car shut down. It seemed forever till he could open the door and swing his feet out, and hear the broken breathing of the victims, the moans, and someone sobbing. The air stank of burning oil and rubber and spilled fuel. It reeked of blood as he approached the victims. Glass scattered like gleaming diamonds and crunched with his every step.

He knelt by the first one, even though he knew there was no hope, and put his hands to the neck to check for a pulse. The flesh so warm . . . the heart so still. A teenage boy, with malt-brown hair, his throat almost gone, eyes staring upward at Wade in stark astonishment. It was his blood he had smelled so strongly, spilled in a huge pool under him, spilling out no longer. Clarkson put the eyelids down, then straightened and started toward the next.

"Shit," someone said. Wade turned slightly and looked.

The man had gotten to his knees, his hands up toward his face, almost completely untouched . . . except for the arrowlike piece of window framing that pierced his throat. Blood trickled out between his fingers. He stared at Wade.

"You gotta help me."

"Don't touch it," Wade told him. "I'll be right there." Disgust rose in his own throat with a burning sensation.

The drunk sank down on his haunches, back braced against the tire wheel of the car, and began a litany of cursing and sobbing. Wade crossed the road swiftly to the other car. A body hung upside down in the shell of the wrecked car, and one look was all it took to determine that the driver had not lived as well. He turned back to three more bodies on the road. The girl had ceased crying and now sat up, her face dead white in the eerie illumination from the cars. She looked at him, blinked, and tried to make a sound. Blood smeared her face, and her left arm hung at an unnatural angle.

Shock, a minor scalp wound, and a broken arm, perhaps even a broken collarbone. She would be all right, though, unless there were internals he could not possibly diagnose now. A group of teens in a car . . . going to see a movie? Coming back from the pizza parlor and pool hall? Just out cruising? They would never, ever, climb in a car again with those friends, expecting the same good, exciting things to happen. Never again.

The boy sprawled at her feet made a spasmodic movement and tried to take a breath. Wade almost froze at the sound . . . sucking chest wound. Then he knelt by the boy and saw the damage. Even with a surgical team, and an operating room and equipment, and time he did not know if he could save him. On the midnight-dark, rain-slicked pavement, with only his hands and the few things thrown in the back seat of his car . . . Wade found himself shaking his head.

The girl in shock let out a tiny sob. "Help him,"

she said. "You've gotta help him!" She tried to get to her feet with a shudder and began weeping.

"Stay there. Just stay where you are. You're hurt, too."

She put her hand to her head, brought it down splotched with blood that looked like ebony patches in the half light from the headlights. She turned her hand one way and the other, not comprehending what she saw on her fingers.

"Hey! I gotta get some help!"

The drunk bellowed at Wade. He looked up and saw the man stumbling toward him, carrying a cellular phone unit in one hand, and the piece of car framing in the other. He had pulled it out, and a torrent of blood began to cascade down the side of his throat. He cleared his throat, or tried to, and toppled to his knees.

The cellular unit was a newer one, about the size of a small toaster, and he had it sealed in a plastic baggy. Wade grabbed it from him, not only for the use of the phone, but for the baggy . . . for the sucking chest wound. The man let it go and began to sob. Wade took his hand and put it into the neck wound, saying, "Hold this and don't let go." The wound was simple enough, clean, the puncture relatively small. Direct pressure would seal it without any problems. The drunk swayed back onto his haunches and sat for a moment, his stubby fingers pressed into his neck.

Wade emptied the phone from the baggy. He shoved the phone at the girl who had stopped sobbing and was now making tiny, breathless gasps, repeating over and over again, "Oh, God, oh, God."

"Call 911."

She looked at the phone unit in stupor.

"Pick it up and call 911. Tell 'em we're about two miles south of the country club on S16."

She looked at him, nothing in her eyes.

"God dammit!" Wade roared at her. "Pick up the phone and make the call!"

She jumped. The jolt moved her wretched arm, and she let out a scream of pain, but that pain seemed to clear the expression on her face. She bit her lip, hissing back the agony, and looked at him. "I can get help. I'll . . . I'll call."

He nodded roughly. He took the baggy and pressed it into the jagged chest wound, easing it in, praying he could get it into place, his tired hands now cold and clumsy, and was having no success when the drunk suddenly let out a wheeze and collapsed onto the pavement.

Wade looked from one to the other. He could save the driver. He knew that, but it would take him away from saving the other. One would be a sure success, the other a desperate bid to do the impossible. He reached for the drunk, and put his hand in the wound, felt the pulsing vein and slick surface, and the tiny tear, warm blood bubbling up around his hand as he compressed and held it.

The boy arched his back, fighting for air, his face already cyanotic. Young, so much younger than the face Wade looked at in the mirror whenever he found time to shave. Had he ever been that young? And if he did nothing, the teen would never move into older years, into the realization of what it was he was meant to do, and who it was he was meant to be.

Clarkson had heard others talk about it, quietly, overheard, rather, because medical staff did not like to admit they had ever come to such conclusions . . . but there inevitably came a time when one flipped a coin and either saved a life or let it go. He did not know what yardstick they measured by, whether it came from within or without, but he only knew as he knelt there that the waste, the sheer waste, of the boy's life sickened him.

He looked at the life sprawled before him, as it died, and took his fingers out of the neck wound, his chilled hand heated by the blood, and reached for the dying teen, and the plastic envelope, and began to work, as quickly and competently as he knew how. He guided it into place, and felt the sucking pressure of the lung as it took in the patch, and the boy took a clear breath, then another. He could not take his hands out of the chest cavity, though, for he felt certain that he was maintaining pressure on a bleeder which he could not see or diagnose, but which his hands told him was there, had to be there, and so he stayed, unmoving, as the far away sound of sirens began to pierce the air.

He knelt next to the boy, his hands buried in him, saving him and watched the dark pool under the drunk spread and then reach a kind of saturation point as the heart ceased to pump. He never knew that he was dying . . . never suffered . . . would never realize the lives he had already taken on this curve.

Clarkson reflected that the dead man was lucky.

When the paramedics reached them, they would take care to load the teen so that Wade could keep the pressure on, helping him step into the back of the van, dislodging him as little as possible. They would take the girl as well, and send for a second unit for the dead, and the one unconscious teen who seemed to have few injuries despite his state.

Phelmans would grudgingly give him an additional twenty-four hours off, for the press coverage had focused on the plight of the young, exhausted doctor, doing whatever he could, on a godforsaken, rain-soaked stretch of road. The news channels would mention the hospital frequently, and good press was always welcome.

There would even be a moment when Phelmans would grasp Wade by the shoulders and say jovially to the news crew, "What do we have here? I tell you what we have here . . . the makings of a damn fine surgeon!"

And the camera would catch Wade looking at his hands in an unguarded, reflective moment . . . looking at his hands as if trying to determine what miracle had anointed him, had given him the means to do the impossible.

Chapter Three

John Rubidoux swung his legs out of his car and stood, his dress blues scratching as he did, and even before locking the door and shutting it, he had a finger between his collar and his neck, trying to ease the stiff material away. He could feel the sunlight being sucked in, already hot against his skin. He didn't remember the collar being that tight or just plain irritating. The driver's side mirror flashed in his eyes, even the heavy-duty sunglasses he wore didn't quite catch the glare. He saw himself reflected in the side windows . . . tall, straight, coat with shiny buttons, police cadet insignia . . . and dark glasses that hid the expression on his face.

The graduation ceremonies for which his family had planned for months would not be taking place today . . . or rather, they would be held, as they were held every spring, but he would not be attending because of the page he had received earlier. Instead, he would be standing in a hospital breezeway, hoping that his police dress blues would grant him access away from the jostling crowds of reporters and TV crewmen. . . . standing just long enough in the hope of seeing the doctor who intended to save the life of the man who'd killed his father.

John spotted the camera trucks littering the far end of the parking lot, and drew away from them, knowing that his uniform would draw them like honey drew flies, not wanting to give them yet another angle to their news story.

Son of murdered cop forgoes his own graduation to protest the court-ordered lifesaving operation granted to the murderer on Death Row . . . film at eleven.

Oh, yes, they would stampede to get juicy tidbits like that. He had no intention whatsoever of finding himself laid open again, his mother, his family stripped and bared, sore wounds probed and poked viciously to see if there was a spark of life or emotion in them. He had seen it before on the outside, and since he had begun training as a cadet, on the inside, and it sickened him almost as much as the events which brought him to the hospital surgical center now.

Sun beat down on him, on the newly parted crease in his hair, he could feel it on a tender scalp that should have been covered by his hat, but he'd tossed that into the back seat. When he took a deep, steadying breath, the faint tang of smog and pollution bit at his lungs. Oh, yeah, welcome to L.A. All you snowbirds, just come flooding in, enjoy the gangs, the freeways, the smog. The death.

The killers.

John strode into the breezeway which connected the doctors' parking lot with the back entrances to the building, found a shady corner, and leaned into it, prepared to wait. He was fairly certain he would not have to wait long; the operation had been set for one p.m., PDST, according to the newscasts, the soonest the surgical team could set it up after getting the court order at nine that morning. The irony of it all had never ceased to amaze John. He wished his father could have had a court order keeping him alive.

It was not enough that a convicted, brutal murderer like Dover could sit on a California death row for ten, fifteen years while his attorneys exhausted the appeals system. It was not enough that he lived, but now that his own body threatened him, the state fought to keep him alive . . . so that it could execute him later, the legal system permitting. He had a brain aneurysm, a fatal, ballooning bubble in an artery, and the only thing John could think was that if it ruptured, it would be too quick and clean a death for a bastard like Dover. But his attorneys had fought for treatment, despite the fact that Dover faced execution . . . and this morning they had won.

Wearily, John put his shoulder to the stuccoed wall

of the breezeway and winced slightly as he did, the shoulder still tender from years of basketball in school and college, reminding himself, thank God, that it was not a knee, because if it had been a knee, he would not have gotten through cadet training. Justice be damned. He waited to make a final appeal, a *human* appeal, to the doctors who would be coming in soon to scrub up and read angiograms and MRIs and decide how they were going to save Dover's life. He would beg them, if he had to, not to operate.

The world did not need Dover. It was infinitely better off without a vicious rapist who violently, permanently, mutilated his victims . . . when he did not outright butcher them. John did not wait just for himself or his family, but for the ten families who had suffered loss and unbelievable outrage, nine dead victims, a half a dozen other scarred victims, and the tenth family like his, a cop's family. Two of the finest had died cornering Dover and bringing him in. There was no sense in a world which would try Dover, and then let him linger, laughing behind bars, at what he'd done . . . a world which would save Dover from the justice his own body perpetrated against him.

It had seemed a strange kind of fortune when the news stories had started trickling out as Dover's lawyers filed their first round of appeals. Immersed in training as a cadet, Rubidoux had not paid too much attention in the beginning to any of the follow-ups to the trial. It had been difficult enough dodging the few reporters who had followed him around the first couple of days as he'd entered the police academy. Scavengers, jabbing and thrusting for any morsel they could steal from the wreckage of his life. Over the months, he had learned to block them out, and even rumors of health problems for Dover had not caught his attention as graduation loomed. Then his mother had called.

She had not cried when his father was killed. Not in front of him or the others, but he knew she cried. Sometimes when he called to check up on her, the serenity would be gone from her voice, the cheerfulness that he had heard his whole life, vanished, her tone hollow and thickened.

But she was weeping when she called him, the noise thin and upsetting to hear, and the words came through almost garbled. "The son of a bitch is dying, and they're going to court to save him."

How she said what she said shook him almost as much as what she said. "Ma . . . what?"

"I said, the son of a bitch is dying, and his goddamn lawyers are going to court for medical treatment to save him."

He remembered looking across the tiny courtyard of the building he lived in, seeing the ferny branches and lush purple blossoms of the jacaranda trees which lined the streets of the old residential area, a sea of smoky indigo, rising above asphalt shingle and tile rooftops. He heard, but it took a few moments to sink in. His body ached down to the bones from the past few days of obstacle course prep and the feeling seemed to sink down into that ache, piercing him.

"Ma, do you want me to come home?"

It was the only thing he could think of to say. It came unexpectedly out of his core, where thought did not seem to exist.

It stopped her crying. She took a deep, shuddering breath. "No, Ruby, that's all right. I just wanted you to know."

"Now tell me again."

"He has a brain vessel that's about to burst. It's likely to be fatal. They refused him surgery, so his lawyers are suing. They're going to get a court order and a surgical team is standing by as soon as it goes through. Is there a God in heaven that keeps this man alive when your father is *gone*?" Her voice rose until it nearly disappeared altogether.

"I'm driving out tonight."

She sighed. Then, "Bring your laundry."

"I can't do that!"

"Hon, I need something to do. Something to keep me from thinking!"

That had been two weeks ago, and it was like when he had first been told his father had died in the line of duty. Everything changed, and nothing would be the same again.

RETRIBUTION

He found himself standing with fists clenched, his jaw so tight the cords on his neck stood out, his temples throbbing with the pressure. John forced himself, bit by bit, to let go, pulling in short, forced breaths. He had not become a cop because of anger. He had done it because of his father's intense pride and belief in the job, instilled in the son as well. If his father had been given a choice to live or die in finding and stopping Dover, he would still have done what he did. John felt that as strongly as he'd felt his grief at the outcome.

Spring heat, hinting at what summer in the basin could be like, washed in from the parking lot, light waves shimmering. His throat had gone cottony. He shoved a hand into his pants pockets, felt a number of quarters lingering in there, and ducked inside the hospital to see if he could find something cold to drink.

The wing entrance lay next to the cafeteria. He could smell coffee on the air and something that held the aroma of meat loaf, and the garishly painted vending machines caught his eye as he tracked down the aromas. He found a relatively unflavored brand of bottled iced tea he liked and plinked his quarters in, grabbed the chilled container and twisted it open, taking nearly half the bottle in the first gulp. Wetness and sweetness flooded his dry mouth and throat in a satisfying tide.

At the far end of the corridor, which probably teed

into the main part of the hospital, he heard doors ratchet open and close almost as rapidly, shutting out a roar of noise and clamor. John froze, bottle in hand, watching as the contingent entered the corridor, headed his way.

One of the three men shrugged out of his coat, throwing it over his arm, muttering, "I'm getting something to drink before we go up," and striding to the machines. The other two, braced by two hospital security guards, stopped and waited uneasily.

John's hand tightened around the iced tea. It surged upward, splashing over his fingers. He looked down stupidly at the spill; the only thought he could focus on was that his quarry had gotten in, gotten past him, and he could not cut them off now, not with security escorting them.

The surgeon fishing quarters out as he approached was nearly as tall as John, raven-black hair combed back, and eyes a piercing blue color. He was older than Rubidoux, but without a doubt much younger than the other two.

His eyes met John's just before he put his hand up and fed his coins in.

John wet his lips. "Don't do this," he said. "Don't keep a murderer alive."

The surgeon's face twitched slightly, but he did not look away except for the seconds it took to find a selection button and push it. When he looked back, his eyes swept John's uniform.

"I'm a doctor," he returned quietly. "It's what I'm trained to do."

He did not move as the container dropped, but kept his eyes fixed unwaveringly upon John.

"He's on Death Row. So what if he dies a little sooner."

"I didn't put him there."

"My father did!"

The surgeon flinched then, hiding his movement by reaching down to get his drink. He opened it and took a long swallow before eyeing John again. The group milling around at the intersection split open for a second, and a pepper-haired man said impatiently, "Dr. Clarkson, I am waiting for you."

Clarkson smiled slightly, as if knowing that John inhaled that name, remembering it for all time. "I have my job," he said. He reached out and touched the police insignia lightly. "You have yours." He toasted John with his soft drink. "May we both do it well."

He turned and loped away, before John could add another word of plea. The guards framed him and the group marched into the bowels of the hospital.

The splash of coldness over his hand brought John back. Looking down, he saw that he had squeezed his plastic container in two. The contents had drenched his hand and the carpet at his feet. He took a swallow of the remainder, found it had gone suddenly bitter, and slammed it into the waiting trash bin.

Had he really expected to make a difference?

He told himself as he left that he had not, but the knot in his throat and stomach told him otherwise; just as his father had always hoped, he thought he could make a difference, and that he had to try. The failure settled in him like a burning ulcer, and it would never leave. Not late that afternoon when he heard on the radio that Dover had nearly died during surgery, but that the brilliant young assistant Clarkson had demonstrated a new technique, saving him. Nor would that sense of defeat leave as Rubidoux went on patrol, and the waves of riots swept by him, and crime, and drugs, and violent marriages. Every triumph eased the burn a little and made his decisions bearable. He wondered sometimes if Clarkson felt the same.

Chapter Four

"Clarkson, I want you to head the team on this one. I'll assist, of course, but I think you've proved yourself."

Wade looked across the walnut conference table at Dr. Kevin Eisner and tried not to let triumph be read in his features, but gave a confident nod instead, thinking how far he had come from Phelmans' disdain of his abilities. "I'd be pleased to." Although pleasure could not describe the well-being he felt. The stories-high windows gave him an excellent view of Los Angeles, haze and all, and of the palm trees far below swaying in a slight wind. He would not trade all the clean air of his former residency for the view he looked at now. "Let me know how the team fills out."

"Good. I'm going to be sending you her full medical charts for you to go over later this afternoon, but I will tell you her surgery is already scheduled for

Wednesday, nine a.m." Eisner paused, his mild brown eyes blinking. "Not to bring a human element into this, but this young lady has two small children at home and a concerned husband, and in my dealings with her, I have found her to be an exceptional person. You might want to step in this evening after rounds and you've gone over her charts, and talk with them . . . let them know what procedures we'll be using and what the prognosis is." Eisner cleared his throat. "They're rather overwhelmed by all this."

"First thing this evening, then." Wade sketched himself a note on the pad in front of him.

Eisner nodded. He flipped through the paperwork he held, turned to Dr. Emilio Chavez, and began to assign another case as Clarkson rocked back slightly in his chair.

In the office which had been given to him, a room with a single bank of windows overlooking hazy freeways and the hospital grounds from a number of floors up, he thumbed through the various printouts and tests. The surgical procedure would be demanding, but Linda Elliot's prognosis was excellent. He should have no trouble as the operation presented itself, and it pleased him to know he could tell her and the family that. It was a benefit of the grueling work that he did . . . the grateful smiles, sighs of relief, and an occasional hug. Sometimes the joy would be so bountiful that he would stand there ignored and yet the tide of celebration would flood him and that would be enough.

And yet, there would always be that time when he had looked into a young policeman's face and found himself remarking that it was his job to save a killer. A fresh memory that, the anger and disappointment looking back at him, and the uneasiness that he had somehow betrayed himself by doing it.

Wade closed the folder and put his Mont Blanc pen on top of it to remind himself to make notes on it before he left for the evening. In the meantime, he had rounds to make, and a family to reassure.

Eight-thirty a.m. on a cloudy Wednesday, he scrubbed up, and by ten-thirty was well into an operation going routinely. At ten-thirty-one, he hit a bleeder that would not stop, weakened blood vessels started to collapse into mush, and the nightmare began from there. Eisner worked elbow to elbow with him, both of them moving frantically and precisely, and when they gave up at eleven-oh-seven and called her death, he hardly had time to take a breath. Warm blood drenched his surgical gloves and splattered his gown. He took a moment, looking down at the body, chest cavity sliced open for a heart massage, a desperate last-ditch attempt to bring her back, and knew that there was nothing he could have done.

The operation should have gone smoothly. He

looked at his hands, turned them over, searched them front and back for the flaw, for the betrayal.

Eisner thumped him on the shoulder. "It happens, Clarkson."

Wade did not respond as the nurses began to clean up the operating theater, preparing for the next surgery, drawing a paper sheet over the body. It did not happen to him. Not any more. Not since he had been anointed.

Clarkson looked at the blood on his gloves, haunted by the thought that he had tampered with the balance of life by saving Dover, and what the retribution had been. He stripped his gloves off and tossed them in the hazmat container in the corner of the theater.

What he did not know was how to get his blessing returned.

Days later, he still struggled. Wade did not feel like a society dinner and benefit as the weekend approached, but the head of surgery had let him know subtly that his attendance was not optional, that there would be many functions like this and it was almost as much a part of his position as a surgeon at the hospital to attend these as it would be to operate. The valet took his car keys as he got out of his new white-and-gold-trimmed Acura Legend and he settled his shoulders into his tux jacket with a deep breath. At the head of the flagstone steps to the Bel

Air residence, Kevin Eisner joined him and flashed him a grin.

"Glad you could make it, Wade."

They shook hands. Eisner looked more relaxed than Wade could ever remember seeing him, his tux jacket open, and brocaded vest restraining what had begun to be a pouching stomach. Eisner nodded in approval at his appearance. "See you took my advice on the tux."

"You're my senior, Dr. Eisner. It would be foolish not to listen to you outside the hospital as well as inside." Wade smiled ruefully. The tux had set him back nearly a grand, and the alterations had topped it. The paychecks coming in were substantially better than those he had received before, but there were debts, massive ones, to be repaid. And then, of course, there was the car. One had to have a car in L.A.

His supervisor tweaked the tux lapel a bit. "You'll need a couple of those babies, but one benefit at a time, eh?" Eisner slapped his shoulder blade. "Abby will be pleased to see how good you look in one."

Abigail Switzer was the major hospital donor who was funding this soirée, a formidable woman from all accounts. Wade unconsciously straightened, bracing himself for the ordeal of meeting her.

Eisner's eyebrows twitched. "A handsome young doctor always brings in the bucks at these things. Unless I miss a guess, she'll be roping you into doing the bachelor auction for Valentine's Day. Take some advice—say yes, and enjoy yourself." The older doctor grinned as he brought his highball glass to his lips and took a sip of what looked to be Scotch on the rocks. His wedding band gleamed in the porch light.

"I aim to please."

"Good. Come in and enjoy yourself. Watch the booze and cheer up a little." Eisner winked. "We can't win 'em all."

Clarkson did not like the analogy of surgery as winning or losing. It was a skilled attempt and nothing of chance should reign within it. But he could not argue with Eisner. Some things seemed beyond his skill at the moment. Uneasily, Wade followed the surgeon into the house, through a sprawling front room and toward the back. Eisner thumped him on the back before saying, "My wife is waiting for me at the tables," and stepping past. French doors to the patio revealed an expansive backyard done up in a Mardi Gras theme, with harlequin masks and golf cart floats being driven along the edges of the lawn, people riding them laughing and throwing out beads and whatnots to the other guests. A lot of flash and glitter and money. There were craps and baccarat tables and a row of what looked to be fortune tellers under mandarin paper lanterns at the far edge of the patio. The sound of a fairly decent live blues band came to him. He could smell cayenne and other spices in the air from the supper tent.

RETRIBUTION

He saw a lot of very well done face and body lifts on painfully thin elegant women, who glided through the crowd. He snagged a drink from a waiter going by, tasted it, found it to be a mild coke and rum and decided he could probably nurse it most of the evening. With Eisner gone, a slight shyness settled around him. He did not feel like socializing or like discussing what had gone right and wrong in the recent high profile surgeries he'd just done.

A tinkle of real crystal reached him, punctuating words from people whose faces he could not actually see.

". . . some people deserve to die . . ."

"Courts really screwed up on that one . . . wonder how long it will be before he takes out another quick mart?"

". . . poor clerk did everything he was told and still got it, point-blank, in the face. Such a shame. I hope we can help the family."

"We'd be better off getting the judge out and pushing for a retrial! Better way to spend our money."

"This is a charity function, not a political agenda, though I do agree with you about Judge Canton. However, a judge has to have a certain confidence in his abilities and judgments . . . an arrogance, if you will, in his training and the decisions he makes. Just like a surgeon."

"Surgeons are arrogant sons of bitches."

A deep chuckle. "Watch yourself, John, we're surrounded by L.A.'s finest here."

"I didn't say they weren't good doctors. I just said they have one flaming opinion of themselves!" The speaker tossed back half a crystal glass of what must be Scotch on the rocks. "And they damn well better have. I wouldn't want anyone putting a scalpel to me if they were shaking in their boots! I don't like 'em looking at me like I was a slab of meat."

The silver-haired man opposite him shook a finger. "You are just a slab of meat. You have to be, for them to do their work."

"The hell I do!"

"No, John, listen . . . just think about it. They hold your life in their hands—like God. If they have to know you, think about you, wouldn't they have to consider what kind of life they might be saving? Wouldn't they? Wouldn't doctors have to look at the soul behind the flesh and wonder if they were doing the world any good by repairing that flesh? No, they have to have the guts to consider you a piece of meat like any other piece of meat. Or, to paraphrase, let 'em all live and let God sort 'em out in the end."

A masculine snort. "And I hope you at least agree that some people deserve to die!"

"On some level, everyone deserves to die. Whether I agree or not is moot. The judge made his decision. The man was let go. Just like that plastic bag rapist. He served his time. The system did what it was supposed to do." The silver-haired man shrugged. He returned his empty wine stem to a platter as a server passed by and got a fresh one.

The fleshy gentleman next to him gave a humorless laugh. "And we all know that he's thoroughly rehabilitated now, cured of putting plastic bags over women's heads and raping them while they suffocated." Sarcasm punctuated the masculine tone. "But at least the court system got a chance to function." There was a pause, then the beefy voice continued, "Not that I want that son of a bitch living anywhere near me. I'd kill him myself."

Wade paused inside the house, not quite ready to plunge into the Mardi Gras scene, or involve himself in the conversation drifting to him. Invariably, someone would recognize his name and connect him with Dover's miraculous recovery. Unlike the plastic bag rapist, appeals had done Dover no good and he sat on Death Row, waiting. Alive, far more alive than any of his victims, and waiting. Wade felt a sudden need to relax and took a long, hard gulp of his rum and coke before backing away from the patio.

Turning around, he went into the house, crossing a plush carpet and wandering through an open door to find himself in a library, cool, quiet, mahogany bookshelves dominating the walls, a couch before a fireplace and an upholstered chaise lounge in the corner under reading lamps. The fourth wall, over the mantle, held a number of paintings. He found himself looking at one of them, somewhat primitive, but evocative, color flooding his vision, and he could feel the sheer enthusiasm of the artist.

Leaning close, he thought he could make out the sweeping signature, small yet flashy. He did not recognize it.

"Quite a talent, don't you think?"

Wade swung around in guilt, to face an auburn-haired woman wearing a bronze satin ball gown, her neck and shoulders no less exquisite than those of Audrey Hepburn. He felt the impact of her presence jolt him down to his feet.

She put her hand out. "I'm Abby Switzer, your hostess. And you are?"

"Wade Clarkson." He shook her hand. She had a firm, if slightly cool, grip. Diamonds, white gold, and emeralds amply decorated her fingers. Her blue-gray eyes seemed somewhat amused. Her upswept chestnut hair complimented her firm chin and neck, despite the twenty some years she must have on Wade.

"Ah! Kevin's new doctor. I approve." Abby moved even with him, with a slight ruffling of her satin gown. "That one was done by Charlie. Have you heard of her?"

"Afraid not."

She nodded. "She is just now getting a reputation. I find that owning paintings gives me a great deal of pleasure, as well as the fact they should appreciate quite a bit over the years. I make it a habit never to collect anything I do not like. And I adore her." Abby took a drink from the tall, slim glass she held in her left hand. "She is only eleven, you know."

"Eleven years old?"

His hostess inclined her head. "Remarkable, I think."

Wade studied the painting again. "Astounding."

Abby put her arm out. "I think you should meet my other guests, Dr. Clarkson."

He took her hand and settled it upon his arm. "I would be delighted to."

Abby laughed, a low, sultry laugh that managed to send a message down his spine, as she stroked his arm lightly. "And while we walk, let me twist your arm into coming to another benefit I run—a bachelor auction. You are single, are you not?"

He smiled firmly under her assessing gaze and she gave a triumphant laugh. "Yes, I think you must be. Well, let's get your fortune told and meet the donors who keep the hospital able to hire staff like yourself."

She swept forward to leave the room, and he was hard put to keep up and escort her. He would remember a lot of things about that night, the fine dinner, the tumbling black-and-white dice at the gaming tables, her subtle and expensive perfume, and the way the gown fell from her body in her dusky blue bedroom.

But what jolted through him, what would sear into him as though he'd been struck by lightning, would be sitting at the fortune teller's table, hearing the snap of tarot cards, and the woman's dark eyes boring into him as she tapped the cards.

Her nails were the color of freshly spilled blood, wet and glistening. She would touch a stone tower being destroyed by thunder and bolts, the whole world being turned upside down. "You will face the end of everything you know . . . if you do not reverse yourself."

"An eye for an eye," she would tell him. "Never forget that. God's law and the law of the universe. Even God's own law finds and dictates the balance."

It would not strike him then, for Abby had stood behind him, delicately, just barely brushing the back of his tuxedo jacket with a rustling of her gown and the perfume of her presence, but she had still garnered all his attention, his own masculinity acutely aware of her femininity. Every nerve in his body had been focused on her and a different kind of balance, the silken balance of a man and a woman.

It would not be until later, lying in her bed, listening to her soft breathing, his own body steeped in sexual well-being but unable to surrender to sleep that his beeper would vibrate on the nightstand, and he would reach over and thumb it to retrieve the message and see his code for emergency surgery report flash in the plastic window.

And when he stood in scrubs cleaning his hands, going over the routine, the smell of the betadine soup sharp in his nostrils, so opposite from Abby's aroma, that the doctor who'd requested him had come loping in to brief him, mask hanging down around his neck, eyes red with fatigue.

"What we have here is a real mess coming up from ER. I don't know if we can save him or not or if the bastard even deserves it, but I needed the best so I had you paged."

"It's all right," Clarkson murmured, concentrating on the scrubbing routine, nails, fingers, palms, back of the hand, wrists, forearms, until his skin felt scraped raw. "What happened?"

"He just got out of prison yesterday for rape . . . and went back out tonight to his old neighborhood. He got caught in an attempt . . . and the whole block went after him. Beat his skull in. Took knives and razors to anything else they could reach. He should be a dead man. The only thing I could think of to do was put him in your hands. You have the technique on bleeders that I need while I work on the head fractures." The surgeon put his shoulder to the door and let Wade go in ahead of him to where the anesthesiologist was doing his best to administer to a living corpse.

He scarcely had time to feel the irony as an assistant pulled gloves down over his waiting hands and he entered the sterile room.

Operating theater lights did little to soften angles or aspects. They were there to illuminate, in the sharpest way, every feature, to emphasize so that the surgeon could perform his best. Flesh hardly looked real, blood sometimes garishly dark. The surgical team, working around the table in efficient strokes, parted slightly to let him approach.

Wade looked down on the plastic bag rapist, covered in fresh blood, glistening. He looked at the man, half flayed alive, his skull beaten badly enough that it had caved in in one spot, and yet the man lived, or struggled to, and Wade knew that the object he looked on *did not deserve to live*. He thought of the one man's definition of surgical arrogance and competence. If he could play God, *wouldn't he have to?* Wouldn't he have to look behind the anatomic technicalities of what he had before him and consider the ramifications? Wouldn't he? *Wouldn't he?*

"Ready," Wade murmured and reached out to touch the man.

When it was over, and the patient gone despite or because of their efforts, the surgeon who had called him in, one of the country's foremost neurosurgeons, clapped him on the shoulder, commending him for his valiant efforts, and asked if he would consider taking on a few more years of residency and join his neurosurgery team.

He did not hesitate with his reply, for surely the brain was the closest thing to the human soul.

Chapter Five

Wade did not watch the local news channels. He could not bear the style of reporting in Los Angeles, which resembled real reporting about the way he resembled a rhino, going for glitz and entertainment value, given with a zeal and smile that hardly matched the horrendous content of the stories the anchors were delivering. The anchors looked as beautiful as the movie-star town they covered, the women young and fresh and ethnically diverse, everything candy for the eye, although he was certain if allowed they might have pithy opinions on the stories they were permitted to cover. He scarcely had time in which to kick back and enjoy anything, and within his apartment walls, where he could be king, he used the remote control to his television relentlessly.

He watched CNN where, to his amazement, some of the local news stories would creep in despite his

vigilance. It was just as well that his surgery schedule
kept him away from the television on the average
day and he did not have to suffer the indignity often.
He picked up the remote to thumb it off, the picture
screen filled with black tie and evening gown society
milling around at yet another self-serving event, reminding him of Abby Switzer in a bittersweet way,
dear Abby, two years gone now of cancer, a lump
that he had discovered himself one night while avidly fondling her breast in their lovemaking. The old
saw about breast cancer being too, too true in her
case, that it had not been painful, had not been discovered until too late; despite all the surgery and
chemo and radiology—and money—nothing could
be done which would save Abigail Switzer. The poignant memory kept him from channeling away from
the glitzy story, a story which quickly materialized
into something more.

"Famed child prodigy and artist Charlotte Saunders, known by art collectors the world over merely
as Charlie, collapsed today at this benefit unveiling
her latest painting. . . ."

Wade sat up straighter in the corner of his couch,
his eyes glued to the television shot of a honey-
haired girl, tall and willowy and still very, very
young, going pale in front of a bank of microphones
and then swaying, dropping so quickly no one could
catch her. The clipping showed chaos, screams, the
mother dropping to her knees, an oily-haired young

man pushing others back, the glitterati screaming in response to the emergency. The camera view was almost immediately flooded with obstacles, but a thin view of the girl remained visible. His trained eyes picked out the still form which then began to convulse, but in a way which he thought he could recognize, not the unconscious trembling of a fainting victim.

He picked up the phone.

"Get me Katsume," he said to the pleasant voice who answered him.

"Yes, Dr. Clarkson," she responded swiftly, knowing his voice instantly, taking no umbrage at his brusqueness. She came back. "He is paged and will return your call immediately."

Wade disconnected, and sat, remote in one hand and the portable phone in the other, dissecting what he saw on the television screen.

"Her agent Federico Valdor acted as spokesman for the family, saying only that the popular young artist, whose works are permanently on display in the J. Paul Getty Museum in Los Angeles, the Smithsonian, and the Museum of Modern Art in New York, had been working at a very demanding pace to finish the final paintings for this show and that she simply fainted. Charlie's paintings commonly sell for upward of a hundred thousand dollars and there is a waiting list to view and bid on her finished work.

This show had been scheduled to benefit the local AIDS foundation and—"

Wade's mouth twisted as the portable rang in his hand.

"Hey, Wade, what is it?"

"What's the matter, Kat, did I interrupt your golf game?"

The Japanese-American surgeon answered with a rich chuckle. "Of course you did."

"Kat, I want you to call the family of Charlie Saunders . . . they're in one of the beach cities in Orange County, I think . . . Newport or one of those . . . and get her into our clinic for evaluation."

"Charlie Saunders." He could hear wheels turning in Kat's deliberate response, then a slight gasp. "The little girl who paints?"

"That's the one. She fainted at a benefit show, and unless I miss my guess, she needs us."

To his gratification, Katsume jumped to the same conclusion he had. "Pediatric tumor?"

"I think so. It wouldn't hurt to put her through the program."

Kat let out a low whistle. "Will do, Wade. But if you're wrong. . . ."

"If I'm wrong, I'll buy you a new set of graphites. And find someone to pay the lab bills."

"That's a deal, buddy. Talk to you tomorrow."

Wade put the phone down. Though the television screen had now moved away to other scenes in other lands, his mind's eye stayed fixed to the image, seeing the girl-woman again, dressed in a strapless ball gown, her pale skin and shoulders emphasized by its darkness. He again saw the faint spasm in her face before she grew even paler and her eyes rolled back. He would need every bit of his training if his suspicions were correct, for excising the problem would be one thing, and doing it without affecting her genius would be quite another.

He put the remote down and looked at his hands, palms up, then palms down. He would need skill and providence on his side.

Chapter Six

INTERLUDE 1
Printed in: *Los Angeles Recorder*

The art world was stunned today when Federico Valdor announced that Charlotte Saunders, known as Charlie to fans and collectors, has retired from painting.

The controversial prodigy made news just a few short months ago, surviving neurosurgery to remove a benign but potentially deadly tumor. Although her health was rumored to have been precarious for days following the surgery, she began to make a rapid recovery and left the hospital for physical therapy and to return to her home sooner than expected.

Speculations on her ability to paint at all immediately rose at Valdor's announcement, but he refused to comment further, saying only that Charlie continued to improve and was expected to make a full recovery. This statement came on the heels of tabloid reports that she had suffered partial paralysis of the right side, making it nearly impossible for her ever to paint again. Those same tabloid papers reported there was suspicion that she had not been the purported artist of any of her works and that her entire career had been a fraud.

Valdor and her family refused to answer those allegations, saying only that Charlie had been through a lot and deserved to have a childhood while one still remained for her. Privately, he was said to have expressed the opinion that Charlie would return to painting in the future as soon as inspiration moved her, as "she was a talented and unique young lady."

Asked for a response to accusations that the neurosurgical team had destroyed a budding genius while saving her life, Dr. Katsume would say only that he, Dr. Clarkson, and the team had done everything they could to save Charlie's life and he was satisfied with the end results. There was nothing physical holding the girl back from painting if that's what she wished to do, once strength and other training rehabilitated her arm and shoulder. "As for artistic expression," Katsume added, "that comes from outside, and we deal only with the flesh."

Chapter Seven

PRESENT DAY

The phone rang. John answered it on speaker, calling out, "Sentinel Dogs," raising his tone to be heard clearly over the muffled noise of his kennel and the tin echo from the filing cabinets as he worked. The archly feminine voice reaching him hurt as keenly as a kick in the gut.

"John, it's me."

He did not respond. His throat locked up, stopping him in his tracks as cleanly as one of his well trained canines. He stood dumbfounded at the filing cabinet of his one-room office and looked about the somewhat organized clutter, as if he expected to see her.

"It's been a while," she said quietly.

Three months and twenty-one days, he thought, his damnable brain doing the opposite of his larynx, wheeling in tumultuous thought and emotion.

"Sorry to be bothering you." She cleared her throat. "This is not about us."

No, of course, the call wouldn't be . . . she was too stubborn and he was too proud, and there was no us, anyway, not any more.

"You need a dog?" *Stupid, idiot thing to say, she hated dogs. . . .*

"No, John I don't need a dog." And she spoke in that patronizing tone which he hated, reminding him of how bad it had been between them and why he should not have been surprised when she left. "I called because I ran across something today, and I thought you might be interested. That dog you trained, the golden, the one that bothered you so much . . . well, the young lady and the dog are going to be at an art benefit auction in Laguna tomorrow night. I've e-mailed you the information and address. That's all. Don't make anything out of this call."

"I don't intend to."

"I know you better than that, John." She gave a lilting laugh and hung up, the laugh reminding him of just how good it had been between them once. Laughter and good times and pleasant sex.

His phone took a few seconds to disconnect, buzzing loudly, setting the kenneled dogs off again, barking in chorus to let him know they heard suspicious sounds. He bellowed, "Shut up!" at them, and they quieted down eventually.

He did not know if the golden retriever had been

the beginning of the end of their relationship, the cause or the symptom, but Julie was right—the assignment had worried at him a lot, gnawing with sharp teeth at the bone, the core, of him. He closed the file drawer slowly, went to the computer and sat down, looking at the screen saver kaleidoscope for a moment before signing on for his mail.

You don't take a dog like a golden retriever, a dog known for its companionship qualities and temperament, and make a guard dog out of it. It would be like deliberately poisoning its personality, the pearl of its existence. There was a reason certain dogs were used again and again in the business, because they were bred for it, they had the aggressive qualities which could be combined with direction, as well as other qualities. But a golden retriever had never been bred for aggression, controlled or otherwise, and he had accepted the assignment with a ton of misgivings.

Julie had talked him into it because of the money involved, not to save the kennel which had been foundering despite his disability from the police department, but to fund him into another line of work. For retraining, she'd explained again and again, nagging him to go into computer programming for months . . . and he had finally taken the assignment because he was desperate for that almighty check. He had not, naturally, used the funds to retrain himself, but that was just another step into the downward spiral of their relationship.

Those misgivings had been compounded the moment Jagger had been delivered to his compound—a sleek, smaller-boned golden, agile, with bright caramel eyes and a feathery tail, complete with his little vest proclaiming him to be a companion dog. He had known the dog was a family dog, but not that he had already been finely trained.

John had sworn at the driver. "Jesus Christ, this dog is already trained. What are you people doing?"

The driver had looked at him impassively, shrugging, "I just brought the dog and the check, sir. You want 'em or not?"

Flint, the Alsatian, hurled himself at the wire enclosure, barking in mad alpha domination at the golden who merely looked interested, his tail giving that ambiguous wag which people who don't really know dogs think is a sign of friendliness. It was Jagger's way of saying that he wasn't intimidated . . . yet.

"You don't take a trained animal like this and reverse it."

The driver rolled his shoulders again and held the leash out.

Jagger looked up at John, and his pink tongue lolled forward a bit in a self-confident pant. Rubidoux looked at the animal, a handsome and happy animal, and his inner self recoiled at the thought, and he wondered if the family was stupid, insane, or desperate.

"Why?"

"Why?" The driver pursed his thick lips in thought a moment. " 'Cause the girl needs protection, sir."

"Whose dog is this?"

"Hers, sir."

John looked from the dog to the driver, who stood in square, thick heaviness, his neck bulging out over the starched collar of his uniform. He looked like a short bull, and whatever his background might have been on the streets or in the barrio, he did not look like he could provide protection, not savvy protection. He might be good for intimidation or brawling, but there was no finesse about him. The driver blinked back at him, dark brown eyes showing just a hint of John's assessment, his swarthy face bland. The eyes remained open and honest.

"You can't do the job?"

The driver blinked slowly. "She lives alone, sir. I drive for the family. But I am just a driver. The dog stays with her all the time." His mouth thinned. "She doesn't want anybody to make a fuss."

"What's the problem?"

"Stalker." His eyes flared momentarily, and a flush came to his full cheeks.

John's stomach knotted a little. The golden whined a bit, growing uneasy at not knowing what was expected of him in the situation, and then shook his head, flapping his ears noisily. He reached for the leash. "All right, I'll do it."

The driver let out a sigh and shoved the envelope at him as well. "Your check is in here. Give me a call when Jagger is ready to be picked up. Feeding instructions are in there, too, plus his command list."

"I'll need at least a couple of weeks."

The driver nodded curtly. "Yes, sir. And . . ." He paused, already halfway back into the car. "Thank you, sir."

John fingered the envelope, fine, watermarked paper rustling at his touch. Jagger whined again as the car left, not a fearful sound, but just one that showed he was alert to what was happening and that he was uncertain about it. He leaned over and thumped the dog on the ribs.

"Good boy."

Jagger lolled his tongue out again, pleased. The feathery tail gave one quick wave. He knew he was a good dog. That had never been in question.

John Rubidoux remembered laughing in spite of his misgivings.

Jagger had been perhaps one of his most successful failures.

John slowed the van down, eyeing the procession of expensive vehicles turning into the hillside home and park grounds where the Peppermill Galleries held residence. He flexed his jaw as if he could ease the neck of his tux by doing so, made a right turn to avoid the procession and eased the van into a spot under a blue gum eucalyptus on a side street. Normally not embarrassed by his van, tonight did not seem to be the time to show up flanked by vigilant guard dogs painted by a talented young local mural artist. As he stepped out, the fragrant eucalyptus tree reminded him that the van smelled of dogs and he flicked a few stray hairs off the elbow of his coat.

This was only the third time he could remember wearing a tux. The first was his high school prom, the second three years ago when his sister Lyndel had gotten married. He'd still had a limp then and had to use a cane. A rueful smile pulled the corner of his mouth in memory at that; he still had the cane at home, a handsome black stick decorated with a silver dog's head. Lyndel had bought it especially for the wedding. He hadn't used the cane in the years since, though there were days when his hip hurt badly enough that he should have. He should pull it out of the dark corner of the closet where he kept it and polish the grip.

John lifted his chin yet again, then started uphill in a long-striding clip to the Peppermill grounds. California pepper trees graced the grounds with their long, almost weeping willow type limbs and foliage, their delicate leaves still green from spring rains, tiny flowers beginning to bud. It would not be dark until almost eight, but the wind off the ocean carried a chill touch to it, and he faced into it with enjoyment. Someone had mowed the grounds in diamond patterns, the grass as thick and lush as a baseball park or golf course. The actual mansion was much farther up the hill, almost completely hidden by huge trees which had probably stood there even before the hundred-and-some-year-old house had been built by one of those sailing merchants who had harbored at Dana Point.

The gallery, set just inside the sweeping driveway and gates, had probably been a carriage house and stables once, converted several times over to other structures, and it now looked as if it had never been anything else than what it was that evening: a wood-and-glass gallery poised among the pepper trees. John found a side entrance open and took it, while cars still edged forward slowly onto the grounds, being parked in the lot behind the gallery and, in some cases, along the long circular drive and back down again. He wondered if the lower lawns would be utilized as well before the evening was out. The upper lawns between the gallery and mansion were filled with three large white tents, and he could hear music already.

John put his hand to his pocket to check his ticket. The $100 donation entitled him to a buffet dinner, two champagne or wine drinks, unlimited soft drinks, and an invitation to bid at the silent auction. Everything else would no doubt be an additional charge. The ticket also listed several nonprofit organizations to be benefited, most of them art community oriented, several of them children's art projects. He slipped it back in the breast pocket of the tux. One of the parking valets eyed him as he sauntered along the driveway, then lifted an eyebrow and turned away to accept the keys to a white BMW.

As he neared the gallery, he could see the canvases on the walls and people milling around inside. Along the tents, there were a number of temporary pegboard walls set up, with numerous artworks hung from them. He wondered if this was an annual event and suspected it was, judging by the groups of people who greeted one another with familiarity. He sensed an ulterior motive in Julie's telling him about the event: Get him there to see the dog, and while he was there, perhaps a little elbow rubbing with the well-to-do might help with his networking skills. Surely among all these people, there would be one or two potential clients who needed to augment their security system with a well-trained animal. Or maybe it was just her way of pounding into his head again just how unsuccessful he was.

He snagged a plastic champagne flute as he entered the gallery; no one asked him for a ticket as he joined the crowd inside. He saw a lot of seascapes, from one end of the California coast to the other, including two of the famous Laguna Beach cove, one of which he liked and one of which he didn't. A discreet look showed him that the one he liked was listed at $12,500 and the one he didn't at $27,000. He took a sip of his drink, found the champagne cold, dry, slightly sweet, and incredibly bubbly, and weighed the differences in his mind between the paintings. Finally, with a shrug, he left the gallery and meandered up the hill toward the tents and the open air art gathering which seemed a little less pretentious even if the attendees did not.

The sea breeze was brisker out on the lawns, and the tents billowed a little, but their cloudlike enclosures seemed anchored securely to the dark green grass, and he wondered where the dog was and whether he would even be able to find him among the crowd.

As he entered the first corridor of exhibits, a loud woof caught his attention, and he turned, looking uphill, to see the golden retriever not straining in his harness, but at full attention, his jaws agape in dog greeting, his tail bannering the air. John grinned in spite of himself, then followed the dog's body to the slim yet determined arm keeping him at bay, and saw . . . not a girl, though they had always called her "the girl," but a young woman holding Jagger. She was not pretty in the face: plain, angled, intense. Elegant satin pants followed long legs up to a slim waistline set off by a vest and a sleek white blouse, a feminine echo of his own tuxedo. She had thick golden-brown hair pulled back and tamed into a kind of knot at her neck, ends curling farther down her back and her eyes were so deep-set he could not see their color.

She frowned at the dog, her gaze sweeping across the area, and he saw a wrongness in her face that gave him pause, before he identified it. One eyelid drooped ever so slightly, sleepily, as did the line of the mouth under it. Stroke, he thought, or some sort of weakness on the right side. That could explain why she'd had the dog to begin with.

Jagger gave a tiny bounce in greeting, front paws off the lawn, settling back down into an eagerness that was almost puppylike. He had filled out a little in the many months since Rubidoux had had him, and he was a handsome specimen of the breed.

John ordered his face into a neutral expression, knowing the dog would read his body language, smell his scent, and listen to the tones in his voice almost simultaneously, and ordered, "Down."

Jagger licked his chops, then dropped to the lawn, relaxing in the harness almost instantly. The young woman almost staggered back onto one heel, the weight of him leaning heavily against her suddenly gone.

She looked at him, her eyes neither blue nor gray, but a mixture of both, as though they were the reflection of a changing and complicated sky. Relief was suddenly replaced by a slight suspicion. "Do you always give orders to other people's dogs?"

"Only when I've trained them and I see them misbehaving," John answered. He forced himself to look down at the dog to hide the momentary jolt he felt when he looked at her. The golden looked up at him, happiness glinting in his eyes. The misgivings Rubidoux had felt during those weeks of training him eased slightly at Jagger's confidence. He obviously still thought he was a good dog. Which, indeed, he was.

John bent over and ruffled the dog's ears. Jagger leaned into his touch and made a little chuffing sound of contentment. When John glanced up, his eyes met hers and he realized close up that the tiny weakness in the corner of her eyelid and mouth only enhanced natural attractiveness, giving it a slightly beguiling slant. If she worried about her disability, it did not show as she offered her right hand. He shook it, measuring his grip carefully, surprised to feel some calluses and roughness in her fingers.

"I'm Charlotte Saunders," she said. "Charlie to friends of Jagger."

"And I'm John Rubidoux."

She nodded. "Ruby," she said softly, as if wondering if his nickname bothered him and if it did, making sure not to let anyone else hear her say it.

"That's me." He found himself defensive, as her blue-gray eyes measured him.

"My father," she added, "could not decide if he loved you or hated you."

John remembered Quentin Saunders as a hard-nosed CEO who had worked his way up through the blue-collar ranks into his position and money. He demanded results without excuses and either got them or found somebody else. Quentin Saunders had not been too happy with the work John had done with Jagger, but had finally capitulated when Rubidoux had insisted on not ruining an intelligent animal with training contrary to his instincts. They had compromised on what to do with Jagger, though John had never felt happy with that compromise. "I could say the feelings were mutual."

Charlie shifted weight and scanned the grounds imperceptibly before looking back to him, and he wondered whether he was detaining her or if she always felt ill at ease . . . or perhaps she was just a little self-conscious. He looked back down at the golden retriever. "How's he working out for you?"

"Oh, he's my best guy." Charlie leaned over and scratched Jagger's chin. The golden gave her a look of immense devotion and happiness.

"Did he help with your . . . problem?"

Charlie gave a little sigh which was followed immediately by one from the dog, and John bit the inside of his lip slightly to hide his amusement at the unconscious emotional rapport between them. She frowned and took a step away from him, and he knew he had crossed some kind of boundary with her.

"My father and a few others overreacted to a situation with my ex-agent, I'm afraid," she answered slowly. "But Jagger here performed heroically anyway. He showed his teeth and Valdor gave up his hope of forcing me back into painting."

"Good. Glad to hear that. He's a good dog. He wasn't cut out for the kind of work your father wanted from him." John cleared his throat. For Jagger to do everything Quentin Saunders had insisted upon, he would have had to deprogram the dog thoroughly and most likely would have ended up with a confused and worthless animal. As it was, Rubidoux was not sure that Jagger would perform the aggressive guard and attack acts they had worked so hard on. Worse, he feared that the dog would begin refusing his service commands, misplacing the aggression John had tried to instill in him.

Seeing him here and now, though, made Rubidoux feel a little more at ease. Happy dog, happy owner. He backed up a step. "Sorry about the painting though. I didn't realize you had stopped."

Charlie tilted her head slightly, offsetting the slant to her features. He wondered if it was a studied act or just something she did naturally. "It happens. Sometimes you just lose the desire."

"I understand that—" John suddenly felt as if he were walking on eggshells, and very unsuccessfully.

"I don't talk about it much any more," Charlie told him. She tugged her mouth into a smile. "Surely you didn't get a tux and come out tonight just to say hi to Jagger."

"Of course not. As an independent businessman, I'm told I should support functions like this." He stretched his neck against the tightness of his collar and flushed as she noticed him fidgeting. "It's called networking in the nineties. And my accountant said, 'You need the write-offs anyway.'"

She laughed. "Well, that's one way of doing it. I'm not sure too many of them here would look you up on a website. They prefer to schmooze. You look like one of the harder working donors. Let me give you a guided tour. There's food and drinks with that ticket and I'm sure you wouldn't want to miss a good meal." She clucked to Jagger who lurched promptly to his feet and squared himself away in his harness.

John followed after her, wondering if he wore the same hungry look on his features that he often saw on his dogs. How did women know? How did they unerringly home in on a signal he was not aware he gave? Or was a man's stomach something a woman could take for granted?

Or, he thought ruefully, as they neared the food tent and buffet line and he could smell the rich fragrance of some mighty good-smelling dinner plates, and his stomach gave off a growl, maybe he had been signaling after all. Some well-heeled folks cut her away from him and began to talk to her earnestly in low tones. She waved him by to the food line and after a sorrowful look from Jagger, John decided that he would get a tray for himself and make a dent in the hundred-dollar ticket. It looked as though his guided tour had ended.

Jagger alternated between watching him hopefully and scanning the people who continued to press around Charlie. No sooner would one group drift away, then another couple or threesome would surround her. John wanted to think that she stayed in order to talk with him, perhaps share the intimacy of dining with him, but that not only no longer looked possible, it looked as if she had not even had that in mind. He filled his dinner plate with an assortment of goodies that made Jagger lick his chops as he passed by to an available table.

He sat down, too hungry to think about the difficulties of eating alone, and had half his food finished when he looked up, and saw Charlie Saunders watching him over the shoulders of the latest conversant to hold her captive. Her look quickly flicked away as if she'd been caught. John suppressed the desire to see if he'd spilled something on the rental tuxedo and put his fork down. He gathered up the tray holding his plate and drink, surveying his plate and realizing it was actually damn near empty. He stood and made his way back toward Charlie, leaning into the conversation without preamble.

"Hon, I'm going back for seconds . . . sure you don't want me to pick up a plate for you?"

She blinked as her face turned rosy, then nodded. "I'm famished. That would be wonderful," she said smoothly, after a twitch of the corner of her mouth. "You know I adore the Chinese chicken salad, and anything with shrimp in it." Jagger flashed him an enormously grateful look as if the dog knew dinner snacks were drawing close.

"Will do." John grinned. "And I think I saw a couple of pieces of chocolate fudge cake that had our names written all over it." He nodded toward the latest group holding her hostage. "You don't mind if I steal her away for some dinner, do you?" The rosy glow to her face took the edges off her plainness, and he found himself enjoying having her somewhat at a disadvantage.

Her audience immediately began to murmur agreement as he swung past, grabbed another plate, and began to assemble her request. By the time he'd gotten her dinner, his seconds and dessert, they were saying their good-byes and Charlie was shaking their hands.

She followed him over to the table which had thankfully remained empty, the slight limp she walked with engagingly, unconsciously, sexy, and sat down with a sigh. She examined the plate as he slid it over in front of her, unrolled the linen napkin from the silverware, and laid it over her lap. "I am not sure how grateful I am for the rescue—I've been avoiding the cake all evening." She dipped a fingertip into the icing, tasted it, and rolled her eyes. "Torture."

Night had rolled in, a black velvet backdrop to the tent, and the candle lanterns on the tables began to reflect their golden glow. He had a plain, hard-boiled egg to the side of his plate, neatly sliced it in two and pressed it into her fingers. "Jagger deserves a little something, too."

The dog responded quickly, moist nose sniffing the air for all its good smells. Charlie smiled wearily. "Actually he would prefer a piece of the cake."

"But chocolate isn't good for him, and he'd just as soon have the egg."

With a laugh, she bent over and Jagger scarfed up the treat with little judgment as to whether or not chocolate cake would have tasted better.

"Dogs," Rubidoux remarked, "are potato chip eaters. Each chip looks irresistible, and they're always ready to eat another."

She more than smiled at that; she burst out with a laugh, a sound so genuine it made him feel like responding the way Jagger did . . . with a feel good all over wiggle. He suppressed it by stuffing a shrimp egg roll in his mouth. She did not say anything for a good five minutes other than "mmmming" at the salad and rolling her eyes in happiness.

"If you want to keep avoiding the cake," he offered, "I'll eat both slices."

"And die a slow death from a dull butter knife," Charlie warned.

John Rubidoux grinned.

A handsome, silver-haired couple paused by the table, as if waiting for Charlie to notice them, and of course she did, swallowing quickly and wiping the edges of her mouth with the corner of her napkin.

"Judge and Mrs. Laverman, how nice to see you!"

They smiled: tall, elegant, well-groomed people. He wore a thick but well-trimmed mustache, and he had a lot of laugh creases at the corners of his clear blue eyes. John had seen a fair number of judges in his police days, but he had never been before this one and found himself wondering what it would be like. Not too many people made him want to remember those past days.

"It's a pleasure, as always, to see you, Charlie." Mrs. Laverman wore lavender which accented her aging gracefully. She leaned over and hugged Charlie's slight shoulders. "Any new pieces tonight?"

"No, no, it's just a retrospective. You know I haven't done anything new in almost ten years."

"Well, it doesn't hurt to ask."

Charlie winced and shook her head. "You shouldn't even wonder! Your pictures are more valuable with me not painting."

Mrs. Laverman reached out and patted Charlie's hands. "Perhaps in a way that's true, dear, but we'd rather see you painting and happy again. We don't collect for value, but enjoyment. Anyway, enjoy your young man and dinner. We'll see you later."

The color on Charlie's face increased markedly as the judge and his wife sauntered away, across the lawn, their heads bent together in hushed talk he could not follow.

She cleared her throat as she looked back to him. "Sorry about that."

"Oh, I think she was referring to you and Jagger."

Charlie had begun to eat again, and gave a little snort-choke, and dropped her fork, holding her napkin up to her face. When she lowered it, she was laughing again.

"Thank God," he said. "I thought I was going to have to perform CPR."

"It's the Heimlich for choking."

"I know, but CPR sounded like more fun."

Jagger chose that moment to flap his ears as if he wanted attention, and Charlie took the other half of the boiled egg off John's plate to feed to him. He sat back in his chair, thinking of what an intimate move that was, and how Julie would have never done it for anyone, under any circumstances, let alone for a dog, and he felt contented.

Charlie looked away from Jagger and met his eyes. She smiled. "You have the look of a well-fed man."

"That I do."

She pushed away her salad, and glanced at his chocolate cake. "Got enough room for that?"

He picked up his fork. "Always! There's always room for chocolate!"

Jagger barked sharply. They grinned at one another and dug in, and if Jagger happened to accidentally get several very fat chocolate crumbs from Charlie's plate, Rubidoux pretended he did not notice.

When they finished, Charlie looked at her watch and made a face. "I've got to go announce the winners of the silent auction. If you come, if you have time afterward, I'll show you the judged exhibition. And my gallery, if you'd like to see it."

He knew very little about art except what he liked and didn't, but he knew the evening was not nearly old enough for him to want to say good night to Charlotte Saunders. He nodded. "I'd like that."

John reached for the plates and cleared them all onto his tray, as Charlie got to her feet, grabbing for the dog's harness. For a moment, her face went terribly pale, and she swayed, blinked several times, then righted herself. He went for her elbow.

"Are you all right?"

She waved her hand at him. "Just got up too fast. Champagne went to my head a bit." Her face went cold and stiff again, and he felt the warmth between them drain away rapidly.

"Sorry, I . . . I thought you needed help."

"No." She straightened her vest and pulled at her blouse cuffs. "It's just a hazard of being in this body."

He took his hand back, and busied himself picking

up remnants. An icy barrier had dropped around her, and he was unsure if it was something he'd done, or something she always did.

She and Jagger started downhill as he finished clearing.

When he reached the lower tent, she'd already been pulled in front of a microphone, surrounded by easels of paintings, etchings, and other artwork, and had been introduced to an applauding crowd. She looked through the milling people, spotted him, and gave a slight nod, acknowledging him, and he had some hope that he hadn't ruined everything.

When she spoke to the tented audience, it was with an ease she had not shown with him, something he realized came from years of dealing with the public and from her own quiet confidence in herself in that particular forum.

"Good evening, ladies and gentlemen. I want to thank you for coming to the Peppermill tonight in support of the many projects this night is benefiting." Charlie smiled, and put a hand down to her dog's ruff, the only slight sign of disquiet in her.

He found a sturdy chair to lean upon as she began a spiel about the local arts programs, the festival, and other charities and opportunities. She introduced a handful of artists whose works had been in the auction, waiting for scattered applause for each, and then began to read off the pieces and the winning bidders. John found himself wishing he'd bought a painting, just to hear what she had to say about it. Jagger watched as people came onto the stage one by one to claim their artworks, his tail waving in slow acceptance and warning, leaning a little against her black-satin-covered leg protectively. Rubidoux watched him as the golden looked up once or twice, whined anxiously, but settled immediately at a low word.

John found himself a little uneasy at Jagger's distress, but he decided it was an outward show of what Charlie must be feeling, on the stage, in front of everyone, using the podium to steady her slight weakness of body, and whatever inner strength she carried to steady her inner self. He found himself watching her more and more, in spite of the fact his interest should be in the dog.

An older woman pushed her way from the back of the crowd, determined to get as close as she could. The wave of movement caught John's attention, his old training immediately surfacing, and he watched her carefully as she drew near his own spot in the audience. She did not have the same casual air of elegance as most of the onlookers, and lines creased a face that had never seen cosmetic surgery, giving her a somewhat careworn look. She wore a hand-painted blue silk dress that was somehow more monied and more comfortable than the formal wear of the other women.

Unconscious of his scrutiny, she gave a tiny sigh of relief as she stood next to John, unable to get any closer to the stage, yet obviously pleased at the progress she'd made. He watched her, wondering if she was a fan of Charlie's painting, for it was painfully clear that she had come to see Charlie.

His policeman's nerves twanged a bit, honed by his years on the force, and his years of working with guard dogs. There were those whose obsession often turned deadly, and he was never so aware of it as he was at that point in time. Who was this woman and why did her eyes fix so avidly on Charlie as she spoke? What did she want—and what was she capable of doing?

On the stage, Jagger paced a step or two and whined, loudly enough that the microphone picked it up, his ears flattening in worry. He glanced up at Charlie once or twice and shook his head uneasily.

Then, Charlie stumbled to a halt, her voice breaking. She put her hand to her temple and looked out, toward Rubidoux, blinking in confusion as though the brightly lit tent hid him from her eyes. "I'm sorry . . . I seem to have forgotten . . ." She swallowed. "I can't—" She put her free hand to her brow, shading her eyes. "I'm sorry," she repeated in bewilderment. "I can't seem to see. . . ." She let go of the podium abruptly, both hands groping for the dog. "Jagger—" she forced out, and swayed.

Then she dropped in her tracks.

A woman screamed.

The woman in blue standing near John blurted in absolute horror, "Oh, God, not again."

Chapter Eight

Jagger immediately dropped into a guard stance, his ears back, and his lips skinned off his teeth. Rubidoux could not hear the low-toned growl he knew had begun to issue from deep in the dog's throat, but those standing nearest could. He knew what it would sound like, a rumbling, burbling growl. Rolling out slow and steady, increasing in fervor and pitch and loudness. A sound born from primitive instincts and vocal cords, provoking an equally primal reaction of fear and warning.

A balding gentleman tore off his tuxedo jacket and threw it over Jagger as his wife knelt over Charlie's form. The dog shot out from under the jacket. Canines shining, he bucked, snarling and snapping, forty-five pounds of animal fury, and swung his head, his nose to the enemy.

"Shit!" The balding man danced back a step. Not far enough to evade Jagger's anger.

RETRIBUTION

He barked and snapped. His teeth grazed the air at the man's knee as he scrambled backward off the platform, gasping. Jagger swung around, targeting her, and his wife scampered after, shrieking.

Stiff-legged, lips curled and ivory teeth menacing, Jagger emptied the stage of anyone who might think of helping his mistress. His ears flattened as he retreated back to Charlie's body, his snarls amplified by the live microphone. At least two cell phones were whipped out of jackets and handbags, their owners shouting, "I'm calling 911."

And the woman beside Rubidoux, her face creased in worry, surged forward. John instinctively followed in her wake as she shouted, "Someone get that damn dog away from her!" She got out something else, words garbled by an emotional catch in her throat that John recognized. His mother had sounded like that rushing through the hospital parking lot the day his father had been shot and brought into ER, only to die. Suddenly he knew the woman in blue had to be Charlie's mother. He had never met her, dealing only with Quentin Saunders, never Mary.

He caught her by the elbow as she gained the edge of the platform. "I'll get the dog."

She blinked at him almost without seeing him. "Can you handle him?"

"That's what I do," he answered. Without waiting to explain further, John took the stage in one step, his long legs bringing him to Jagger in a second step.

The wooden platform gave under his weight, almost like the springboard on a pool. The dog shifted uneasily, unnerved by the sudden sway and trembling of the boards under his paws, and by Ruby. Guilt flickered through his caramel eyes as if Jagger suddenly realized he was not doing the right thing. Snarling still, he cast his eyes on John as if looking for guidance in a world gone suddenly awry.

"Good boy," he said. "Down." He watched the dog calmly, levelly.

Jagger stopped growling, and his lips quivered a little, his brown gaze flicking to Charlie and back to Rubidoux. The tail came out, wagged very slowly and stiffly, showing his aggression, acknowledging the fact that he might no longer have domination here, warning of his intent to protect himself if threatened. Like a barometer, Ruby watched the tail and when it seemed to him that he'd relaxed even more, John moved his hand to catch the harness. Jagger erupted, teeth gnashing, and barking sharply in warning.

John did not withdraw, but froze until the golden quieted to take a breath. He snapped his fingers. "Jagger, down."

Charlie rolled slightly, letting out a faint moan, and the dog's ears went up and back, and he whined, in clear distress. John looked down at the dog, in almost as much distress, seeing what he had feared might happen, warring inside the animal. The companion or service training was in conflict with the guard training and without a conscious Charlie to give him commands, Jagger did not know what to do or how to react.

Someone just offstage, at Rubidoux's elbow, said, "I've got a stun gun. Use it on the dog if you have to."

A stun set to disable a human could kill a dog. Yet John knew that they might have to resort to that if he could not calm Jagger down. He stifled his protest. He had no time to waste persuading them otherwise, as Charlie's body twitched in the faint convulsions of the unconscious.

He looked into the caramel eyes, focusing, aware that Charlie lay just beyond, her fallen body framing the dog's, a background of beauty and distress.

"Jagger. Down." And he made two clicks at the back of his throat, similar to the little metal cricket he used in training.

Jagger shook. His tail tucked between his hindquarters in agonizing conflict. His lips curled back. The golden ruff at the back of his neck quivered as if to rise. His ears shifted. John looked into his torment steadily. Then the dog blinked, and, with a whimper, went down.

John let out the breath he didn't realize he'd been holding. He put his hand to Jagger's head and patted him gently. "Good boy. Good dog."

Jagger whined miserably and dropped his head to

his paws, no longer secure in his doggish estimation of himself and his world. Rubidoux reached for the harness. "It's okay, I've got him."

Mary Saunders moved past him in a swift rustle of silk and blue, crying, "Charlie!"

Not far behind her, he recognized Judge Laverman and his wife. Mrs. Laverman put a hand on Mary's shoulders. "The paramedics are on their way."

Mary sat down unceremoniously on the temporary stage, pulling her daughter's head and shoulders into her lap, smoothing stray tendrils of golden-brown hair from her forehead, crooning, "Oh, Charlie, Charlie."

Mrs. Laverman traded looks with her husband. "She's been working hard, Mary," the woman said softly. "Perhaps she is just tired."

Mary Saunders rocked her daughter's unconscious form ever so slightly, her eyes brimming with tears still unshed. "Oh, God," she mumbled. "It can't have come back. It can't!"

Mrs. Laverman put her hand on Mary's shoulder and patted her comfortingly. "Don't even think it."

Frowning, Mary eyed Jagger. "That damned dog."

"It wasn't his fault, Mrs. Saunders. If you need to blame anybody, blame me."

"And who are you?"

"I'm the man your husband hired to retrain him."

Mary's face quivered with expression, as she soothed the hair from Charlie's face and crooned to her. Then she looked at John and nodded, as if to acknowledge him as one of the culprits. John stood in uncomfortable silence.

And no more words were exchanged between them as the EMTs came running up the driveway and sprinting across the lawn. Jagger lurched to his feet, growling anew. John corrected him, although the harness could not tighten on his throat as effectively as a choke chain, but he got the dog's attention. As John worked to keep Jagger calm, someone from the philanthropic organization came to the mike and announced free champagne in the buffet tent to disperse the crowd. They went, still looking back curiously, as the paramedic team straightened her body and began to take vitals.

Mary stood to one side, her hand to her mouth, as if she could smother unwanted thoughts the way she could words.

As a gurney was brought up the drive, one of the techs nodded to her, saying, "You can ride in the van with us if you want, ma'am."

"Thank you," Mary Saunders murmured. Her glance flickered to the dog.

John volunteered swiftly, "I'll take Jagger home with me, if you don't mind." He fumbled a card out of an unfamiliar tux pocket and pressed it into her hand.

She looked at him. "Thank you," she repeated, her

voice sounding as if it were on automatic, but gratitude flickering in careworn eyes.

Mrs. Laverman slid an arm around Mary's shoulders and gave her a quick embrace. "Don't worry, dear," she said. "It can't be a tumor again. It simply can't be."

Charlie's mother shuddered, but whether it was because of the other's touch or her words, John could not say. "It's been ten years," she answered. "I thought—we'd both hoped—that it was all behind us finally. Now this."

Jagger whined and pressed close to John's legs, as the gurney carrying Charlie was taken back down the drive to be loaded in the paramedic van, and Mary followed slowly after.

He ruffled the dog's ears thoughtfully.

The strokelike weakness in her right side. The artist who used to paint brilliantly and now didn't . . . or couldn't. . . .

What had been taken from her then, saving her life yet changing it irrevocably, and what more could be taken from her now?

John felt his throat grow tight, gripped by emotion, as he watched the van doors slam shut, and he could no longer see Charlie's still form on the gurney or the techs bending over her, or Mary Saunders standing stiffly afraid in the corner of the vehicle, looking down at her.

As the paramedics drove off, he found himself

making a tiny sound from his throat, not unlike the whine which came from Jagger.

She had a headache. It was bad enough that sleep could not hide the pain from her, though she tried to stay adrift. Jagger lay on her legs heavily and she felt as though she could not move at all, suffocating under his weight and heat. He was not supposed to get up on the bed, and most nights he didn't. Still, there were some nights when he crept up, and she was just as grateful for his company as he seemed to be for hers.

Tonight was not one of them. The throb that ached through her skull also seemed to have brought an incredibly bad taste to her mouth, pasty and foul. Charlie shifted slightly, trying to get out from under Jagger's body, and wake. Cobwebs seemed to be all around her, thready remnants of a nightmare she could not quite remember, yet that still clung to that thin veil of awareness between dream and consciousness. It held a haunting similarity to the dreamworld that used to seize her before . . . to the Midnight that would cloud her entire mind and body. . . .

Charlie shuddered uneasily, trying to throw off the darkness cloaking her.

She flung a leg out, muttering, "Jagger, get *over*," and tried to open her eyes.

"Charlie, honey, it's your mother. Can you hear me?"

Charlie pried one eyelid open successfully, though the blurred vision which met her did no good at all. What was her mother doing there? "Mom?"

A blur of light and shadow converged into a large blob that leaned near her. "It's me, honey. I'm right here."

Sitting on top of Jagger, if Charlie could judge the position properly. She slid her legs farther away from the heaviness. With a tongue that felt as sticky and foul as an old turpentine oil rag, she tried to lick her lips. "Jagger's too heavy . . . make him get down, Mom."

"The dog isn't here, Charlie. Do you know where you are? Do you know what happened?"

She peered through the one eye which would stay open, though not focused, and managed to shake her head. A touch, quick and cool and damp, brushed her forehead.

"You're in the hospital, honey. You fainted on the stage during the benefit."

Dismay shot through her. "Oh, no. No. . . ."

Back in the hospital again. Of course that could not be Jagger on her legs. Jagger came after the hospital . . . no, even after that. Before Jagger, she'd had a dog named Monte. But the hospital had come first. Always first.

Charlie closed her eyes.

And before the hospital, Midnight had come.

The aching throb pounding her skull suddenly became secondary to the drumming of her heart. She let out a tiny groan, one that was not supposed to escape her lips, but she seemed to have as little control over her lips as over the rest of her. She hated hospitals, she despised them, and if she was in one, she did not wish to stay.

The weight from her leg lifted suddenly as her mother stood up and moved to the head of the bed, adjusting the pillows behind Charlie's head.

Charlie wet her lips and opened both eyes successfully, gazing around. She knew the look of the room when it met her eyes, and the banks of monitoring equipment sitting with the green screens and tiny blips and floating lines.

"Take me home, Mother."

"Charlie! I can't do that. There are tests scheduled. We have to know what happened."

"I didn't have a chance to eat till eight o'clock, that's what happened. If you won't take me home, I'll call Daddy." Charlie struggled to bolster herself upright in bed, and look her mother in the face.

Her mother's lips thinned.

Quentin Saunders, like Charlie, had a poor opinion of hospitals while Mary had the opposite, fully embracing the miracle which seemed to have saved Charlie's life the first time around.

"Charlie, I don't like it when you threaten me. They have an MRI ordered."

She shuddered. She could not stand the confinement of the coffinlike enclosure, had never gotten used to it, her panic growing worse with every exam taken in it. Her heart began to drum faster at the thought of lying in the noisy tunnel for even a minute, let alone the thirty to sixty minutes she knew they would ask her to endure. She wet her lips.

"Mom, every time I trip or forget something or get a little dizzy or nauseated or something goes wrong in my life does not mean the tumor has come back." She pushed the sheets aside and swung her legs over the edge of the bed.

Mary put a firm hand on her shoulder. "You're not going anywhere. Quentin is coming down—I don't have my car here. I came in the van with you and the paramedics." She sighed, and then put a hand out to help Charlie sit up. "You don't know what it's like," she added, her tone conciliatory. "Seeing you faint like that again, remembering last time—"

"Mom, I live in this body. I have a far better idea of what it's like than you do." And she had no intention of staying in the hospital for another minute while they tried to understand what had happened. "I've got deadlines to meet for the Kensington buildings and I'm not going to make it if I'm lying here while they stick pins in me for a week as if I were some kind of voodoo doll." Charlie scooted to the edge of the bed, then she realized she had nothing on but one of those soft cotton gowns that hung open in the back. "Where are my clothes!"

"Hanging in the closet. A little rumpled, and I don't know if dry cleaning can save your blouse. . . ." Mary's voice trailed off. She made a slight movement with her hands as if embarrassed at retreating into a mundane subject like laundry.

Sitting at the edge of the bed, a wave of unsteadiness swept Charlie. She clenched her eyes shut for a desperate second, ducking her chin so that her mother could not see it pass through her. When she opened her eyes, she looked for Jagger who should be curled up in one corner or another of the room.

"Where's Jagger?"

"Oh, Charlie, he was dreadful! He snapped at everyone who tried to get near you. Poor Cameron Mott had to run for his life. He tried to throw his jacket over that dog to get to you—"

"I would have snapped at Cam myself." Charlie tried to shrug, and ended up wincing at a sudden tenderness in one arm. Thinking of the event organizer, she added, "Call Janie first thing in the morning. I want Cam's tickets refunded even before he thinks of asking for his money back. But Jagger . . . you didn't just leave him there? Or call the pound?"

"Of course not. Some young man seemed to know what to do, he got Jagger to lie down. He said he would take him home."

Charlie stared at her mother in amazement. "You let some stranger take my dog home?"

"Charlie, I wasn't worried about Jagger at the time." Her mother's mouth went into a hard, thin line, and her eyes glistened.

She took a deep breath. "Mom, I know, I'm sorry. But I need Jagger and you don't even know who has him!"

Her mother took a crumpled business card out of her purse and tried to smooth it between her fingers. "He gave me this. I will call him first thing in the morning." Mary Saunders said that firmly as if no one in the world would want to keep a dog longer than absolutely necessary.

"Mother, sometimes I just can't believe you." Charlie put her feet to the cold floor and stood, holding onto the railing to steady herself. She reached for the card. Relief struck her at the name. "This is Ruby."

"You know him?"

Charlie felt her face warm slightly. "We had dinner together. He was pleased to see Jagger." She waved the card. "Put this in my pants, wherever they went to." Her mother watched in disapproval but said nothing as Charlie stood. Instead, she reached into the small wooden closet, rummaging through a plastic bag which turned out to contain Charlie's underwear, and then spread out the evening pants, vest, and torn blouse, slipped the business card into the pants' pocket, and neatly put everything back.

RETRIBUTION

A nurse hurried in, frowning as she took in the erect Charlie and the monitors. "What are you doing up?"

"I need the bathroom," Charlie answered. She found herself losing strength and sat on the edge of the bed.

The furrow in the woman's face deepened. "Bedpan."

Charlie shook her head. "Just point me in the right direction."

The woman hesitated, then took the IV stand and untangled it from the monitor cords. "I'll go with you." She unsnapped the leads dotting Charlie's chest from the heart monitor, tapped in a code, and made ready to escort Charlie. "I have to get you ready for the MRI, anyway."

Charlie trembled. "Not tonight."

"You're not leaving here without one. Don't worry, we located your doctor and he's ordered Valium by IV." The nurse put a firm hand on her arm, and resigned, Charlie shuffled after her.

When they returned from the bathroom, her mother seemed to be asleep, having finally collapsed in the chair in the corner, and Quentin stood over her. He put an arm around Charlie to guide her back to bed, his square face creased with his intense dislike of the hospital. He had nursed his invalid mother in and out of them for the last ten years of her life, and although Charlie scarcely remembered the step-grandmother she saw little of in that time, she knew how he felt. The nurse moved the IV stand back in place and left briskly.

She squeezed his arm. "It's all right, Daddy, everyone's just overreacting."

He tucked the sheet around her legs, before looking at his Rolex. "Your shot should be here any minute, the MRI is scheduled in about twenty." How he knew, she did not know, but she did not doubt that he had already been to the nursing station in the ER and probably knew much more about what was going on than she did. He brushed his silvery hair off his forehead. "I knew I should have come tonight."

"No, you shouldn't have. Just an ordinary art auction, and you needed the rest." Charlie sighed and looked at her mother. "So did Mom."

She plucked at the hem of the hospital sheet.

Quentin Saunders, his near black eyes sharp, his face creased from years of work in the sun as well as behind a desk, watched her. "What happened?"

She shook her head. "I just fainted."

"You don't just faint." Quentin perched on the edge of the hospital bed. He wore casual clothes like some men wore suits, impeccable, creased, and with authority. "You're like me, a workhorse." He patted her sheeted foot. "You missed your last appointment for a checkup."

"Of course not. I went in, it was clear—"

"Don't lie to me, Charlie. That's the first thing the doctors out there told me." He eyed the IV, the small cotton ball and Band-Aid on her arm where someone had drawn blood, though she did not remember it, the leads to the heart and other monitors. "Why did you do that?"

She looked into dark eyes that had negotiated tough contracts the world over, and she was the first to blink.

She exhaled. "All right. I didn't go in."

"Why?"

"I feel great. And I hate that thing, you know how I hate it."

He nodded slowly. "I understand. You're not leaving here tonight till they take a look at you."

"Daddy—"

He put up a hand. "This is not negotiable."

She felt cold.

Quentin Saunders said, "You have to trust me on this."

The nurse bustled back in with a tray, syringe rolling around on top of it. The sight of the needle made Charlie queasy and she fastened her attention on Quentin, as the nurse took her wrist, checked the information on the plastic bracelet and said, "Tell me your name if you can."

"Charlotte Saunders," she answered lowly. Before she'd finished, the woman snapped the end of the syringe off and plunged the medication into the IV shunt. Her stomach clenched at the thought of the MRI coffin. The nurse emptied the syringe and pushed her gently into the bed, saying, "You won't be out, but you won't care."

Efficiently, she put the railing up, brushing Quentin aside to do so. She paused, looking at him. "You the father?"

He nodded.

"They're asking for someone down in administration, for the insurance information and background."

Quentin smiled gently at Charlie. "You have your calling, and it looks as though I have mine." He patted her foot again before stepping away and then carefully putting his hand on his wife's shoulder.

Mary shuddered awake. He leaned down and kissed her forehead. "I am here, and I am gone again. They need me downstairs. She's almost ready for the MRI."

She smiled tremulously. "Hurry."

"I will." He gripped her shoulder as if infusing his strength into her, and left the curtained area.

Charlie settled into the hard pillow, unwillingly, but feeling the lassitude creeping over her, a welcome melting of flesh and blood and nerve. She put her hand on the railing. "Mommy . . ."

"I'll be right there with you, honey."

Charlie nodded, her eyesight blurring. It was becoming difficult to focus. She closed her eyes.

* * *

As Mary trailed after the bed, the orderly in scrubs wheeled it through half-lit corridors to the Radiology department. She watched them transfer Charlie's almost totally limp form to the bed of the MRI, and strap her down lightly, admonishing her not to move. She stepped back into the operating booth as they took her daughter's blood pressure and checked her before switching on the equipment. Its noisy, resonating hum began, and Charlie's still body rolled slowly into the enclosure.

Behind her, a tech stood at the bank of monitors and screens and a second tech stood waiting to inject the dyes for the second phase of the MRI when signaled. Her daughter disappeared from sight and Mary watched the monitor instead, Charlie's face even bleaker in the black-and-white video quality of the screen.

"She claustrophobic?" The male tech looked bored. His thin, stringy brown hair was combed back, and braided into a tight little pigtail at the back of his neck. His scrubs were rumpled and a coffee stain trailed down the front of the top.

"Didn't used to be. But she's had so many of these. . . ." Mary's voice trailed off.

"Yeah? How come?"

"She had a pediatric brain tumor."

"That'll do it. What, two, three times a year follow-up?"

"Three times a year, first two years. Now, twice."

He nodded. He began to hum a flat, unrecognizable tune, as he made adjustments and lined up the first scans on the monitors in front of him.

Mary wanted to ask him what was happening, but she knew he would not tell her. If he saw something, he would not comment. It would be up to the staff doctor to read the MRI and interpret it, a formal declaration, and that might not be for a day or two. Everything in writing, carefully worded, precise, not to protect the patient, but the hospital. She shifted her weight.

Music was being piped into the enclosure, and she became aware of its overflow, it vaguely matching the tuneless hum of the tech. He pointed at some stiff plastic chairs in the corner of his booth. "Going to take a while, might as well have a seat."

She took the chair, almost thankful for its discomfort, gouging her behind the shoulder blades, hard as a rock on her bottom, keeping her awake. In spite of it, she must have dozed, for a muttered exclamation from the tech seemed to jar her into awareness.

"What is it?"

"Don't know." The tech rose out of his chair, blocking two of the monitor screens slightly.

"What do you mean, you don't know?" She stood. "What's happening?"

"She's out right . . . I mean, she was practically totally under." The tech touched dials. Mary shouldered him aside a little to look at the monitors.

She had been at enough of Charlie's tests to realize that the dye had been administered—she'd been asleep for thirty minutes without realizing it—but could see nothing else untoward about the displays. "What is it? Is she in danger?"

"No, no . . . just . . . look at the brain activity here." He tapped a finger on his screen. "Those aren't sleep waves . . . but she's out . . . look." And he indicated the video which displayed Charlie's form inside the narrow tube.

Mary looked at her daughter, eyes closed, body still. "What is it?"

"I don't know. Strange, huh?" The tech pulled his pigtail around to the front and tugged on it absently for a moment. "Sorta like a poltergeist, I guess." He grinned, showing a broken tooth, and make eerie noises.

"That's not funny. She can't be hurt in there, can she? I want it shut down immediately."

"The machine's fine." The tech cleared his throat. "I'm sorry, ma'am. I didn't mean to upset you. Can you have a seat? I'm almost done here."

Mary held her ground, alternating her study between the video picture of Charlie and the monitor showing the MRI scan. "It's not a reaction to the dye?"

"No, ma'am. She's fine. Except she is showing brain activity on some level I've never seen before." He clucked. "Let the docs figure that one out."

"But her heart rate . . ."

"Everything else seems to be fine. Might be some kind of reaction to the Valium." He shrugged. "Weird."

Mary shifted her weight. She stayed on her feet for ten more long minutes till the noisy throbbing of the MRI shut down, and Charlie's quiet form came sliding out of the enclosure. By then the activity seemed to have stopped, and the second tech had brought her bed around, and the two techs transferred Charlie back onto it. Mary quickly tucked the gown and sheets around her into some slight form of modesty. Charlie's eyelids fluttered slightly.

"Mom."

"Right here."

"I'm . . . groggy."

"It's all over. We're going back to observation now." Mary patted her daughter with a confidence she did not have.

"I want to . . . go . . . home."

"As soon as they let us know." She lengthened her stride to keep up with the bed as the orderly took over outside the Radiology department and began to push Charlie back down the corridor.

Charlie nodded and took a deep breath.

The doctor was waiting for them in the room and looked up from his clipboard wearily, a young, thin Asian doctor, his hair sticking up in the back from a recent attempt to get a few hours of sleep, a wrinkled and threadbare white lab coat over his hospital scrubs.

"She can go. We'll read the test results when we can and have them sent to . . ." He paged through forms on the clipboard. "Dr. Katsume and Dr. Clarkson."

"You're releasing her?"

"Soon as the Valium wears off, which shouldn't be too long, a minimum dose was ordered for her. All the rest of her vitals seem fine."

"And that's it?"

He looked at her through tired black eyes. "That's all we can do for now. She seems stable. If the MRI shows something, your own doctors will handle it. I'll have a wheelchair brought up." He paused at the room's doorway. "Is there someone here who can help you?"

"My husband should be in the building somewhere."

He nodded. "Saunders? I'll have him paged." The doctor disappeared out the door before Mary could say yea or nay.

She sighed.

Charlie stirred on the hospital bed, kicking aside the tangled sheet. She grasped the railing and tried to sit up.

"Charlie, wait a minute."

She gave a wobbly shake of her head. "I want to go home."

Faintly, Mary could hear Quentin being paged to patient discharge. She moved to her daughter as Charlie stubbornly clung to the railing on one side of the bed and tried to lower it on the other. "Let me help."

Charlie gave a little laugh. "I don't think I . . . have . . . much choice."

The phone rang sharply. Mary jumped, caught her breath, and then answered it.

"Everything all right?"

"Everything is fine, they're releasing her."

"It'll take me a minute to bring the car around, then."

"We'll wait for you in the lobby, dear."

He made a noise, one she was familiar with, not a grunt or a sigh, but a noise in between, that he often used when making a decision of some type. Then he said, "Be there as soon as I can."

"We don't even have a wheelchair yet, so don't hurry."

"All right." The phone line went dead.

Mary replaced the receiver, and stepped to Charlie. Already her daughter looked more alert as she reached for her garment bag of clothes. The IV had been removed and Charlie clumsily began to peel off the connectors to the heart monitor. Silently, Mary stood there, and helped her daughter when she could, almost as if afraid to touch her.

*   *   *

Charlie felt frail. More than her mother's action made her feel that way. The Valium seemed to have numbed even basic motor skills.

It took more time than she thought getting dressed. She seemed to have reached some kind of mental block as to what to do with each item, how to put it on and fasten it, what she really wanted to do with it, and the sheer effort of the concentration it took her to deal with dressing made her afraid. She did not look at her mother once while she did so, knowing that her mother might read her confusion from her face. An attendant came with the wheelchair and waited for Charlie to step into it.

Mary pushed a wing of ash-blonde hair from her face and said, "We should wait in the lobby for your father."

"All right. Are you going to sign me out?"

"I think that's one of the things he's taking care of." Mary hesitated a moment, then moved to Charlie's right side, and put her arm out, so that Charlie could lean slightly on her.

And Charlie did so, something she hadn't done in years, and her mother looked up at her, gave a short smile, and the glistening in her eyes dissolved to a tear that rolled down her face slowly. "I haven't . . . I haven't had to help you like this for six or seven years."

"And you won't again, either." Charlie gave her a brusque hug. "I'm fine, Mom." She took a deep breath. She could not always remember what it had been like those first few years after the operation, the weakness, the physical therapy, the recovery to the point where she could get along quite well, even without a service dog. The weakness, the trembling, the disorientation, the inability to hold her right hand steady enough to paint . . .

The loss of desire to paint anything at all.

The emptiness.

The frailty.

Midnight coming.

She did not want to go back.

Never.

She took a deep breath as she settled into the wheelchair. "Let's see if Daddy is waiting for us yet."

Chapter Nine

INTERLUDE 2

When Midnight comes, it is unrelenting. Total. A complete blackout of all five senses, like death. But it is not death, because once its curtain, its cloak, has fallen over her, it brings back the senses one by one.

Sharp.

Acute.

Painful.

But they are not her senses, they do not belong to her, they belong to this creature of darkness that possesses her. They ride piggyback on her own, thrust into her, latched on with grappling hooks, piercing her with agony.

She sometimes thought of Midnight as that Hellraiser creature from the Clive Barker books and movies: needles everywhere, raw nerves and bringing horrifying visions with it.

Visions.

Nightmares.

Owning her soul completely until she could some-how, some way, put them down on canvas . . . exposing them to the light of day.

Many of the nightmares seemed not nearly so awful or frightening once she translated them into paint. Some were even quite beautiful.

"A colorist," they said of her. "Symbolic. Some-where beyond Picasso and between Chagall and Dali. None of any of them, and similar to all."

Valdor, at first her agent, and then someone who had tried to take total control of her life, had often whispered in her ear, "That's because you transform it. You take the rawness of what you see, and you purify it. You reflect it, and the essence of you, your innocence, your goodness . . . heals it."

She did not believe that.

Valdor wanted her to start painting again. He lived expensively and gambled even more expensively, and he had grown more and more desperate as the years went by.

She only knew that between what Midnight brought her and her hands put on the canvas, the visions changed.

Except for the two.

The first two paintings of a trilogy she would never finish.

Because when that tumor had been cut from her brain, Midnight had been excised with it.

And she could not paint any more. She had not even tried for the first six months. That had been taken up with learning how to crawl, how to walk, how to stand and gain balance, and eat and dress herself again. She made progress so rapidly that she hardly noticed the toil, and then came a point when the weakness still remained, and she knew she would never be the same again.

Quentin had gotten her the dog then. He helped her stand and steady herself, pulled her when she was too tired to walk on her own. Carried things for her. Warmed her. And when he'd gotten too old to help her any more, Monte had been retired to the same foster family who had raised him from puppyhood to training, and Valdor replaced him. A crutch . . . only he leaned on her far more heavily than she leaned on him.

She had not consciously done it then, and she realized now that Federico Valdor had insinuated himself into that position purposely. Urging her to depend on him, taking up the brushes again. Always insisting that he had her best interests at heart.

She had not been able to do so.

Eventually their bickering turned to quarreling, and quarreling to vicious, controlling fights and hatred.

And Quentin had gotten her Jagger when Valdor

left, though he never really left. He stayed on the fringe of her life like a lingering remnant of the weakness which plagued her.

A reminder that something had struck which could never be completely cured, but would always have traces, remains, which must be endured.

Valdor had never considered her foray into commercial art as successful. Her weavings, her collages, her textile creations adorned banks, lined entire corridors of office buildings, and continued to earn her a substantial living, so that the fortune she had earned before was never touched. She would probably never have to worry about money the rest of her life if she lived modestly, yet her career was something he scorned. "Wallpaper," he scoffed, "was not art." And, of course, he did not have a percentage of her commercial career. And though the paintings she had done previously continued to go up in value, there was no doubt that their worth would be greater if she returned to her career, bolstering it with growth and new examples of her talent.

She did not know or care. She bought the Laguna bungalow she and her mother had lived in most of her young life, moved away from the modest mansion in which Quentin and her mother lived, and she was happy. Her hands grew calluses from the weavings and the loom, her back sometimes ached from bending over the potter's wheel and worktable, her jeans were often flecked with minute pieces of paper lint from making her own papers and masks.

And if she thought of Midnight at all, it was only in memory.

If it was inspiration, she would live without it.

If it was hell, she knew that someday it would return.

Chapter Ten

The attendant was wheeling her out of the elevator, when her beeper went off. She brushed the appliance, then looked at them. "I'm sorry. We're shorthanded tonight."

"I'll take her from here," Mary said softly.

The young woman hesitated, her burnished brunette hair swinging about her face. Then she sucked on a lip. "I could get into trouble . . . hospital rules. . . ."

"They need you upstairs, and we'll be fine. We'll leave the wheelchair by the information desk."

The attendant had already backed up a step, retreating to the elevator. "All right." She smiled at Charlie. "You feel better now."

Mary Saunders guided the chair into a quiet corner of the lobby. "I'll go find Quentin." She brushed her lips across Charlie's forehead, her mouth dry, trembling, and Charlie felt the concern and worry her mother restrained.

"I'll be fine."

Her mother hurried off with a faint click of her low heels.

The lighting was subdued in the hospital lobby. Charlie absently checked for her watch, but her mother had not returned it to her, so she looked around the several alcoves of furniture and magazines, anywhere, for a clock. She finally spotted one on the wall in the glass-enclosed gift shop which was shuttered for the night. A plain-faced dial of a clock, its somber black hands rested at ten after three. Yet, even at this hour, one of the other lobby niches held a family, leaning close to one another as if for strength, murmuring quietly, their faces showing the strain of their vigil.

One brown-haired child had succumbed to sleep, his face bunched up against his mother's elbow in a rubbery, uncomfortable position, but his snuggled contentment apparent. Only he seemed at peace. The man and woman and brother all fidgeted and watched the elevator banks against the far wall with furrowed brows. That was the elevator, Charlie knew, which the doctor came down in after surgery.

In her own fatigue, she found herself staring, thoughts wandering off into a kind of blankness, and she looked away quickly, hoping they hadn't noticed. Instead she looked down at her blouse, tucked hastily inside her vest, because the buttons had been torn from the front, done her mother said, by the para-medics to check her vitals. The black sequined vest which matched her satin trousers seemed unharmed, and for that she was grateful. Evidently its two buttons had been easy enough to open quickly. Her bra had been cut into shreds and she had tossed it into the trash, along with the plastic bag from the hospital which had held her other garments. Self-consciously, she drew her vest closed a little tighter.

An aquarium bubbled in the corner, a tall and thin rectangular glass world, with fuschia and ivory sea fans as a backdrop to the saltwater fish who swam seemingly heedless of the hour. She watched it, knowing that the window to the sea was soothing as well as entertaining, far less stressful than a television set, yet as compelling to watch. Her neurosurgeon from years ago had had two such aquariums in his office. She could not count the times she had spent, nose nearly pressed to the glass, watching the fish and eel and hermit crabs among the rocks and flora. After the operation, she had found herself eerily identifying with the hermit crab, her own head bound in a turban of bandages, the rest of her venturing out into the world only when she could hope it was safe.

There was no hermit crab in the hospital tank. There was, however, one of those eels, peeking through a porous lava rock, his brown sleek self darting in and out as a brilliant fish ventured too close to his lair. She had never seen an eel eat a fish, so she thought it was to protect his territory.

A shadow fell across her view and she drew back quickly, prepared to see her mother. Instead, the dark-haired boy smiled shyly at her. His T-shirt had a small grape-colored stain on it, his round stomach peeked through a tiny hole, and he wore knee-length shorts meant to sag.

"Lady, could I borrow some quarters? My dad wants some coffee and we ran out of money."

"You've been here a while, huh?" Charlie reached inside her vest, to an inner pocket, where she always kept money folded up and secreted. She withdrew the bills, found a one crisp except for the crease in the middle, and gave it to the boy. "You can put this in the vending machine."

"I know," he said wisely.

She nodded. She could not tell if he was school age or not, but she knew the wisdom of children when it came to drink and candy machines. "Well, there you go."

"Thanks." He started to turn around, then looked back. "My sister . . . she was in a car accident. We don't know if she's gonna live or not."

His need for her to understand touched her. Charlie smiled briefly in sympathy. His brown eyes darkened for a moment. "You can pray for her if ya want."

A sharp whistle sounded across the lobby, directed

at him evidently, for he flinched. He added, "Gotta go," and dashed away, holding the dollar bill gingerly. Charlie swallowed a small lump in her throat and looked back to the aquarium as if she were drowning and the small, brilliant light of the tank were the sun to show her the way to the surface. She did not want to be here. She fought down an overwhelming moment of panic, wondering where her mother could be.

A janitor came through with a small carpet sweeper, cleaned the area of the lobby briskly and quickly, leaned to the aquarium and snapped the light off. He smiled at Charlie.

"Even fish have to sleep sometime," he said apologetically.

She nodded. She continued to watch the darkened tank, although the fish were nearly impossible to see now, and the eel withdrew entirely into his rock. The janitor worked his way around, humming off-key to himself, and then there was silence again except for the sound of the aquarium pump, and the faint voices from the waiting family in the other alcove.

She closed her eyes briefly and sent a small prayer for their daughter, whoever she was.

"Charlie."

Startled, her eyelids flew open, her body jerking in reflex.

He stood very near her, so close she wondered how he had gotten there without her knowing, unless she had dozed for a moment or two when her eyes closed. His face was shadowed in the dimness of the alcove, but she would know it anywhere, dark hair smoothed back, dark eyes intent on her, dark goatee neatly trimmed, his ivory shirt gleaming from the depths of his dark and expensive suit jacket.

He removed a handkerchief from the inside pocket of his jacket and handed it to her silently. She took it, careful not to actually touch his fingers, and realized a tear or two dampened her cheekbones. She dabbed at them, drying her face.

He refused when she tried to return the handkerchief.

Uneasily, Charlie wrapped it about her hand. "Thank you, Valdor."

He inclined his head. "Are you all right?" His dark gaze swept the wheelchair.

She paused before answering. "I will be."

"May I sit?"

So formal. Always, so formal. Born in Europe, educated in Italy and France, like his father and grandfather before him, his fiery intellect bent entirely toward the arts. He discouraged use of his first name, Federico, which Americans invariably tried to reduce to Fred, preferring to be addressed by his last name, even in intimacy. He had spent most of his youth in San Francisco before going to Europe to finish his degree in business and art, and he had scarcely a trace of accent in his voice, but his mannerisms, his culture, his outlook, his whole persona were indisputably Continental. He even far preferred to gamble in Monte Carlo rather than in Vegas.

At one time she had thought it incredibly sophisticated. Now she thought little of it one way or the other.

He sat down anyway, taking care to pluck at the crease in his trousers so that it would stay in place.

"You were there tonight," Charlie said, suddenly realizing that though she had never seen him he had to have been among the crowd.

"I was."

"Why?" The calm in her tone surprised her.

"I heard of the show. I came because I hoped . . . you had started painting again."

"I will never paint again."

"You cannot say that. No one of us knows what our future holds."

A small sigh escaped her despite her effort to rein in all her emotions. Valdor's eyes flickered slightly.

"I can say that I don't feel like painting again."

He countered, "But we both know your feelings change. You are mercurial, like the wind."

She was not, and he knew it, and about the only major feeling she had ever had change was her love for painting—and he knew that, too. She ignored the dig. The palm of her right hand itched a little, missing the feel of Jagger's harness in it, and the protection he gave her. Valdor would not be sitting opposite her now, a cool, composed smile on his face, if she had Jagger with her.

She had to wet her lips to ask, "Are you back now?"

"Perhaps." His flint-colored eyes watched her keenly. "I am still your agent, Charlie."

"The contract expires in a year."

"It does not matter. I have your best interests at heart. I always have had. There is no one else who could represent you in the fashion that I can."

She had to concede him that. Valdor was a flawless businessman. But it was his relentless pursuit of her to begin painting once again, his somewhat questionable advances from some of her investments, that had made Quentin urge her to cut him off, and they had done what they could, changing accounts and locking him out. Then Valdor had gone into a rage, and things had escalated from there, fired she knew by his need to pay his gambling debts and her father's determination that she would not be scorched as well. After that initial blowup, things had subsided somewhat.

He adjusted the French cuffs on his shirt. "Are you ill again?"

"It was nothing," she said defensively. "A busy day, I fainted."

"You do not faint, my dear."

"I did tonight!"

He appraised her for a few seconds. "And you do not get frightened easily." He raised an eyebrow.

Where in God's name were her mother and Quentin? Had the hospital swallowed them whole? Charlie added firmly, "And I am fine now."

Valdor stood smoothly, as though aware time was no longer on his side. His expensive suit fell into unwrinkled lines on his compact body. The fourteen years' difference in their ages did not show on his face. "I wish you well, Charlie. I have always . . . wished you well."

Faintly, she said, "If you stay in the area, my father will get another restraining order."

He tilted his head. "Of course. And you still have your ferocious dog . . . somewhere . . . I assume."

"I do."

"It is not necessary, my dear. I have only your best interests at heart. You must paint again, Charlie, because that is your soul, and you cannot continue to deny it. Nor can you let the critics say that you were not genuine, not a talent. You need to return to canvas."

She closed her eyes against the pain briefly, then looked outward again. "Valdor—"

But he was gone, as silently as he had appeared.

Charlie began to shake.

She was still shaking when her mother finally came

out of a corridor, leaning on Quentin, her hand full of papers, her face furrowed.

Charlie found the strength to stand quickly. "Let's get out of here."

"I should work for the United Nations. We've been trying to coordinate the hospital with your clinic. Phone numbers, faxes, doctors . . . no one is happy about this."

"But your mother settled things." Quentin patted her arm. Mary looked up at Quentin, and her face immediately smoothed, as it always did, the love lines in her expression beginning to glow.

It was enough for them to be worried over the one thing. She shoved aside every intention she had of telling them about Valdor, despite her misgivings.

He pressed gently on Charlie's shoulder. "Sit down, young lady, and let me wheel you to the curb."

His presence behind the wheelchair settled her a little, solid, formidable, his low voice rumbling something to her mother who walked, birdlike, quickly, fluttering, to keep up with them. "Let's go home, get some sleep . . . I'll cancel my golf game tomorrow . . . and then we have to make those doctors happy, so we'll make some arrangements."

Charlie sighed. Her mother slipped her arm around her waist. "You're coming home, of course."

"No. I want to sleep in my own bed. Besides, I don't know when he's going to bring Jagger back."

"Where is Jagger, anyway? Someone has him?" her father asked sharply.

"John Rubidoux. He came to the benefit, too. Jagger knew him immediately."

"He made such a fuss over Charlie, Quentin, I don't know what I'd have done. No one could get to her!"

"Good dog, that. So Ruby took him?" Quentin made a grumbling sound. It cheered her to hear it. She hugged him. "All right then. Sleep in your own bed. I'll send Pedro after you when you call."

"I'll make a brunch," her mother said cheerfully.

Sandwiched between them, Charlie rolled to the lobby doors. A small body darted in front of them, blocking the exit as it opened.

"Lady! Your change." He held out a grubby hand, a silvery quarter flashing in his palm.

She looked back, and saw a fatigued figure in hospital scrubs, talking to the man and woman, and the woman's face was wreathed with smiles, and the worn-down man was pumping the doctor's hand up and down vigorously. She had no need to hear the words to know the outcome, and smiled faintly. She pulled her money out again, and pressed a ten into his hand. "Go celebrate," she told him.

His button-round eyes widened. He gulped. He flashed an all-over grin and ran off, waving his money in triumph.

"What was that all about?" Quentin rumbled in

her ear as they went through the doors and into the parking lot, an evening wind off the coast chilling the air.

"Survivors," she said. "We need to stick together."

Chapter Eleven

He had doubted the address as he pulled into the winding drive, the street lined with unpretentious bungalows, but he began to change his mind when he saw the cars sitting in the driveways, convertible BMWs, more modest but equally pricey Mercedeses, and the last of his doubts was erased as Jagger stuck his head out the passenger window and let out a loud "Woof!" of approval. John decided that, despite the small size of the homes, the hillside view of the Laguna cove and beach far below must be worth the price. It was hardly afternoon and he'd already embarrassed himself by calling earlier and obviously disturbing her from the sound of her voice. He'd found, beside the embarrassment, the throaty tones awakening him sexually, as he thought of being beside her in the morning, that voice in his ear in person. After a sentence or two, the cold composure had returned to her voice to his dismay. He rang off quickly to let her go back to sleep, and to put a quick check on his own responses after agreeing to come by after one.

Towering palms and ficus trees straddled the boulevard, this street carved into the hill when front yards and boulevards actually existed. Ruby found Charlie Saunders' address and pulled in, parking behind a late model Honda Accord. Jagger verified it, his tail skimming the air in happiness, beating John's arm.

Jagger looked as if he was going to take the most direct route to the ground, through the window, when John snatched at his harness.

He gave the correction and added a "Hey!" for emphasis. Jagger put his ears back remorsefully and sat down on the car seat. He rolled caramel-colored eyes as John got out and closed the van door, but he waited until John opened the door and gave him the signal to get down.

Still, no training in the world could keep Jagger's feathery tail from whipping into furious motion nor from a front shrub getting watered as they approached the door. Jagger did not wait for John to knock or ring the doorbell, he let out another belling "Woof!" and they could both hear a light voice answer, "Jagger! Just a minute!"

The golden retriever shook himself vigorously in pleasure. He looked up guiltily at John and John sighed, answering, "You're right, bud. We're both goners." The dog, however, could be certain of his reception.

He was in the process of removing his baseball cap and running his fingers through his hair with his free hand when the carved oak door opened abruptly. Jagger pulled the harness out of his hand as he bounded inward, slid to a stop on the parquet flooring in the foyer, and gently leaned on his mistress' leg, quivering in contained happiness.

No less was the look of joy on her face as she rubbed his ears and then glanced up at John.

Charlie made an odd face. "I can't thank you enough for taking him. My mother would have just left him, I think. And Ollie—the man who owns the Peppermill Gallery—would have been beside himself. I don't know what would have happened to him!"

"Any time," he got out. He ran his fingers around his baseball cap.

Jagger sat on Charlie's foot and whined at Ruby.

She smiled faintly. "How about we start over? Hi. I'm Charlie Saunders. I limp a lot, I used to paint, and I have this terrific dog."

His heart did a funny skip beat in his chest and he coughed slightly to hide the fluster he felt. He took the hand she held out.

"Won't you come in? I have a brunch for a small kingdom in the kitchen, with my mother's orders to eat all of it. You'll save my life if you're hungry."

"I . . . ah . . ."

"Please. It's the least I can do for inconveniencing you last night." She gave that lopsided smile. He felt his objections go sliding off in his chest somewhere. He saw that she leaned on the door to steady herself and quickly stepped in.

"I'd appreciate that. Besides, I'd like to talk to you about Jagger."

"All right."

He put his arm out, gently and discreetly nudging the aforementioned dog out of the way, and Charlie shifted her weight to him. She smelled of soap and something else, very faint, he couldn't identify. Something herbal, but light and refreshing.

She talked to the dog all the way into the kitchen, and he found himself grinning widely at the silliness of her words and tone, much as Jagger was doing. A small round oak table sat in a nook that overlooked a wide green yard and glass doors leading to them. One of the chairs had a white dish towel wrapped about its back rungs. At a word from Charlie, Jagger gripped the dish towel and tugged the chair away from the table's edge so she could sit.

The table was laden with goodies. A basket full of freshly baked muffins, their aroma filling the air, sat in the center. A silver chafing dish with serving spoon laid over it sat next to it, and a small round silver casserole on a hot pad was nestled next to a pot of jam. A carafe of what looking to be freshly squeezed orange juice reigned next to faintly blue-colored juice glasses.

Charlie grinned. "You just missed the delivery truck."

He reached for expensive-looking paper plates and silverware, setting her place first and then his before sitting down. "You weren't kidding. This is enough to feed an army."

She flushed as though slightly embarrassed. "The delivery service won't deliver for less than four, so . . ." She spread her hand over the dishes. "That's what Mom ordered. I also told her you were bringing Jagger back. She wanted to be sure you were fed, too."

He opened the chafing dish. Slices of crisp bacon and patties of browned, spicy sausage lay on doilies, along with four slabs of thick ham. The smell made him instantly ravenous, and Jagger whined slightly, as though affected the same way. He looked at Charlie.

"Bacon, sausage, or ham?"

She held out her plate. "Bacon and sausage, please."

He grinned. "Good, 'cause I'm having all three." He served her with pleasure. She opened the casserole dish where creamy scrambled eggs lay nestled over cooked spinach and chives. For a few minutes, no one talked as they passed the muffins and cold butter back and forth, poured orange juice, and divvied up the eggs. He found another serving dish hidden under the napkins and it yielded country style potatoes.

Charlie sneaked a potato wedge down to Jagger before diving into her eggs, then she made an appreciative sound and rolled her eyes.

He had already devoured a blueberry muffin by then, and sliced off a sliver of what had to be genuine Virginia smoked ham. He sat back for a moment, savoring the ham.

"This is good—"

"Excellent food—" they blurted together, and then Charlie began to laugh.

Jagger sat at alert attention by her side as she slipped a small piece of bacon down to him. "I'll have to ask Mom where this place is."

"Do that, and let me know. It beats the local fast food hands down." He sat back, poured himself some coffee from a white thermal pitcher, and inhaled the rich fragrance of good, ordinary java. He drank it half down and beamed in satisfaction.

Charlie fussed a moment over a piece of bacon, doing more crumbling of it than eating, and he sensed that the time had come for them to talk. He looked at her and smiled. "Ready?"

She closed her eyes as if bracing herself, before looking at him. "What is it about Jagger?"

"You know he stood guard over you. It was hard to get to you to help you."

"Isn't he supposed to do that?"

"He is supposed to follow my command to cease when I give it."

"And he didn't?" She quirked an eyebrow.

"Not at first. He was very confused and upset. Charlie, a scared dog can hurt himself or someone else. Someone wanted to use a stun gun on him—it could have killed him. Plus, if you had been in cardiac arrest, we couldn't have gotten to you easily."

"But that's the point, isn't it? No one is supposed to be able to get to me."

"On command."

"I didn't have time to give a command . . . or rescind it." She frowned as she picked up a muffin and opened it, steam escaping, so she could butter it. "What do you suggest?"

"A refresher on his basic training, what he was meant to do."

"The institute won't be happy."

"He's too good a dog to ruin." He refilled his coffee mug and poured some for her. She lightened it with cream, but took no sugar. He watched her and looked away before she could notice him taking her in. The buffer zone she set up with just a faint coolness of her expression and tone had dropped into place again, but not as severely as before.

Charlie thought a moment and put her hand gently on Jagger's head. "Could you do it?"

"I don't know what methods they used. I would

probably confuse him more and that would do the opposite of what he needs right now."

She nodded, the corners of her mouth turned down. "I'll call. I just hate to . . . lose him . . . for a couple of weeks." She ruffled the golden's ears. "But, if you think so, I'll do it." She picked at her eggs with a fork, stirring them around a bit, but not eating.

"He's worth it, isn't he?"

"Of course!"

"I'll make the call if you want."

Charlie looked at him, some happiness returning to her blue-gray eyes. "Would you? I know it's an inconvenience, but I can pay for your time."

"I wouldn't charge for this."

"Yes," she said firmly, "you would, and will."

John hesitated a moment, unsure of his footing, then said, "I am not treating you like a charity case."

A certain awareness flickered through her eyes. She picked up a fork, then set it down. "I apologize," she said. "I have a certain cactus-like charm, I'm told."

"Strictly defensive. But you don't need it with me." He put his napkin up on the table. "I won't take money for trying to repair work I did badly the first time. I can't speak for the foundation. They may charge you an arm and a leg for putting him through the motions again."

Her lips moved a little. "And your charm is equally prickly. How soon do you want to start?"

"Any time. But it should be soon."

She nodded, and her golden-brown hair tumbled over her shoulder with the movement. "All right." She smiled at Jagger. "We'll just have to bite the bullet, huh, buddy" The dog put his head on her knee and whuffed at her.

He found himself doing all the eating, as though the somber mood had taken hold of her and would not let go, and he was angry at himself for doing that to her. But it had to be done, he knew it, she knew it, and most of all it seemed the dog knew it.

He polished off a third muffin and looked at her nearly untouched one. It struck him that part of her plainness came from the sharpness of her features. "You should eat a little more."

Charlie had been staring off at the backyard in thought, and looked at him guiltily. "I'm sorry." She picked up the peach cobbler muffin and picked at its edges. "When are you going to take him back? I hate to lose him, even for a day."

He found himself saying, "Well, if they'll let me observe, maybe I can go out to their training site and see what they're doing. Maybe I can come over here for an hour a day and refresh him, and you won't have to give him up."

Her eyes sparkled. "Could you?"

For a look like that, he'd jump the moon. "I can try."

"Oh, please! We'd be miserable without each other."

"I'll call first thing Monday."

Jagger lifted his head from Charlie's knee and looked at Ruby, his jaws opening and his tongue hanging out happily.

Something rattled at the side of the house. He barely caught the sound, but Jagger's ears went up instantly. The dog shot out of the kitchen, his nails scrambling for a hold on the planked flooring as he cornered.

John got to his feet.

"What is it?"

He shook his head. "I don't know."

Jagger let out a sharp warning bark and Rubidoux could hear him charging across the house to the front. "I'll find out."

He was out of the kitchen before Charlie got to her feet and limped after him.

"He never does that."

Then either something was wrong, or the dog's training was beginning to collapse at a greater rate than John had feared. He entered the living room to see Jagger frozen at the large front window, snarling, his paws on the sill, his head thrust through the drapes. The hackles rose on the dog's back and he dropped his snarl to a low, continuous growl.

Ruby snapped his fingers. Jagger immediately dropped, but his eyes kept going back to the front window, and his chest rumbled with that low, warning growl.

As Charlie came in and braced herself on the back of a living room chair, he went to the front door. "Stay inside," he said, "till I see what's upsetting him."

She nodded, her face a little pale.

John canvassed the entire outside of the house first, circling it, to see if anything had been flushed to the sides or back, but found nothing other than a trembling hibiscus shrub, one of its fresh yellow flowers dropped and crushed to the ground. He trotted around to the front window, where he could see Charlie watching.

He knelt down by the soft dirt of the flower bed. A half imprint of a shoe marked the soil.

From the size of it, a man's shoe.

He looked at it a moment, thinking. Broad daylight. Bold, but not unheard of. Perhaps even a utility repairman.

Or perhaps not. He straightened and saw Charlie, still watching him closely. He did not want to alarm her and there was no real reason to call in police.

Only now, he had an excellent reason to try to keep Jagger with her, twenty-four hours a day, as he was meant to be.

He reentered the house and gave Jagger the command releasing him from guard. The dog trotted to Charlie, and she leaned on him gratefully.

He did not want to tell her, but he did. "I found a shoe print out there."

She wavered. "No."

"Probably just a phone or cable man. But I'll make whatever arrangements I can to try to keep Jagger with you."

"Good." She nodded absently, as though her thoughts had suddenly gone elsewhere.

"I can't see calling the police, unless you can think of a reason."

She shook her head quickly. "No, absolutely not." She dug her fingers into Jagger's golden hair.

He did not know her well, not nearly as well as he wanted to, but he knew then she was lying.

Chapter Twelve

She awoke, barefoot and standing, pale moonlight shivering through a slanted shade on the window, brushes in her hand. Charlie looked at them in wonder and touched their bristles, new brushes, never used, their heads still soft and clean, resting in her hands as though she had taken them up to paint again.

The closed-up studio lay in soft gray and dark shadows, various easels and cabinets and tables casting strange shapes around her, muted by the lack of lighting in the night. She never came in here, not even to clean. Someone else, occasionally sent by her mother, did that. Otherwise the door to this studio stayed locked, as shut away from her as the life she had once had. She had converted a third bedroom into a studio at the other end of the house, the only new portion of her home, knocking down walls and extending them, putting in ceiling fans and huge windows and a great long wall which often acted as a kind of work space for the textiles and other media she used now. It was busy and cluttered and well used, that room, spacious, airy, light.

But this room was the part of the house which gathered the best sun and had the view of the cove, and to which the sea breeze came at night without benefit of fan or machine. She had kept it as she had once used it, unknowing, unwanting, untouched.

She trembled. Jagger lay close to her feet, snoring quietly, and she knew that she had been standing on the enclosed porch for a while, at least long enough for him to settle. Yet she had no memory or dream of leaving her bed and walking to the studio, or any hint of the need that drove her to pick up the brushes. She looked at the easel with its canvas, untouched, awaiting her for . . . how many years? Almost ten.

Midnight had come, and carried her away, bringing her here.

And she did not even remember the trip.

Charlie dropped the paintbrushes. They bounced off her feet and scattered on the floor, one rolling to a rest under Jagger's nose. The dog opened his eyes, sniffed at the instrument incuriously, and then shut his eyes again.

She stared at the bare canvas, afraid she would see that she had . . . somewhere . . . somehow . . . touched it. Touched it unknowingly as Midnight had touched her. Finally she put her hand out and stroked the canvas. It was old and she could feel the dust upon it, layered by its exposure over the years as it waited on the easel to be prepared and used. She would have to have new canvas, she could order it in the morning, paint thinner, new paints—

Charlie inhaled sharply.

Unthinkable. What she planned was unthinkable. She swayed, her right leg feeling its weakness, and she grabbed for the edge of the worktable, a sturdy, plain pine table, its surface stained here and there from its usage over the years, and as she looked to make sure she could steady herself, she saw the tube of paint.

Uncapped, coiled upon the palette, ready to be used in prepping the canvas. A thickened blob leaked from its silvery mouth, looking venomous in the pale moonlight.

She had almost put her hand into it, though she doubted if the paint could actually be used, it was far too old, it would have separated and then dried. Charlie lifted her hand to sniff it lightly. She had already put her hand into it. She could smell the linseed oil very faintly. She had opened the paint during her sojourn with Midnight.

She ruffled her hands across the table, darkened in the night, searched and found them, open, her wooden box of charcoal and sketching pencils, the drawer holding them slid out, her fingernail catching a ragged edge of the battered box, bringing up a splinter. The momentary pain stabbed and she flinched, recoiling, then pulled the splinter out. In sheer reflex she sucked on the wounded fingertip, tasting the grit and woody flavor of charcoal.

Charlie brought her hands down and stared at them, turned them over and looked at her palms and saw the faint dusting of charcoal on them.

She cast her gaze about the studio, wondering what else she had done. In the dim light, she could see little more than shape and shadow, though the easel was placed where the moonlight caught and highlighted it, and she realized then she had moved the stand and canvas. The notion made her shiver.

What had she sketched upon the canvas? What had she drawn in pencil and charcoal? What lay there to be prepped for actual painting? What had she seen? What had Midnight brought to her?

Charlie swung back on the easel, shaking. She grabbed a leg and dragged it over nearer to the beacon of light coming through the blinds, afraid to turn on the overhead fixture, afraid to flood the room with illumination, afraid to see what she might have done. She stumbled away from the worktable, caught her lazy foot on a paintbrush and fought to right herself, to keep from pitching forward and crashing into the easel and table, threw her hands out, clutching at air, at nothing, at straws.

Jagger scrambled up and into her legs, his weight

catching her, and she grasped for his ruff, finding her balance. He whined anxiously and licked his chops in reflex as her grip pinched at him, but he never winced or yelped, instead leaning against her as though knowing he was her only anchor in the dark night.

Never since she had left Valdor had she felt so terribly, achingly alone.

She had been lucky last time. She had lost some motor coordination, had some right side motor weakness. That she had coped with.

This time, she might not be so lucky. She could well lose herself.

Charlie let herself drop to one knee, looping an arm lightly around Jagger's warm neck. The dog responded with a hot, wet tongue to her face, a quick lick of reassurance. She hugged him closer and felt her throat tighten and an unwanted tear roll slowly down her cheek.

How could it have grown back so quickly, so devastatingly? Her last scan had been clear, normal, as had all the others, and only weeks ago . . . and the first time, she had gotten ill slowly, over months and months, years by the time it insinuated itself so fiercely it could no longer be overlooked.

This time . . . mere days, in comparison. As though it had a rationality to its malignancy, as though it had cut a trail into the mind and body it well knew, so that it could find its way back speedily.

How long did she have? How long could she hide it? Did she have any hope at all of staving off Midnight until it could touch her and her alone? How long would it be before others noticed, before she could not work at a steady pace, before she would begin to miss deadlines?

How much time did she have before her mother would know? Before the endless hospital corridors would swallow her up for testing and treatment, before the surgeon would shave her head once again and take a scalpel and bone saw to her skull, and carve away whatever it was that was killing her, and carve away as well whatever it was that made her alive.

"Oh, God," Charlie murmured softly, and laid her cheek to Jagger's head, feeling the soft hair and warmth, and she cried until the dog squirmed in her hold, his pelt wet with her grief.

Chapter Thirteen

Charlie woke to the insistent drilling of the alarm clock/radio. Jagger sat by the edge of the bed, his ears pricked in doggish anxiety at the sound of a noise he rarely heard, as she struggled free of the bedcover. Only slightly successful, she pounded her hand upon the radio until she hit a button and squelched it. Jagger whined, licked his chops, and flicked his ears forward and back. She lay back for a moment, still entangled in blanket and sheets, and stared at the ceiling. Her face felt crusty, and as she rubbed at it, she could also feel fine, golden dog hairs sticking to her skin.

Charlie reacted in disgust. "Oh, God." She sat up, peeling both sets of sheets up with her and then shedding them like a second skin to get out of bed. As she put out a hand both to greet Jagger and brace herself on his frame, she looked at her bed. Not only had every corner come untucked, but the mattress itself had slewed around on the frame, hanging over the far edge by nearly a foot. It looked more like a wrestling pit than a bed.

She shoved the mattress back in place and collapsed on the corner. Her eyes felt raw as she rubbed at them. The clock/radio began its insistent drone again—she had evidently hit the snooze button—and Charlie lay down on her stomach to reach it and tap it off correctly, staring into the face of the appliance, trying to remember why it was necessary to be up so early after such a horrible night. She turned her cheek to the satiny blue mattress and stared into Jagger's caramel eyes. Now that the dog was awake, he would need to be let out. Because of security concerns, Charlie did not have a dog door built in to the back of the house, and normally Jagger kept to her flexible schedule with little trouble, but the undeniable fact of that matter was, once awake, he needed out. He whined a little and made as if to lick her nose, not quite reaching her.

"All right. All right." Head pounding, she got up, swaying across the hardwood floors, Jagger pacing happily at her knees. Every morning was a good day to him, every anticipation his doggish skull could hold an excellent one. Exercise, play, food, and visiting. More play and food. Sleep. As she unlocked the rear door and opened it for him, she saw that he had cowlicks of hair going every which way in the ruff of his neck as if someone had taken hair mousse to his golden hair.

As he bounded past her into the yard, two mourning doves taking flight and winging off over the back wall, Charlie felt her jaw drop and the quick, sharp edge of her grief, her tears, her keening in the night returned to her. She shut the door and ran through the house to the studio, threw herself on what should have been a locked door, a door which swung open violently, nearly dropping her to the floor.

Charlie balanced herself on the doorknob, looking in, squinting as the shades could not hold back the flood of morning light into the room. The easel had left marks on the tile where she had dragged it. Paintbrushes lay scattered next to the worktable. Even the faint smell of oil paint came to her, though that tube she'd found open last night had been mostly drying. With a shudder, Charlie stepped into the studio and looked at the canvas which lay facedown on the workroom floor, toppled from its easel pedestal.

She could hear a faint bark from the yard, Jagger telling her he was done and wanted to come inside and eat. Ignoring it, she dropped to one knee, hands trembling, and reached for the canvas to turn it over.

The confident slash of charcoal and pencil, detailing the impressionistic picture which would be painted there, met her eyes. Took her in. Gripped her. Even the insistent barking from the rear of the house did not register as she looked at the skeleton of what would be a painting.

Did not recognize it at first.

Then she saw it. An interior scene, looking out a window into an exterior. Benign. Unimportant. Harmless, perhaps even pleasant. Palm trees, cars on a street below, far below from the perspective, other tall, impressive buildings outside, inside a desk with its chair rolled back, or perhaps its occupant lolled in it, looking out the same window the painter and viewer were drawn to, daydreaming. An office of moneyed influence, quiet, powerful, yet totally nonthreatening.

Charlie closed her eyes a long moment in relief, then opened them and stood, bracing herself on the worktable, as she lifted the canvas back onto the easel. The pounding in her chest and ears slowly almost immediately as the anxiety began to ebb away.

She tightened the vise into place, holding the canvas. "Midnight, you've lost your grip." She backed up a step and took a second look at what she had sketched, before shrugging and turning away. She would finish it, Charlie thought, already knowing what paints she needed to buy to restock, what she would need to mix to bring out the color of the couch she'd drawn in hastily yet convincingly. It would be one of those oxblood leather couches, with brass nail head studs instead of welts edging it, a piece of furniture bespeaking quiet, conservative, old money. The blue of the sky outside, the metallic flash of expensive cars parked down below, the bloom on the myriad of potted plants lining the vast windowsill. All that and more she knew instantly; having sketched it, she now had to paint it.

She crossed the house quickly to let Jagger back in, singing over and over a line from a popular song that was going through her head. "How bizarre, how bizarre,"

Jagger tossed his head and slobbered on her hand, joyously awaiting breakfast. Charlie caught a glimpse of the kitchen clock, and suddenly remembered that today was the day scheduled for the wall textile installation at the Kensington corner office suites. Grant Kensington would be there, as well as her mother, the two of them planning a charity benefit for one of her many auxiliaries, and Charlie had made reservations for the three of them to have lunch. She had forty minutes to shower, dress, eat, and be on the site before the delivery trucks and workmen arrived.

She got there fifteen minutes later than she'd hoped, but the first of the delivery trucks appeared another ten minutes after that, just as Grant Kensington's XK8 Jag pulled into his designated parking slot. Jagger recoiled ever so slightly in his harness and against her leg as the powerfully built businessman swung out of his car, a paper cup of coffee in each hand. Grinning at her, he swung a hip into his car door to close it.

"Good morning, Charlie! Everything underway?"

"It will be. Everything should be installed and ready for the dedication next week, right on schedule." She took the hot disposable cup he shoved at her, returning his smile. The Kensington office suites would house his corporate offices, planning and sales and property management, and the room left over would be leased out to those interested. Though Grant had not said anything to her, Mary had told her that there was already a two-year waiting list to get leases for available space. The office building was intended to be, and would be, a showplace for all that Kensington could do for its clients. She had met Grant through his father Oliver and through hers, and though Grant had been businesslike and easygoing, there was no doubt in Mary Saunders' mind, at least, that Charlie and Grant ought to see more of each other. Her mother seemed to be unaware of the fact that Kensington had a male partner and absolutely no sexual interest in Charlie whatsoever.

She pried the plastic lid off her coffee, preferring to drink it from the rimmed cup rather than through an insipid hole in the plastic covering. Grant toasted her.

"Ready to take me up on moving your design studio here? I have just the corner for you. You can take an upstairs loft, high ceilings, as much room as you need. We can even install a private elevator." Grant tossed down a gulp of steaming coffee that made

Charlie blink. He must have a throat of iron inside as well as out. "Dog run for Jagger here."

"I'm comfortable at home."

"Charlie, you need more room. You need a showroom as well as a design studio and a work area. You're limiting your potential if you keep working out of that closet."

"I don't feel like expanding my operations. We've discussed this. Right now, it's hands on for me, and that's the way I like it. Besides, if I need to rest, I'm there."

He bounded up the walkway and turned to wait for her. "That's why I mentioned the loft! I can have a retreat built in there for you, small, noise-proof bedroom, private bath. You can take an elevator half a story up, close the door, and *viola!* You're home again."

Turning slightly away from his enthusiasm, she watched as the delivery trucks marked with the name WindRiver Mills circled and drivers and installers began to unload. It was always a bit of a shock to see textile designs she had worked so intimately on being delivered in massive carpet rolls, and it was always a bit of a thrill as well. WindRiver was one of the nicest mills she had ever found to work with, a small family business, flexible to her needs and designs and delivery timetables. In slow periods, the family refused to reduce their payroll, always finding a way to tide their workers over, and even in busy times, they were never too busy to work with Charlie. Even Quentin spoke begrudgingly well of WindRiver.

As she approached with Jagger, the lead installer made a motion with his hand, and the hand trucks carrying the massive rolls halted. He made another motion, and his crew removed a roll and unwrapped it carefully, laying a good twenty feet out on the pristine sidewalk for her to see. Though she had already viewed the product at the factory, the sight of the carpetlike wall covering took her breath.

"Oh, the dye lots are spectacular. Look at that color!"

Grant Kensington, slightly behind her, gave a low whistle of appreciation.

The foreman, Harry Ramirez, let a swift look of unadulterated pleasure pass over his seamed face before signing with his hand again, his crewmen scrambling to rewrap the roll and get it back on the trucks. With one eye watching the delivery, the foreman unrolled his diagram of the office suites, with her installation instructions, and ran his blunt finger over the areas. "This right, ma'am?"

"You've got it down pat." She smiled at the foreman.

"It's always a pleasure workin' with you, ma'am." Two twists of his wrists and he had the plans rerolled and tucked in his back pocket. "We should be out of here by three."

She had calculated two days for installation, but it looked like WindRiver had sent a crew of triple the size she'd contracted for. That meant that work was slow at the mill itself, and though she would not have to pay for the extra manpower, it was temporarily available. She smiled at Ramirez. "Tell Papa George that I should have another nice run to order soon."

Ramirez nodded, already swinging about, hands and arms in motion, setting up the delivery and installation crews.

Grant tossed back the last of his coffee as he held the lobby door open for her, crunched his cup and made a basketball crosscourt toss into the wastebasket by the lobby reception area. "Charlie, you know you're paying for those extra men."

"No, I'm not."

"Of course you are. It's built into the cost. There's no such thing as a free lunch, anywhere, anyway." Kensington shrugged into his Armani jacket. "You need to work with vendors who can give you volume prices."

"Grant, I don't order enough to get that kind of price break, and you know that everything I do is one of a kind. They have to program their looms, everything, just for me. WindRiver is not only willing to do it, they do it beautifully. Their textiles are quality, commercial grade, and they deliver when they say they're going to. What more can I ask?"

"An extra ten percent discount per roll," he returned, as he put his wide palm over the elevator sensor.

"Are you unhappy with my pricing?"

"Of course not. I don't see how you stay in business."

Charlie smiled slightly. "And if you're happy, and I'm happy, why change things? If it ain't broke, don't fix it." She sipped down the last of her coffee, letting him take the empty from her hand, watching as he crunched it and gave it another long toss across the lobby, unerringly hitting the wastebasket and dropping in.

Shaking his head, he said, "Wasted potential," checking his watch as the elevator doors shut them in. "I've got calls until your mother gets here at eleven. We should be ready for lunch by eleven-thirty."

"Fine. I should be free by then. Harry's men know what they're doing, I don't have to watch them like a hawk."

"Good! I want Mary to see the office space I'm holding for you." Grant's mouth quirked slightly, and Charlie knew she'd been sandbagged. With her mother on his side, his persuasive power more than doubled.

"Dirty dog," she said.

Grant grinned even as Jagger threw his head up and wriggled slightly at the humor in her voice.

"Not you!" She ran her hand across the golden's head. He sighed and leaned against her, content. She looked up to find Grant watching her seriously and she found herself blushing. He flexed his shoulders and eased his neck in his business collar, looking away nonchalantly.

It was that game, she thought, of looking at one another, trying to determine if there were possibilities, if there should be possibilities, if there was an interest, a bond, a commonality. In their case, it was business, in most cases, sexual attraction. She'd spent a fair amount of time with Grant Kensington over the last six months, but he had been fairly aloof until recently. And, although the knowledge he was looking at her differently now pleased her because of Kensington's financial acumen, the pleasure was not nearly as intense as the personal attraction she had felt with John Rubidoux at the art show and when he'd brought Jagger back. It was one thing to have her career validated, and another to have her—would she call it soul?—validated.

Mere moments could hardly compare to weeks, and yet they did.

Charlie found herself clearing her throat as the elevator gently bumped to a stop on the main corporate floor.

The bare walls of the office building floor stared at her. She saw that they had been prepared for the installation of the textiles she had designed. Grant gave her a pleased look. He ushered her out of the elevator with a wave of his hand. He let Jagger take her forward into the corridor.

The dog bounded ahead, pulling against his harness, almost dragging her into the open hallway. Grant quickly grabbed her elbow and righted her.

"This will make the building come alive," Grant said.

"Yes," she answered. "That is the intention of the design." Charlie smiled slightly, and looked at Grant. "But then," she added, "you knew that. That's why you hired me."

Jagger barked sharply as the freight elevator at the other end of the corridor began to open. The installing crew came out with a clatter of ladders and tools, followed by the massive hand truck with the wall covering. As soon as the dog saw Ramirez, he settled down, being very familiar with the foreman.

Charlie dropped her hand to the dog's head and patted him gently in reward. Even though Grant knew she would not be parted from her dog, she did not trust that he would be accepted in the office building if she moved her business there. Jagger would not be happy confined in a dog run. She had no intention of letting him pine away behind a chain-link fence without company or the chance to do work that he so clearly loved to do.

Kensington looked at her and said, "I think that

we should go upstairs and see what I have put aside for your office and let the crew work in peace."

Charlie gave the command for Jagger to jog along beside her as they returned to the elevator to go upstairs. Grant leaned casually against the far wall of the enclosure, his face carefully neutral. Charlie did not know what he was thinking and that bothered her slightly. However, he knew that her mother would be at the offices soon to go over the charity functions Mary had planned with Grant and the elder Kensington. The dog shivered a little as the elevator lurched back into motion. No matter how much Charlie worked with Jagger, he seemed unable to accept elevator movement. She understood and did not scold him, not liking to be shut in close spaces herself.

As the doors opened once more, they stepped out onto the top floor of the building. It was not an extremely tall building, for Grant had planned expansion later in wings rather than height. He felt that this design was better suited to the oceanside community. Charlie thought that he was more than right, that this was part of Grant's genius: to determine what was right, what was beautiful, and what was efficient. The Kensington building would be a stunning showplace without the need for height to make it stand out.

As she looked along the flight of the building, Charlie realized just what an elaborate floor space had been saved for her. The bank of windows faced the ocean. She could see the blue-and-gray waves as they crashed onto the beach far below. Jagger looked toward the windows as if he could also see the Laguna Beach cove below, his tail flagging. Grant smiled widely.

Her mother came out of a doorway cut into the crude open space. She wore blue again, as she frequently did, an elegant pantsuit which her body filled well and made look much less pretentious. Mary beamed.

"Grant, this is incredible. Surely you don't mean all this space for Charlie."

"I do. This entire wing, if she needs it." He braced a shoulder against the white wall—a vast, empty space which was so much like a canvas awaiting creation.

Jagger whined a bit and bumped her knee. Charlie blinked and glanced down at the dog, her thought chain broken, feeling a little lost . . . what had she been thinking? And what bothered Jagger?

Mary turned around and took in the ocean vista. "The view is breathtaking. The building brings it all in, yet from the highway below, this sets into the hillside very naturally. I think you have more than a bit of Frank Lloyd Wright in you, Grant."

The builder-architect chuckled, but his eyes were on Charlie. She could feel them as she began to pass across the expanse, mentally measuring the current room in her house to the footage here. It was like comparing her bedroom closet to the Grand Canyon, a drop in the bucket. Of course, the open space would not stay open, there would be additional interior walls added. There would be a showroom, an office, filing and storage area, workroom. The potential for having her own loom set up crossed her mind. Charlie stopped her careful heel-toe walk to look up and see the one permanent wall looming before her.

It was as though she were the miniature and the wall a normal sized canvas. Or perhaps she was not the artist at all, but the brush, soft and supple, ready to deal out color and structure at the whim of the holder. . . .

From a very long way away, she could hear Jagger whine again, but it did not seem significant, barely audible, unimportant. Something rubbed at her knee again, she scarcely felt the touch.

Something else tremored through her being, a great, deep, dark quake rumbling toward her, vibrations so low on the sound register she felt more than heard it, knew it was shivering toward her, even the very marrow in her bones pulsed to its drumming voice. She stared at the empty wall, her face small and insignificant, the area not flat but concave, like a maelstrom getting ready to inhale her, a canvas insisting, demanding that she fill it, an urge more important than even breath itself.

* * *

Mary watched her daughter with no small pride and pleasure . . . and pain. It was still difficult to see the slight halt in her step, the tiny sway in her walk, the unconscious dependence she had on the large dog to steady herself, the nearly imperceptible weakness of her right arm and hand. She could remember the time—it seemed like yesterday—when that had not been the case, when Charlie had been a normal, healthy young girl, growing in leaps and bounds.

Charlie had never walked when she could run, had never known a moment of stillness except when perched on a stool in front of her easel, and then her young face had transformed into something beyond childhood and even adulthood. As Charlie stood now, looking at the walls and office spacing, not seeing what was there but what might be there someday, constructing it all in her head, in that wide and explored territory of the mind and imagination. Mary crossed her arms over her chest lightly, hugging herself, pleased that Charlie seemed to be so intensely drawn in.

Grant Kensington had been leaning against the opposite wall; now he drew near, frowning.

Voice pitched for Mary's ears only, he said, "She doesn't like it."

"Oh, no, quite the opposite. She's thinking. She's just sketching through the possibilities."

He rumbled in satisfaction. Then, Grant added, "Good. I'd like to have her here."

Mary looked at him and saw what she'd hoped to see, that Kensington's interest was not totally business and, though shrewd, self-serving. She smiled encouragingly. "Charlie is a wonderful girl, and I'm not saying that because she's my daughter."

Jagger whined slightly. Mary ignored the dog, continuing to smile. "She's made me very proud." She wondered why Kensington did not respond and felt for a moment like she was picking at a scab, trying to elicit a reluctant response.

"She's very talented, even now."

"Without the painting, you mean?"

Grant flushed slightly as if he had compromised himself and nodded brusquely.

Mary tilted her head. "I agree. Very, very talented. I think she enjoys her life more now than . . . before."

He lifted an eyebrow.

She chose her next words carefully. "She never liked the controversy over her age, her style, her training or lack of it, the speculation that her paintings were critiqued because of who she was rather than what they were. The ones who cheered her artwork embarrassed her and the ones who criticized it hurt her. She was, I think, a little relieved after."

Jagger complained again, louder, sharper, the noise cutting into her. Mary pivoted back around to see what bothered the animal.

The golden retriever stood against Charlie's knee as if bracing her, his ears pricked, his tail down and steady, unhappy, his jaws agape as if he might be ready to pant in distress.

A coldness shot through Mary. "What is it, Charlie?" she asked sharply.

She heard her mother's voice as if from very far away or perhaps even under water, blurred and bubbling so much that she could not make sense of the words, even if she tried to focus, which she gave up, because other words filled her hearing and color flooded her eyes. . . .

Two male faces, up against the wall. Both flushed, sweating, their expressions twisting with intensity. For a half second, Charlie felt embarrassment as though she had caught them in a sexual act, for one of them was Grant Kensington, but then she caught the emotions which steamed off them and it was hatred, pure and jolting, and she realized they were fighting, struggling, and one had pinned the other against the wall she stared at dumbly. An argument of words, escalating into action, the air shimmered with the heat of the fight and she could almost hear what they were saying, almost paint the impact of their actions. She blinked, losing the vision but not before she finally recognized the second man's face, Michaeljohn, Grant's partner—and she thought then that the sexual overtones she had perceived and then dismissed were not that incorrect after all . . . and she realized that this space had been kept aside, planned, for Grant's partner Michaeljohn, and the fight had destroyed those plans. Grant's invitation to her was meant only to fill a gaping void in his life, in his building. Her vision blurred as violence erupted, two massive men wrestling with one another, crimson drops falling like sweat from Michaeljohn's face, their throats erupting with vile, angry shouts of recrimination, fists swinging. . . .

She took a step back in shock as the jolt hit her.

Jagger barked, his voice shrill in canine warning, as Charlie buckled, falling half on him and onto one knee. Mary pitched forward and immediately pulled her daughter into her arms, smoothing Charlie's hair from her face.

Her daughter had gone incredibly pale and though her eyelids fluttered open, there was no recognition in her eyes. "Charlie!" Mary cried. She shook her daughter gently.

Charlie took a deep, shuddering breath, her eyelids moving again, and then she looked at her mother blearily. "What time is it?" she asked shakily.

Chapter Fourteen

"Don't be ridiculous. I was up half the night worried about this installation. . . ." Charlie's voice faded away and she looked glancingly at her mother. She could not keep her eyes steady on her mother's face, and she could not look at Kensington at all, still shaken from the vision of his face contorted with primitive emotion. "There's no reason to send for paramedics."

Mary responded, "Charlie, you can't go on like this."

Grant had propped her back up against that huge, towering, blank wall and squatted near the two of them, one knee of his buff-coated suit touching the concrete flooring, almost a part of their group yet not quite, as if wishing to yield some personal space to them. Jagger lay quietly against her legs, but his caramel eyes stayed alert, watching. Mary's mouth pinched slightly and she added, "Charlie, this is serious. We both know it."

"I did not pass out. I just got very disoriented."

"You didn't stay on your feet." Mary Saunders straightened, walked to the bank of windows across the corridor, looked out them wordlessly for a moment.

Charlie took the respite for what it was and inhaled deeply a couple of times to steady herself. She exchanged a look, but no words with Grant whose face had returned to that studied neutral expression he had worn earlier, a kind of businessman's poker face. The contrast to the raw emotions she'd envisioned made her tremble. She brushed her palm over Jagger's flanks. Instead of responding warmly, the dog flinched as if something unpleasant shivered down his body. Puzzled, Charlie drew her hand away.

Mary returned. "We'll talk about this later." The line of her mouth pressed tiny wrinkles into her face, creases which Charlie suddenly realized had been there for some time, were etched there, and which she had never noticed before.

Charlie started to get to her feet. Grant rose and offered his broad-palmed hand. She took it, his warmth such a contrast to her chilled fingers that it almost felt as if he burned her. Jagger got up, too, and shook himself vigorously, his vest and harness flapping about him. She looked at her watch. "Let me go down and check on the installation. I should be ready for lunch in about an hour."

"Good," Mary said lifelessly. "That will get us in before the crowds." She sounded as though she did not really care, but responded automatically, having gone through a lifetime of planning lunches to a business world's schedule.

Charlie went to the elevator. Grant's shoulder brushed against hers. The touch shocked through her like a static discharge, vision swirling in her mind, a palette of emotions and colors. She said quietly, pitching her voice so that her mother could not possibly hear her. "You meant this wing for Michaeljohn, not me."

He shot a glance at her. His expression stayed casual, but this time with great effort. "How do you know that?"

"It's enough that I know, isn't it? Anyway, you're miserable without him."

Kensington frowned. "What makes you think that?"

"You're not?"

He shuffled his feet. "Charlie, this is not the kind of thing I would discuss with anybody."

"I'm not asking you to discuss it. Just observing. That floor space and the loft—it's not my career you're interested in—it's his. And I think you should tell him that."

Grant pressed the signal buttons for her. "Is this common gossip?"

"Of course not!" She took a breath to steady herself. "You laid this wing out long before you hired me to design textiles for it."

He nodded then, as the faint vibration of the upward moving elevator became apparent. "I see. And this is your advice?"

"My advice is never to do anything you regret."

A very slight smile curved his mouth for a moment. He inclined his head. "Sounds . . . profound and practical." He added, "I should come down with you, but I have a call to make, and," he murmured apologetically, "I'd like to show your mother the rest of the floor. There is a corner office, not as spacious or grand . . . which you might consider?"

"Of course." Charlie nodded and let out a grateful breath as the elevator door opened in almost immediate response. "I'll meet you at your office."

"If there's any problem—"

"There won't be," she returned briskly and entered the elevator. She studied the elevator floor, unwilling to see her mother, and waited for the doors to close and the vehicle to carry her away. Jagger strained at his harness, pulling toward the exit anxiously.

"It's all right, boy," she said soothingly.

His tail dropped unhappy. She rubbed the back of his ear. For a second or two he ignored that comfort, than gave a low whuff and leaned into her fingers, eyes closing for just a moment in enjoyment. "What an attention span you have," Charlie kidded him.

The tail lifted till nearly level with his back and waved briefly.

When the elevator stopped, she could already smell the adhesive though it was faint and not too objectionable. As she stepped through the doors, the sight and sound of the installation met her eyes.

She had designed the textile to be installed as a runner, framed top and bottom. The bottom board was being put in now along this section of the wall and she got her first chance to truly see the finished work.

Against cream-colored walls which held the very faintest tint of sea foam green, her work ran like curling waves, an ocean current that carried with it serenity and strength, pierced now and then by an aquatic form or sometimes driftwood or other vague shapes of flotsam. It cooled the eyes to look at it, broke over the senses as she hoped it would, and made her yearn to touch it, to see if it was yarn or water which filled the wall.

Charlie's face warmed with pleasure and satisfaction. She paced down the corridor, Ramirez's workmen busy, hardly turning their heads to notice her, as they stretched and hung the design. Staple guns and the sound of the compressor powering them hummed loudly, punctuated by sharp grunts of effort and the occasional rapid-fire comment in Spanish, some of which she could interpret and most of which she could not. This ocean wave theme would be repeated throughout the building, although the coloration was different for each level. Down here, on the main floor, the ocean was at its deepest, most commandingly blue. It would warm as the floors ascended, until the top floor was the color of the intriguing waters of the Caribbean, blue-green and inviting. At night when the building depended on artificial lighting, the walls themselves would have a more perceptible greenish tint, soothing, she hoped.

Charlie crossed her arms over her chest to stand and watch. The chair rail baseboard went in smoothly and any paintwork which needed to be done would be done by hand with a detailing brush, just as she had planned. The top railing framing the covering looked as if it would go in as smoothly.

It filled her senses to stand there and look upon it, and made her proud to see it even better than she had imagined it. Looking at it that way for the first time, she realized why WindRiver had asked her if they could buy the design from her and offer it as part of their line. It was both highly commercial and highly decorative. She would have to consider the mill's offer more seriously. But in the meantime, to look at it, experience it, consumed her. This was fulfillment and this was, in spite of what Valdor thought, art. It was as full of conceptualization, movement, color, and texture as any Rembrandt or Monet or Dali. Though he'd grown up in it and made

172

his living by it, nothing filled Valdor that she could see, except his hunger for gambling.

The thought of Valdor hounding her again troubled her slightly, and the temporary peace she'd gained looking at the walls fled.

Charlie frowned.

Wade Clarkson settled into his leather chair, chafing his hands together lightly, still smelling of the antiseptic soaps from scrubs, his shoulders slowly loosening from the tension of the operation, his mind readjusting to the pace. He was done for the day except to finish his dictation and look over some charts. A vague restlessness swept over him. He decided to handle his voice mail before dictation.

He picked up his fountain pen and made notes on the calls before he heard George Laverman say briskly, "Give me a call back."

Wade smiled to himself. Old George must already be noodling on the wager set up for their next golfing date. He couldn't blame him really, a grand was stiff, but the proceeds would all go to the same charity the tourney had been set up for. He needed some amusement and decided to yank George Laverman's chain. He dialed the number.

"In chambers, Laverman here."

Without preamble, Wade said, "If a grand is too much, we'll knock it down to a hundred."

George laughed. "No, a grand donation is acceptable. Just be prepared to write that check." The judge paused a moment and said, "Actually, I called about Charlie Saunders . . . wanted to know how she is."

"Charlie? Haven't seen her in months. Fine, as far as I know." Wade rocked back in his chair and rolled his shoulders to ease his neck a little and shifted his attention to the painting on his left wall, the one real artifact Abigail had left to him, the painting both she and he had enjoyed so much, a painting which might now be worth more than a quarter of a million dollars and which he would unthinkingly swap for her life if such a swap could be made. He had never expected her to will him anything at all, her trust set up to benefit the hospital and other charities, and the painting had been both a shock . . . and a poignant declaration. Abby, sick and in pain as she was, had taken the time to alter her legal papers so that he might have it. He swallowed tightly.

"You didn't hear then? She collapsed at the art auction down here Sunday night."

Wade sat up. "What happened?"

"I was hoping you knew. They took her to Sunrise Hospital."

He scrubbed his jaw. "Let me check around. Hospitals don't always share their information, but I should have been notified." Inwardly, his gut recoiled. The distance between Los Angeles County and Orange County might as well be measured in continents, and the exclusive Scripps Hospital complex down in San Diego County was just as uncommunicative. He made a note to call Quentin Saunders as soon as he found out what Sunrise had to say. The family should know that he'd heard, and he wanted Charlie in as soon as possible. "She fell·or what?"

"She got a little confused and then fainted."

He exhaled. "I'll get back to you, George."

"Do that."

His secretary had gone to lunch, so he dialed for records and asked for Charlotte Saunders' file. After long moments, in which he heard inane chatter and background noise, the clerk came back to the phone line. "She's in the computer, but the physical file isn't here, it's been checked out."

"All right, then, who has it?"

"Looks like psychiatric."

He muffled his reaction before thanking the clerk.

"Should we call it in, Doctor?"

"No. I'll get it myself."

Wade disconnected, lurched to his feet, and made his way to the wing holding the psych offices.

Elyse Roseburg looked up as he knocked on the doorjamb to the inner office. "Hey ho," she said, as he leaned partway in, and grumbled good-naturedly, "I thought I had a guard out there."

"She went to lunch. Real people do that." He looked at the doctor as he stepped in, her lips as thin and sculpted as her eyebrows, the only thin part about her somewhat rumpled body in a dark, pinstriped woman's version of a power suit. She had just taken her glasses off, their imprint still on the bridge of her nose, a single folder in her hands as she crossed her legs and sat back.

"The implication is that I am not real." Elyse smiled. "Is that how you feel about what I said?"

He laughed. "Is it possible to have a genuine conversation with you, Dr. Roseburg?"

Her face warmed. "Of course it is." She chuckled. "To what do I owe this invasion?"

"Somebody in your office has Charlotte Saunders' file."

Elyse tapped a manilla folder on her desk, her manicured nails glittering. "As a matter of fact, I do."

"Good. Open it up and tell me what Sunrise Hospital may or may not have sent me." He took the big barrel chair opposite her desk and settled into it.

Elyse arched her razor-thin brows and opened the folder. "Nothing here . . ."

"Probably because someone downstairs is looking for that." Wade smiled thinly. "It's like pulling teeth to get these smaller hospitals to share information with us. They are always afraid we are on an ego trip about our patients—"

"And we're not?"

"It's not ego. It's a matter of funding, as you are well aware." He put a hand out for the folder.

Elyse closed it, handing it over. "Do you know when she was due for her checkup?"

Wade considered Roseburg, thinking. "Should be soon. Why?"

"Her annual was scheduled nearly four months ago. She called and canceled it, and hasn't rescheduled."

"What?" He leaned forward so abruptly in his chair that he nearly lost his hold on the file. "Why didn't someone notify me? Isn't there a flag on that file?"

"Yes. The file's been in my department because I review Charlie's case once in a while . . ." and pale, tailored Elyse Roseburg had the grace to blush slightly. "She's an incredible case study of artistic creativity and actual brain function . . . if only I could understand why she no longer paints."

They had been over that before, the two of them, off and on for years. Wade rubbed his hands together now, unwilling to get back into the discussion as to why the removal of the tumor had disrupted Charlie's creative ability as well as motor ability. Right side versus left side—there should have been no correlation. But this was not the concern now. The fact that she had missed her checkup was.

"No one called to reschedule her appointment because the folder was in your department."

Elyse nodded. She passed the folder over wordlessly.

Wade accepted it, flipped it open, laid it out, and glanced over it. The days seemed to go by in a blur now. He could have sworn it had not been so long since he had seen Charlie, but it had, and then some. This was his fault, too, as much as it was Roseburg's clerical staff, but he would not admit that. Could not. He considered the chart in front of him. He would have Sunrise fax whatever they had on her, unwilling to wait and see if there were reports floating around downstairs in someone's in-box waiting for the folder to turn up. He inclined his head slightly and rubbed at his tired eyes again.

Elyse smiled kindly. "Time to get those reading glasses?"

He stared at her. "Really trying to get on my good side, aren't you?"

She leaned forward in her chair. "And how do you feel about that, Dr. Clarkson?"

"Like calling your husband, taking him golfing, humiliating him for eighteen holes, then letting him go home to take it out on you."

Elyse let out a peal of laughter. "Son of a bitch, you would, wouldn't you?" She added kindly, "For what it's worth, she doesn't seem to be at risk any more."

"True," Wade responded. "Until last Sunday. She collapsed at a benefit. I'll have to get her in here as soon as possible."

"Oh, no."

"George Laverman just phoned me to see what

the prognosis was. Imagine my embarrassment to be totally in the dark."

She pointed to the open doorway. "If you can ever forgive me, I'd like to see the file again when it's updated. In the meantime, I have another file to review before the victim . . . patient . . . gets here."

He nodded and stood. There was more that he wanted to say—to rage about—but this was a colleague, and he did not make a habit of burning bridges. She knew that her slip was only one in a chain of them. Still, he hesitated, to give her an opening to say something.

Elyse paused as if she had read his mind. "Wade. I owe you and your staff an apology. I hope that nothing we did kept Charlie from getting treated promptly."

"Me, too," he answered as he went out the door. It was not good enough, but it was something.

He resettled at his desk after leaving word that he wanted all records forwarded to him ASAP, and that Sunrise was to fax him copies at his personal number, even though his secretary was still away from her desk. He went into his office, and sat down, and looked at the painting, shutting himself away with his memories of Abby and a child prodigy and a tumor.

Chapter Fifteen

By three-thirty the installation was finished as promised, and Charlie stood wearily, leaning against the framing for an office doorway, appraising it. Lunch with Grant and her mother had been hurried and strained, with Mary watching every bite she took as if she could blame nutrition for failing her. In truth, Charlie could scarcely remember what she'd eaten, though it sat uneasily in her stomach now. She'd been working nonstop since returning, directing the workmen, making sure the appropriate dye lots went to the proper stories for installation.

She made a mental note that the Caribbean colors needed to be warmed a little more for future runs, if she sold the design and scheme to WindRiver. Of course, that was part of the illusion of the textile, to cool the body through the mind and vision, saving a little on air-conditioning costs. Even a degree or two made a big difference in a commercial office building, and it had been proved that colors could affect body temperature as well as mood.

Her leg ached. She bent over and rubbed it, knowing that she should start wearing her brace again. It was light-weight aluminum, velcroed shut, a far cry from the appliance she'd first worn years ago. She did not like to wear it now, but understood that the leg had an inherent weakness and even with constant exercise, it might never carry its share of the strain of supporting her body and walking. The alternative to wearing the brace when she needed to was having the leg break under stress, and that would hamper her even further.

If only wearing leg braces were as fashionable as eyeglasses and teeth braces seemed to have become.

Charlie let out a wry laugh, interrupted by the vibration at her waist of her beeper. She reached for it, and read that her bank wanted a call or personal visit as soon as possible. She blinked at that. Perhaps she had forgotten to roll a CD when it had matured. She thumped back a yes in response to the page and straightened, signaling Jagger. Harry Ramirez, engrossed as he was in getting his crew to clean up, leaving the area impeccable at the other end of the corridor, saw her movement.

He lifted his head. "Leaving now, Miz Saunders?"

"Yes, Harry. It looks wonderful."

"Thank you. I'll tell my boys that." He waved his hand, followed by a few lilting words in Spanish, and the workmen nearest her lifted their faces and beamed at her.

Charlie gave a last brush of her hand as she entered the elevator. She stopped at the central floor where Kensington had been installed since the building was first even barely habitable, disregarding the havoc of the continuing building and customization around him, or the noise of the crane layering and finishing up the floors above him. Jagger pulled her out eagerly as soon as the elevator doors opened once more.

The contrast between the Kensington-occupied part of the wing and the rest of the floors was incredible, like seeing a portal into the future open when all this space would be filled, painted, papered, rugs and tile laid down, furniture arranged, and most importantly, peopled. She had not had a hand in it, of course, but she'd seen the conceptual printouts from the designer and thought that her wave runner textile would fit in, and now that it was installed, she felt a burn of triumph that she had been correct.

The receptionist lifted a finger, smiling, even as she spoke into the headwrap microphone, and pointed toward Grant's half-open office door. Taking that as a signal to go on in, though she usually met him in the conference room across the lobby, she went in the direction of what Jagger had already recognized as her mother's voice, who had obviously not left the building yet, no doubt gently bullying Kensington into underwriting as many of her charity projects as she could cajole him into.

Across the office threshold, she limped to a halt, then, stunned, felt Jagger pull his harness out of her grasp. Her mother shifted weight in a wing-back chair to face her, and Grant Kensington slowly swung about in a massive high-backed leather chair to smile at her also. Beyond him was a window she recognized from her preliminary sketches; the view below of the palm tree lined drive heading into the complex dropped away below the road to the Laguna shores. Charlie blinked, dismayed by both the likeness and wrongness of her drawing.

Her mother petted Jagger as the dog thrust his head into her lap. "I was just telling Grant what plants he should have on that window ledge."

Charlie remembered to breathe again. The ledge, so lushly inhabited in her vision, sat bare and open.

Grant smiled. He'd taken off his cashmere coat, and loosened his tie, his collar open at his heavy throat. "Actually, she was insulting me, I think. She told me this looked like the office of a stodgy old tax attorney."

Mary laughed. "Sometimes the truth hurts."

Kensington raised an eyebrow. "Does it?" He looked at Charlie.

The built-in bookcase that dominated one wall of the room, the window, all, all as she had seen . . . but no sofa, no blooming plants on the sill. Charlie caught herself frowning slightly. "The truth? It does, I think." She tried to let out a slight laugh, was not sure if she succeeded or failed. She glanced at her mother. "Mother, I've had a call from the bank and they'd like to see me as soon as possible. I'm really tired . . ."

Mary got to her feet immediately. "I'll drive. We'll have your car picked up." She leaned across the desk and took Grant's hand. "I took up far too much of your time, but I think you'll be pleased with what we're going to achieve."

"The achievement, Mrs. Saunders, is all yours. All I have to do is sit back and reap the goodwill. Are you sure I can't do anything else for you?"

Her mother's face creased in an expression which Charlie knew well, one of humor and pleasure. "That's part of my talent, Grant, to make you think you're doing none of the work! I'll fax your secretary a timetable by the end of next week, so you will know where you stand."

Grant chuckled and would have given her another rejoinder, but his inner office phone line buzzed. Mary took Charlie's arm and the opportunity to retreat gracefully, as Grant picked up the receiver and swung about in his great chair. Jagger trailed along behind them, his ears and harness flopping about him.

"I can tell you're still tired," her mother said brightly. "You look as if you had seen a ghost."

"Sorry. I promise to go home and rest, but the bank sounded anxious."

"What is it?"

"I didn't call them, they just paged, and I sent back an affirmative." She checked her watch. "I'll need to call from the car, they should be closing in minutes."

Her mother drove a Catera, and Jagger had to sit in the back. Mary took a folded up towel from under the front seat and put it down for him. The dog sniffed at it with scorn, but he sat on it as directed. Charlie could not help laughing.

"He won't stay on there, Mom."

"Oh, yes, he will," Mary answered with the authority and experience of motherhood.

Charlie had the bank on the cell phone before her mother pulled out of the driveway, passing the last of the WindRiver trucks.

"This is Charlotte Saunders, responding to a page."

"Oh, yes! Bev Ackerman wanted to have a word with you. Can you hold a moment?"

Charlie responded, then listened to the hum of the line. She had dealt with several vice presidents over the last few years; the branch of the bank she used seemed to be a training ground, but Beverly had been there for two years now, a near record. She sounded tense when she answered.

"Is it possible for you to come down here, Miss Saunders? I'll have the doors opened for you."

"Is there a problem?"

"We are not . . . sure. I'd rather discuss this in person."

"I'm driving down now."

"Thank you, Miss Saunders, I'll be waiting for you."

Charlie disconnected, puzzled. She looked at her mother and shrugged. "They'll keep the doors open for us. She wouldn't say anything over the phone."

Mary frowned. "I can't think of anything they might be worried about."

Charlie sat back in the bucket seat, more tired than she wished to admit, and was glad to be a passenger. She looked out the window at the quiet streets and storefront facades of Laguna as her mother drove. It was a comforting thing sometimes to relinquish control. Sounds came from the backseat of Jagger scratching at his towel and then lying down with a doggish grumble.

"I didn't mean to spend nearly the whole day with Grant," he mother remarked, slowing the car.

"Is he underwriting what you'd hoped?"

"That and more." Mary glanced at her, and smiled. "He has a very keen sense of finances. He knows that he is buying advertising as well as goodwill and tax write-offs. Gets it from his father."

Charlie nodded. She did not ask, because the memories still brought pain to her mother's face, but she watched the streets go by again, and wondered where her talent came from, what twist in the DNA strand gave her the need to create. She no longer remembered her father, though sometimes in dreams she thought she might. It was not natural that she did not remember him, she had been eight or nine when he died. It was as though her memories were too painful and she'd shut everything away, all the good as well as the shock of his sudden death. She let out a small sigh.

Mary patted her knee. "Your father had not an artistic bone in him," she remarked.

Charlie tried not to startle; her mother had a way of doing that, and she supposed the train of her thoughts must have been obvious anyway. She brushed a strand of hair behind her ear. "Then, where do you think—"

"I have no idea. Some things are just buried inside of us, and sometimes they are never allowed to bloom."

"Then you don't know . . . you don't know what might have been inside him."

Mary's expression creased thoughtfully. Reluctantly, she said, "True. I have always thought I knew him well—certainly better than anyone else in his family—but we had such a short time together, really. He worked so hard all the time I don't think he did anything to relax but watch TV. He would hold you, put you up to his shoulder and just sit, unmoving. Sometimes I wondered who was comforting who. He'd stay like that for hours, and I didn't have the heart to get mad at him for spoiling you. He always told me, you can't spoil a child by loving it. Not the kind of love you give with material things, but the love you give by holding and being there."

Charlie saw the bright sparkle in her mother's eyes and realized she was on the verge of tears, and looked away, her throat aching.

Her mother skillfully pulled into the bank parking lot. Charlie had to coax Jagger out of the backseat and he shook himself vigorously, harness flapping about him, after he jumped down to the asphalt. She wished she could shake off her weariness as she palmed the grip on his lead.

The shadow of the bank manager wavered at the door as they approached and Charlie knew Beverly Ackerman had been waiting for them. Keys scritched in the lock and she let them in, her long face creased and her mouth tight, scanning the parking lot quickly before closing and locking the doors behind them. The harshness of her dark navy business suit did nothing to ease the paleness of her face or soften her angular body.

"Sorry to bring the two of you down here."

"It's all right, Bev. Is there a problem?"

The bank manager took her by the elbow and drew her into her cubicle which was only partially open to the long ell-shaped bank and lobby. "I'm really not sure."

Jagger reacted to the strain in the woman's voice by dropping his head and whining edgily, pushing against Charlie's leg. Mary glanced down at him, frowning, but Charlie just ignored him. "What do you need from me?"

"I need an okay for a twenty-five-thousand-dollar cashier's check from your account."

"What?"

Mary Saunders' head jerked up and she swung her gaze across the bank, blinking.

Charlie swallowed. "Who ordered the check?"

"Federico Valdor. He's waiting at the nook at the other end of the bank. I told him I would have to check availability of funds to make a draft like that, that most of your money was in CDs."

Mary sat down in one of the cubicle chairs. "Valdor is here?"

"Yes, Mom . . . I saw him the other night." Charlie held onto the harness grip so tightly she could feel her fingernails cut into the palm of her hand.

Her mother looked at her, the corners of her mouth drawn into fine lines. "He has balls."

Beverly Ackerman shifted weight awkwardly. "Then there is a problem? I have him listed on your painting account, but limited to five thousand. And any drafts out of there have always been signed by you. I checked."

Charlie sighed. "I'm going to go talk to him."

Mary put her hand up. "Not without your father!"

. "Let me handle this, please."

Her mother's mouth opened, then closed, with a small exhalation of sound, but she made no other protest as Charlie ordered Jagger out of the cubicle. The dog's nails clicked on the marble tiles of the lobby and Valdor heard them coming. He stood up, his face washed in surprise, which he quickly smoothed away, much as he unconsciously and quickly smoothed away wrinkles in his suit as he awaited them.

"Charlie. I should have wondered what the delay was."

"Valdor, you know you're not authorized for my personal account."

"The escrow account is all but empty. There's very little happening with your paintings right now, Charlie; resales are all I can expect to get directly, and the licensing rights statements have not come in yet. I was just pulling out an advance against my commissions."

"You could have asked."

"And face an inquisition from Quentin and you?" He shrugged, not even rumpling his elegant hand-tailored shirt with the movement.

Jagger lowered his head and a deep rumbling started in his chest and began to burble out his throat. Valdor shot a wary glance down at the dog.

"You can't wait thirty days?"

"If I could, do you think I would subject myself to this?"

"Do you have a gambling debt?"

Valdor raised a thin eyebrow and declined to answer.

"My paintings don't bring in those kinds of earnings any more."

"New ones would."

They stared at one another, Charlie feeling uneasily as though he were a hunter and she some kind of cornered prey. "I am not painting any more. We've discussed this a million times."

"I've earned that money. I made you what you are . . . were."

"You have been living well off me for twelve years. You have other clients."

"Don't make me beg, Charlie." Valdor took a step forward, and Jagger's growling increased in volume. Valdor's face paled.

"Then tell me the truth." She was too tired for this, too tired to argue, too tired to cope with him. Her bones felt cold and aching.

"I owe money to . . . people I shouldn't." He swallowed.

"And you thought robbing me would solve that problem?"

"I'm not robbing you. I've worked hard for you for years—"

"This is my account, Valdor. My money, my earnings after you and taxes take their cut. Twenty-five thousand dollars is a big chunk of it."

His hand twitched slightly. "I haven't any choice."

"You can sell the paintings you own."

His mouth twisted bitterly. "They're too valuable. I may need them later. All of this could have been avoided if you would just start painting again." His eyes glanced away, and she realized then he'd already sold them. He'd squandered everything.

She lowered her voice, anger snaking through it, "All of this would have been avoided if you could have stayed away from the casinos!"

"I could sooner stop breathing."

"That sounds like that may have to be one of your options." She took a deep breath. Jagger shook at her knee, quaking with the same deep emotion she did. "I don't owe this to you." She turned her head slightly and raised her voice. "Beverly." She looked to make sure she had Ackerman's attention. "Cut that check. But make it for five thousand. He isn't authorized for any more, and after today, he isn't authorized on my account at all."

"For the love of God, Charlotte—"

She stared coldly at him. "Five thousand. Take it or leave it."

Beverly Ackerman appeared from her cubicle and keyed her way behind the counters, opening drawers and busying herself.

"Thank you, Charlotte," Valdor said with difficulty.

She looked back at him and felt her eyes narrow slightly. "And I want you to terminate our contract."

"Now?"

"Yes, now! Sit down, grab a piece of paper, and resign from the contract. You're a thief, and I caught you red-handed, and I want nothing, absolutely nothing, more to do with you!"

"Charlie, don't treat me like this. . . ."

"Me? Treat you? How many paintings have you sold and not reported commission on? How many checks did not even get this far? How far will you stoop to pay your debts?"

He raised a hand and it hung there, palsied, trembling, as if operating with a will of its own, framed by the expensive French cuff and jacket sleeve, then he moved forward to sit down at an empty desk and do what she asked.

With a snarl, Jagger lunged at him.

The harness whipped through Charlie's cold fingers. It jolted her forward and she let out a cry as it yanked away from her, pitching her nearly face first to the bank floor, and all she saw was the golden-red flash at the corner of her eye and the vicious snarl as Jagger went for Valdor.

"My God!" gasped Bev Ackerman as Charlie hit and sprawled upon the marble tiles, one knee cracking down and her wrists taking the rest of her fall.

Jagger moved in a blur; his teeth sank into Valdor's wrist and the man let out a scream, high and effeminate, of sheer terror and pain.

Charlie shouted, "Jagger!" her throat going raw with the violence of her cry. The dog hesitated a moment, then braced himself, teeth locked into Valdor's arm, paws spread for traction on the slick floor.

"Federico, don't move!"

He stood gasping with pain, his face gone gray-white, the dog pulling his wrist slowly and inexorably down. "Charlie" he wheezed, and tears began to stream down his face, "call him off, for God's sake."

"Jagger, down!" She grabbed a nearby chair seat and tried to pull herself up, but her leg had gone numb at the impact and though pain shot through it, it was still numb, unresponsive, as she tried to claw herself back onto her feet.

The dog's ears twitched, but the menacing growl kept rumbling from low in him, primeval, muffled by the sleeve in his jaws. Jagger took another bracing step, catching himself on a chair pad under the desk and finding solid traction at last. Charlie drew a sobbing breath.

Behind her, Mary said, "Beverly, don't use that on him."

Charlie twisted her face around, to see Beverly holding a taser in her hand. The breath left her lungs as if she'd been punched.

"Don't kill him."

Valdor looked up and swayed, beads of sweat popping out on his chalky forehead. "Do it!" he pleaded.

"Charlie, I can't let your dog rip someone apart." Bev Ackerman's hand shook.

"You know Jagger—I bring him in with me every time I come. He's let kids climb all over him, he's never so much as whined in protest. Bev, that thing could kill him."

Valdor let out a sound, not so much a groan as a stifled shriek as Jagger set himself and took a firmer grip.

The bank manager's face stayed pale as she advanced from the counter toward them, the device in her hand aimed at the golden retriever.

"I'll get him," Charlie promised. "Just let me get him." She snapped her fingers. Jagger flinched, rolling his caramel eyes. He pulled at Valdor, who gave a squeak of pain.

"Charlie, for the love of God, he's hurting me."

"Jagger! Down!" She pulled herself up the back of the chair with arm strength alone, climbing as though it were a ladder, holding onto it for dear life . . . her independent life, Jagger's life . . .

She snapped her fingers again and shrilled out, "Release!" and added one last time, "Down, boy!" And then bit her lip hard, to keep the sobs welling up in her throat from choking her voice away entirely, muffling her next words. "Good boy."

A ripple moved through his fur at her words. Jagger shook his head one last time, Valdor moving with him, trying to keep the teeth from rending him, his skin so pale, the tears streaming silently down his thin face.

Then the dog let go and dropped to the floor, his tail down and stiff, his gaze steady and relentless on Valdor. Bev Ackerman inhaled deeply, leaned back against the tellers' counter and dropped the taser there and blinked at Charlie.

She took a deep breath and groped for the harness. The hand grip slipped into her fingers and palm, cold, hard, familiar. Jagger's ears flicked and he backed up against her, once more under her control. Charlie stared at Federico Valdor.

"Take your check," she managed. "And get out!"

Valdor wrapped his hand around his wrist, crimson slowly seeping into the ripped fabric. "My wrist. My suit."

"You've been compensated." Charlie swallowed. "That check should more than cover it."

Glaring, he sidled to the desk where her mother had sat as if frozen, the check blank in front of her where Bev Ackerman had placed it. Mary looked at Valdor as if newly awakened. He grabbed at the check as Mary Saunders signed it, her own face pale, her eyes darting first to Charlie for approval before taking up the pen. He snapped the paper crisply in his hands, torn cuff sagging from his wrist.

"This all could have been avoided, Charlie."

"How?" she said, and the bitterness in her voice surprised her most of all.

"Paint again. It's in you, you know it is, it never left."

"It was cut out of me!" Her voice quavered. "Get out before I call the police."

Charlie turned her back and heard, but did not watch, Valdor race for freedom out the bank doors and into the late afternoon. She lowered herself into the seat of the chair she'd been clinging to and heard her mother cross the lobby and Jagger put his head on her knee.

"Charlie," her mother said softly, tentatively. "Are you all right?"

She could hardly breathe as she wrapped her arm around the dog and felt his heart pounding in his chest, twinning the beat of her own heart. "I don't know, Mother," she sighed and began to sob.

Chapter Sixteen

The skies had begun to gray late in the day and the air felt heavy with moisture. John left his office and stood for a moment, then laughed, catching himself much like the Alsatian Flint, three pens away, nose to the wind, wondering if it would rain. The rainy season was tailing away with little measurable rainfall to anticipate between the spring and late fall. But he could smell it now, on the air, and in the ache in his leg where the bullet had lodged in his bone, and the dogs could smell it, most of them at the back of their pens, under the roofing, their noses between their paws, and their tails curled around themselves for warmth. He wondered if it would really rain, thinking of the tourists scurrying away from the amusement parks, their faces damp with bewilderment. Below the canyon, light faded quickly, the ocean churning dark and gray, rising up to meet the sky. He would feed the dogs extra tonight, for this kind of weather went straight to their stomachs, telling them hard times might be ahead, to eat and prepare for it. Actually, what lay ahead was a smoggy and hot, dry summer, and their deeper instincts were already making them shed their coats in preparation for it. He could not, however, argue with the immediacy of their stomachs. John grabbed a stripping comb off a nail on the nearby pen post, pulling tufts of hair out of it and letting them drift on the breeze, watching them trail away like dandelion seeds.

Flint paced back and forth in the front of his pen, his charcoal and black coat still lush, his dark-brown eyes appraising John and then returning to the matter at hand which was nothing that Ruby could discern with his meager human senses. Coyotes, perhaps, on the other side of the hills or maybe it was the coming storm or perhaps a young possum had been in the sheds again, eating at the dry kibble stored there. Whatever it was, Flint in his confidence knew he could handle it, and did not look to share his anxiety or triumph with John.

John sauntered to the exercise yard and opened its gate. He could let Flint run with any of the dogs. Flint exerted a quiet dominance over all the other dogs Rubidoux had currently, and there would be no fighting. The Alsatian had merely to curl his lip, revealing his ivory fangs, or lower his tail, and the others dropped into subservience immediately. Hans, across the kennel, flung himself at his door, whining in anxiety to get out and run. The youngest of all John's charges, Hans needed the exercise and companionship. John decided to let the two run together.

As he approached Flint's kennel, the dog watched him with confidence, and a friendly wave of his tail. John released the latch, and Flint bounded out, gave him a quick slurp across the back of his hand and raced to the exercise yard. Hans gave him a bit more trouble. John had to bury his fingers in the shepherd's ruff and collar to make sure Hans stayed with him and entered the yard. When he released him, Hans took off with a joyous yelping bark and launched himself right at Flint. The older dog stayed his ground and took the full weight of the shepherd, scarcely moving, letting out a low growl and raking his jaws across Hans' flank as the other rolled to the ground, still wiggling in excitement. The shepherd quickly went to his back and stayed there a moment till Flint made a noise deep in his throat and trotted off. Hans got to his feet and loped after him, safely behind, but close enough to have been a part of Flint's pack, if Flint had a pack. John laughed at how quickly Hans contained his enthusiasm and watched as the dogs settled into a jog, examining the yard, its grass, its smells, its scent posts, the trees in the corner.

In the far corner, Sultry lifted her head and gave John a mournful look. Due to whelp in about two weeks, the dog passed up no opportunity to let him know she was heavy with pups and miserable and hungry. He would run her alone because she was always bitchy in temperament and her current condition made her even worse. As the dog was not his, only boarded with him, he took even better care of her than he did his own kennel—and there were those who said John coddled his dogs shamefully, that a guard dog should be lean and hungry and unhappy. John had never found that to be true of any coworkers whether two-legged or four-legged. Fit, yes . . . starved for education, food, or companionship, never.

He filled Sultry's bowl and pushed it under the gate. She got to her feet and walked over, her sides bulging with her unborn, one of them kicking energetically, visible even through her sleek pelt. With a grumble, she nosed at her bowl, then began to wolf it down. John chuckled at her, poking his fingers through the chain-link fencing and scratching her head. She stopped eating long enough to lick at his hand, then turned her attention back to her food. He made a note to recommend that her owner have the vet look at her in a day or two, a week earlier than her scheduled appointment. He did not see how she could go another ten days or more before whelping.

Comb in hand, he got two dogs out and groomed them thoroughly before the feeding, gathered in Flint and Hans and returned them to their pens with dinner bowls just as the portable phone in his back pocket began to trill. He kneed the door to Flint's enclosure closed while getting the phone.

"Guardian Dogs, John Rubidoux speaking."

No one spoke. He could hear an open line, though he was far enough away from the office that his reception was not crystal clear. He put a hip to Flint's gate to keep it closed while fumbling one-handed at the latches, and repeated a little louder, "Guardian Dogs . . . may I help you?"

"John."

He stopped fooling with Flint's pen—the Alsatian wasn't going anywhere—and straightened. The pit of his stomach reacted. He had never thought to hear from her again and had been trying not to think of it, pushing it out of his mind these last few days, and his reaction told him he'd been stupid to think he could. "Charlie? Is that you?"

So faint, he could barely hear the answer. "Yes."

The bitterness, the fear in her voice, abruptly made him stop thinking of himself. She was in trouble. "What is it? What's wrong?" He turned around in the kennel yard, facing toward the office, trying to clear the reception up. "I can barely hear you."

"Are you busy?"

"I'm out back feeding the dogs. Look—can I call you back?" He immediately hated himself for suggesting it, he would lose that contact—

"No . . . no . . . I'm sorry, I didn't mean to bother you . . ."

"Charlie." He found himself putting the same sternness in his voice that he used with a young, worried dog, determined not to lose her attention, her call. He cleared his throat. "Tell me what's wrong. I have to close the pens up. If the signal goes, I'll call back. You're at home?"

"Yes, but I—"

He cradled the phone between his ear and shoulder and finally got Flint's door locked. "If you won't tell me over the phone, then I'm coming over as soon as I get the kennel locked down."

Still faintly, she responded, "That's not necessary, really."

"It is necessary, I can tell from your voice. What's wrong with Jagger?"

The faraway sound of her words dwindled until he thought he'd lost her entirely, and then he heard a slight noise and realized she was crying. He shoved another food bowl into a pen with the toe of his work shoe. "I'll be there in twenty minutes."

"It's not—"

"Thirty minutes, tops. I'll be there." He hung up, so she would not argue with him anymore, and so that he could not hear her crying.

He finished feeding and cleaning the runs, letting everyone but Sultry have a good five-minute romp in the yard before collaring them and returning them.

All of the dogs gave him a mournful look as he shut them in for the night, knowing he had short-changed them. He scratched ears and jaws through the chain-link diamonds, apologizing to them, and tossed in chew bones before running to the office and getting his van keys. He looked at his clothes. Casual slacks and a T-shirt tucked in, and Rockport walking shoes. Ruby decided he did not have time to change. He was running close on twenty minutes now and it would take him longer than ten minutes to get across the southern part of the county. She would have to overlook the dog hairs and wrinkles and one or two knee-level slobber marks. He had the feeling that she was the kind of girl who would.

Jagger was bouncing up and down in the living room front window as he pulled up in the driveway and turned off the engine. He could see that the drapes had been drawn, but the golden retriever had gotten in between them and the glass, his paws on the low sill, his nose making wet marks on the immaculate panes. The sun had set, the glowering clouds now a fine rose color, like pink lemonade, and Charlie had the house lights on, their golden glow seeping from behind the drapes and backlighting Jagger.

As Ruby approached the front door, Jagger let out a muffled woof and disappeared. Seconds later, he could hear a scratch on the other side of the carved door. Long minutes passed before the doorknob began to turn in response to his knock and he winced, seeing in his mind the limping progress Charlie had to make to answer it. Jagger's head bumped the door frame, pushing the door open wider, his caramel eyes brimming with welcome that John did not find echoed in Charlie's gray-blue eyes as it swung inward to reveal her. The color seemed leeched from her skin, leaving it as pale as milk, and a neoprene-and-aluminum brace was strapped about her right leg outside her jeans.

"What happened?" He put a hand out to steady her, but she did not take it. He dropped his arm awkwardly.

Charlie swayed as she moved aside to let him in. Her lower lip trembled very slightly, fear and tears darkening her eyes to a fathomless blue. "I'm going to lose him, John . . . and I don't think I can stop it."

John had dropped his hand to the dog's head and froze with it there, not quite touching it. Jagger threw his head back, bumping John's fingers, and wiggling all over at the touch, accidental as it was. "Did he do that?" Ruby stared at the brace.

"No . . . no!" She shook her head tiredly and closed the door behind him. "He attacked someone in the bank this afternoon." She sagged into a chair, her slight figure almost disappearing in the cushions, her fingers still curled tightly upon the dog's harness.

"What do you mean, attacked? Tell me what happened."

"He jumped at someone, caught him by the arm."

He sat on the couch, on edge, leaning forward, his elbows on his knees, watching her, watching the dog. He would be more worried, but Jagger had done what he'd been trained to do, not snapping at legs but going to immobilize the arms. "Not on command."

"Of course not!" Anger replaced the weariness in her face briefly, and brought a lightning quick color to her face.

"What I meant was, are you certain you couldn't have cued him somehow, even if you didn't mean to."

Charlie frowned then, catching the edge of her lip slightly between her teeth in thought. "Possibly," she murmured, and looked down at the dog thoughtfully.

"Tell me what happened."

Haltingly, she told him about the call from the bank, and the illicit withdrawal attempt. He stopped her when she said his name, frowning, "I know that name. Isn't he the one Quentin accused of stalking you?"

"My father called him that, but I was never in any real danger."

"You told me Jagger went after him once before."

"Yes, but—" She looked at him with hope. "Do you think I set him off?"

"I think Valdor set him off. He should not have tried a takedown without being commanded, but I don't think he's going to go after just anyone. He knows the man's scent, and he shares whatever emotions you feel about him. Fear, anger, resentment— any of those, and he would have acted on his own instinct to attack." John leaned back on the couch, thinking of an additional matter. "Who was here the other day?"

Her eyelids fluttered slightly. "What do you mean?"

"When you thought you had a prowler . . . who was here? Could it have been Valdor?"

Again, that slight tint of color, welcome on her pale face. "Possibly. I don't want to think it was, but possibly." She reached down and ruffled the dog's ear. "Jagger would have known, though, wouldn't he?"

"He would have scented him, been reminded today, taken your reaction as a cue. Dogs are territorial. Valdor made an attack on his territory then, and he threatened you today. Jagger reacted the only way he knew how, the way I trained him." John nodded to himself. "Makes sense that way."

Charlie smiled slightly. "And it has to make sense."

"It does. Or we have to consider putting him down."

"You can't retrain him?"

"I don't know how much good it would do if you couldn't trust him any more. Goldens are protective dogs, but not aggressive. They will drag you out of the water to save you, but they will not go for another human. Or they should not."

She eyed Jagger, her blue-gray eyes shadowed. "I will always trust him."

"What about your leg? He knock you off balance?"

"When I get tired, it seems to get weaker. This is a precaution. I don't want to stumble and hurt myself."

"You said you fell in the bank."

The corner of her mouth pulled. "I'm still black and blue. It wasn't his fault, he just lunged and I had hold of the harness. Something had to give and it was me."

John shook his head, answering. "You can't have that, Charlie. Jagger has to perform the way he was trained to do. He can't be knocking you off your feet or hauling you around."

"Can't you do something? Retrain him?"

"I train guard dogs, security dogs. I've never even attempted to do with a dog what the companion trainers do. They're specialized and they're good."

"You're good."

He tried not to hear the hope in her voice. "Charlie, I can't . . . I can't do what you want me to."

"You don't know what he means to me."

"He's a working dog, a service dog, and there's no place for aggression in his training. I told your father that—"

"Then undo it! Take it away!"

"Charlie, I don't think I can."

Jagger looked at him and whined slightly at the agitation he must hear in their voices, the flaps of his ears moving so that they pulled back defensively, close to his head. He could see pain reflecting from those animal eyes, pain without comprehension of what had happened.

"You did this to him," Charlie told him.

"You don't have to push guilt my way."

"That's not what I meant," she protested faintly, and he knew that that was exactly what she had meant, and now regretted saying.

He shifted uncomfortably.

Jagger moaned and put his chin on his paws. Rubidoux saw what he had always feared and looked up, to see Charlie watching him, an echo of the same agony on her face.

"He gives me the freedom to be myself." Charlie waved her hand at the house. She dropped her hand to her lap and he noticed that the jeans she wore, faded and comfortable looking, bore paint spots and that she wore an old shirt over her T-shirt like a loose jacket. It, too, had various stains and splatterings on it, reminding him of how intensely her work was hands on, of how any physical weakness would affect that ability, that drive. She took a slight breath as if steadying herself. "But more than that, he's here with me. He's part of me, and I owe him. I can't stand to see him unhappy and he is. He doesn't understand. And if they take him away from me now, he'll never understand, he's only a dog—but it'll break his heart. Can't you help us?"

John exhaled slowly. He didn't know how he could—but he knew he could not say no. "I'll try," he answered.

The sense of relief he expected did not cross her face. The corner of her mouth tightened a bit, then she leaned forward and said determinedly, "Do not *try*—that implies failure is a possibility. I can't, we can't, afford failure. You have to *do* it, John Rubidoux."

"All right then . . . what's your schedule like tomorrow?"

She brushed the palms of her hands across her knees as if cleaning them. After a slight hesitation, she answered, "I just finished a job. I'm clear for a few weeks."

"Good. Tomorrow morning, here, early, eight o'clock. Is that all right?"

A wistfulness moved through her eyes and across the curve of her slightly tilted mouth. "I was going to say, it couldn't be soon enough, but that sounds pretty early." She dropped her hand down and leaned over to ruffle Jagger's ear. "We'll be waiting for you."

Charlie closed the door behind John Rubidoux and exhaled a long breath of relief. Jagger raced to the window and put his paws on the low sill, as if he watched John leave. She saw his golden feather tail tentatively wag, then lower and stop as she heard the sounds of the van pulling away from the house. Only then did she leave the door, chirping for Jagger so she could steady herself with his harness, and head for the studio.

She stood in the doorway, making no move to go in, but the door was open and blocked so it would stay that way. She had done that the moment she had gotten home from the bank. The delivery she'd ordered had been left only moments before Rubidoux arrived, and she swept her gaze across the room where a dozen new canvases waited for her, most of them landscape size, a few portrait, and two much bigger, leaning across the wall. On the worktable, boxes of oil paints were stacked, the purchase order delivery sheet still sticking out from the corner of one of them. Two new tins of odorless paint thinner stood side by side, along with a hand-rolled paper bag of brushes and a cardboard box which contained a mix of sketching pencils and markers.

How odd, she thought, to have been in a computer database, after years to be able to call up and say only, "Deliver the usual and bill me," and no one would blink or think of doing otherwise. Of course, she still bought nearly everything she needed from the same art supply store, but she had not bought these items since her recovery.

Charlie felt her mouth twist slightly. It would not be long before someone noticed what had been ordered, and think, and whisper, and another would hear, and make a call, and surmise, and another would listen . . . and soon the whole colony would think and wonder. Is she painting again?

Jagger whined slightly as if impatient with her stance at the threshold, but she did not wish to go in right now. Charlie put a shoulder to the doorjamb, leaning, as her head began to hurt with a dull, not quite realized headache. She did not know if she would ever go back in, but if she did, she knew she had to be prepared. She thought of the irony. If Valdor had just waited one or two more days. . . .

On the easel rested the landscape she had begun the other night. The white canvas was now faint umber, and she had started to block in color over her sketching. She could smell the faint odor of the few paints she had found still in good enough condition to use, as their wetness dried on the canvas. The aluminum mahl bar stayed where she'd left it, on a left-right diagonal across the picture so that she could rest her wrist upon it while painting. It was a thin, light, yet strong bar with a knob on one end to anchor on the frame and then lay across the canvas, almost but not quite touching it, so that the artist could use his strength on painting rather than holding the arm and hand in the air steady. The mahl bar had changed little in design in centuries, only in its composition. As she did with Jagger, she would be leaning on it, depending on it. She had scarcely used a bar when she was younger. This one had been a gift from Kirk Miller of The Open Door Gallery—who had given her lessons briefly—and whom she always thought of fondly whenever putting the glories and mysteries of reflected light in her paintings.

She should call him, she thought. His faintly accented, gentle voice from the South would respond in delight, and she could picture his thinning brown hair tousled back and his frameless glasses perched on his nose, a good-looking man, talented and enthusiastic with the chivalry of his background and education. She really should call him.

But she would not, not just yet, because though he had taught her the joy of painting, it was Midnight who dictated to her.

And she was waiting for Midnight.

Chapter Seventeen

He found them waiting in the backyard for him, the grass still a little damp with morning dew, and Charlie putting away her scoop as she cleaned up after Jagger. The golden bounded to the fence to greet him, his vest and harness flopping on his flank and shoulders, his doggy face split open and tongue lolling in pleasure. A good breakfast and a run had made his canine day, and John chuckled, thinking it would be nice to have such simple pleasures satisfy him as well. He reached over the top of the tall gate and unlatched it, letting himself in.

Jagger started to bounce up. "Off!" Ruby shot at him, and the dog caught himself and twisted back to the ground ears twitching in surprise as if the command to be mannered were scarcely used. Charlie gave him a slightly embarrassed look.

"Sorry," she murmured.

He chuckled in spite of himself at the abject expressions on both of their faces. "Spoiled and well-loved dog."

"Coffee?"

"When I'm done working him," John answered. He took the harness in a businesslike grip, the golden retriever responding immediately, and he began to walk Jagger through elementary obedience commands. The dog paced by him easily and willingly enough though once or twice he cast a look at Charlie as if to ask if Ruby needed to be obeyed or not. Each time, John checked him smartly, not giving the golden the chance to even consider disobeying him for another second.

Charlie winced as though the correction hurt her and stepped back onto the patio, and slipped into a cushioned outdoor chair, picked up a section of the newspaper and began to flip through it. John turned his attention fully to Jagger though he could have sworn Charlie continued to watch him somehow. He could hear the ruffle of the newspaper as she thumbed through it, yet the feeling of her eyes on him stayed.

He worked the dog briskly, putting him through his basics over and over, watching Jagger gain confidence as he did what was asked of him quickly and even happily. When he finished, the dog was panting from the light exertion, his tongue hanging out, and he headed for the water pan by the sliding glass door as soon as John released him.

Charlie dropped the newspaper. "That's it?"

He checked his time. "Nearly an hour of basics. That's enough for today."

"But," she sat back, and pushed a wisp of hair away from her forehead, "I don't understand."

"He needs to know he has to obey. Whatever is asked of him, whoever is in control of him at the time. He did well after a few initial hesitations. When he's in harness, his attention is supposed to be fully on whoever is holding that harness."

Charlie smiled wryly. "He was looking to me for the okay."

John nodded. He took a patio chair and seated himself. She pushed the morning paper in his direction, picked up a thermal pot and filled a coffee mug for him. She pushed it over, too, without meeting his gaze.

Further explanation still seemed to be needed. "It's not harsh on him."

"I don't like seeing him jerked that way."

"It's a correction, and it doesn't hurt him. It gets his attention, when done properly. It also tells him that I am the stronger, I am the one in charge."

She crossed her legs, still not looking at him. "Alpha dog."

"You say it like you don't believe it."

"I think these theories go in and out just like psychological fads with people."

He shook his head. "Dogs are pack animals and

216

that remains a basic instinct in them. I can walk into any household which has a dog and tell you who the real head of the place is just by watching the dog interact with the family . . . and it's often not who you think it is."

"It's the one who sets out the kibble."

He smiled a little, looking at Charlie, wishing she would tilt her face so he could look into her eyes. "Sometimes, but it's more than that. It's the leader and the one the dog respects. I can tell who the dog fears and I can also tell you who the dog will ultimately follow. Sometimes it's the man of the house, sometimes it's the woman, sometimes it's one of the kids. It's whoever barks and gets the action." His mouth twisted wryly. "The family dynamics can be real interesting, and if you have a very dysfunctional family, often you have a very dysfunctional dog. There's no real pack leadership or security."

"You're saying I'm dysfunctional?" Her face did move then, as she stared at him, but that was not the reaction he wanted.

"Not even remotely that." He cleared a throat going dry. "I'm saying that I'm responsible for ruining a good dog and I'm hoping I can undo it."

"Cut to the chase."

He nodded curtly.

Charlie smiled faintly. "How did he do?"

"He did real well. Not only that, he enjoyed it. He knew he was doing well. He was confident about it."

The both glanced toward Jagger, who lay full on his side, splayed out in front of the glass door, his muzzle wet, his paws already twitching in some doggish dream.

"Where do we go from here, then?" Charlie asked softly, as a mother might who feared to wake her sleeping child.

John leaned forward, putting his elbows on the patio table, to tell her. "I continue training the dog. Then, I retrain you."

"Me?" There was faint surprise in her voice.

"You. Otherwise, both he and you will revert to old habits."

She frowned. "You expect me to . . . correct . . . him like that?"

"I expect you to reinforce his training and manners."

She shifted in her chair, away from him. "I can't do that."

"It doesn't hurt him, and I am not telling you to haul him around. A jerk for attention, sharp, sudden. It's not a punishment and it isn't meant to be. You use your voice, too."

"Do you think I want him cringing when I talk to him?"

"Like a child, he knows from your tone if you're happy with him or not. And like a child, he accepts that. He accepts that sometimes you're pleased with him and sometimes you're not, and it in no way affects the overall bonding you have with him. But he's more relaxed and confident if he knows he can please you, can do what you expect of him. What I am doing is resetting lines of communication between you and strengthening them."

"By being cruel."

"By being consistent. So that he knows what to do and when to do it."

She shook her head. "I can't do that to him."

"You have to learn to be firm."

"I won't hurt him."

"You're not hurting him. And we both know it's far more damaging to let this go."

Charlie's mouth thinned and she looked away from him, saying, "You can't come back tomorrow. I have an appointment in Los Angeles."

"Thursday?"

As if it were painful to do so, she nodded slowly. "Thursday." She looked at her right hand reflectively. "I don't know if I'm strong enough for this."

And he knew she was not talking of her physical strength. He picked up his coffee mug to keep himself from reaching for her, because he knew she would reject him and he did not think he could stand that. "You'll be fine," he said soothingly.

She looked at him almost as though she were not able to see him.

"I'll be here Thursday morning," he added, to hide his discomfort.

* * *

Valdor sat in the car, his neck growing damp as sun warmed up the dark car's interior, and pulled his binoculars down from his eyes. From the terraced hillside, he had a decent view of the backyard of Charlie's domicile, though blue gum eucalyptus and palm trees and immense ficus wavered in and out as a growing breeze rustled them. He could see what he had not been able to determine last time, that she had had the bungalow built onto, perhaps as many as four hundred additional squares. Studio? Workshop? It had to be. Still working out of the home. . . .

He took his silk handkerchief and cleaned the eyepieces of the binoculars, then put them up again, gazing down the hillside. She had that man here again, the one he'd seen pacing around the house when he'd been forced away last time. Boyfriend? He was having difficulty reading the body language, but he did not think so. They sat opposite one another at the table, not close, and there was no touching intimacy between them as far as he could see. He had parked and begun his surveillance in time to see the man working with the golden retriever.

Valdor pulled his lips from his teeth in a slight grimace as his wrist ached holding the binoculars up. Damn dog. He'd needed six stitches to close the wounds, though most of them were puncture marks, which stitches would not help. Not to mention the

Saville Row suit ruined almost beyond even an expensive repair.

He swept his ocular view across the house again. There was a security system, Quentin would have insisted upon it, and he'd seen the small warning sign staked in the front yard, and the camera, and sensors about the windows and door . . . but she would not be using it. She hadn't that day when he was there, and he doubted she ever did unless she was leaving for an extended time, a business trip perhaps or vacation with her parents. She would think now as she had thought when he was in charge of her: The world was generally a benevolent place and she was too unimportant for it to notice her anyway.

The cell phone on the front seat beside him chimed softly. Valdor lowered his binoculars to his lap, hesitated, then reached over and picked it up.

"Federico."

"Yes," he confirmed, though he knew the oily voice well and knew that the owner of it undoubtedly recognized his own.

"How are you doing, Freddie?"

He inhaled sharply to keep his temper. "I am busy, my friend. Can I call you back later?"

"Now, Freddie. You know that I'm the one who tells you when I want to talk to you and when I don't."

Valdor swallowed tightly. "I sent you a payment."

"Barely enough to cover the interest. And, as I recall, you said you'd have the whole amount for us today."

"Things didn't work out."

"*Things didn't work out*," the speaker repeated without a trace of humor in his voice. "Why not, Freddie? Why didn't they work out?"

He could feel the collar of his shirt growing damp. Valdor tugged at it uncomfortably. "You'll get your money."

"Of that, I have no doubt. It's when that I am wondering."

"I have an investment . . ."

A slight, dry and humorless chuckle. "As do we."

"It's going to take me a couple of days."

"We've been patient with you, Freddie."

He swallowed. He hated being called Freddie. Valdor inhaled deeply. "I will have the money within two weeks. The full amount, plus the interest. Take the four grand . . . as a bonus. Free money. Just give me two weeks."

"A bonus, Valdor?"

"Yes. For being generous with your . . . time." He tried to swallow again, but his mouth, his throat, had gone rigidly dry.

"Intriguing. With our interest rate structure, hardly anyone ever offers to pay more."

"I am. But I need the time."

There was a pause at the other end of the line,

during which he heard nothing but the faint hum of the cell phone connection, but he could imagine a whispered exchange. After long moments during which his shirt drew damp in his armpits his caller said, "My friends and I are agreed. Two weeks, Valdor."

"Thank you." The words rasped from his parched throat. He should have repeated them, but they galled enough that he did not.

"If your . . . investment . . . doesn't pan out this time, I don't think I need to tell you what our recourse will be."

Valdor hung up. *No, they didn't* He opened the collar of his shirt and peered down the hillside terraces again.

In that bungalow, relatively unguarded, relatively accessible, were two or three Saunders painting which would be worth a fortune to him. The Peppermill Gallery had more paintings, but it was highly secured, and he could not risk it. Here, he had only the girl and the dog to worry about.

And if the paintings he was certain were there had gone somewhere else, then there was the girl herself. Quentin Saunders would see that no harm came to her . . . would pay to ensure her life.

There was only the dog to stop him.

Valdor lowered his binoculars again.

One way or another, the dog would have to go.

Chapter Eighteen

Wade walked into the inner lobby where he held his patient consultations. A sort of neutral ground between the outer waiting room, the inner office holding the receptionist and the nurses' work areas and the insurance clerks, the exam rooms and his own office, the rippling light from the wall stand aquarium seemed to diffuse the flowery wallpaper against which it hung. Charlie, pressed against the aquarium glass, looked up as he reached for the back of the chair he generally used, and he was struck by the faint dark lines under her eyes and the shadow of worry. He had watched her cross the threshold of puberty into young womanhood, but it always surprised him a little to see her; she seemed forever fixed in his mind as that child prodigy, that painter who made a physical effort to take both her talent and the furor accompanying it in a grown-up's stride.

Her mother looked much the same as always, a

little heavier than she should be, a little simpler than her moneyed status, a little older than it was necessary for a woman her age to look. Her reflection in the highly polished conference table flattered her even less. Mary Saunders did not seem to notice his eyes on her as she reached out and took her daughter's hand, squeezing it lightly.

The golden retriever sprawled at Charlie's feet looked at him alertly, giving a wave of his feathery tail, before dropping his chin to his paws. Wade assessed him for a moment before sitting down, placing the file on the table in front of him, and looking at Charlie, who would not meet his eyes. He smiled warmly in spite of the atmosphere of anxiety, a smile he neither practiced nor felt, but simply wore.

"Charlie. It's been a while. Dr. Katsume saw you last time . . . and I would have seen you for your last scheduled appointment, but our records show you called and canceled it. So it's been, what, more than a year?" He would normally have asked how she had been, but under the circumstances, it did not seem appropriate. She looked at him, and then away again. Mary Saunders shifted as if to say something in her daughter's stead, then pressed her lips together, and remained quiet.

Wade looked kindly at Charlie. "I am not going to tell you that if you'd made that appointment, this would never have happened."

Charlie took a deep breath. It brought some measure of color to her face, still plain, but with an underlying prettiness that he supposed came from her own basic nature, the corner of her mouth drooping just slightly. It gave her expression a slight intrigue. "Would it have?"

"We might have detected it earlier, but the truth is, we could not have prevented it." Wade folded his hands and leaned forward slightly, resting on the folder. "We have a new lesion in that quadrant, and it appears to be significant in size and pressure from the tests run on you. I would like to have you schedule some appointments for additional tests here, at our clinic, so I can make a determination as to the best course of treatment."

"Operable?'" Charlie's blue eyes fixed on him.

"I don't know yet. But techniques are changing every day. The gamma knife makes things possible I could not have done ten years ago."

Mary Sunders blurted out, "It was benign last time! How could it be back?"

"If I could answer that, I could prevent tumors, and none of my patients would ever suffer from one." He stated the obvious. Wade unfolded his hands, reached over and patted hers in a gesture meant to be comforting. "And it is probably benign this time as well. It is the growth and pressure which makes it deadly."

Charlie seemed to flinch. "How soon do you need me?"

"As soon as we can get you in. There won't be anything new, Charlie, you've been through these before."

"I know."

He patted her shoulder. "I'll have Kris set you up as soon as she can get you in. If there are openings today, are you prepared to stay here?"

Mary answered, "Of course we are."

Charlie traced her fingers on the conference table-top. "Suppose I refuse?"

"Charlie! You can't be serious!"

Charlie looked at Wade, ignoring her mother. "I have that option, don't I?"

"Everyone has options, Charlie, but refusing medical attention is not a wise one in your case. You will be creating additional problems, serious ones, which are totally unnecessary and avoidable. We have the advantage now to sidetrack complications. We're here to help you, not hurt you."

Charlie shifted in her chair, putting her right leg out, wearing an aluminum support brace over her tailored trouser leg, and looked at it as the dog moved slightly to avoid being hit or jostling her. "That's what you said last time."

"There is some risk in every operation, no matter how routine. And," Wade cleared his throat slightly. "What I do is scarcely routine." He opened the folder to the black-and-white printout of the MRI done when she had been hospitalized. He tapped his finger on the swirls of black, gray, and white. "I want you to take a look at this. I'm going out to find Kris and have her begin making arrangements. Talk about it. Tell me what you want to do."

He pushed away from the table and knew that Charlie would not utter a word till he'd shut the door behind him, although he could hear Mary Saunders begin to stutter in bewilderment as the lobby door clicked shut.

Kris, a tall, willowy young woman with dark hair and beautiful skin that set off her hazel eyes, began efficiently tracking down schedules and making calls as soon as he asked her. She could not arrange anything sooner than forty-eight hours, however, which, he reflected, was probably just as well. He would make a private call to Quentin Saunders to apprise him of the situation. Quentin would see that things got done.

Mary Saunders looked suspiciously bright-eyed as he stepped back into the lobby, carrying the schedule Kris had entered into the office computer and printed out for him.

"Here're the appointments we've had set up for you, as well as any prepping instructions you need to know. She managed to get them all into a day and a half, so we can get through this as quickly as possible with as little inconvenience as possible. The sooner I have readings on my desk, the sooner I can tell what it is we're going to have to do."

"Is it . . . is it in the same area?"

He looked at Charlie. "Close."

"And what will you cut away this time?" Her lip trembled. "What of me will you take away forever? How much of me will be left? Will I need a cane or a wheelchair?"

Wade put his hand on Mary's wrist as she took in a breath sharply, to forestall anything she might say, and answered levelly, "As little of you as I have to. You have to trust me, Charlie. Trust in my skill and my training and my desire to see you healthy." He took a breath. "To not do this, to think that by ignoring it, the tumor will go away will leave us fewer and fewer options. It seems to be growing quickly since it reestablished itself. Time and hesitation and fear is *not* on our side."

"And what is?"

"My skill. Your youth. Your earlier medical history. The hope that this, once again, will be benign. And ever-growing technology. The gamma knife, new laser technology, the whole gamut means that I might be able to handle this much less intrusively."

Charlie caught her lower lip between her teeth, as if to stop its trembling. She stood, the golden retriever immediately scrambling up as well. "Thank you, Dr. Clarkson. I'll let you know." She took the printout.

"Charlie!" her mother blurted, then shot Wade a look of apology and got to her feet to hurry after her daughter, who was already out the lobby door and disappearing into the outer waiting room.

Wade watched them go, Charlie's lithe body swaying with the tiniest of limps, her hand secured about the dog's service harness, watched her thoughtfully, before gathering up his file and returning to his office.

Her mother scarcely said two words to her as they settled into the backseat of the car. Jagger sprawled on the floor between their feet, seemingly unaware of the hump in the floorboards or dismayed by it, his chin on the toe of her shoe. Mary continued to look out the passenger window as though the rushing freeway and traffic beyond it carried some sign of salvation. Finally, she said tightly, "You can't be serious."

Charlie sighed. "I was never more serious."

"Charlotte! You have your whole life ahead of you. You're talking about throwing it away."

"What kind of life is it if I end up a vegetable?"

"He said nothing about that—That's not foreseeable."

"He said nothing about this last time either, did he?" Charlie looked at her leg brace. "He took away my painting . . . my leg, my arm, my hand. What is he going to excise this time?" She put her hand on her mother's shoulder and shook her. "What if I forget you? Forget myself? What am I then? An amusing turnip who used to be a person?"

"Oh, Charlie!" Her mother turned from the car window and leaned over, and took her in her arms, and held her tightly. "That won't happen this time."

Her voice muffled, Charlie said bitterly, "You can't promise that. He can't."

Her mother said hoarsely into her ear, "I can't promise you that we won't die in a car accident before we get home, either. *It happens, honey, and God only knows why it happens.* But he will do his best for you, and he is one of the best, and that's all we can ask."

"I can let it go."

"You know you can't. The tumor could blind you, paralyze you, suffocate your functions one by one with seizures." Her mother rubbed her shoulders, gently, her hand palm down, soothingly, as she held her. "Jagger can't save you from those, sweetheart."

Charlie found a strength in her mother's embrace. She took a deep breath, and did not try to move away. She would endure the clinic again, she knew she would, but she did not know what she would do beyond that. Fear seemed to have crept into her and settled deep into her bones, replacing marrow with icy crystals of dread and hesitation. It was as though she were permanently on the threshold of Midnight, caught between being truly alive and slowly dying. One or the other would be preferable to where she found herself now.

She signaled Pedro to let her off at the foot of the hill, on Pacific Coast Highway itself, rather than going up to her street. Her mother stroked her face before tucking a wayward strand of hair behind her ear. "You should let us take you all the way up."

"No, really. Jagger needs the walk, and I want to buy some juice and vegetables."

"Get something for lunch, too."

The small family grocery store behind her was famous for the sandwiches from its meat counter. Charlie smiled faintly. "I will. Do you want me to run in and get something for you and Dad, too?"

Her mother shook her head. "No. I imagine he ate at the club, and I have some leftover shrimp calling my name." Mary Saunders hesitated, then caught Charlie's hand. "Call me later."

"I will if I have time." Charlie saw the dismay sparked in her mother's face. "Mom! It's not like I didn't just see you."

"I worry."

Charlie laughed softly. "You'd worry even if I did call you."

"You know what I mean."

Charlie gently took her hand out of her mother's. "And you know what I mean. I need to go home, do some design work, and relax. That's what you have to do, go home and relax."

"I have a charity fashion show to set up."

"Then do that." Charlie backed out of the door frame. "We're stopping traffic. Go home, Mom, I'll be fine."

Mary Saunders closed the car door reluctantly. "Call!" she shouted as the car began to pull away from the curb, easing back into traffic.

Charlie nodded and waved, and waited until the tide had carried them off before turning into the small store.

May, the Korean-American woman who owned and operated the store with her family, smiled pleasantly, her moon-shaped face and dark eyes lighting as Jagger pulled Charlie in. The floor sloped unevenly, buckled slightly from the great earthquake of 1933 which, from Long Beach south into Orange County, had shaken foundations everywhere. The little store had been a family-owned store then, as it was now, although the families had changed, and the building, coast, and neighborhoods around it had changed, too.

"Good morning, Miss Charlie," May giggled slightly. "Almost afternoon, nearly. Did you want to order a sandwich? The counter is empty, my husband is in the back."

"I'll wait. Do you have chicken salad today?"

"Sure do."

"Good." Charlie moved to the cold case, where vegetable and juice drinks sat in icy rows, waiting. She picked out a carrot-and-wheat grass drink, and then an orange raspberry juice as well. As she passed the checkout counter, May leaned over and pressed a small dog bone into her hand, smiling. Charlie bent over and offered the treat to Jagger, telling him, "This is from May."

He took it and she waited while he chomped it down and then wagged his tail happily. May smiled largely before returning to her textbook, opened discreetly behind the electronic register. She was always studying something. Charlie went down the gondolas, picked up some free-range eggs, went to the fresh, organic vegetable and fruit bins and picked up some arugula and radiccio, an avocado which looked temptingly ripe, some butter lettuce and swiss chard, all of which looked incredibly crisp and tender.

May's husband Delman came out from the back of the butcher area, straightened a clean apron, and smiled at her. "What can I do for you today, Miss Saunders?"

"How about a barbecued beef sandwich and a chicken salad sandwich to go?"

He nodded and briskly went into motion. Jagger whined slightly, pressing his head against her brace.

The beef sandwich she'd have for dinner as well as her salad, knowing full well that at least half of it would go down Jagger's begging jaws. The sauce-rich sandwich tantalized both their taste buds as Delman served it up on a long, freshly baked roll, wrapped it in waxed paper, deftly twisted the ends, then wrapped it again in light foil He made the chicken salad as quickly, the wax paper crackling as he twisted it, and then put both in a paper bag. "That it for today, Miss Saunders?"

"All I can think of."

He smiled broadly. "Would you mind if I stuck a bone in for Jagger?"

"Not at all."

He fished out a bone from under the counter. It had been boiled, from the looks of it, perhaps to make broth, but still had plenty of meat hanging from it and one large knobby end. He rolled foil around it and added it to the paper bag. Jagger licked his chops in anticipation.

She laughed. "I think he knows that's for him."

Delman grinned. "You two have a nice day, now." He went back to cleaning his counters as she gathered in the paper bag which was already redolent with savory aroma.

Jagger escorted her to the small checkout counter by the front door, his head bumping her brace from time to time.

"Piggy," she said quietly to him, as she put her basket up and watched May begin to unload. Jagger continued to bump her leg without remorse.

May giggled as she emptied the basket and totaled

up the items. "He knows what smells good," she noted, her short, slim fingers flying over the register keys.

"His idea of heaven is to come shopping here with me." Charlie could not help but smile as she ruffled the dog's ears. "How is your son?"

May's and Delman's son was a budding young artist, one of many helped by the local colony art programs. May's face brightened even more at the mention of her child. She reached out and moved a poster board toward Charlie for better viewing. "He drew this," she said proudly. "His was chosen out of several hundred."

Charlie looked down. She saw a starred night, a highway, a car with blaring yellow headlights staring into the darkness, some childish words about driving safety . . . the colors were bold, garish, in wide strokes, reminding her of something she had painted. The poster caught her, ensnared her, she could not look away.

Jagger whined and bumped her knee again. Charlie heard him as if from far away, muffled, as though she lay underwater. The car in the poster began to slide sideways, careening off the asphalt highway, sliding, headlights skewing wildly into the night, across the stars, the moon, until the car came to a tumbling halt, the jolt popping a door open and a young woman falling out.

She staggered to her feet, leaning upon the car,

blood streaming from a gash across her forehead. Charlie blinked and watched, her hands growing ice-cold, the only part of her she could feel . . . the rest of her being had narrowed into this singular focus, the nighttime drama unfolding in front of her. She was sight and sight only, with no other sense or flesh.

Another set of beams pierced the darkness. The highway looked as if it glistened, with rain or dew, wetly ebony, lights wavering as they streamed across it. The young woman clung to the side of her vehicle as the other car pulled near. Rescue was at hand. Charlie could see the relief on her face as the other car stopped, and more light illuminated the dark as a car door opened and stayed open. A figure stepped out of the car, big, burly, masculine by its very size. Moved toward the girl. The figure carried light in his hand . . . and that light flashed up . . . in her vision, the young woman looked toward the figure, toward Charlie, opening her mouth, beginning to scream.

The light flashed up and down, up and down, swinging violently as the object bludgeoned into her head again. And again. And again. Until, still silent, face cascading with blood made black and muddy-looking by the night, she sank to her knees, slumped into nothingness. The figure grabbed her by the collar and dragged her to the open car door and shoved her inside. The door closed. With that movement, all light winked dark.

Jagger nosed her again.

"$17.59, Miss Saunders . . . are you all right?" May peered at her over the handled shopping bag of groceries on the counter, blinking in concern.

"Am I . . . what?"

"Are you all right? Should I call someone for you? You look very pale."

"No. I . . ." Charlie looked at the child's poster. "I . . . I'm fine." She handed May a twenty-dollar bill. "Keep the change, put it on my account." She took her groceries in her arms. The pungent smell of the barbecue sandwich hit her sharply. "I'm sorry. I was thinking." She took a deep breath. "Your son is quite an artist."

"Thank you." May gave a little bow. "But not like you."

"Thank goodness for that! He should have a longer career." Charlie tried to smile. Her face still felt frozen and numb. Jagger pulled her toward the door and Charlie let him.

What had just happened to her? What had she just seen—or imagined?

Shaken by the violence, by the coldness which seemed to dwell inside her still, she let Jagger pull her uphill toward the residential streets, his tail flagging. They made this walk at least once a week if not more often. He knew where they were headed: Home.

Or hell.

*　　*　　*

By the time they reached the house, she had broken into a light sweat, her muscles trembling with the effort. She sat down and ate mechanically, her mind's eye centered on the vision, her hands plucking a bit at a time off the chicken sandwich and feeding it into her mouth, and to Jagger. A bite for me, a bite for you. . . .

She recognized that picture. Not the child's poster, but the picture she had seen. Not a movie, but a flat, two-dimensional rendering.

Charlie shot to her feet. Limping, she hurried through the bungalow to her studio, and went to the small built-in bookcase in the corner. Her various ribbons from art shows sat mounted on easel boards, gathering dust and webs from daddy longlegs spiders who seemed to be everywhere in the house, ribbons and small plaques, and a few local magazines. She picked them up and thumbed through them, knowing she had kept them because she was featured in them. The dust clung to her fingers. She wiped them off with one of her new painting rags. Yellowing pages turned stubbornly in her hands.

She recognized herself with an odd feeling in the pit of her stomach. Looking at photos ten years old and older . . . she was both inside and outside that child caught in time. She looked at a figure somewhat waiflike, hair combed back and held with one of those clips, so trendy then, still popular now, sticklike legs in satin pants, vest and a silk shirt, leaning self-consciously against an easel.

Jagger came in, chuffing impatiently at the thought of a half-shared chicken sandwich still lying on the kitchen table, while she thumbed through the photo retrospective of the gallery showing. Some of the paintings were well captured by the camera lens, many others she could only catch glimpses of. She had forgotten them, not all, but a few, but it only took a passing glance to refresh her memory. She put a shoulder to the bookcase and, leaning upon it, paged through the first of a dozen magazines she needed to examine.

The phone rang.

Charlie looked up, drawn out of her memories, and frowned slightly. Jagger sprawled near her, having given up on the sandwich, and hardly moved when she stepped around him to get the portable in the bedroom. Late afternoon shadows laced the room, curtaining it.

The phone rang a second, and then a third time before she reached the appliance, its tone eerily flat. She answered it, to hear a buzz on the line not unlike the dial tone itself, and a void before someone answered back.

"You know who killed me," the young woman said.

"You know."

"H–hello?" Charlie stammered. "Who is this?"

"You know," the unfamiliar voice repeated.

"What are you talking about? Who is this?" The cords of her throat strained and her fingers wrapped tightly about the portable phone. Charlie shook. "Tell me what you want!"

The voice faded, barely audible. *"You know."*

The line went dead. And then the dial tone resumed, from the background static buzzed to a loud droning in her ear. Charlie dropped the portable. It bounced on the corner of her bed. Stunned, she looked back toward her studio.

Jagger came walking in to find her, his head down unhappily, whining, his caramel eyes anxious.

John pulled the van up in the driveway and stopped. The interior of the vehicle reeked with the smell of freshly made onion-and-water bagels, and the rich aroma of newly brewed coffee. He swung his legs out, then gathered up his offerings. Jagger scratched at the house's front window, his nails clicking eagerly. Ruby grinned at the dog's excitement and hoped it was a reflection of the greeting he might get from Charlie this time.

He knocked on the door, to hear resounding barks from the golden retriever, but it was long moments before the door opened hesitantly. Charlie leaned on the edge of it, bracing herself, her face pale and drawn. Tangles of her hair trailed about her face, and she smiled of paint. The only color about her was the smear or two on the shirt and trousers she wore. She held a brush loosely in her hand, almost as if unaware of it, the paint still glistening damply.

"Charlie?" he said anxiously.

She blinked, almost as if not really seeing him. Then she made as if to close the door, barring him. "Go away."

"Are you all right?"

"Go away. I'm busy . . . I can't see you today."

He put his body in the gap between door and threshold. "What's wrong?"

"You can't come in." Charlie put her hand up as if to fend him off, her fingers stained with paint, trembling slightly. Faint indigo stains of tiredness hung belong her eyes. She tried to block him, but he took her by the elbow and let himself in, steadying her.

The faint smell of oil paints hung in the air. Jagger came dashing up, still in harness, but it had slipped about him, hanging from his side, half unfastened. He pawed at John and began to slobber at the scent from the paper bag full of bagels. The living room looked as if a whirlwind had hit it, newspaper flung everywhere and on those papers, canvases lay or stood, propped up against sofa and chairs and wall. Bright, glistening canvases gleaming with fresh paint, bold colors that struck him before he even looked upon them . . . ten . . . maybe twelve of them, trailing down the hallway and disappearing.

"My God," he muttered, and shut the door behind him. He put his arm around her shoulder and held her to him, afraid she would move away warily, and more afraid she would topple. "Did you sleep at all last night?"

Charlie took a deep breath at his touch and relaxed against him slightly. She looked at her hand and the paintbrush she still held as if it were a foreign object. Her fingers opened stiffly and the brush fell to the floor, where it landed upon one of the strewn newspaper. She looked at John in bewilderment as if he had awakened her, shadows thinning in her blue-gray eyes.

"Is it Midnight yet?" she asked faintly.

Chapter Nineteen

John felt her tremble as he guided her through the house and into the kitchen, the only place he could find away from the paintings. She sat down numbly. Jagger bounced at him impatiently, nosing the paper bags, backing off only when John dropped them on the kitchen table. He looked and saw the water bowl in the corner nearly dry, only a thin puddle of liquid on the bottom.

He got both of them water and brought hers back. She stared at it, then curled the fingers of her left hand about it. Jagger pushed his face into his water bowl, lapping noisily and continuously.

"It's almost eight-thirty," he told her. "The dog acts like he's starving. Has he eaten? Have you? Did you even sleep?"

She sipped at her water aimlessly. "I don't remember. I don't think I did." Charlie shuddered. "I've done some painting." She considered her hands, small streaks of color on them. "Haven't I?"

"The house is full of them."

She closed her eyes, a bleak look on her face. "I need to look at them."

"You painted them."

"I need to look at them!"

Not comprehending, but trying to keep her calm, he answered. "Not just yet. You can barely stay on your feet. Let me feed the dog, take care of him, then we'll go . . . look."

Charlie nodded, slumping down in her chair.

Jagger trotted across the kitchen as he went to the pantry and found the large bag of kibble propped up against the storage shelves. The dog's tail began to beat a tattoo against the air and he licked his still wet chops in anticipation as John filled his eating bowl.

"Go ahead."

The golden hunkered down, and whined, but made no move to the bowl. Charlie stirred and said hoarsely, "Dinner, Jagger. Come on and eat."

At her signal, Jagger leaped toward the bowl and began to wolf it down, his noisy crunching filling the small room. John opened the refrigerator door and found a carton of orange juice, nearly full, stowed next to the carton of low-fat milk. He poured them each a stout glass of orange juice before sitting down.

"Tell me," he said, "what you want to."

She wrapped both hands around the juice and took a long drink, before setting the glass down with a sigh. "I have to look at them," she told him. "Before I can tell you anything."

"Look at them? The paintings? You just finished them."

"I know." Charlie glanced away from him, checked Jagger, who was polishing off the last of his kibble nuggets, then looked back. "It's hard to explain."

"I have nowhere else to be this morning." He polished off his orange juice, still vaguely hungry, got up and made himself at home at her coffee maker. "Try me."

"It's the way I paint, sometimes."

He busied himself with the filter and the coffee, sensing that it was easier for her to talk if he was not looking at her. "Listening. Making plain coffee here, unless you'd rather have one of these flavored—"

"No. No, that's fine. Thank you."

He could hear her take a deep breath. Studiously, he kept his eyes on the coffee, measuring it out, savoring the smell of it, finding the filter.

"I started having nightmares after my father died."

"Quentin is not your father?"

"No. My father died suddenly when I was eight. I don't remember much before then. They told us I was severely traumatized by his death. I wouldn't know. I can't remember . . . but I started having these nightmares."

"Nightmares or night terrors?"

She downed her orange juice, then met his eyes. "Night terrors?"

"Nightmares are dreams. We all get them. Night terrors . . . are different. They shake you to your very core, and often you can't even remember them. Sometimes you bolt out of bed and run—" he paused.

"Night terrors," she repeated slowly. "Close. All I know is that when I wake, I paint. I want to paint, I have to paint. What I've seen, what I've felt . . . painting is how I deal with it. Once or twice before the tumor, I painted at night, not knowing."

"And last night."

"Yes." She put a fingertip to the rim of her juice glass, captured some orange pulp hanging there, and sucked it from her finger. "It comes on me, some great soft dark cloud . . . sometimes I think I'm going to suffocate . . . when I was little, I called it Midnight."

He stood in front of the coffee machine, smelling the fragrance as the steaming hot water began to hiss through the coffee grounds, and the dark brown liquid began to trickle through, and the aroma wafted up. "Like a seizure?"

"I don't know. I think so."

He set up two mugs from the cup holder tree. "I guess it stopped when you had the tumor removed."

"Everything stopped. No Midnight, and no desire

to paint anything whatsoever, for any reason. It was as though I had had the artistic eye cut out of me."

"But you're still an artist."

"Textiles, conceptual art, yes. I enjoy the designing, the textures, the weaving, the play of colors." Charlie watched his face as he pushed a mug of coffee into her hands. "But I could not paint any more."

"You tried?"

"For a while, after the physical therapy. The weakness makes it difficult, but I could do it." She sighed. "I just didn't want to."

"And now Midnight is back."

"With a vengeance. And so is a tumor, evidently."

He sat down abruptly, hiding the shock he felt, the cold fear. "That's why you fainted."

She nodded slowly, wordlessly. A single tear escaped her right eye, glistening and rolling from her slightly drooped lid. "What am I going to do?"

"What you did last time." He put a hand out to cover her right hand. Her bones felt slight and frail under his, her skin slightly cool. "Do what you have to and get over it."

She smiled slightly. "You make it sound easy."

"Hell. Nothing is easy. But easy and possible are two different things." He sipped his coffee carefully. "How certain are they?"

"Fairly. They want me to repeat the tests, to be certain. Then . . . I have a microneurosurgeon . . . he'll want to do surgery as soon as possible."

"Is it malignant?"

"It wasn't last time. There are no guarantees this time."

"Never are." John felt himself smile wryly. He saw her put her coffee mug down. "Ready?"

She nodded. "I have to see what I did."

He leaned over the table, and with the ball of his thumb, gently wiped away a streak of blue just at the corner of her mouth. Charlie gave a nervous laugh. She did not, however, move from his touch. He fancied she even turned into it momentarily.

She stood and though Jagger trotted over expectantly, she moved to lean on John. The dog made a chuffing noise. She glanced at him. "Lie down," she ordered. He did so, turning round and round on the planked flooring before making himself comfortable.

"I'll take him out for a run after you're finished with the paintings." He felt her settle her balance on his arm. She gave no indication of hearing him, her attention was on the hall.

He escorted her past the canvases. Her face paled again, her glance sweeping over them, from the three standing against the hallway walls, to the seven which lay about the living room.

Five of them were hastily painted, the strokes thick, the night and stars and highway rendered in heavy, suggestive, impressionistic movements. He watched her as she glanced over each quickly, then went back and pondered each painting as deeply as if she were an art critic dissecting them. Then she said, "There is a story here. Chronologically. Help me arrange them."

She directed him. He picked up and moved the still wet canvases, swapping them back and forth, with her correcting him and pointing until she stopped, and looked again, and then seemed satisfied.

"Now look at them . . . and tell me what you see."

He rocked from foot to foot uneasily. He looked at the paintings . . . dark . . . nights illuminated with twinkling stars and car beams . . . cut by scenes that made him nervous.

"I've painted a murder," said Charlie faintly.

He did not know how to answer her.

She shivered, her shoulder brushing his. He put an arm around hers, steadying her, warming her. "You've painted fear, that's all." He could not understand the emotions inside her that drove her to paint the scenes before him, but he knew the violence had not, could not, come from inside her. Not from the person he was coming to know. "Fear and the aftermath—I don't see a murder here."

"There's a missing scene." She shook her head. "Regardless. Murder." Charlie inhaled deeply. "And I've done it before."

"What?"

She left him, limping through the house, and coming back with a magazine in her hand. "The Peppermill still has this on loan. It's part of the Lavermans' collection. The photo isn't real clear, but it's here."

He took the periodical from her. Charlie sank to the edge of the couch, her gaze fixed back on the canvases. "You met Judge Laverman and his wife at the benefit."

John nodded absently, only half looking as he studied the magazine photos. His trained eye, from the past, made it hit him before he could try to view it as art . . . a crime scene sprawled before him. It had nothing to do with the new canvases in her house, but was nonetheless bizarre and disturbing, even the half frame of it which the camera had caught. He looked up at her, hoping to hide his expression, but could not, and she saw it in his face.

"Oh, God," she said faintly. "What have I done?"

Quentin Saunders strode up, and grasped Wade's hand in a firm handshake as he rose to meet him. "Doctor. Good to see you again. With a little more notice, I could have cleared my calendar and taken you to lunch." Quentin released his hand, but not before the impression of a man who had made his living through physical ability as well as business acumen was made.

Wade sat back down. The resin chairs on the patio were slightly less than comfortable, but the clarity of the view of the coast and the refreshing ocean breeze more than made up for it. "Coffee is fine. George Laverman is meeting me for lunch while I'm down here. This just gives me a chance to talk with you in person."

Quentin frowned, creasing his lined face, and shifted his chair slightly. Wade looked at him, realizing the graying hair had gotten more and more silvered over the years, the lines deeper and deeper around the eyes and mouth. The neckline had begun to sag, almost imperceptibly, but it was there. Wade looked at Saunders and felt time beginning to touch himself as well. Saunders waited until the waiter brought his coffee and set it down in front of him.

"Is this about Charlie?"

Wade inclined his head.

Quentin made two tries to pick up the tall, curved mug. "And a phone call would not do." He paused. "How bad is it?"

"I wish I knew. Preliminary readings of the MRI from Sunset indicate a new growth, but, frankly, their equipment doesn't have the clarity ours does, and Charlie has refused to undergo new tests."

"What?" Coffee splashed onto the glass-topped bistro table and spread, almost like a puddle of blood.

"That's why I'm here."

"And you let her walk out?"

"She's an adult now, Quentin. There isn't much I could do. I had the clinic schedule her anyway, and advised both Charlie and her mother that she should not try to ignore this, that it will only make things more difficult in the long run."

Quentin folded both of his huge hands around the coffee cup, dwarfing it. "Is it cancer this time?"

"I don't know yet. I am optimistic that it may not be, like last time, but I won't know until I go in . . . if she lets me." Wade looked into Quentin's eyes. "You have to persuade her, Quentin."

"She'll make your appointments," Saunders answered grimly.

"Charlie is frightened."

The other flinched slightly, a muscle ticking in his jawline. "She knows you, she knows Katsume. You saved her life."

"She went though a lot. This is not the kind of thing anyone wants to repeat, no matter how successful the first treatment was." Wade stood. "Just call the clinic and confirm, if you can get her in. If not, reschedule. Try to bring her in as soon as possible, Quentin. The growth of this tumor seems to be rapid. Every day can make a difference."

As he passed by Saunders, he dropped a hand to his shoulder, and squeezed. "We all love her. We all want the best for her."

Saunders gave a shaky jerk of his head. "God knows, I don't want her to go like my mother . . . comatose for two years . . . barely alive . . . God knows, someone like Charlie should have her whole life before her."

Wade patted him. "My team and I will do everything we can."

John brought Jagger back in from his run and sat down on the couch, where Charlie still stared unblinkingly at her paintings. He took her face in his hands, gently making her look at him.

"What on Earth makes you think you've done something wrong?"

She looked back at him, her lower lip quivering slightly. "John, look at the magazine again."

"I don't need to."

She took a deep breath. "But I do."

He let go of her and reached for the magazine. This time, she turned the page. Wordlessly, she pointed to another painting.

Stunned, he looked from the magazine's slick rendering, to the paintings in front of him, and back again. This painting showed a confrontation and, put together with the ones she had just finished, the tale of a killing became clear. "Charlie, how . . . ?"

She touched the magazine. "I painted that nearly eleven years ago." She took the magazine from him and closed it. "Do you know why we have art?"

He watched her face. "Tell me."

"To express, teach, and inspire." Her expression

went bleak. "God help me," she repeated. "I've inspired someone to become a murderer."

"You can't know that."

"I can." Haltingly, she told him what she could remember.

Sometime as she spoke, he reached out and drew her onto his lap, holding her, cradling her, listening to her flow of words, thinking his own thoughts, his body independent of his mind, feeling her next to him, the fragrance of her hair, the slight taint of oil paint from her skin. He tried to blanket her, to warm her, to give her strength. He felt himself begin to react to her nearness.

John rubbed her shoulders lightly before deciding to put her aside, back on the sofa, his desire totally inappropriate to what he had intended, unable to help himself. As he shifted slightly, to gather her up and move her, Charlie stopped talking abruptly, and tilted her face up toward his. She kissed him, catching him offguard, her mouth soft and gentle, not quite meeting his lips.

He almost pulled away but not before she kissed him again, this time seeking his mouth and finding it, hers parting slightly, hungrily, and he gave an inaudible groan, wanting to answer her.

She drew back. "Let me feel this," she said.

"Charlie . . ." He reared back slightly, fighting himself, yet did not push her away, unable to.

She ran her hands lightly over his shirt, parted the

neck of it, bent her head and kissed his throat, trailing her lips up to his jaw, over his chin, searching for his mouth again. "Let me feel something besides cold and afraid and alone . . . something besides Midnight."

He touched her hair, soft and silken, its golden-brown strands tangling about his fingers. She turned her head and caught his hand and snuggled her face against his palm.

He found breath enough to say, "Are you sure?"

"Of this, yes."

He pulled her closer, and kissed her back then, possessing her mouth, gripping her shoulders tightly, tasting her lips, her tongue, her mouth, velvety soft and open to him. Sometime later, he managed, "Tell me no . . . just tell me if you want me to stop . . ."

She murmured many things to him over the next moments, but "no" was never one of them.

Chapter Twenty

He left her curled on the couch, an old and worn afghan tucked around her, and went through the house looking for paper, before going out to the van and finding a pocket-sized notebook. Jagger yawned at him when he came back in, and flopped over, his flank to the edge of the couch, guarding Charlie with his very body . . . even if he was practically sound asleep.

John walked his way through the paintings again, then opened the magazine and sketched the death scenes, both of them, and then added whatever details from the new paintings he could put into words. Lovemaking had quieted her soul, and set his into motion. His years on the force and his continued association with it had taught him that nothing was impossible, that sometimes the mildest of people had a venal streak. But that her paintings could inspire that, he doubted. He could tell her in words, but he could do more—he could prove it. And would.

He hated to wake her, and shook her shoulder gently. Her eyelids fluttered, not quite opening.

He bent close and kissed her cheek. "I have to leave for a while. I'll bring lunch back with me."

Charlie smiled. With a slight sigh, she burrowed back into the couch pillows and afghan, drifting away again. He pulled a long golden hair away from the corner of her mouth, not wanting to leave her . . . ever.

He locked himself out as he left, scanning the street. He looked up the terraced hillside and down, then got into the van.

Most of the desks were empty when he walked in, got his visitor's ID and clipped it on, the station cleared for lunch. He headed to the back to see Hubie Valenzuela, his leg aching in memory of times spent in similar police stations in other cities.

Valenzuela did not smoke, but he chewed cigars till they were pulpy messes, and had one hanging out of his thick lips now as he looked up and caught sight of John rounding a beige-hued corner.

"Ruby! Coming in to sign up for league?" The beefy officer swiveled around at his desk, shuffling papers, searching, cigar drooping.

"No, but I suppose you won't let me out of here till I do."

"How's that leg of yours? I need a shortstop this season."

John shook his head. "Good arm, no legs. You know that."

Valenzuela muttered around his cigar, found a tattered manila folder, and fetched it out. "I'll put you in right field, then. Again." He flashed a grin at John before sketching his name onto the latest roster in bold strokes. "Meet at Impy's Pizza in a coupla weeks, I'll give you a call." He bent his head to the desk, resorting papers, and then looked up when Ruby did not move away. The rest of the squad room had all but cleared.

He raised an eyebrow. "You don't wanna be in right field?"

"No, that's fine. I'm used to it." John grinned at him. "Actually, I have a favor to ask."

Valenzuela kicked around to face him. The cigar worked in his mouth, bobbing up and down. "Favor." He cleared his throat.

John looked at his computer, smiled slightly, and did not answer.

"Ermmm." Valenzuela shifted uneasily. "Ruby, you know the rules."

"It could be important."

Valenzuela sighed. "This for you?"

"Girl."

The cigar dropped from his mouth. "You've got a girl?"

"It has been known to happen, but she's not mine. Just a friend who has some trouble."

Valenzuela retrieved his soggy cigar, picked some lint off it, and jammed it back in his mouth. "Ruby . . ."

He held his hand up. "If I don't tell you, you won't know."

Valenzuela sighed. "Better be some girl."

John did not say anything.

Valenzuela cocked his arm to look at his watch and his eyebrow twitched in mock surprise. "Lunchtime!" he said in delight. With the toe of his shoe, he glided a bottom drawer in the desk open, leaned over, and fished out a bulging paper bag.

He stood up and said to Rubidoux, "I'm supposed to sign off at lunch. Sometimes I forget. It's a bad habit, but this is a secured area. I doubt anybody will try to use my computer anyway." He turned his back on John then, and headed away from his desk to the corridor which would make an elbow bend before reaching the lunchroom.

John waited until Valenzuela was officially out of sight before gaining the chair, sitting down and swiveling around in it until he faced the monitor. He took his notebook out of his shirt pocket and flipped it to the page where he had begun making notes. Then he brushed his gaze over the keyboard, licked his dry lips, and began to type in earnest. The light in the tower blinked as the hard drive whirled into search mode, and the various data banks he could access displayed on the monitor.

John scanned them quickly, picking out the most logical ones to tap into. The breakdown and barriers between local, state, and federal agencies into computer data banks had been slow at first, but now he could see that technology was rapidly bringing them together while maintaining the separate jurisdictions the agencies had always fought over. A few of the frustrations he had experienced as a cop had finally begun to erode away, unfortunately pressured by the mounting numbers in crime statistics. It had been neither politics nor common sense, but necessity forcing those changes. He rolled his tongue across the back of his teeth, deciding whether or not he wanted to go into the FBI violent crimes folders, hesitated, then settled for local.

He ran his fingers across his notebook, trying to sift through the details and sketches he had scribbled down, and enter them as a coherent inquiry to search the database. The computer could not make an intuitive leap from the information he was providing. Either it would find a match for the details he had gleaned from the paintings or it would not. Not finding a match did not mean the crime scene did not exist. By the same token, he told himself, finding a match did not mean that Charlie had ever been there or seen it . . . or precipitated it somehow.

As possibilities scrolled up on the monitor, he

flinched. Endless deaths . . . death scenes . . . victims. . . . He felt a momentary sense of helplessness, like weightlessness, adrift in a sea of troubles which he could not solve or help or prevent. John took a deep breath to put space between himself and what he scanned, toughening himself. It did not matter then and it did not matter now. What mattered was that he cared and tried. A drop at a time into what seemed to be a bottomless bucket . . . it was all he could do, and have the faith that it would help. He found a few possibilities and opened them up, reading the confidential details more closely and looking at crime scene sketches and photos, trying to determine if there was a match.

The grisly details gleamed before his eyes, the computer screen somehow more harsh and jarring than he expected. He browsed it, did not find what he was looking for, left that file, and opened another.

And then another.

And then another.

He took a look at the clock and saw that he had precious little time left. He closed that file and pulled up the last real possibility he had been able to sift out.

And stared at the screen numbly, trying to read what he looked at. What if she were right . . . what if what she drew inspired someone who saw it to kill . . . what if what she saw made someone crave that splash of crimson, that jolt of anger, whatever it was that made a killer kill . . . The computer brought photo scans down what seemed to be infinitely slowly, one line at a time, achingly revealing its crime scene. It was almost as agonizing as watching the actual act take place and being unable to do anything about.

As brutalized flesh began to take form on the screen, the hard drive lights blinking steadily as the modem worked to download the imagery and files, Rubidoux leaned closer to the screen. Wordlessly, he found a scrap piece of paper on Valenzuela's desk and tried to sketch down the bare essentials, body placement, the artifacts considered significant that were found on the scene, pencil scritching across the writing surface, sending a chill down the back of his neck. It was what he had both hoped and feared to find.

He had a match. Or what seemed to be a match. He leaned forward and studied the main photo of the crime scene. The environment was all wrong though. This woman had been found outdoors and the details he'd taken from Charlie's painting indicated an indoor setting. Yet the body, the wound placement, the instruments of death scattered by her in the ruts of the road . . . He rocked back in the chair and swiveled slightly.

It was not until he paged to the actual file and forensic reports that the chill down his back turned his whole body cold.

Murdered elsewhere. Body dumped and displayed, but the feeling of investigators was that she was carefully placed just as she had been originally. Fibers found gave them an idea of the place of death, fitting in a surrealistic way, what Charlie had painted. This was not the death from the series of paintings, though.

Someone tched. John jumped as Valenzuela leaned over his shoulder.

"That was a nasty one."

"You saw it."

Valenzuela shook his head, tumbling his blue-black hair over his forehead. He stuck beefy fingers into his hair and tried to comb it back into place. "Naw. But we all talked about it. She might have been pretty, once, before somebody carved her up. She was killed in her condo and thrown off the 15. For a while, we thought she was one of a serial spree. We all felt pretty bad about her until . . ." He blinked, his brown eyes darkening a little.

"What?"

He shrugged. "The investigating team pulled together a bio on her. Turned out she was dealing drugs about half a block from the nearest high school, three blocks from the local elementary school." Valenzuela reached over John, and keyed in for a printout. "Lunch hour is over." He gave a thin smile. "Some people deserve to be dead."

"You know who did it?"

Valenzuela shook his head. "Never found out. A lot of blood went somewhere. She was sliced to death. Found two boxcutters in the dirt beside her, the kind you see lying around in a grocery store back room or a warehouse. Still had cardboard and tape fibers on the razor blades, besides her blood and tissue. But theory was someone used something else on most of her, cuts were pretty clean."

"Jack the Ripper?"

Valenzuela laughed coarsely. "Nah, nothing like that. No sexual mutilation. We think a pimp or pusher got even with her. I don't think anyone has even tried very hard to solve the case." He put his thick hand on the back of the swivel chair and rocked it. "Come on, before you get us into trouble."

"One more."

"You know, I thought maybe you were looking up parking tickets or something. Get up."

Ruby rose slowly. "One more, Val, we're already in."

"Ermm," Valenzuela said as they traded places. "What are we looking for?"

"Roadside. Young woman driver . . . looks like she might have been forced off . . . bludgeoned."

Valenzuela coughed, and this time the pulped cigar flew under the desk where it stayed in a damp puddle on the old linoleum floor. "Ruby, you're seeing the wrong kind of women. Was the body ever found?"

"I . . . don't know. You tell me."

Valenzuela looked at him. "You're talking about one of the most famous MP cases around here if it hasn't." His blunt fingers tapping loudly, he closed down the data banks and signed off his access code. "We don't even have to look in here." He stood and plowed his way across the squad room, as other police began to filter in from lunch. He drew John off to the side and pointed out a bulletin board. "Ortega Highway. We hoped she would be like Denise Huber . . . we'd find her body eventually. Never did."

John leaned close to look at the crime scene photos tacked up on a bulletin marked, "STILL OPEN." There were a few other scenarios up there: a small child whose nude and battered body had been found in southern Orange County; a popular church leader killed in what had probably been intended as a simple burglary; a tragic hit-and-run from several Halloweens past. But it was the Ortega Highway collage which drew him. The actual crime scene showed little, but there was an artistic rendering of enactment which caught his eye.

Nighttime, curving stretch of road, a car spun out of control. He stared at it.

Charlie's most recent paintings. She had caught the road almost exactly, the thin stands of California oak and eucalyptus on the Ortega, two-lane road, the curve. The starry night.

Valenzuela tapped it. "No body," he said. "Blood on the scene, though, and drag marks, and indications of a second car. Driver, young, white female, about twenty-two at the time."

John closed his notebook. From the make of the car, he could tell the scene was at least eight or nine years old. "How long has this one been open?"

Valenzuela rubbed his chin and shrugged. "Ten years, maybe. Want me to check on it?"

He nodded. "When you get a chance."

His buddy let out a rich chuckle, then coughed. "Like my desk is always empty and I'm always lookin' for something to do."

Ruby nodded. "I know, Val, I know. But this could be important. I'll see if I can get something from the newspaper library, too."

"You do that. Everything's on computer now, probably be faster than waiting for me." Valenzuela nudged him. "Bring the new girl to Impy's if she can play softball. Hell, bring her even if she can't!" He walked off, laughing softly to himself, unwrapping a new cigar and sticking it in his mouth.

John drove back to the house, uncertain what to tell Charlie. He had not thought he would find anything to match what she had painted. But he had . . . not once, but twice.

Could she be right? Could someone have admired her nightmares and then gone out and enacted them?

The world was full of sick people. Anything could be possible. He was not sure if he wanted to prove that to Charlie, if he wanted to reinforce her fear that she'd contributed to it.

Another car sat in front, at the curb, and John got out slowly. He hesitated to even head to the front door. She had been alone at the art auction . . . alone whenever he'd come by to help with Jagger . . . but that did not mean she was alone. Though when they'd made love, her response to him had been as eager as his to hers, as though she had been as lonely as he had. He stood on the front sidewalk and debated with himself whether to go in, or go home and call, and come back later.

Or if he should come back at all. *You don't sleep with your clients, idiot*, he told himself.

He heard a raised voice, and it did not sound pleasant, and he strode quickly to the door.

An officious looking man with a piece of paper in his hands faced Charlie, who looked frazzled and worn still, Jagger at her side, his lips curled, both her hands wrapped about his harness.

Before she could speak, or John could say anything, the man slapped the piece of paper at Charlie. "The dog goes. You can't find me the vaccine records, then we'll quarantine him for two weeks. It's that simple, lady. He bit someone. We have a complaint. I'm taking him."

Chapter Twenty-One

"No . . . no, you're not taking Jagger," Charlie said, drawing back, hauling with her strength on his harness. The golden lowered his head and let out a low, unhappy whine.

She looked past at John, her eyes bright with both fear and appeal.

The thin-shouldered, wiry man set his heels, his stubbornness rippling through his uniform. "Ma'am, this is just like a warrant. You don't have any choice!"

John reached into his back pocket and got his wallet out, flipping it open in a smooth move. "You must be the call I got," he said to the animal control officer. He flashed his kennel credentials and business card at him. "I get your overflow animals. Guardian Dogs."

As the county employee bent his head and attention to the wallet, John stared at Charlie. She winced and seemed to try to take a deep breath. John made an impatient move. "This is the dog, right? Bit somebody? Want him for quarantine? Look, my time is money. I got a contract for the overflow. You called, I came."

"I didn't call," the man said. "I don't have the pickup truck with me today . . . came over here on the rush. But I don't make these calls."

John sucked on a tooth unhappily. "Somebody called me. You can take him if you want . . . hope you got a muzzle . . . he looks like he could bite somebody else . . . but I have to bill the county anyway, for my trip and a day's board. Even if I don't take the dog."

"I can't authorize that."

"You don't have to authorize it. I got my license right here. Copy of my contract." John slipped out the copy, unfolded it, and waved it in the air. The county used him mainly for emergency evacuations during fire season, when brushfires often left homeless animals ranging behind. He even had held a horse for them once, at the rear of his acreage.

The county employee blinked through his frameless glasses and scrubbed a hand over a head that showed freckled, balding scalp through mousy brown hair. "Who called you?"

John said, "Don't have a name, but they had my contract number." He smoothed out his copy and began to read it off.

"Forget it." He took his own paperwork, holding it to his chest like a shield. "Sign for the dog."

Charlie looked from one to the other. "You're just going to hold him?"

"That's all, ma'am, like I tried to tell you. Until you can get a copy of that rabies certificate from your vet or quarantine is over."

She released one hand from the harness, visibly relaxing. John frowned slightly at her. "Have you got a muzzle, Miss?"

"He won't need a muzzle."

John scratched his head. "I've got one out in the van. You'll need to take his harness off. I have a leash I use."

"He won't fight you." Charlie put her chin out.

The county employee looked as though that was the start of the argument where he came in, shoved a pen and his forms at John, backing up to the door. "Ma'am, you settle that with Mr.—ah—Rubydoo." He ripped apart the paperwork, dropped a copy on the end table, and bolted out the door. Jagger gave a resounding bark as if personally responsible for the rout.

She dropped the harness wearily as John kicked the door shut. She leaned against the couch and watched Jagger as he lunged to the front window, still barking.

"You're a dog catcher?"

"Pardon me, Miss, but we like to be called animal

control officers. And, no, I'm not a dog catcher." He smiled. "I am just kennel help." He refolded his paperwork carefully and slid it back into his wallet. "Actually, I get the dogs and cats from burn areas, usually, the healthy ones. I board them till their families are located and can take them again, or until the shelter has room."

"Really?"

"Really. That was a valid contract I showed him. So, officially," he grabbed Jagger and pulled him away from the window. He shook the dog affectionately, adding, "Your ass is mine, dog."

Jagger slurped him.

"I don't think he's impressed," Charlie observed.

"He will be when I put him in the lockup."

"Will he get fed in there?"

"Of course, twice a day, kibble to order—" He stopped as he realized she was watching him.

"At least he won't starve." Charlie faintly emphasized *he.*

John stood, baffled. She watched him with a look of faint amusement. He spread his hands. Jagger sat on his foot, tilted his head and looked at him curiously. "What did I do? No reward for saving him?"

"You," she said, advancing on him, "forgot lunch."

She reached him, and slid her arms around his neck. "No lunch, no reward."

He looked into her blue-gray eyes, smiling eyes,

despite the faint shadows of tiredness below them, and felt himself stir again, wanting to make love to her again, but not frantically, hurriedly, as they had that morning. He wanted to stretch out on an immense bed, and explore her, and have her touch him . . .

He managed to say, "I think I can handle that."

"I hope so," Charlie told him. "I am very . . . very . . . hungry . . ." And to prove it, she began nibbling on his lips.

John forgot what he had planned.

George Laverman laughed, leaned over, and refreshed Wade's iced tea with the carafe left at the table. "You seriously didn't tell her that."

"I did," returned Wade. "The best way to get even with Elyse is to yank her husband's chain. She adores him." He grinned as he picked up his drink. "Besides, she's a good colleague. It wasn't her personally who had the file, it was one of her staff, and I can pretty well be damn sure it won't happen again. At least, not to one of my files."

"And what about Charlie Saunders?"

Wade sat back in the upholstered dining chair, the ambience of the room muffled, quiet, dignified, wide glass windows affording yet another view of the beautiful Laguna cove, while sheltering the diners from ocean winds which could be downright cold during the winter. It was late spring, though, and he would have liked to feel the sea spray on the breeze. "I don't know," he said, finally. "I think Quentin will make sure she comes in. Until I get a look at it myself, I don't have the slightest idea."

A waitress, young, pretty, vibrant, came by with a bread basket filled with freshly baked bread and folded the linen napkin back a corner to expose it, letting the smell escape further. She left.

Wade watched her walk away. She was about Charlie's age, and walked with a bounce of good health, strong limbs. He looked back at his place setting. Charlotte Saunders should have suffered no ill effects from his surgery, but he had not been quite skilled enough, then. Though it probably had been a slight stroke during recovery. He was not sure—could never be sure—that he had not done the damage himself.

On the other hand, she was lucky to be alive. Fortunate that he had been able to excise the tumor, and that it had been benign.

Blessed to have had a good surgical team working on her.

He smiled at Laverman, as he caught the judge looking at him. George finished buttering a slice of the fragrant bread and said, "You never married, did you, Wade?"

"As the saying goes, I'm married to my job." He lifted his glass to hide his expression slightly. "Doctors make poor husbands."

"I would have to disagree with that. Look at you. You damn near work banker's hours. You can't tell me that you get hauled out at two in the morning to answer somebody's emergency call. Your operations are scheduled like clockwork."

Wade laughed. "All right, then." He took a drink and set it down. "I just never found anyone I wanted to marry. And the longer I go, the more set in my ways I get. Nobody could measure up to Abby."

"She would be pleased to hear that." George dabbed his napkin to his mustache, cleaning off the butter and crumbs. "She was a wonderful hostess, a smart intelligent woman . . . and she had an ego."

He smiled in memory. "She had a lot to be proud of."

"You got one of her paintings, didn't you?"

"Just the one, one of Charlie's."

"I bought the others from her. She said she wanted to give the fund cold, hard cash."

"I haven't seen them in years."

Laverman plucked himself another piece of bread, as the waitress came back and served up cold salad plates. "The Peppermill is just around the corner and up the hill. They're doing a retrospective on Charlie's works, have most of the ones which are kept in California there right now. I'm out of the courtroom until tomorrow morning. Have time to go to the gallery with me?"

"I'd like that. This might be a good time to remind myself just what a remarkable young lady she was."

"Abby always did have a good eye for promising young talent." George winked at him over a forkful of crisp lettuce, streaked with carrot slivers and radiccio, his voice full of innuendo.

Wade chuckled. "Wait till I get you out on the greens," he said. "I will remember every word."

The judge laughed heartily. A few diners turned to look, smiled, then went back to their luncheons. Nothing untoward could surely be happening in this muted dinner house, perched on the cliffs overlooking the ocean, on a day clear of fog and smog. Surely nothing.

Wade smiled and smoothed his napkin over his lap, speared a bay shrimp on his silver tines, and crunched it between his teeth. He enjoyed his salad thoroughly, and they regaled one another with golfing tall tales as the grilled salmon steaks came, and then pretended to fight over the check; but as well off as Wade was, he could not match Laverman's wealth, which had nothing to do with his career as a judge. He and his wife had both been born into money, old money gone West, which was one reason they had known Abby. She knew how to cultivate and network money.

He followed Laverman's Mercedes through the streets, guiding his Jag, thinking that he liked the community, the colony of Laguna, with its narrow inconvenient streets and neighborhoods, stubbornly refusing to knock down and overbuild on its pricey ocean view lots. George's house overlooked the canyon itself, where the grounds and bowl for the Laguna Festival of the Arts, and Wood Chip Celebration, and other outdoor art expos reigned year-round, amidst the tourism and the arts. Laverman did not take him to his hilltop home, however, but up to the grounds of one of the old railroad magnates, where what had been a carriage or gatehouse was now a restructured, modern, and yet whimsical art gallery.

A banner strung across the front carried the July and August dates of the upcoming Laguna Arts Festival and the expositions at the Wood Chip Celebration. Wade had to duck under it slightly to enter the gallery door. George brushed a finger across his mustache, smoothing it. Inside, the building seemed far bigger than out, its ceiling nearly two stories high, its walls filled with art, movable and permanent walls making more exhibition space. One wing seemed open, walls bare, an easel set up, a work in progress, an unframed, newly finished canvas done in acrylics leaning at the foot of the wall, placards in a half-open cardboard box nearby, as if waiting for a new show to be set up. A battered, rolling table with two drawers held what appeared to be someone's collection of new and well-cared-for brushes, a tray of paints, a pad of disposable paper palettes, and other supplies. There was, however, no sight of the artist.

George moved purposely to the northern end of the gallery, waving off a thin, freckled, redheaded woman who lurched to her feet from her desk.

"Relax, Janie. Dr. Clarkson here owns a Saunders, and I wanted him to see the exhibit."

"Ah." She wrung her hands in slight embarrassment, gave an awkward bow, then reseated herself at her desk. "Do you need me, Judge Laverman?"

"No, no. I'll just walk him around. Don't let us interrupt you."

She smiled faintly, setting her freckled complexion into animation, then looked down. Whatever it was she was working on drew her attention back completely, and she did not seem to notice as they walked past.

The phone rang twice at Wade's back and began a third ring before she picked it up to answer, though the three of them were the only ones there.

Laverman spread his hands. "Here you have it. Janie has been working on getting "Retribution" on loan permanently from the Norton Simon in Pasadena, but with the exception of that pair, this is a pretty good retrospective of Charlie's works. Janie asked Charlie's help in getting them hung chronologically. Yet even these very early ones, have a real sense of color and movement. In the later ones, she shows the little training she was allowed to have—"

"Allowed to have?"

"That's right. Quentin and her manager, Federico Valdor, they were both pretty shrewd when it came to marketing Charlie. They sensed that her appeal came from her youth and the fact that she hadn't been molded into someone's idea of what she should be artistically. I disagree. The paintings I own came after she worked with Kirk Miller of The Open Door Gallery and he gave her the ability to do things she'd been struggling with before. Art hasn't changed much in hundreds of years, but when an artist has to figure out every aspect of it herself, it can take a lifetime of experimentation until she finds herself free to do what she wants." Laverman folded his arms over his chest, tucking his chin in, his lanky athletic body momentarily at rest, gazing at a painting.

Wade merely responded, "I know what I like." He moved along the wall slowly, eyeing each and every painting. There was one of a monarch butterfly resting on a wild thistle, a child's view of change and promise, done with an imprecise hand, even then obviously not trying to convey a photographic sense of the scene, but the feeling of a wild thing, free flight, caught and balanced for a moment.

Another painting caught him, a row over, its canvas streaked with darkness, fear, action, and reaction.

He found himself staring at it for a very long time till George said, "Remember that one?"

"No," answered Wade faintly. "I don't think I do."

"Abby didn't like it. She said it was like looking into someone's dark soul. My wife doesn't like it either. Once Janie gets insurance set up, we'll probably leave it here on permanent exhibit. Unless the Norton Simon wants to buy it from us, or the L.A. Museum of Modern Art." Laverman shrugged in his sports coat. "Nothing wrong with making a profit now and then."

"Indeed," said Wade, moving past the picture reluctantly. The hair on the back of his neck seemed to have lifted uneasily, and stayed that way, as he looked into the mind of the artist. He tried to remember the discussions he had had with Elyse over the years specifically about Charlie, but the only thing he could recall was Elyse's interest in what sparked the creativity, not what the creativity symbolized.

Laverman stumbled slightly, and Wade hurried to brace his elbow. His friend made a wry face and straightened. They looked at one another. Wade knew, of course.

George said, "I don't think I will be making that golf tournament this year."

"How bad is it?"

"They won't give me any more painkillers. I suppose I could resort to buying marijuana off some of the people I find in my courtroom, but that is not a choice I find savory." He gripped Wade's arm. "I am going to need you soon, Wade."

This was something that remained unspoken between them. George was dying and had no wish to suffer, nor did Wade expect him to. He nodded. He knew that George would not wait till his body began to give out on him, as well as the pain growing to be unbearable. "Just let me know." He released George's arm. His friend straightened proudly, continuing the tour of Charlie's works.

He took another step along the wall, trailing Laverman, as George spoke about awards and gaining recognition and touring Europe and England until her eventual collapse, but he only half heard his friend's voice.

Was he the only one who could see the tortured visions before him? Who could glimpse the workings behind the paint, the humanity past the canvases, the hope and dismay they held? Whose gaze raced along bold swoops of color, done by a brush held in a hand which must have been moving rapidly, joyously. The effortless way she suggested outlines, and brought the viewer's eyes to the details she wanted them to see, and left others in the background, ghostlike, suggestive, almost subliminal.

He paused and drank them in. He could not let her die. She had to live, perhaps to paint again someday.

She had to.

And he had to be certain she did.

Chapter Twenty-Two

Charlie put her head on his shoulder, and shifted so that her right leg lay between his, and John smiled to himself, put his arm around her and brought her in even closer. He looked at the ceiling of her bedroom, which had faint, barely noticeable cloudlike designs, and thought of absolutely nothing at all.

She rubbed her palm on the flat of his stomach. "So tell me where you went this morning."

That jolted some of the well-being from him. He smoothed his hand up and down her bare arm, feeling the silken quality of her skin, trying to decide how to tell her.

"I went to see some friends," he said finally, "about your paintings."

"The new ones."

"And the ones in the article."

She did not move away, but he could feel tension

return to her body, and he kept rubbing her arm, her shoulder, as if he could will it away. "What kind of friends?"

"Old friends."

She moved her leg, touching him, his leg, the old wound which had forced him into disability. She'd asked about the scar when they had been exploring each other, learning each other's bodies, and was remembering it now. "Police?"

"Yes." He still did not want to tell her, and realized from his very reluctance, that he had. He gripped her roughly and pressed her close.

After several long moments, she said, "Tell me all of it."

"I found something that seemed to match."

"You did." She paused. "Which one?"

"Both of them actually."

She buried her face against his shoulder. He could feel the warm dampness of her tears, though she made scarcely a movement. He kept caressing her shoulder. She rolled away from him, sat up, and started to dress, sniffing hard, stifling back her tears. "Someone took my nightmares . . . my Midnight . . . and went out and made it real."

"That's not what I said."

She paused on the threshold to the bathroom door. "You said what you found matched them."

"I found some details that were similar. I can't make a match until I get more information." He left the bed as well, pushing Jagger off his socks, and pulled them on.

"You would have told me if it was nothing." Charlie smiled ruefully before she disappeared. He heard the shower running while he finished finding his clothes and dressing. He fixed himself a cold drink, went to the kitchen phone, and checked his messages. There was one from a prospective client, and another from Sultry's owner, checking on her, asking how close to whelping she was. John knew he'd have to leave.

Charlie padded barefoot into the kitchen, dressed in worn jeans and a soft cotton shirt that she had only buttoned two buttons on, showing the slight cleavage of her breasts, and her navel, and stood, toweling her hair dry. He hung up.

"What do I do now?"

"You wait until I do some more research. One thing I can tell you. The murders go way back. Ten yeas, at least."

"What if . . ."

He put a finger on her lips. "What if you didn't have anything to do with it?"

"But what if I did? Those paintings have been in private collections for years. Now they're on exhibit again. What if whoever it was starts again?"

"Charlie, you don't know that they will . . . or they won't. You don't know that you're responsible. How can we trace someone who wandered in and out of . . . how many galleries . . . ten years ago?'' He took her wrist and pulled her to him. "Don't feel something you don't need to feel."

"Don't tell me what to feel! I need to . . . I need to be alive again." She clenched her fist and punched him, not to hurt, but as if to emphasize. "I didn't know how dead I was till I felt those brushes in my hands again. How numb. How blind. How deaf . . ." Her words broke off.

He pressed his jaw to her head, feeling her golden-brown hair tickle his face. "I have never met anyone more alive," he told her.

"Then," she answered hoarsely, "help me stay alive."

He left Jagger with her even though there was a possibility some county official might show up at the kennel to make sure he was in quarantine. He let Flint out with Hans again and while the two tussled with one another and Flint let Hans race around him and snap playfully at his muzzle, John went to check on Sultry. She was lying on her side, panting, and rolled an eye at him.

He knelt beside her, and put a hand on her tummy, and checked her teats. Fluid beaded on them. John muffled an angry word. Her owner would not schedule the vet visit he'd suggested and now it looked as if she was in labor, early, and he had no idea for how long. He petted her face, stroking the dog, and told her soothingly he'd be right back for her.

He already had the whelping box ready in the corner of the storage room, warm, dry, solitary. He put down fresh newspapers and towels, got a leash, and returned to the bitch. She'd gotten up on her feet, and her tail wagged slightly as he clipped the lead on her.

As the dog settled herself into the high-sided wooden box, he called the vet and the owner, then went out, rounded up the boys and penned them up. Chow would have to wait till he had time.

He phoned Charlie just to let her know he would be busy for a few hours.

"Puppies," she said wistfully.

"Looks like it. I'll call you later." He hung up before she responded, as Sultry let out a low groan.

Puppies that might be caught, or turned sideways, or too big for the bitch to deliver. Complications he did not want right now. John made sure the front gate was unlocked, squatted next to the whelping box, and began to help Sultry bring her litter into the world.

Charlie cleaned house. She took the paintings and moved them to her studio, trying not to look at them, unable not to, eyeing them. She lined the wall with the canvases and hurried out, sweeping up the newspapers and stuffing the trash bag full of them, then opened up windows. She could smell the paint. It seemed to permeate the bungalow and she was sure anyone coming to see her would know. She found an old can of deodorizing spray under the sink and walked through the house with it until Jagger began sneezing and pawing at his nose.

Charlie took pity on him, letting him out into the backyard, where she took the paper and sat herself for a few moments. Her skin felt raw, incredibly sensitive where she and John had touched, melded, and she sat there, paper across her lap, not reading, not seeing, her thoughts turned inward to memory. When the phone rang long minutes later, her eyes fluttered, and she reached for the portable as if waking from a dream.

"Charlie. Thank God you've got that damned voice mail off," Quentin blustered in her ear.

"Hi, Daddy. I'm sorry." She switched hands. "You have me now."

"Good. I saw Clarkson today. What is this nonsense about not going in to the clinic? I thought we had that all straightened out."

She looked at the yard, its lush greenery, the hydrangeas in the corner beginning to bloom, the impatiens along the shady wall already blossoming, Jagger racing across the grass as a mockingbird scolded and dove at him. She thought of Midnight, descending on her, curtaining all that away from her. But did it . . . or did it lift a curtain from her eyes that most people could never have lifted? And what, if anything, might her illness have to do with any of it? Her gift, her paintings, her sight, Midnight. "I thought so, too," she answered softly.

"Look, you know I have no love for hospitals."

"I know, Daddy." She cherished the memory of the woman who had helped her learn to walk and eat again, silver-haired and sharp-nosed, soft-spoken, who told her to call her Nana, and treated her as if she were her own grandchild, who had fallen ill not long after her own slow recovery and lay helpless for almost two years before her strong body finally gave up and followed where her soul had already passed.

He said gruffly, "We've no choice in this, honey. I'll go in with you, if I need to. Let me know so I can rearrange my schedule."

"No . . . that's all right. Mom will go, I'm sure. And it's just the usual string of tests. I've done it all before," she added wearily.

"Then why haven't you gone in?"

"Dad . . . what if I need surgery again? What's going to happen to me this time?"

Silence on the other end. "There're no guarantees in life."

"I want one this time."

"What do you mean, Charlie?"

"Don't let them leave me a vegetable. Don't leave me that way."

"I won't, honey. Whatever it takes."

She felt a sharpness go through her, and pass, a sense of relief.

"I'll be there if you need me." Quentin cleared his throat. "I'll be the first one by your side . . . and I'll take care of things, do you understand?"

"I don't feel very brave right now." She sighed.

"How bad is it?"

"I'm having seizures again. I don't know when they're going to hit, I don't know how to stop them . . . and I don't know if I can survive them."

"God almighty. How long has this been going on?"

"A couple of weeks. I hoped . . . I thought . . . it can't all be happening again."

"You don't give up on us, honey, and we sure as hell won't give up on you. We have a contract, you and I."

"Thanks, Dad. I'll call later and tell Mom when to pick me up." Charlie disconnected, then rubbed her forehead. A slight, dull ache started to center itself behind her eyes, and she wondered if that was where it was. Hidden. Lurking. Searching out her mind and sinking into it. Charlie shuddered and put the phone back on voice mail, not wanting to talk to anybody else. She wished she had been asked to go along with John and see the puppies being born.

He had said to her, "Maybe next time."

She took those words and held them to her, a

promise, as if they could keep her afloat in times that seemed determined to drag her under. She sat outside until dark fell and beyond, watching Jagger chase lightning bugs and that persistent mockingbird which must have a nest somewhere in the trees bordering the yard, and thought that night was never as dark as the inside of her mind.

The vet left and John cleaned up. The owner was out of town, in Vegas for some trade show or other, but would be back on the first short hop in the morning. John hung the old towel on its hook and took a look back into the storeroom, where Sultry lay nursing eight fat wiggling bodies which looked more like sausages than pedigreed shepherds. He watched them with pleasure before going to the phone to call and tell Charlie. Outside, it was late, the hills unseeable through the night, and the faint hint of fog and heavy moisture seeping into the air.

He got her voice mail and, disappointed, left a brief message. She was resting, he hoped. The sound of her on the recording was not enough to make him happy. For a moment, he thought of dialing it back just to hear it again. John laughed at himself and instead went to his computer. He had some research to do, the world literally at his fingertips.

He finished close to one a.m., stretched in his chair, and checked Sultry again, who decided she wanted out. He helped her out of the whelping box, disturbing only one of the little fat sausages, who made a grumpy noise before pushing around hungrily in the towels and papers. Sultry hesitated, as if to go back and settle down again, but he grabbed the ruff of her neck, urging her out the door to the exercise yard.

At the sound of him, immediately both Flint and Hans were at their kennel gates, silent, dark shadows, eyes glittering in the faint glow of the moon, watching him, almost wolflike. They did not bark or otherwise give sound, which he encouraged at night. They would not bark until they knew there was a quarry, and then they would bell like the Hound of the Baskervilles until they attacked and brought him to a halt.

Sultry paced back and forth, marked her spots, looked out at the hills, and her black moist nose moved as if she could smell coyotes on the evening air, threatening her litter. John looked up into the foothills, too, wondering where the coyotes were, for he had no doubt they were up there, their senses even keener than the dogs he had kenneled.

He shook himself, tired, and urged Sultry to finish so they could all go to bed for the night.

In the hills, along a darkened curve, a car sat just off the road, its occupant low in the seat, watching the occasional headlights as the beams began to approach, drew near, swept over him, then passed on.

A feral uneasiness pulsed in his veins as he watched, debating, weighing, judging. A silent sentry, he seemed to attract no notice, which was as he desired. He sat, and watched, and felt his blood running through him, knowing the spurt of it, the wash of it over his hands, the faint coppery tang to its warmth. He wondered if the lights caught his eyes, if he would reflect it. That was the least of his thoughts. He sat and watched and wondered.

Who to kill and who to let have safe passage.

Chapter Twenty-Three

Hubie Valenzuela woke at the insistent sound of a beeper. It buzzed and vibrated like an angry insect, dancing along the nightstand. He reached out and thumped it once or twice before it woke up his wife. He grabbed it up as he pried his eyes open and tried to focus on the dim light of the beeper window. He held it close; that made the numbers even fuzzier to read. Mumbling, he fumbled out of bed and went to the bathroom, closed the door, and snapped on the light.

His wife said faintly after him, "Get your glasses." The blankets made a soft whispering noise as she pulled them over her and resettled in their bed.

Valenzuela sat on the toilet lid. He rubbed his eyes. Not only did it seem impossible to read decently any more, but his eyes got crustier and crustier. Getting older was hell. And he did not feel any happier when somebody told him it was better than the alternative.

Stubbornly, he refused to reach for the drugstore-bought reading glasses and peered at his beeper.

He found a cigar, unwrapped it, and began to chew. He wanted to smoke it. Christ, George Burns lived to be a hundred smoking cigars. But Della hated the smell. So he chewed. At this rate, he doubted if he would make it to half of George Burns' age.

He squinted at the beeper message again. It was his code to contact the station. He could have guessed that. The portable was in the bathroom, where it always was. He picked it up and dialed.

"Valenzuela. What is it?"

"Looks like a homicide during a home invasion robbery or maybe it was a follower."

"You need me?" They shouldn't, but they had beeped him for some reason.

"Homicide thought you might want to come in and look at it." A pause. Then, "You need to see it."

"Give me the address and twenty minutes." Valenzuela found the scratch pad he kept on the sink, next to the portable phone, and the pencil, and scribbled down the location. Portable phone, toothpaste, and his wife's skin cream, the essentials of their bathroom, second only to toilet paper. Sleepily he flipped up the toilet lid and sat back down, wondering why he needed to see the crime scene.

It was nearly forty minutes later, not twenty, for the address was in a tony section of the area, almost out of his jurisdiction, the ranch house back in the canyons, purple shadows almost hiding it from the road. The garage door was up, nice looking luxury car parked inside, already surrounded by the chicken-shit yellow tape cordoning off the area. Hubie mouthed his cigar. Coroner was here, detectives' cars, and two patrol cars.

He parked across the street on the cul-de-sac. The fact that the house had probably been entered through the garage door made it a logical follow-home robbery situation. He flashed his shield as he ducked under the tape, but the kid minding it hardly looked at him. Hubie was not sure if that was because he had a reputation . . . or because he could not be missed because of his physical description. He plowed across the front lawn and in through the front door, because the garage was teeming with evidence collectors.

Just inside, he could smell it. The coppery tang of blood, unmistakable, already beginning to turn bad, like rank meat. Body decomposition was a lot stronger, but Valenzuela could smell the more subtle qualities of spilled blood. He thought maybe it was because he did not smoke—better nose. A lot of rookie cops he'd been around had never been able to smell the difference between fresh blood and older blood. Of course, in the dry air of this part of the state, blood cured quicker.

He worked on the cigar a little, running his lips

and tongue around it. The air was thick with the scent. A box of disposable foot shields rested on the sofa-back table in the foyer. As he heard voices and followed them, after putting booties on his shoes, the aroma grew heavier and heavier. When he entered the bedroom, he could see why.

Crime scenes like this were why the word blood-bath had been invented. His jaw dropped, the corner of his mouth just barely keeping a grip on his cigar. "Holy Mary Mother of Jesus."

One of three, suited investigators turned to him, face obscured by dust mask, body lumpy and unrecognizable inside the protection garment, intended to keep the blood and crime scene from being contaminated—or from infecting the investigator.

"Stay where you are, Hubie. Believe it or not, we're trying to find a spatter pattern."

He stopped in the doorway. His stomach made a noise, and he was unsure if it was one of revolt or hunger. Blood splashed everywhere. It ran down the walls of the bedroom in rivers. It pooled wetly in two or three spots on what had once been a plush, ivory carpet. It dropped sluggishly from the ceiling. The mattress held the body, which looked marble-white, drained of all fluid, and drowned in it.

"How much blood can one person hold?" escaped his mouth, appalled.

"About five liters, female. About six, six and a half,

male." The investigator shifted. "And I think we're looking at about all of it."

A second investigator turned, holding a flower vase in one hand, and he recognized Melanie Ramsey behind the protective suiting, her dark, luxuriant hair bound up by the tissue cap. "Looks like he collected it in here. Then . . . splashed it everywhere."

"God damn Jack the Ripper. Don't you dare let the media in here." Valenzuela swallowed. "We'll have a circus."

"They'll find out no matter what we do," Ramsey said grudgingly. "They always do."

"Anybody look at the body yet?"

"Throat's been cut, no sexual mutilation that we could see, the M.E. will have to tell us if she was raped first . . . or during . . . or whatever." Ramsey turned away, and continued her slow, careful sweep of the crime scene.

From what he could see where he stood, more than the throat had been cut. The nude body was criss-crossed with slashes, all of which had been bleeding, which meant they had been pre-mortem. Yet, from what he observed, there had been no great struggle. Nothing overturned, the bedding not twisted or pulled at, her clothing in a pile kicked to one side, but nothing seemed ripped or torn. He hummed to himself around the cigar butt. The victim had been sliced again and again, but did not fight to protect herself. Why?

He blinked as another flash went off on the still camera recording the scene.

There were footprints here and there. Hubie looked down. None crossed the threshold, either in or out.

The murderer had to have been covered in blood.

"Which begs the question . . . do we have blood traces anywhere else?"

"If we do, it's minute. We'll know more later."

Valenzuela nodded morosely. The whole house seemed to be carpeted in this ivory plush rug.

Had he been deliberate enough to stop, remove his shoes, and tiptoe out? The neighborhood was remote, deep in the canyons, the woman alone. But how would the killer know no one might be close behind? How would he be sure a husband or lover would not interrupt him? Or did he even care, so caught up in the act, that all caution had been thrown, like her blood, to the wind?

Obviously the victim had not been given a chance to scream, if she had even thought to, silent as well as passive, perhaps not even aware her life was at stake. So the neighbors were not a factor. Yet one of them had seen the open garage door and called the police. And from the smell of the blood, they had come not long after the time of death. So, if he thought he had time, that he would not be found, he was wrong. But he had acted as if he had all the time in the world. A cool murderer, yet not—one who danced in the blood he spilled.

Or had he been prepared to cause this kind of bloodshed? Had he brought coverings for himself, head to toe, followed her in, subdued or drugged her, suited himself, then slaughtered her. Stepped out of his coverings, and left.

Hubie realized why he'd been called in, and sighed. Someone very nasty was out there killing and enjoying it, and very liable to do it again.

Chapter Twenty-Four

Sated, Valdor pulled his car to the curb and parked it, and sat back. He inhaled a deep breath of satisfaction before reaching for his binoculars to scan the street below; the night lowered around him, fragrant with hibiscus and night-blooming jasmine, and even ginger. He could see little in the bungalow. The lights had all been on all night until he had grown too bleary-eyed to watch, as if light itself could be a sentinel, fending him off.

He had not dared to creep close to examine the house, or what Charlie was doing, knowing only that she had been there alone. Had she been closeting herself against fear? He enjoyed the thought for a moment. She deserved to feel the icy streak that arrowed through him. She was spoiled, sheltered from the cold, hard world. He had been that way once, and now had no haven. Perhaps if she understood what he faced, she would relent. Perhaps what he planned would no longer be necessary.

RETRIBUTION

It was more likely Quentin had told her to leave the place ablaze with electricity. There was no mercy in Quentin's hard eyes. Charlie had learned that from her stepfather. He'd seen the same scorn in her face when she'd told the bank how much to cut his check for. No quarter given, especially not to an inferior foe. Valdor frowned, sweeping the binoculars along the view site.

Tonight nothing could be seen.

There was a certain, quiet satisfaction in being totally alive when all the rest of the world slept, every nerve in his body functioning, pulsing, learning, sending. It was part of the allure of gambling, being alive, the intensity of the moment. Part of the allure of several things.

Valdor thought of the woman again, and smiled. She had not been cheap, but she had been eager, not quick, but enthusiastic, and lingering, teasing him to unleash heights he had never suspected of himself. The overall event had been truly unforgettable and satisfying. Too bad he could never return to her.

He put up his binoculars. The sutures at his wrist itched slightly, giving him another feeling of smugness. The dog was gone. Despite all Quentin's plans and protests, Charlie had stubbornly remained independent of all but the dog. And without him . . . Valdor had Charlie at his mercy whenever he wanted.

The sensations he had been swimming in slowly

began to dull. The drum of his heart slowed, the pace of his breathing evened. The faint smell of his sweat on his body cooled. He would return to his hotel and sleep as well, drugged and sluggish like the rest of the world.

When he rose, he would lay his plans, and then execute them. He would have his money and his vengeance, too, and be safe from retaliation.

The palms of his hands itched. But he had no table waiting for him, no dice, no cards.

Soon though. Very soon.

Valdor started his car up and left the unaware neighborhood.

Charlie woke to a dull throbbing and winced a little, as the morning light streamed brutally in through her bedroom window, and knew it was late, that she had slept in. The throbbing in her head grew louder, and Jagger let out a bark, from somewhere else in the house. His nails scrabbled on the floor as he came dashing back into the bedroom.

The pounding in her temple kept time with the insistent beat on the front door. She yelled out, "Coming!" with only faint hopes they would hear and stop banging. It had better not be that officious weasel from the county again.

She eased out of bed, her body slightly sore in places she was not used to, and she blushed a little as she realized why. She had slept in a T-shirt and panties, so she grabbed a pair of jeans and tugged them on, first one leg and then the other, hopping down the hall. Jagger ran around her in a circle, not in harness, obviously feeling his oats, and flashed his teeth in a lopsided doggish grin. The rules went with the harness, no harness, no rules. He ran back and tagged her, excited. That eased Charlie somewhat. He must know who was at the door.

He beat her to the door, of course, but she had the advantage of being the only one of the two of them who could open it. He jostled her in eagerness and she felt the same, for it must be, could only be, John.

Heart racing, she threw the door open.

He stood there, hand still up in the air, his flesh red from knocking, a tentative look of worry on his face. It changed, evolved, as their eyes met, and he grinned.

"It's late."

"I slept in." Jagger wound between her ankles, nearly dumping her unceremoniously on the ground. She nudged him aside.

Ruby laughed. "Nice welcome."

"Really." She kneed him aside even more to let John inside. As he came in, however, the grin faded from his face.

"I tried to call earlier. You still have the voice mail on."

She reached for his hand and then saw he was

carrying a leash. Puzzled, Charlie shut the door. "What is it?"

"The county called early this morning to verify that I had Jagger. I'm going to have to take him, Charlie, and kennel him, at least for the time being."

"What?"

"I'm sorry. If I don't take him, someone else will. At least you know he'll be with me, warm, well-fed, he knows me."

"Oh, John." Charlie sagged against the wall. "How long?"

"The full two weeks unless the vet can find his rabies certificate."

She inhaled sadly. "I haven't called yet. But since the practice was sold, it's been chaos over there." She looked at John. "Can he be with me days and locked up at night?"

"He has to be quarantined. I don't have any choice in this, honey." John put his hand out, took her arm, and pulled her to his side, then slipped his arm about her waist. "I don't have time today, but tomorrow, if necessary, I'll go over there and look through the back files myself."

She gave a rueful laugh. "That could be more heroic than you know. Old Baez did not believe in computers."

"If it springs Jagger early, it's worth it." He snapped the lead onto Jagger's collar. "I've got to take him now, in case someone decides to be really efficient and come by to check up on us."

Jagger looked from her to John, his tail threshing the air, obviously thinking he was going for a run, not a care in the world. She ruffled his ears. "My tests are scheduled this morning." She checked her watch. "In fact, I should be picked up any minute!"

"It'll be all right."

She wrapped his arm a little tighter around her. "It has to be."

"Don't think. Don't worry. Just do what you have to do today, and we'll handle the rest of all this later. Understand?"

"We," she repeated faintly.

"That's right. We. You, me, and eight new puppies."

"Eight?"

"Do you even listen to your phone calls?"

Embarrassed, she answered, "I haven't had time this morning . . ."

John gave her a squeeze and a quick kiss, saying, "I'll call you then . . . and take your line off voice mail. I want to be able to talk to you. I think you'll be please with what I found out."

She felt her face warm as he let himself out the front door. She stood poised for split second, in case he should return and kiss her again, but he did not. Charlie put her hand to her cheek, touching it, before pivoting and managing as quick a dash as she could back down the hall to change clothes.

Clarkson checked the operating theater clock as he left. It was just after eleven in the morning. He began to strip off his scrubs, lightly bloodied as they were, rolled them up, and dropped them in the waste, the container labeled "Infectious/Contaminated Waste Haz Mat" and marked with the state code for the proper disposal of the material as well as the company the hospital used to collect it. He stripped off his gloves, mask, and booties, disposing of them as well. The container smelled strongly of blood.

Wade ran his hand through his hair before stepping to the sink and scrubbing again, just for a precaution, and then prepared to leave. The beeper at his waistband went off. He collected it, wrists still dripping, as he juggled toweling himself dry and thumbing the beeper off. The voice recording intoned, "Charlotte Saunders' MRI has been completed."

Nodding to himself in pleasant surprise, he grabbed a fresh pullover top from the shelves marked "large" and tugged it on, headed down the halls to his office. He had a report to finish on the operation just concluded, some letters to dictate, lunch, and then another operation slated for one-thirty. As Laverman had suggested to him, his day was scheduled like clockwork.

But there was little methodical about what he did once he got in the operating theater. Every case had its own unique challenge. His skill, the technology which gave him that skill, was forever being tested. Unlike Laverman, who had to rely on casebooks and precedents for his decisions and rulings, every time Wade went in to operate, he was in some sense trailblazing. He wrote his own precedents.

The news that Charlie had come in as scheduled felt gratifying. The day had started out well, and was continuing the same way. Quentin Saunders had done what he had promised, and gotten his daughter in for an examination. He would call down and make sure the report was on his desk by three. Wade would have to pull a favor or two, but he felt time to be of the essence. Mothlike, Charlie Saunders was flirting with flames which would consume her, and only he could quench them.

He passed through his offices. His office manager, Rosa, trailed him partway, saying, "I paged you."

He shot her a smile. "I caught it. Let me finish my dictation on this last one, then I want you to get radiology on the line for me."

"Right." She nodded and turned on her heel, a white-and-blue blur of action and reaction. She already knew what he wanted, that MRI and a copy of the reading on his desk as soon as he could get it. She would help him move heaven and Earth to achieve that.

Wade settled into his chair. Despite his reputation and that of the clinic, most of his patients were everyday people. Good people, unique people, all valuable in their own small ways, cogs in a machine that could be thought of as commonplace and ordinary, of worth only to other cogs turning in their own small ways, dependent upon it. Unique and worthwhile, but mundane . . . and conceivably lost in a universe made up of many such folks. It was rare when a case presented to him also presented a life that was such a commodity that the whole world would be lessened by its loss.

Such a person was Charlie Saunders. He would not lose her.

If it took all of the skill he had and more, he would have to stretch, to extend himself. Today Charlie had taken the first, hesitant step into his care, committing herself into his hands.

He would not fail her.

The dogs greeted Jagger's arrival with their usual fuss until Ruby yelled at them to be quiet, then they settled down. They all pushed their noses through the chain-link gates, but none of them would know Jagger except Flint. The Alsatian came to the fore with his usual dominant attitude, secure in himself and his position in John's pack. Jagger slowed as he paced by John's side but stopped somewhat reluctantly as Rubidoux halted to let the two touch noses and renew their acquaintance.

Some dogs were remarkable in their ability to associate scent with memory. He watched the two sniff at one another, Flint rumbling low in his chest, Jagger neither subservient nor dominant, his tail down but steady, and then Flint left off threatening and seemed to recognize that Jagger had been around before. The golden retriever shook himself, collar and lead rattling, before giving John a look, as if to tell him he could move on now. Ruby trotted Jagger down the row to the first clean and empty kennel isolated at the row's end, opened the gate, and put him inside.

Once in, Jagger gave him a look of accusation and betrayal from caramel eyes as John shut the kennel door and locked it. "Better here than county," John told him. "And hopefully you'll be sprung tomorrow."

The dog circled the pen before making a chuffing noise and lying down. He put his head on his paws, gazing at John mournfully.

"I wouldn't lie to you, pal. You're better off here than anywhere." He coiled the leash and pocketed it, before going in to check on Sultry. He had an appointment that he did not wish to miss.

A young woman about his age opened the front door and gave him a lookover that was neither friendly nor hostile. He straightened slightly, introducing himself, "John Rubidoux, LAPD, retired. I believe your mother is expecting me?"

She said, in a slightly teasing voice, "Kind of young to be retired, aren't you?" as she allowed him inside. Thick in the hips and overly bosomy, she showed him inside, and if she was disappointed that he did not rise to her line, she did not show it.

The house, like its outside, was humble middle-class inside. Carpeting, a neutral beige, showed traffic wear in areas. The furniture, neither new nor old, sagged in a spot or two. The paintings on the wall had no doubt been bought at one of those mall shows, an unremarkable study of flowers in a vase and a mountainside brook. John found himself looking at them critically and turned his eyes away, thinking that Charlie had already affected him in ways he hadn't even known.

"I'm Becky," the young woman said. "Mom is sitting in the family room. Her quiz show just finished." She paused. "Mom watches a lot of TV these days. Especially Bob Barker. She says he cheers her up. Always pleasant, upbeat . . . better than the talk shows." She shuddered slightly and then said, "Try not to upset her, would you? It's hard enough to have her living with us right now, and my husband . . ." she trailed off, leaving unsaid problems which John would just as soon have not been told about. She raised her voice. "Mom. John Rubidoux is here," stumbling a little over his name.

Becky guided him around a corner to a sunken family room, an add-on, where a woman sat in a battered recliner. At their appearance, she thumbed a remote, and the room, which had been filled with clapping, and cheery music, and the sound of a winner's excitement, abruptly went still. She looked toward John, thinning gray hair, skeletal face, a birdlike woman who appeared decades older than her years.

She stared for a moment as if caught by total surprise.

"I'm John Rubidoux," he said, stepping down into the room. "LAPD, retired. We talked on the phone last night. . . ."

"I remember," she snapped, and popped the recliner into an upright position. "I hope to God you came to tell me you finally found my daughter's body."

Chapter Twenty-Five

John put out his hand. "Mrs. Finley. I'm sorry, I did not mean for you to . . . I don't want you to think I misrepresented myself. I am retired from the department. I'm not here in any official capacity."

She looked at him sharply, then seemed to deflate, shrinking in on herself, becoming even smaller and more frail. The recliner, upholstered in a heavy olive material and built to hold the heftiest of American working men, dwarfed her. "I don't understand."

"If I can just sit and talk with you. It is about your daughter, but I don't have any answers."

Becky said, "Mom. . . ." She did not finish, but looked at John.

Her mother flapped a thin hand. "Let him stay. I'll talk to him. It's been years anyway since anyone has even called us about Linda."

"Are you sure? Mr. Rubidoux—" Her daughter shifted uneasily.

"I'm not here to upset matters."

Finley gave him a hard look. "Retired? Why?"

"Disability. Perp caught me in the leg with a bullet. They put me back together, but it keeps me from doing the things I need to."

"No longer fit to be one of L.A.'s finest, huh?" She pulled her stick-thin legs up and tucked them under her. "Becky, you go and do whatever you have to, to make whatshisname happy. I'll let you know when I don't want to be bothered any more." She pointed at the nearby sofa, beat up and crouching on the floor, one end littered with newspapers and TV guides. "Have a seat, Mr. John Rubidoux."

Becky turned, gave John a wink, and padded away to somewhere at the other end of the house. The faint sounds of pan lids and running water could be heard, cabinet doors opening and shutting.

"Mrs. Finley—"

"Edna. Mrs. Finley was my dear old mother-in-law." The woman smiled, and for a fleeting second, John caught a hint of a humor that must have been readily apparent once.

He pushed papers aside and sat down next to six weeks' worth of TV Guides, the covers of every one turned and folded to the crossword page, which had been done in ink.

"You want to ask me about Linda. Well, you already know she's been missing, is probably dead, and no one has been able to find her body for me."

Edna gave a sigh that made her birdlike chest rise and fall tremulously. "I need to know what happened. I've given up that we will ever find out who might have taken her. But I need to know if she's alive or not." She held a fist to her chest. "They say a mother knows. Well, I'm a mother and a damn good one, but I don't know. The police don't know. They have a word for it today—closure. I need closure. When they found Denise Huber's body, they thought maybe he'd stuck Linda in a freezer somewhere, too. But he didn't know anything about it. When that Marine confessed to killing that girl on the Saddleback Campus and four or five others, I thought, 'He's the one.' But it wasn't him either." Her face narrowed. Her eyes grew suspiciously bright. "I need my daughter, dammit, dead or alive."

"You still have a daughter."

She sniffed, and tucked a pewter-gray strand of hair behind her ear. "For which I am grateful, and she knows it. Don't give me any of your pop psychology. I get enough of that shoved down my throat by Oprah Winfrey and Sally Jessy Raphael." Edna laughed without humor. "Actually, Becky was my favorite. She and I have both been carrying that guilt around with us. Linda was a good girl, but she didn't have the brains and grades that Becky did."

He took his notebook out. She eyed it for a moment, then nodded, familiar with the ways of interviewing policemen. He cocked his pen. "Can you tell me what you remember? I was researching what I could through the newspaper back files. . . ."

"October 19, 1987. Almost eleven years ago. She had been working, then had gone to night class at Saddleback College, and then went out for a beer nearby before heading home. She'd had a fight with her boyfriend. He thought she was flirting with somebody at work, they fought, so she left and headed back here. But when she was upset, she liked to drive. The Ortega Highway, back roads, just sort of run the aggression out." Edna Finley took a deep breath.

"She was a good girl. When she disappeared, at first the police didn't tell us much. They suggested she'd run away." The woman plucked at the crocheted blanket over her knees.

"She went for a drink after class . . . and then had a fight with her boyfriend? Was he in her class? Did she meet him somewhere? Anyone in her class involved?"

Edna Finley frowned, the expression in her eyes absent, thinking, remembering. He knew the look, and waited patiently, his pen ready. "He was lucky to graduate high school. She knew him from then, but she didn't date him till she started working. He was a mechanic. More than that actually, he worked for a shop that built Indy cars . . . you know what I mean?"

"Race cars?"

She nodded. "Indianapolis 500. Mears, Ongais, they all had shops in the county then, and others hoping to make the circuit. He was just a kid, but he liked cars, and he was good with them. He helped her keep hers repaired. She had an old, beat-up car. It was all her dad and I could afford to get her. So they dated. But he was jealous, worried about her, worried she didn't love him."

"Did she?"

She shrugged, her pointy shoulders rising and falling. "Who knows? She told him she did, she told me she did—but she also said, 'There's a lot of other guys out there, Mom, who knows who I'll end up with?'" Edna Finley smiled faintly, as if she could hear her daughter's voice in her head.

"Was he violently jealous? Ever hit her? Stalk her?"

"No, nothing like that. But they had a fight that night. She came in with a guy from one of her classes. He made fun of Sean. She tried to defend him, that made him madder. They had a couple of beers and they started to argue, so she left. She called me first to tell me she was going out for a drive and she'd be home in an hour. So I'd know. She was like that." She paused, her quick eyes darting over him, watching him take notes. "Sean had her car fixed. He called it . . . what . . . a sleeper."

"A sleeper?"

She bobbed her head up and down. "Yes—a

316

sleeper. He put a big engine in it, rebuilt—
could move—a big engine that that kind of little
didn't usually have. Linda loved it. She loved having
all that power right there. She said no one could box
her in on the freeway. They used to laugh about it.
She could pull away from a light faster than anyone,
even cars meant to go fast. Sean was very proud of
the condition he kept her car in. He'd done body-
work on it, got it painted for her. It was nice looking
by the time . . ." Her voice trailed off. She waved a
hand in bewilderment.

"I assume Sean was questioned about her
disappearance."

"When they eventually decided to start questioning people." Edna rearranged the afghan, pulling
her sharp knees up to her chest, hugging them. "I
don't think he did it. He cried. He called me almost
every day asking if she'd called, if I'd heard
anything."

John didn't say anything. He knew from personal
experience that, although it was rare, sometimes the
main suspect stayed in the center focus, helping the
family, offering to assist the police, enjoying being
the center of attention vicariously, even controlling
and setting off events surrounding the case, manipu-
lating and feeding off media frenzy. In an infamous
nationwide child kidnap, molestation, and murder
case, the killer was the most helpful of any of the
people involved with the missing child, even hand-

ing out flyers and setting up a volunteer office in town to field calls. A cynic would have said he did all that to keep clues from pointing to him. That had not been the case. He had been involved in the center of it to enjoy the controversy, the drama he'd caused, enthralled by the fear, the mourning, the media titillation over what the child's fate could have been, and eventually was. At the trial he announced that it kept the good feelings going for him, like a never-ending orgasm, almost as satisfying as the molestation and murder itself. When the grief-stricken father shot him to death outside the courthouse, public outcry demanded the father be set free, and he was.

Ruby looked up from his notebook, feeling Edna's piercing gaze on him. "You're thinking almost as much as you're writing," she observed.

He nodded. "You can take the boy out of the police, but sometimes you can never take the police out of the boy."

Finley grinned. "At least you're listening," she shot back. "What else?"

"Do you remember what time she called?"

Edna blew out a long breath. "Around eleven, eleven-thirty. I remember it was during the eleven o'clock news. I went to bed, cause I always heard the girls come in. I knew I'd hear her, it would wake me."

"And she never came in."

"No," said Edna tightly.

John looked back at his notebook, not because he

had to refresh his mind, but because he had to look away from the primal anguish on her face. He flipped a few pages back and forth, giving her time. Then he asked, "When did the police decide something might have happened, that there might have been an abduction?"

"Took 'em three days. By then, most of the evidence where she went off the road was gone. Tire prints, that kind of thing. They brought in one of those dogs to sniff around—"

"Tracking?"

She shook her head. "No. One of those dogs trained to look for blood. They told me the dog's reaction was positive. And they could see what looked like blood traces in the photos . . . and drag marks. So they went over the car. What they determined was that she spun off the road, hit her head on the steering wheel, most likely. Got out of the car, dazed and bleeding. And disappeared into thin air."

"Someone might have forced her off the road."

Edna Finley shrugged again. "No one saw anything. That stretch of highway was pretty deserted at night, then."

"Why did the police think at first that she might have run away? Where would she run without the car?"

She licked her dry lips, tongue flicking over her small mouth quickly. "She'd been in some trouble. They weren't real sympathetic about it. There was talk that she had disappeared on purpose, maybe even that Sean had picked her up and helped her hide."

This was information John could not possibly glean from the newspaper, or even from the police reports. "Tell me what kind of trouble."

"She had a drunk driving trial coming up. She didn't do it, she took the blame for a friend of hers who was driving, but she was accused of manslaughter."

"She told the officers she was driving? In a case where there was a vehicular death?"

"Linda was like that. She took the rap for her girlfriend. They didn't think it would go to trial. It happened on the freeway, he was drunk himself and stepped out of his stalled vehicle, right in front of them. No way they could have missed him."

"But you say Linda wasn't driving."

"No."

"So the police thought that she might have been avoiding the trial."

"That was the general thought when they did a background check on her, and found out who she was."

He felt a twinge over the assumptions he and his coworkers had sometimes made, snap judgments, undeserved but there all the same. "So they bore down on Sean? Thought he helped her disappear and avoid the trial?"

She nodded several times. "It wasn't true, of

course, and eventually they decided they had a case of some kind. Probable homicide, based on the photographic and blood evidence. And they started investigating. They started looking at Sean again. Nearly tore the kid apart. And we, my husband and I, we kept waiting for her body to turn up. Somewhere. She never did."

"What happened to the DUI charges?"

"Well, Devon felt awful about everything. She confessed that she was driving, her father got her a good lawyer, and the charges were dropped. Like I said, he stepped out into the freeway traffic. There was nothing they could have done."

John did not respond to that. A sober driver made quicker, better, safer responses than a drunk one. But it seemed to him that Edna Finley did not deserve to pay the price she'd already paid. He closed his notebook. "Mrs. Finley, if I showed you some photocopies . . . do you think you could stand to look at them?"

Her attention hopped away and back again. "I thought you said you didn't know anything about her body?"

"I don't. As far as I know, it hasn't been found. This isn't that kind of picture. But I'd like you to take a look at them, if you would." He pulled out a folder and opened them. He'd taken photos of Charlie's paintings, had them developed and then made color copies, slightly enlarged, to show the detail.

Finley's hand trembled slightly as he passed the folder over to her. She dropped her knees so that she sat cross-legged, and set the photocopies in her lap. She took a look at the first one, sucked in her breath sharply, then lay them out, spreading them around. One started to drift off the recliner and she snatched it up in midair.

"What is this?" she said sharply.

"I'm not sure. I was hoping you could tell me."

"These are paintings."

"Yes."

She stabbed a twig thin finger at the papers. "This is my daughter's car. And this is Linda. Hard to see her features real well, because it's shadowed. Night time. But this is her." She looked up, her eyes snapping with anger. "Who did these? What kind of maniac would paint something like this?"

He leaned forward intently. "Someone as tortured by Linda's death as you are," he answered softly. He put his hands out for the copies.

Finley blinked at him, then gathered them up, and the folder, and started to pass them back. Holding them in midair, she began to cry, quietly at first, and then with sobs that made him ache to hear them.

Behind him, at the step to the family room, Becky said, "I think it's time for you to go, Mr. Rubidoux."

He stood slowly. "Mrs. Finley, I am sorry to have hurt you with this—"

Edna looked at him, her sharp face streaming with

tears. "Did she see it? Did she see it happen? Why didn't she tell anyone then? Why, in God's name, didn't she say anything then?"

He sorted the photocopies neatly into the folder, gathering his own thoughts as he did so. "She didn't see it. She dreams it, Mrs. Finley, and until this afternoon, she thought she might be going crazy."

The woman looked intently at him. "What makes you think someone who dreams about murders isn't?"

John fed Sultry her nursing mother's meal and put his feet up on the desk, dialing Valenzuela's line at the station. Hubie answered with a muffled grunt, masked by the wet cigar in his mouth.

"It's Rubidoux."

"Hey! Hold on a sec, I gotta talk to you." There was some background noise, papers shuffling, the squeak of a chair, then the line went on hold status.

He made himself comfortable, listened to Sultry clean out her food dish, and the puppies make soft noises as she climbed back into the whelping box with them. Jagger lay in the corner, not sleeping, his caramel eyes fixed on John, as if he could ponder Charlie's whereabouts and John's thick-headedness about returning the dog to her just by staring at him.

Valenzuela came back on the line. "John-boy!"

"I wanted to let you know . . . I went to see Edna Finley this morning."

"Ah." Then Hubie asked, "How is she?"

"I don't know how she was before. Looks frail, but I think she's tough." He added, "It's not my department, and I don't want to step on any policy toes or anything, but I think she'd appreciate knowing that her daughter has a place on the 'Unsolved but Not Forgotten' board."

"I'll give her a call, then. Hard to tell with people, you know. Sometimes they just want to forget it and let it go away."

"Not this lady."

"Thanks for telling me."

"Thanks for letting me have a look-see."

Hubie made a noncommittal grunt, then said, "Now it's my turn."

"Okay." John rubbed the back of his head, stuck a CD into his computer, and began to listen to Natalie Merchant sound as only she could sound when backed by 10,000 Maniacs.

"Who is this girl?"

"Somebody I met through the dogs."

"Somebody special?"

He breathed deeply. Then, "Yeah. I think so."

"Do you know what you're getting into? 'Cause I'm going to have to ask some questions, John."

"What do you mean?"

"Why or how she got you interested in murders from ten years ago."

Protectively, John answered, "She doesn't have

anything to do with them, Hubie. She's just a kid. Early twenties. And like you said, we're talking ten years ago." No matter how awful the killer, chances were time had dealt with him, one way or another.

"No boyfriend, ex-husband, stepfather? We're not dealing with a witness here maybe, or repressed memories?"

He dropped his feet off the desk and straightened in his chair. "What the hell are you talking about?"

"You started it, Ruby. You pulled up that case on Holly Gardner, the pusher who was sliced to death with box cutters. I'm not asking questions just to make myself look busy. You know what my workload is like."

"I know that. What's going on?"

"I spent most of last night at a crime scene. Nasty. Woman, lived alone, looked like a follow-home robbery, but nothing was touched—nothing but her." Hubie cleared his throat. "Blood everywhere, John. Hard to take."

It must have been bad if it bothered a seasoned veteran like Valenzuela. Something icy dropped into the pit of John's stomach. "Tell me."

"She was sliced to death. Looked like he bathed in it, then stepped out of the room without an evidence trace. Killer left a box cutter behind." Hubie breathed heavily. "Whoever the son of a bitch is, he's back."

Chapter Twenty-Six

"I want you to bring her in, Ruby."

"I can't do that, she doesn't know anything." He also knew that Valenzuela did not have enough to force Charlie in now, but that Hubie was very concerned, or he would not even be mentioning it.

"She knows enough. I saw you flipping through your notebook. She didn't just pull details out of thin air and neither did you to get a match. Listen, I've known you since you opened that kennel up. Worked with you. Played with you. Hell, got stinking drunk with you more than once. Talk to her. See if you can understand what's going on, and then talk to me."

"You know if I had anything, I'd tell you, bro."

"I know I'd like to think you would."

John looked at the folder on his desk, flipped it open, and stared at the paintings. How could he explain them? He found words, rearranged them to his satisfaction, then said, "When I figure out what's going on, Hubie, you'll be the first to know."

Valenzuela grunted, as if he could hear John dancing with the truth. "The media is going to be crawling all over this by tonight's evening news. I am withholding the box cutter as crucial evidence, just so you know that. As for the girl . . . I am trusting you on this, John-boy."

"I know you are." He hung up. He stared at the photocopies. He had not been asked to trust Charlie, but he did. She was innocent. But how was he going to convince her of the fact and protect her? Was it herself he would have to shield her from or someone out there, someone who had been watching her before, and had returned to watch her now?

How did she paint what she painted? What happened to her when Midnight fell and brought her such terrible visions?

He closed the folder abruptly, unable to look at the paintings any longer.

He shut his eyes.

In his mind's eye, John could not shut away the view of the body, the slices, the box cutter. He could not ignore the implication. Valenzuela would not.

He reached for the phone and dialed Charlie. After four rings, the cool, impersonal recording for her voice mail came on. He hung up without leaving a message.

*   *   *

Clarkson eased into his chair with a weary sigh, his hair still wet from the shower, dressed in his casual suit, his day finished, and the report he wanted sitting in its slipcover dead center in his desk even though it was three-thirty. A pleased smile curved his lips. He pulled it out, scanned it, then, frowning, picked up his phone and called down to radiology, asking for Stein.

Stein answered briskly.

"Jeff, this is Wade. Thanks for rushing that interp to me."

"No problem, but you owe me big-time on this one. I haven't thought of what yet, but I'm working on it. Maybe a Rolex."

"Get real."

Jeff Stein chuckled benevolently. Wade thought of his big, burly, charcoal-headed bulk squeezed into an office chair, sequestered away, reading X rays and MRIs and CAT scans for half his workday.

"You pretty sure about what you came up with?"

"Fairly sure. You'd have to open her up to be certain."

Clarkson read the report over. Under the circumstances, he felt a little unsure about his best course of action. He would doubt this was even Charlie's report, but the faint scarring of her previous operation was unmistakable. He looked at the patterns of the soft tissue, and then the movement of the dye as it traveled through, frame by frame, and then returned to Stein's report, unorthodox as it was.

"Wade?"

"Yeah, I'm still here, sorry. Sorry to keep you hanging on this one, Jeff. You're sure?"

"It's a relatively new phenomenon, but the increased sensitivity of the imaging seems to be bringing it out."

He nodded absently before realizing the other doctor could not see him. "All right then."

"If you want to see her, give her the news, it's my understanding she's still in the labs down here."

"Still? Can you guys get any more efficient down there?"

Stein laughed. "I know, I know, there's a lot of room for improvement down here, but it's not my department holding her up! Talk to phlebotomy."

"I will . . . next board meeting. If you can get hold of her, do that. My desk is cleared for the rest of the day."

"Will do. I'll put this one on your tab with the rest of the favors you owe me!"

"Do that." Wade chuckled. "Good luck collecting."

"Oh, I'll collect all right. Yup, a Rolex is looking better and better." Stein cackled in his ear and then hung up.

Wade picked up a highlighter and began to earmark portions of the report of particular interest to him, reading and interpreting for himself, and deciding how it was he wanted to handle Charlie Saunders. He called Elyse's number and got her voice mail.

"Roseburg . . . I need to talk to you about Charlie. I've got her MRI in front of me and there are some implications which might involve your area of expertise. Give me a call when you've got time to discuss the case with me." He caught himself with his eyebrows knitting as he hung up. He did not like voice mail. It always left him with a vague, unsatisfied feeling. He swung around, booted up his computer, and waited patiently for it to bring up his desktop, accessed his account and addressed her over the hospital e-mail system, knowing that her computer was always on and never far from Elyse's awareness. One way or another he should have her attention flagged.

He finished, signed off and returned to the paperwork in front of him. He underlined the key words: *consistent with*, read a few more lines, highlighted *characterized by*, and kept reading. When he finished for a third time, all he could do was rock back in his chair and stare at the wall and the painting it held, pondering what it was he intended to tell her, doctor to patient. What course he would advise her, and what he could possibly do to preserve that intense, creative flame which had already dwindled to a mere spark. He was a physician and a damn good surgeon, but there were limitations to what even he could heal.

*   *   *

He had put away the reports and was deep in his other paperwork when Rosa notified him that Charlotte and Mary Saunders were in the outer waiting room. He pushed down the intercom button. "Good, show them to the conference room. I'll be right there."

Charlie looked pale and her eyes were bloodshot as he came into the room, but she reached out and gave him a firm handshake as he settled himself, her case file in his left hand. Mary Saunders, wearing blue again, emphasizing her eyes, seemed to hover over her chair rather than sit in it.

"I'm pleased you came in, Charlie. I know it's an ordeal, and it seems to be a particularly slow one today."

Charlie smiled slightly. "I think I have read every magazine I ever wished or hoped to read today."

Mary shrugged. "It made sense to stay here, rather than run back and forth between here and Orange County."

"If I had been free myself this afternoon, I would have made some calls to speed things up. Actually, this worked out well. I was able to get some preliminary results."

Mary reached over and took her daughter's hand, and gripped it, as if she could transfuse sheer strength of will by doing so. "That's what we anticipated."

"I want you to understand that even with the tests in front of me, I can't be a hundred percent certain. Because of that, I am going to proceed with caution for the moment."

"Caution?"

"Yes. I know that last time we scheduled surgery as soon as possible, but this time is different. We have some time to play with, the discovery is fairly early, some of your problems are asymptomatic, and I want to consult with several oncologists as well as Dr. Katsume before we proceed any further."

"Two days ago you told us time was of the essence." The older woman's features settled into uncomfortable lines.

"And it still is, make no mistake about that." Clarkson smiled. "You are in my hands. I want the best treatment available for you."

"If you are talking about consulting with oncologists . . . does that mean you think it's cancerous? And that it's inoperable?"

He leaned forward and smiled even more comfortably. "It means that it's in your best interests for me to consult with other experts. The tumor does not have to be malignant to respond to some very effective methods of chemotherapy."

"Then I do have a tumor, and it might be inoperable."

"Charlie, I did not say that. I said, it's best for me to consult with doctors in other fields, and determine the proper, most promising and successful course of treatment for you."

Charlie had been meeting his eyes steadily. Now her gaze faltered and slid away, unable to meet his any longer. Her mother took a steadying breath and said, "What can we do in the meantime?"

"I would like to be kept apprised of any further problems, worries about your daughter's health. Keep in close touch with me. Ask me questions if you have any doubts or anything that needs to be addressed. I'll be setting up appointments with my colleagues, but it's near the end of the week and I don't imagine I'll be able to talk with anyone before early next week." He talked to Mary Saunders, but he kept his eyes leveled on Charlie. Quiet, unsure, plain but appealing, talented and afflicted Charlie. "If you need to talk to me, I'll be here."

"When will you know if you need to cut again?" Charlie spoke very softly. Her mother frowned slightly, as if she could not quite hear what was said.

"Soon," he answered. "Very, very soon. But that may not be the answer this time."

Charlie's gaze flickered, looked up, caught his momentarily.

There, there was that spark. The one he valued, the one he'd seen in the paintings, the one he needed to keep lit.

"Trust me," he said.

"I am trying to," Charlie told him faintly.

Chapter Twenty-Seven

A glittering palace. Soft music and the faint blue tinge of cigarette smoke. The electrifying sound of the machines as they signaled jackpots with racing lights and the jangling clink of the coins as they tumbled out, their metallic noise magnified by the bins they clattered into. The soft step of high-heeled women in satin-and-Lycra costumes, and silken stockings, and legs that seemed to go on forever, as they strode across the carpets, calling softly for drink orders with lips painted red, faces framed by tumbling hair. Time stood still, ticked only by the sound of the roulette wheel as it turned, the lit and unlit squares on a keno board, or the croupiers as they racked in chips and called for bets, winners and losers alike.

He was in Vegas . . . not as magnificent as Monte Carlo, with its full tables of baccarat players as elegant in their dress as in any moviemaker's imagination . . .

but it did not matter. Vegas might be an inexpensive girl who could look like a queen and often did, her perfume not as subtle, her voice and vowels not as cultured or continental, but her allure, her passion, her ability to arouse him and capture him just as potent. Atlantic City, her sister, called to him as well, throaty, earthier than the voice of the Garibaldis, and heard just as avidly.

He walked the aisles of tables and dealers and slots, rolling two chips between the fingers of his hand as was his habit, looking for the quiet signs of attraction and luck, for he felt it welling up inside him, the power, the canny ability to know a winner. The rush . . . it came thrumming up through the blood, rolling, bubbling, unstoppable, likened to the unstoppable force of nature when an oil well is first drilled and black gold struck, booming out of the hidden, the below, launching upward, upward until it exploded, carrying everything with it. Or being born on flood tide, white-water ejaculation, winning, seizing the moment, risking all, and snatching triumph out of thin air. A tubular ocean wave, a perfect curl upon which he surfed endlessly, his body a hard, throbbing bullet hurtling forever.

There were those moments, of course, when the rush and fortune abandoned him. Those were the times when his suit became rancid and sweat soaked in the armpits with desperation as he tried to woo it back, tried to formulate the equation, to reduce the odds, to calculate the pay out, to squint his eyes into the dark wells of despair and find an answer. When ill fortune coated him like a sour crust. When his every attempt lay limp and flaccid, and nothing availed him.

But those times rested where he did not have to dredge them up. They shadowed him now, but he did not care . . . the feeling of omnipotence brought him erect, stood him tall, hardened him, and he swept his gaze across the casino, knowing it was his to conquer, and that luck would lie with him that night. It would be she who courted him, attracted by the way he walked, the command in his eyes and voice, the seduction of his hands. She would be enslaved by him, and kneel for him, and do whatever he wanted of her. He could feel it in every fiber of his being—

"Feel this, Valdor?"

Something cold and hard lay across his throat. It was not edged, but it bore into his cartilage and thorax, making it hard to breathe, choking, pressing, and he woke thrashing from his dreams.

Dark stayed across his eyes. The towel or whatever lay across his face let only the edges of light seep around it. He panicked, tried to raise a hand, could not, his limb jerked back into place, and bonds chafed across his wrist. The cold object rolled on his throat. He tried to swallow.

"You sleep late, Fred."

"What are you doing here?"

"Don't panic, Freddie. This looks like a nice little motel. Be a shame to soil their mattress."

"I have days yet . . . he agreed to time."

The metallic object against his throat, thin, rolling up and down over his Adam's apple, pressing, hurting. Then it moved away, and a sharp prick stabbed at the base of his throat. "Know what this is, Freddie?"

Oh, he knew all right. Pewter cold, long, thin, and deadly, end glittering with sharpness.

"Ice . . . ice pick," he got out. His nose started to swell. He was going to cry, and could feel his sinuses tingle in spite of himself, his eyes brim.

"Jackpot," the unseen man said. And laughed.

Despite himself, Valdor felt his bladder go, warm liquid trickling out, hot, vinegarlike smell.

Valdor started to plead for his life. "He told me . . . he agreed . . . I told him to just keep the five thousand. I'll have the money!"

"Relax, Freddie."

The mattress jerked and moved as the assailant stood.

"This is just a reminder. This is just to let you know that we know where you are. You got your time, but when your time runs out, don't even try to run."

The bond on his right hand loosened.

"Count to fifty, Freddie, then you can take your

hand out, and get up, and look if you wanna." The other snickered. "And order some towels. Take a shower. You peed yourself. You stink."

Heavy steps across the floor. A door opened and slammed shut.

Valdor lay very still, until his damp legs grew cold, and his heart stopped drumming, and then and only then, did he begin to count. When he was finished, he pulled his right hand free, grabbed the towel from his face. He sat up and screamed and threw his shoes at the door, cursing Charlie until his throat went raw and he could hardly breathe and someone next door pounded relentlessly on the wall, yelling at him to shut up. Valdor balled the towel between his hands, pressed it to his face, and began to sob in anger.

Later, after he'd showered and changed, he flashed a twenty at the maid, who was still cleaning rooms on the fifth floor, for new blankets and sheets, took his clothes to the cleaners, and found a corner restaurant which served weak coffee and brisket sandwiches he could cut with his fork, and he sat and waited for darkness to fall. He would find out why the lights had blazed all night at Charlie's house. With no dog to stop him, he would make her pay for all the humiliations she had heaped on him. Every one of them, throughout the years. Every God-damn last one of them.

The sky held a faint purplish tinge by the time

RETRIBUTION

John finished his kennel chores, locked Sultry in the storeroom, her puppies all snug by her side, and the bitch giving him a proud yet protective look over her litter. He rushed through the runs in the exercise yard, every moment nagging at him, and Jagger pushed at his hands with an anxious whine as if feeling what he felt.

Charlie had not called him, nor had the voice mail been lifted. What he had to say to her, he could not tell her over the phone. He wanted to be at her side, for she would take it hard, and he could not let her take the blame. She would recoil, he knew that, once he told her about Linda Finley and Holly Garner. She would retreat to some faraway place behind her blue-gray eyes, and thank him politely, and turn away.

He wondered if . . . somehow . . . some way . . . she had discovered that same similarity ten years ago. If that discovery had been what stopped her from painting. If the shock of it had wiped the memory from her mind as completely as the desire to create. If knowledge had scooped the will out of her as neatly as a scalpel had scooped out a tumor.

Jagger pushed and whined at his knee, and pawed at the gate as John maneuvered him back inside so he could lock it. The golden's ears hung limply, and his feathered tail barely swung. He nudged his nose through the chain-link diamonds, marking Ruby wetly. John stuck his fingers through to scratch the top of Jagger's head lightly. He felt the same worry the dog did. Neither of them figured that the day would go without Charlie calling, without hearing her voice, without her welcoming them back to her.

He checked the locks on the gates, turned his beeper on, and headed for his van. As he strode across the lot, a muffled bark or two followed him, and a high-pitched, warbling howl of utter despair. It made him ache to hear it.

A light shone in the front room, a side light which barely threw any illumination at all out the window, and he did not feel very reassured to see it. It was the sort of light left on by someone to protect against the dark when they were gone or expecting to come home late or they'd left on a timer to fool burglars. It did not look as though Charlie were even home.

Nonetheless, he tucked his folder under his arm, took his baseball cap off uneasily, and rang the door-bell. Because it made him feel better, he pounded the ball of his fist on the door two, three, four times, venting his frustration. When the door yanked open abruptly, he nearly went to his knees on the doorstep and he made a startled yelp.

Charlie stared at him as if he'd gone mad.

John lost his grip on the folder, and papers cascaded everywhere. She bent to help him pick them up, looking, slowly, at each paper before she handed it back. "What were you doing with these?"

"I could use a drink," he said. "Anything cold and wet."

He had already all but fallen in. She took a swaying step back to let him in the rest of the way.

"I was working in the studio," she told him, "weaving on my loom."

"You didn't take the voice mail off."

"Oh. I didn't notice, really." She turned, saying, "Let's talk in the kitchen."

He followed her, her manner more distant than cold, and when he sat at the table, he noticed that she had put kibble down, as if forgetting that Jagger was not there. She poured him a soft drink and sat down opposite him, and watched him as though they were strangers still.

"Charlie . . ."

She put her hands on the table. She looked at her palms, face up, as if reading the lines, and she must have been, because she gave a little laugh, saying, "I have a very long lifeline."

"Charlie, what is it?"

She shook her head. "The hands can't lie, can they?" She traced the line with her index finger, showing him. "I should have shown this to Dr. Clarkson."

"You saw him today? I thought you wouldn't see him until the results came back."

"He left word for us after the last lab." She rubbed her forearms lightly, and he could see the faint thumb-sized bruise on the inside curve of one elbow where someone had clumsily taken blood.

Not another word did she have to say, and he didn't want to hear her say it, but he had to know just how bad it was going to be. Had to understand how it was he was expected to brace himself, to know that he was going to lose her after having just found her. "What did he say?"

Charlie still would not look directly at him. "I want you to keep Jagger," she said lightly. "Retrain him for someone else. Don't let him be alone too long—" Her voice choked to a halt. She made a stifled sound, and could not get another word out. He leaped up. His chair crashed to the floor behind him as he pulled her up, lifted her into his arms, and carried her from the kitchen. She hunched over in his arms, making tiny, strangled noises, and the front of his shirt grew damp as he bore her through the house until he collapsed on the living room couch, Charlie cradled in his arms. She wept. And he cried with her.

When he had finished, and she slowed, he smoothed her hair back and just held her. Her weight in his lap did not stir passion as it had the last time he'd held her like this only . . . had it only been a day or two ago? But he felt tremendously possessive, as if his hold on her could keep the inevitable from happening. As her breathing quieted, he whispered, "Tell me what he said."

Charlie rubbed her nose on her shirtsleeve, child-like, and took a deep breath. "He said he was going to have to consult on treatment. His partner, the clinic oncologists."

"There is a tumor."

She gave a jerky nod.

"You told me was a surgeon."

"Yes. But he didn't mention surgery."

He tightened his arms. "Even if it's inoperable, that doesn't mean terminal. Or malignant."

"No. It doesn't. I keep telling myself that—" She wrapped her arms about his neck, crying hoarsely into his shoulder, "I'm so scared!"

"I know. I know you are. You and me both." He fished a clean if wadded up handkerchief from his back pocket and gave it to her. Charlie unfolded it, folded it neatly, and then proceeded to massacre it. She blew her nose with a vengeance and dried her face vigorously, then clenched the poor handkerchief in the palm of her hand.

"I couldn't talk to anyone."

"I understand." He caught a trailing strand of hair and moved it back over her brow, and smoothed it into place. "You may owe Jagger extra kibble, though."

"Life goes on, huh? A dog has to do what a dog has to do."

He nodded. "Sometimes that's the best view. A day at a time." He rubbed his chin over the top of her head, pressing her near to him. "He didn't tell you to expect the worst."

"No. It was just such a shock. The tumor . . . well, I knew it had to have come back. I had myself all prepared for surgery. Then . . . for him to say what he did . . . everything just came to a stop. I went numb."

"Tell me what he said. As much as you can remember."

Haltingly, she repeated what she could. John listened. Tried to find loopholes. Found every word as hard to listen to as the first. When she was done, she lay limply against him, grieving, now too spent for tears. And he understood. He did not know what to do.

So he lied to her. "You can't give up. He has options beyond surgery. You don't know what he has in mind."

Charlie made a furtive movement. "Do you think?"

"I think. And I hope." He squeezed her reassuringly.

After a few long moments, she asked, "Why did you have copies of my paintings?"

He did not want to tell her. To heap devastation on despair. But he sensed that she had reached a kind of emotional numbness. He'd seen it in disaster victims before—a point at which nothing else could hurt or touch them. He started with the lesser first. "I went to see a woman whose daughter disappeared."

She sat up and drew back slightly to look into his face. "And?"

He could not quite find words.

Her mouth drew into a bitter line. "John."

"The paintings matched the scenario fairly closely."

"Life imitating art." She shuddered. "Maybe this is all for the best. I can't go on like this."

"What are you talking about?"

"I can't live thinking I created some kind of monster. I don't want to." She gestured with her hand. "Maybe it's just as well Clarkson hasn't got treatment in mind."

He heard the defeat in her voice. His protest roared out of his chest. "Don't you care give up on me! Dammit! Don't you dare quit!"

She sat up straighter, and took his head, and held it to her chest, and then it was she who rocked him, crooning lightly.

Valdor crouched by the side of the van, the wavering pale beam from the far side of the street barely giving him enough light to read the logo. He fished his dry cleaning slip out of his pocket and scribbled down the information before creeping near the house, parting shrubs and slipping in between them. A block away a dog barked faintly, a small dog, its voice in falsetto. In this house, nothing seemed to stir. He moved from window to window and stood in stark amazement at the old studio window, where curtains had been eased back for daylight, and he looked in.

He could see a row of canvases against a wall, only faintly visible in thin, reedy light spilling over from the hall, but he could tell they'd been filled. It made his heart soar and he stood, trembling, at the discovery before pulling himself away and continuing to the side window at the living room, where blinds hung a bit crookedly, perhaps from the dog's big head pushing them aside so he could look out. He could see the two of them on the couch and the moment of intimacy made his mouth twist.

No dog guarded her now. And she had paintings, more paintings than he ever dared hope for, and they had looked new and fresh to his critical eye. But now there was another obstacle in his path, and he drew back from the window, and sat silent in the night, and decided what to do.

John waited till his anger subsided, then he sat back, and she released her hold on him, and he knew what it felt like to be so spent that nothing else could faze him. Whatever else he might have told her, he held back. It seemed pointless at that moment. Charlie stretched, then relaxed against his chest as he leaned on the couch back.

"What are we going to do?"

He shifted. "Do you date your paintings?"

She shook her head. "No. Sometimes I put a year after my signature. Mom used to pencil in the year on the back if I didn't. Most artists don't."

He brushed his lips across her hair. "I think it's possible you read something in the newspaper. Heard something on television. It sank into you. Days, weeks later, you painted it. I think you saw something that made you identify with their grief, their loss, and when you couldn't take it any more, you took up your brushes. You purged it."

"My paintings came after the fact." She considered it. "I don't remember it."

"No. Because all you remember is Midnight."

She ran her fingers through her hair. "So maybe I don't create psychos."

"I would hope not. If I can track down the date on the first painting of that series, it will tell us."

"If the painting isn't dated, it's possible Valdor has a record. He kept close track of the ones I finished, and the showings and sales." She smiled slightly. "And what if you're wrong?"

"I don't think I'm wrong."

He prayed he wasn't.

His beeper went off. John checked it and saw his neighbor's phone number in it. Charlie got off his lap to get the portable phone for him but before he could dial, the beeper went off a second time.

This time the code was that of his security system.

Something at the kennel.

He called his neighbor first. She answered hastily, excitedly. "John, your dogs are loose. They're running all over. Hans got hit by a car, he's not bad, I've got him here in my kitchen—"

"They break into the office?"

Charlie watched him anxiously.

"I don't know."

"I'll be right there. Call the vet." He stood. She took the portable. "I'll be back as soon as I can."

"I'll be up. Phone first." She pinked slightly. "I'll take it off the answering service."

He leaned down and kissed her gently, a brush of lips, and then she was pushing him out the door.

"I'll bring Jagger back."

"Just go," she urged him.

He hurried into the night.

Chapter Twenty-Eight

Charlie went and washed her face, and ran a brush through her hair, then found a tie-back and secured it loosely at the base of her neck. She felt faintly hungry and realized she hadn't eaten since lunch in the clinic cafeteria. Tomato soup sounded good. She would make iced tea and have soup and then go through her catalogs in the studio, to see if there was any hope at all of dating her paintings more closely after years that seemed like an abyss in her life. In the morning she would call her mother and see if she had copies of Valdor's records.

Moving through the bedroom, she stopped and put her brace on. The crunch and rip of the velcro straps as she positioned and then repositioned them for security sounded loudly in the empty house. She nearly tripped over the food dish in the kitchen, bent over, and picked up Jagger's bowl. She stowed it in the pantry, faintly guilty that she had not followed through getting the paperwork for the county. There would be a tomorrow and a day beyond that and a day beyond that. She couldn't see forever . . . but then, who could?

When the iced tea maker started to dribble hot tea over a mountain of ice, she went to the studio and browsed through the built-in bookcase, running her hands over the spines of old photo albums used for scrapbooks. She had labeled them herself and Charlie paused for a moment at the firm, expressive, and yet obviously young hand printing on labels which were now curled, edges yellowing, the scotch tape holding them to the spines discolored and peeling back. Ten years ago she was a child, and John Rubidoux had been a young man.

She chose a scrapbook and brought it down, wiping the dust off with one of her paint rags, and opening it. It smelled musty and old, faintly disagreeable. Quentin had smoked then, and it seemed the smell of burning still lingered in the pages. She turned them. A leaf which must have once been brightly red and yellow with autumn, now pressed to brown inside its waxed paper. She had written something on it.

Charlie turned the album to read the pencil markings which had skidded and plowed stubbornly over the waxed paper. Fall, Big Bear Lake. Quentin's cabin. The memory curved her mouth. She had called it a cabin, but it had been one of a hundred or so condos, at the foot of one of the premier skiing mountains in Big Bear. He had owned it for an investment, and the two-story unit paid for itself during the snow and ski season. They visited it on off-seasons, she, and Quentin's mother, and her mother, and Quentin. It had a balcony upstairs, living room, eating nook, small kitchenette, and downstairs were the bathrooms and bedrooms, two of them, and a small corner which could be used as a den or another sleeping area.

Blue jays, squirrels, and an occasional raccoon reigned on the balcony. They bought peanut hearts and mini-marshmallows and threw them out to be eaten. The squirrels were gluttons for the marshmallows although the white, puffy objects would make them drool and fill their cheeks almost to bursting. Charlie ran her fingertips over the waxed paper. That was before the collapse. They had not gone back after the operation. She had never asked why, and it seemed that some wordless knowledge had come to her that the condo had been sold to pay for the bills her mother's meager insurance had not.

She turned a few more pages. A lock of hair. A diploma from middle school. A plane ticket.

She smoothed it out. Her first plane trip, to San Francisco, her two paintings in a new art portfolio bag nearly bigger than she was, Valdor on the other arm, carrying her overnight bag and his suit bag.

Charlie swiftly turned a few more pages, the plastic covering bristling, the faint smell of smoke still reaching her. Then she lifted her head, uneasiness stirring in her.

That was not tobacco she smelled burning. There was a faint touch of wood, and hemp, and perhaps even a sharp, acrid scent of paint remover.

She dropped the scrapbook. Even as she turned, she could feel it in her eyes and nose.

Smoke. And fire.

By the time he reached the kennels, the vet's car was in front. He found Dr. Longmont walking out with Hans in his arms, back leg bound in a temporary splint. The shepherd looked at him dully, chin lolling over the crook of the vet's arm.

The vet motioned with his chin for John to open the rear door and the two of them laid Hans down as gently as possible on the backseat.

"How bad is it?"

"The splint's precautionary. I'm not too worried about internals either. Doped him up a bit so I could manipulate him. Lucky dog. The car stopped, according to your neighbor, or tried to. He more-or-less bounced off the bumper." Longmont pulled on his beard, wiry and graying like the hair on his head, which he wore long but kept tied back, looking much as he did in the photos of him during his hippie college days, which hung on the wall in his office, though he had not been gray then, or balding.

"Looks like someone wanted to create problems, but had more trouble than they expected once they let the dogs loose."

"I can only hope."

Longmont's mouth was nearly hidden by his mountaineer style beard as he grinned. "Me, too."

John shook his hand. "Thanks for coming."

"No problem. The bitch seems all right. Someone tried to get in your office as well, but she evidently scared them off." He ducked his head as he got into the driver's seat. "I'll call you about Hans in the morning. If I get busy, you call me."

"Will do." John started to back away, then added in afterthought. "Say, do you know the guy who took over Baez's practice?"

Longmont nodded. "Young kid. Older wife." He smiled. "They specialize in reptiles and birds. Why?"

"He was the vet for a client of mine before he retired. She needs her dog's records, needs to prove rabies vaccination."

Longmont thought a moment, then said, "I'll call 'em in the morning. Everything's boxed up. I know how Viktor kept his records. They'll never find it." Longmont started the car, smiling faintly. "Although there is a certain logic to it."

"What?"

"He kept the rabies certificates filed under Old Yeller." Longmont grinned widely and waved.

Laughing, John backed into his driveway and let

out a piercing whistle, guaranteed to call cabs in New York. Running shapes came out of the darkness, bounding beside him, barking excitedly. Flint, Jake, Hooper. They went into their pens after a cautious approach, their security and faith in their shelter disturbed by events earlier. He checked each gate. None had been damaged maliciously, just swiftly unlatched and opened. He went to the last kennel in the row, Jagger's temporary quarters. Its gate swung eerily in the evening breeze, and there was no sign of the golden retriever anywhere.

"Jagger!" He whistled and chirped.

Flint paced up and down his run, and gave a low growl. John stood, wheeling about in all directions, but no dog came in answer.

Unhappily, he trotted to the office. The outer door also swung open, but there was damage to the frame. It looked as if someone had taken a tire iron to it, popped the doorknob and latch completely out of the frame. He ran his hand along the splintered wood, then stepped in and immediately, savage barks and ivoried fangs lashed at him.

John scrambled as Sultry snarled and crouched, protecting the inner doorway to the storeroom. Behind her, newly roused pups let out tiny mewlings of noise, only now becoming aware of the world of sound as their puppy ear workings had begun to open to it. He snapped his fingers and the canine dropped to her chest, blinking, lips curled.

He calmed her, talking to her, giving her the commands she knew so well. The bitch finally let out a low whine, in apology, and rolled to her side. He put a hand down and rubbed her gently.

"I know, girl, I know. Good girl. Guard those babies of yours. It's all right now." He thumped her rib cage. Then he reached up, got a lead hanging off the hook on the wall, and snapped it to her collar, to take her out to the exercise yard. He searched the grounds and looked up into the foothills behind, but there was no sight of anything four-footed wandering the night.

All the dogs had stayed close despite their loosing. All but Jagger. Had he run off . . . or had someone taken him? It was a twenty-minute crosstown run to Charlie's. He wondered if the dog had decided to go home on his own. Across streets and highway and even deserted stretches where coyotes claimed territory. It was not that far, but the dog had never been that way before.

He didn't know how he could return to Charlie's without him, but it looked as if he had no choice.

Charlie staggered away from the rear of the kitchen as blue-gray smoke curled toward her, choking, stinging her eyes. Orange-red tongues licked up the far corner and back of the house, eating into the textile studio, where the walls were thinner, not the adobelike thickness of the original bungalow. She ran back to the living room and dialed 911, blurted out the address at the operator and added, "This is old Laguna. The big trucks can't get down the streets!"

Swiftly, the operator replied, "I'll note that, Miss. Get in the clear and wait."

Charlie dropped the phone without responding. Her textile works would go up in a flash. She had no hope of saving anything there. But on a diagonal, the painting studio stood, and that was where she ran.

The lights flickered and went out. In darkness made thicker by smoke and growing heat, she got down the hall and into the studio, grabbing up canvases, staggering to the front door and throwing them as far as she could onto the lawn. She could hear the faint, faraway wail of a siren and prayed that it was for her home. She turned and bolted back inside, using her hands to propel herself down the hall.

Glass crackled and exploded at the rear of the house. It shattered like chimes and there was a whoosh, a tremendous intake that seemed to make her ears pop. The sliding glass doors must have gone, and the air being sucked in now fed the inferno to new heights. She could feel the reflected heat, already intense.

Her leg threatened to buckle under her. Charlie gasped, her throat burning, her eyes clouded with tears and smoke. She grabbed more canvases, not heavy but bulky . . . four, five, and stumbled back to the front door. Someone met her there, pushed her aside roughly, grabbing the paintings from her. She could not see his face, staggering on the threshold.

She turned back to get the last of them. She could hear the retired Navy officer across the street begin to shout orders for hoses. Bent over, holding the hem of her shirt to her face, she hobbled to the studio a last time to salvage what she could.

She got the last of the paintings under one arm, and the scrapbook she had been reading. Smoke began to curl in, along the floor, rising quickly, sucking the air out, bringing immense heat with it. She reeled back, knowing she might not get out this time, suddenly afraid.

She thought she heard sirens or it might have been the scream of her own pulse in her ears. Bumping along the dark corridor in which smoke even obliterated the light of flames, Charlie hunched determinedly. Her leg gave out. She fell, coughing and gasping rawly for air.

She heard a dog barking, loud, frantic. She crawled toward the noise, clutching the scrapbook and last of the canvases she could carry. Her lungs felt as though they would burst, as if she were drowning.

Like a cloak, a blanket, smoke covered her. Dragged her down. Heat rolled through the house. She could hear windows all over begin to crack and shatter. It seemed to be all she could hear.

Somewhere that dog kept barking. Sharp. Insistent. Charlie pulled herself to the noise.

She called out as she drew near what must be the front door . . . though she could not see, no longer had any sense of where she was in her own home. Her voice failed her.

Charlie sank to the floor, gasping.

A form burst through the smoke and began to paw and nip at her, wet nose to her heat-shriveled face, grasping at her wrist and then the shoulder of her shirt, pulling, nudging. Teeth sharp enough to cut through her lassitude. Pain brisk enough to make her gasp for breath.

Charlie tried to rouse for Jagger. She could hear sirens shrill and near, then cut off sharply. The dog dug at her and, coughing heavily, she started to crawl after him.

Her lungs failed her. She sank down a last time. Jagger swiped her face and let out a mournful howl. It was the last she knew.

Ruby saw the dark clouds flowing into the evening sky, and then the abrupt stop of sirens nearby, and he felt his heart begin to thump uncomfortably. Fire . . . close . . . too close . . . to Charlie's. As he pulled the van into the terraced hillside, he could see the engines blocking the lower end of the street, and he did not take time to look any further. Jumping the curb, he pulled to the street above, rammed the van into a driveway and jumped out, leaping side yards and back fences, getting to Charlie's the quickest way he knew how, as smoke billowed gray as water hoses hit the conflagration.

There were no words to form his thoughts. He vaulted the last side gate into her driveway, the air and drive slick with water and steam, and ran to the front, where a wispy-haired woman was gathering up what looked like paintings, pulling them out from the path of firemen laying more hose down. He grabbed the nearest slickered fireman. "Did she get out? Did you get her out?"

The fireman shrugged him aside. "Let me do my job. Go around front." He braced himself as the hose line he held suddenly filled with incredible pressure, threatening to knock him off his feet.

John made his way to the front of the house, already his mouth and nose and throat full of the pollution, the smoke, the awful smell of the fire. The headlights of the fire trucks cut across the lawn. He could see a fireman/paramedic on his knees, giving CPR. He leaped forward and pulled the man back, and saw that the limp form in his arms was that of the dog.

Jagger lay stretched out, his golden-red form still, his paws red sores. Some lavender-haired woman he had never seen before, a chenille bathrobe clutched around her, sobbed.

"He was so brave. He kept running back in for her . . ."

The fireman gave him a puzzled look and John let go of his shoulder. He stood up and looked at the woman.

"Did she get out? Is Charlie out of there, for God's sake? Someone tell me they got Charlie out!"

The woman looked at him, and began to bob her head in nervous reaction. The fireman working on Jagger jerked his face aside suddenly as the dog let out a choking gasp and then began to breathe, his tail thumping the grass weakly.

"We wouldn't 'ave found her, but he took us to where she collapsed. She's over on the other lawn. Smoke inhalation. Pretty bad. Soon as we can get the ambulance up here, they're transporting her." The fireman stroked Jagger. "This is one damn fine dog."

He picked Jagger up in his arms and carried him over to the other lawn, where he could see two firemen/paramedics kneeling beside Charlie. He knelt down, laying the dog next to her, her face obscured by the oxygen mask and bubble which the tech pumped to a regular count.

The tech looked at him, in answer to his unvoiced question, and said, "The sooner we get her on a ventilator, the better. She's not burned, but these artists types . . . that's nasty stuff when it gets to burning. Her lungs are trying to shut down."

Her face looked pale under the smear of smoke

and ash, her eyes half-open but unseeing. John found that numb spot deep inside himself expand and swallow him. All he could do was put out a trembling hand and try to straighten her tangle of hair, to smooth it away from her face. "I'm here," he told her. "Jagger's here. The worst is over, you're going to be fine."

One of the hosemen came around from the side yard, calling, "Captain!" He ignored the rescue scene on the lawn, heading to the truck where hose units were still being monitored as they pumped.

The captain looked up.

"What is it, Jacobs?"

"I think we've got a pretty clear-cut case of arson back here."

John rocked back on his heels.

Chapter Twenty-Nine

Valdor watched in agitation as the narrow streets boiled with activity and he saw the opportunity he had created slip through his fingers. Scattered paintings on the lawn were being picked up and leaned against a thick, well-trimmed hedge that separated one lawn from another. He slipped through the night, wove his way inconspicuously through the curious and the helpful, but he could not get close enough to the canvases. Twelve of them! Twelve! Nearly a million dollars' worth of art stacked haphazardly, exposed to the over-spray from the fire hoses and the ash drifting in the air.

Quentin's long, lean car pulled up, and Valdor recoiled into the fringe of bottlebrush bushes and crape myrtle framing a house, watching as Quentin boiled out of the car and immediately begin to take charge, shouting hoarsely, confronting the EMTs as they lifted Charlie's limp form onto a gurney and began to roll her down the street to the only access point the ambulance had had, the bigger fire engines blocking most of the available space. Quentin carried and used his cell phone the way some people used guns, pointing it as he gave directions, making calls, giving Mary a quick squeeze for comfort as the woman leaned over the gurney, her shoulders shaking.

Valdor pressed his forehead to the cold, indifferent stucco of the structure he hugged. The window of opportunity was being shut before his very eyes, and he rubbed his throat where the point of the ice pick had drawn blood, and he swallowed with difficulty. Still, he waited. Saw the new boyfriend heft up the dog . . . damnable creature . . . had chased his car down the street till Valdor had thought he'd lost him . . . and observed as the man and dog were ushered into Quentin's car.

Jane Gilley from the Peppermill came running up, a light windbreaker over what looked to be pajamas, and hugged Quentin, then Mary, and helped Mary get into the medical transport with Charlie. Quentin hand-waved the transport out through the labyrinth of cars and emergency vehicles, then turned to Janie. The wispy redhead listened intently to Quentin and walked over to the hedges, and began to gather up the paintings.

Valdor let out a vitriolic noise and smothered it with the back of his hand till he left his own teeth marks in his flesh. Janie would take the paintings back to her gallery—Quentin would see to that. Shrewd, emotionless except when it came to his wife and stepdaughter, he knew what Charlie had risked her life to save. Still on the cell phone, he returned to his car. Bright, leonine headlights pierced the night as Quentin pulled forward, illuminating the hedge so that Janie could see and mentally catalog what she dealt with. The two men leaned their heads together briefly, consulting in the interior, as Janie returned to her minivan and eased it down the street until she could pull into a driveway. She began to load the canvases quickly, efficiently, seemingly unaware of being in the spotlight of Quentin's car. One by one the valuable pieces disappeared from his sight. Tears crawled to the corners of Valdor's eyes.

Now he could give no quarter. It was his life or theirs. He slunk farther back into the bushes and shadows and disappeared.

Quentin slipped into ICU behind Mary, and put his arm about her waist, knowing that she had no eyes for him at the moment, all her attention on Charlie's quiet form, monitors humming and beeping softly in the hospital room, the pump and quiet hiss of the ventilator keeping Charlie breathing. She took a shivery breath that made her rib cage press into his arm, and he knew that she had just recently stopped crying. He put his lips to the side of her head and kissed her gently.

"Where's Jagger?"

"Ruby took him back to the kennel in my car. He'll bring it back here."

She stroked his forearm absently. "They got her in here as quickly as they could."

"What's the prognosis?"

"Smoke inhalation. They'll evaluate her in the morning, see if they can take her off the ventilator. If that's all it is." Mary tried to take another deep breath and he tightened his arm about her in support.

"All?"

"She's comatose, Quentin. It could be . . . they said they put in an emergency call to Wade Clarkson . . . they say the brain wave patterns are showing abnormalities." She pressed a tissue to her face as if she could hold back the flood of emotion.

He did not want to say to her what he felt he had to. "Mary, the captain says there is evidence the fire was started on purpose."

She shook. "No!"

"Arson inspectors will be on the scene first thing in the morning." He smoothed her hair back, exposing her brow. "Hon, we have to be prepared for this. Charlie may have started that fire. Either in some kind of delusion or possibly even suicidally."

His wife began to tremble in his hold. He braced

himself for her protest, but she did not say a coherent word, mumbling a nearly inaudible sound. They had a contract. Charlie had insisted. Had she planned this? He looked at the white-sheeted form of the young woman he'd raised and loved as his own daughter. "You have to be ready to be there for her. Give her whatever she needs, whatever it is." Mary felt warm in his arm, vibrant, so alive. So much of what he loved about Mary had always been in Charlie. Till now. All of it seemed gone, drained, stolen away, and only the faint noise of the ventilator seemed to be giving her life. Cold fingers seemed to press the back of his neck. "Let's go get some coffee. Decide what we're going to do. Plan our options."

She made a furtive movement as if to edge away from him, then surrendered, as he guided her out of the ICU cubicle. She combed her ash-blonde hair from her face and leaned on his arm. "I can't believe Charlie would do something like that."

"Come on with me. It's going to be a long night." Quentin Saunders supported her easily and guided her down the hospital corridor, familiar to him as the back of his hand, and his jaw tightened.

Midnight came. It brought her to the ER at Sunset, ushered in by the throbbing lights of an EMT van, and gurneys being unloaded, sobbing victims on backboards and in neck braces, blood-splashed, techs rushing out to meet the paramedics halfway, exchanging the bags of Ringer's lactate and vitals. "Female, white, mid-forties; male, white, early fifties; car crash; male appears to have chest compression and injuries, possible broken ribs, concussion; female was wearing seat belt, but the impact drove her sideways into the passenger window, multiple lacerations in the face and torso, possible broken right arm. . . ."

Sliding doors opened to swallow up the gurneys, injured, and techs, shutting away the moans and cries of pain and shock, leaving on the EMT van, its lights strobing the darkness.

It left her watching, ghostlike, over the exterior of the hospital.

A moment of silence followed, almost contemplative, then a car door opened, its yellowish interior light slicing across the darkened breezeway. A silhouette exited and stood, as if watching the drama which had passed beyond the emergency room entrance. Figures in scrub greens and county uniforms could be seen through the wire-reinforced windows of the swinging doors as they escorted their charge. The silhouette stood unmoved by the drama, then turned and took a side door into Sunset Hospital.

Three floors up, a skeleton crew of nurses and orderlies worked the late shift.

A shadow moved across glazed brown linoleum floors. Midnight brought her after the shadow, made her watch, drew her after it. It stalked the rooms quietly, pausing in each corridor as if to gauge direction by drawing it from the wind, from paranormal senses, from the sounds of suffering on these upper floors. A darkness without cloud or chill, it drifted through the passageways, occasionally stopping for long moments, then moving on, as though whatever it searched for had not yet been found. At the end of each floor, the fire exit stairway door opened and clanged shut, as the shadow moved on.

Finally, it halted outside a room, a semiprivate room in critical care where sounds of moaning could be heard with each breath, a keening, heartbreaking testament to the pain of living. A hand reached out of a dark sleeve to push the door open. The volume of the moaning rose like a banshee, then quavered away into momentary silence.

The shadow stepped in, and if it was Death, it had a firm tread.

An elderly woman lay under a thin yellow blanket and a white hospital sheet, her bedding twisted around and underneath her wispy frame. Lank white hair straggled across the flat pillow, emphasizing her sallow features and the only spot of color in her face were her lips, chapped pink with a crust of a yellow fever blister across one withered curve. As he watched, she took an agonizing breath, and her moaning began again. He seemed to be the only witness to her struggle. The other bed lay empty, its mattress stripped bare and awaiting sterile sheets only when a patient would be assigned. The bath-

room door had swung open, its beige interior unin-
habited, the medicinal smell of the disinfectant last
used to clean it still lingering.

Another odor hung amid the faint antiseptic smell,
an odor of disease and decay, and the foul discharge
of every hard-fought-for breath. The woman knotted
her bony hands into her covers fretfully as she slept,
and suffered, and dreamed.

He stood watching, his presence an ombré sliver,
an abyss of light and hope, falling across her bed
and face.

When he moved, it was to take a small pillow resting in the side chair and lightly press it across her
face. It was almost as though he did not intend to
smother her, but to shield her from the sight of what
he would do. The movement woke her with a waving of a frail, blue-veined hand and a shake of her
palsied head, the pillow slipping away under his
slight grasp.

Her eyes met his, drowsy and pain-ridden, yet no
fear shadowed them.

She licked dry and peeling lips, a tiny, furtive
movement of a tongue that seemed no moister.
"Help me," she said. "So much pain. . . ." The claw-
like fingers that curled about his, drew closed in
soft prayer.

He said nothing for a moment, then answered,
"Don't worry."

He moved his hand to his pocket, withdrew a

small glass vial and syringe, and swiftly filled a dose. Reaching for the IV tube and connection, he injected the dosage, adjusted the drip, and stepped back. Both syringe and empty vial he pocketed, then gently put a hand out and stroked tangled strands of hair away from her frail expression. He kept his fingers pressed lightly to her temple, where a blue vein pulsed valiantly, and then began to tremble under his touch.

He stood impassively in the long moments it took her to die, as the tides of midnight swept over her, a riptide of drowning into nothingness she futilely tried to resist. Her hand brushed feebly at his, scraping, as if she could pull him away. Midnight kept Charlie from helping her, but she felt every drumming effort of the heart to keep pumping, the lungs to keep expanding until she ached. The old woman's mouth opened. Her chest sucked for breath as if she truly drowned, growing weaker and weaker as her life ebbed away. Her hand fell back to the sheets.

He took the long, deep breath she had been fighting for. He held it as if clearing away the fascination and power of her death, and stepped back. He left the room after one, last look back, and when he left, he was cloaked in Midnight . . . and Charlie lay stranded in the hospital, alone, bereft, struggling.

The monitors in Charlie's room flickered and danced with life, spiking unexpectedly, the recording strips of paper cascading out of them, inked lines

darting in impossible directions, her eyelids fluttering. She might have been dreaming, violently, her
arms and limbs reacting to the stimulus . . . or she
might have been suffering a seizure. It was difficult
to discern, even with the monitor readings.

He stood at the foot of the bed, watching. The tape
around her lips holding in the ventilator tubing kept
her mute, but her fingers twitched as if signing
words, emotions, though her face showed no sign of
consciousness. Then, motor movement seeped away
from her body, and the monitors subsided into nor-
malcy, and vitals even slipped below that of normal.
He watched them momentarily. Charlie seemed to
slip farther into nothingness, her chest rising and falling only because the ventilator dictated that it
should.

He reached out and yanked hard. "God help us
both, Charlie."

Midnight tortured her again. Visions pressed on
her, kneeling on her till her throat ached and she
could not breathe. Her mind swirled. She felt herself
twitch, willing muscles to run, to carry her away,
body caught in the stasis of sleep, thoughts impris-
oned within Midnight. It fell on her with a crushing
weight. She could not breathe. She ached and burned
and hurt, her throat and bronchials raw, and she
tried to open her mouth to gasp down air, to swallow
it whole, to push Midnight away from her.

Charlie's eyes blinked. Tubes and tape covered her mouth and nose. She could not breathe! She began to claw at it, weakly, futilely, trying to free herself.

On the other side of the horseshoe unit, a sharp alarm went off. Nurses began running in and out of a room at the far end of the hall where he could hear the sharp whine of a defib powering up, the light outside the room blinking in a life-and-distress signal. No one paid any attention to his presence in the unit.

Quentin saw her eyes open. She looked at him and he thought his heart would stop in his chest. She shook her head, hands desperate at her face. She looked at him, throat straining, and he knew he had made a terrible mistake. The ventilator sat silent, suffocating her instead of pumping air in. He grabbed her hands, pushing them away, ripping tape off her nose, and then her mouth, pulling the tubes from her.

She sat up, coughing and choking like a drowning person, pawing at him, and then she began to breathe, jaggedly, huge gulping breaths. Color flooded back into her face. She bent over his arm, holding onto him, coughing and inhaling. Quentin held her tightly, realizing how close he'd come to losing her.

"I've got you. It's all right now. Just breathe slowly, in and out of your nose."

My God, he'd nearly killed her.

RETRIBUTION

He found the call button and pushed it anyway, even though the monitors should have brought them running, knowing that the drama at the other end of the hall held their attention. Charlie clung to him, still coughing, but taking in air. As he moved to hold her even closer, his feet tangled in a loose cord where the ventilator had been unplugged.

No one answered till he began shouting, roaring, for help.

Chapter Thirty

White light flashed in her eyes. Charlie put out her hand, her mind fuzzy, her throat and chest still aching. "John?" She caught a hand at her face and grabbed it, holding it tight. She kissed it, pressing it to her cheek.

The hand extricated itself gently from her hold. "This is Dr. Clarkson, Charlie. I want you to wake up, if you can, and let me check your pupils again." Aside, the deep voice said, "Who is John?"

"John Rubidoux . . . he's a trainer. He's been helping with Jagger." Quentin coughed slightly in embarrassment.

The bed moved under her, lifting her, and she blinked out at them, her stepfather and the doctor. The ICU ward at their back remained a dim background. Quentin paced back and forth.

"Dad, don't make it sound like I've been sleeping with the stable boy."

Quentin halted in his tracks. "Well? Have you?"

She felt her face warm. "I don't have to answer that."

Clarkson took her pulse, his hand almost hot on her wrist. "I'd say she's been a bit too busy dodging fires anyway, Quentin."

He shrugged his shoulders heavily before saying, grudgingly, "I want to thank you for driving down here I the middle of the night."

Wade leaned over Charlie, his face intent on hers, his hand holding a pinpoint flashlight, catching her wide-eyed and making her see spots as he checked the pupil reflex. He put his hand out, two fingers extended. "Squeeze my fingers, both hands."

Then, conversationally, he said to Quentin, "Think nothing of it. I don't like hearing the news I heard earlier. She seems to be much better now. She's off the ventilator. According to the charts, she's already had one inhalation therapy. They might even release her in the morning. So where's Mary?"

"I sent her home." Quentin rubbed his face as if trying not to acknowledge his own fatigue.

Wade Clarkson bent over her again. His dark blue eyes looked at her, piercingly. "So tell me what happened, young lady."

"I smelled fire at the back of the house."

"Just like that?"

"No. John was over. He left . . . to check on the

dogs at his kennel. I went in, fixed some ice tea, and went to my studio to look through my bookshelves."

"And that's when you smelled fire?"

He put her hands out in front of her, balancing them on his, dropping his suddenly, checking motor reflex.

"Well, not just like that."

"Charlie, are you having seizures again?" He did not look at her as he pulled her chart and reviewed it, walked to a monitor and picked the tape up to check the readings that had spilled out of it.

She did not answer right away. She look at Quentin, who made a face of encouragement.

Wade Clarkson said mildly, "Charlie, I need to know what's happening in that mind of yours. There are things tests can't tell me."

"Yes." Ashamed, she stared down at her hands, folded the hem of her sheet down, smoothed it.

"I need to know, if you can tell me, what the seizure feels like. Before, during, after. If you get any warning. If you smell anything or things seem peculiar somehow."

"Midnight comes."

He had dropped the hospital chart back in place and begun making notes in his own file folder. He paused, pen in midair. "The middle of the night?"

"I told you once," she reminded him.

Wade smiled slightly. He drew a stool up and sat by the side of her bed. "As special as you were, and are, I have to confess . . . I don't remember every moment Dr. Katsume and I spent with you. Tell me again."

"It's like . . . it's like a black cloud that covers me. And in it . . . voices. Visions. I don't remember what they are."

"Do you usually lose consciousness?"

Charlie looked at him. "I'm on the inside, I don't know. I think I do."

"And what happens afterward?"

"I paint."

"Always?"

"Usually."

"Do you paint other times?"

"I did. Until the operation."

He nodded.

"Is every seizure you have Midnight? Or only some of them?"

That gave her pause. She started to shake her head, then realized she was wrong. Clarkson noticed her hesitation and said to Quentin, "She's describing a fugue state. I would say from the tumor causing pressure, except that—" He stopped abruptly and stood. He spent a moment as if searching for the right words, then asked, "Charlie, are you painting again?"

"Yes."

Quentin started. "Those were new canvases?"

She nodded.

"Janie's got them at the gallery. She'll have the sense to catalog them."

"I need to see them, Quentin."

Charlie went cold. "Let me show them to you."

The doctor considered her a moment, then inclined his head. "If they discharge you, and you feel up to it. If not today, then perhaps tomorrow. I'm staying with the Lavermans today. George asked me down for a round of golf and dinner. Personally, I think he's sizing me up for the tournament." Wade laughed softly.

"I can't thank you enough, Clarkson," Quentin said again, and pumped his hand.

"You can thank me by convincing Charlie to trust me, and work with me. I don't want to have to open her up to see what's going on in that interesting skull of hers." Clarkson looked at her then, really looked into her eyes, measuring her. "I want you to trust me, Charlie, and to confide in me. I want you to tell me what it is you see, and hear, and when you need to paint, or want to paint." He stopped as the elevators doors opened suddenly on the floor, and a dog's bark rang out.

Clarkson turned and frowned, and put his hand on Quentin's upper arm. "Don't let her be disturbed further tonight."

"But that's John with Jagger—" she protested.

"Not tonight, Charlie." Quentin stepped out the cubicle, blocked John in the hallway. Jagger bounced a little in his harness, excited to catch her scent, looking for her. John gave her a look through the windows. She waved at him, and his face softened a little.

Clarkson shifted weight. "Tomorrow," he said, stepping over and blocking her view. He checked his watch, correcting himself. "Today . . . you'll show me the new paintings, agreed?"

Vaguely uneasy, Charlie murmured, "Agreed."

"Good. Contact my pager."

He stepped out of the unit then, patted Quentin on the back, swept his gaze over John, and went on to the elevators. John and Quentin exchanged a few more words before he waved at her, and mouthed something.

Charlie fell back onto the hospital bed as he took Jagger and left. She was not sure what he had said . . . she thought it had been, "I love you." The thought warmed her.

Hubie slogged through the wet debris and char beside John, his nose wrinkled at the smell, the aftermath, and said, "So what we have here is a fire of dubious origin."

John skirted a garden hose. The chill of coastal fog on a very early morning lay about them. He had not changed clothes, showered, or eaten. He'd called Hubie to pick him up as soon as it was light enough to see the damage.

"How is she?"

"I don't know. They wouldn't let me see her. Immediate family."

"That's a crock."

He looked at the graying edge of the sky, outlining the house. Axes had been taken to the tile roof. The front half looked like an eggshell ripped apart, its edges charred, dripping still with the water soaked into it. He did not know structures. All he knew was that the place did not look livable to him. "Nothing I could do about it. She's supposed to be released sometime today."

"So you think she was a target here?"

An arson inspector passed them, stared a moment, recognized Hubie, gave a wave and a nod and continued on, after cautioning, "Don't touch anything."

Hubie shouted after him, "Let me know what you find!" He raised his cardboard coffee cup to his lips and chewed on the rim, his ever-present cigar for once not there.

John sipped at the cold swirling mass still left in his cup.

Hubie eyed him shrewdly. "So what do you think happened?"

He shook his head. "I have no idea. But I think my dogs were let out on purpose, to get me away . . . and I know she didn't do it."

"She had two studios in the back there?"

He nodded.

"Sounds like a fire waiting to happen to me." Hubie chewed on his cup some more. "Everything right there for a pyro to play with. The paint thinner alone. . . ." He stopped and toed a sodden rectangle of what looked to be a photo album, edges blackened.

John squatted, opening it. He flipped through pages. Clippings of young Charlie, framed by Quentin Saunders and her mother, with a sardonic looking, dark-haired man standing behind them. The family had their eyes fixed with pride on an easel and painting bearing an enormous rosette ribbon, but the young man was looking at the camera, his gaze avid. John pinpointed their names in the caption. This, then, was Federico Valdor, the manager/agent who had parted from Charlie so bitterly.

He straightened, to find Hubie looking over his shoulder.

"They get younger every day," the cop observed.

"This was ten, eleven years ago," John muttered.

Hubie eased the album from his hands. "Who is Cassius?"

"Cassius?"

"Yon guy with the lean and hungry look, to quote Shakespeare." He tapped the clipping.

"Used to be her manager. He's the reason Quentin brought her dog to me." In the car, on the way over, John had reluctantly parted with enough information to keep Valenzuela mollified.

"The one Jagger bit a couple of days ago?"

John nodded.

Hubie closed the album. "Let's go take a look and see what I can find on him." He let out a sharp whistle. One of the team of investigators straightened and turned, looking at them across the debris. "Got anything yet?"

"I'd say we have isolated the origin, and it looks like an accelerator was used . . . looks like we have a definite case of arson."

"Thanks." Hubie grunted. He waved good-bye and trotted downhill to where John had retrieved his van. "Looks like we have a definite suspect, although it sounds to me like a case of killing the goose who laid the golden egg."

John shifted uneasily. "I can't argue with that except that, when the goose is gone, those eggs get rarer and pricier."

Hubie grinned. He crumpled his coffee cup and threw it to the floor of his car as he opened the door and slid in. "Follow me down to the station." He chuckled. "You still think like a cop."

"Bad habits are hard to break," John told him.

Hubie's thick fingers stabbed at the keyboard, his gaze intent on the monitor's display. "So what we have here is somebody who lives way beyond his means."

John leaned in, reading the bad check charges, the

detail of suit by a famous local heiress and art patron claiming fraudulent brokerage charges on acquisitions of artwork, and a forgery charge which had been dropped by Quentin Saunders. "That tracks with what Charlie's told me about it."

Valenzuela hummed as he refined his search. "Okay, so maybe he would torch the house to get her out and maybe lift some paintings in the havoc. But none of this relates to the paintings themselves— a con man is not a stalker. In other words, he's after the paintings because of their worth, not their content."

"I don't know that there is a connection. I'd be thrilled to find out there isn't. As far as content . . . she is scared spitless she's inspired someone to go out and do these things. You ever heard of anyone motivated by something like that before?"

"It's a crazy world, Ruby, you know that. Hardcore porn magazines, sociopathic genes, who knows what motivates some of these guys? If we knew, we might be able to stop it before they get started. Still, the fire doesn't fit the killer's pattern. I think we're dealing with nonrelated events. Valdor may be a weasel, but that doesn't mean he's a serial killer." His fingers tickled the keys. He leaned forward intently. "On the other hand . . . Hel-lo."

"What?"

"Two counts of rape, both dropped. One about ten years or so ago, the last one three years ago, and she claimed he used roofies on her." Hubie opened his desk drawer, got a cigar out, and began to unwrap it enthusiastically. "Valdor is not a nice guy sexually either. Big man, has to drug 'em unconscious first!" He snorted derisively.

John opened the photo album uneasily. Could they have been fueling each other, Valdor and the young artist . . . one feeding the other's fantasies, the other fueling the creative flame? He could not deny that the gap between killings seemed to match the gap in her paintings. It gave him a bad feeling in the pit of his stomach.

Hubie sat back. "There're no easy answers. I'll ask around. I don't need to tell you we're a long way away from building a case, even for arson."

John stood, closing the album and replacing it. Hubie put it in an evidence bag and tagged it, then dropped it unceremoniously in the bottom drawer of his desk.

Valenzuela arched an eyebrow at him. "And I don't need to tell you we've got a bad feeling about this, and to watch your girl like a hawk." He reached forward to his in-tray and pulled out a folder. "You didn't see this," he said lowly, his cigar working in his mouth. He opened it and spread out a few photos.

John leaned over his shoulder and the impact of what he saw made him reach out and grip the edge of the desk. "My God."

Clearing his throat, Hubie shuffled the photos together and closed the folder cover over them. "Autopsy report shows no sign of sexual activity or molestation. She had had a drink or two, but that's about it."

"Who was that?"

"Dinah Woolsey, daughter of one of south country's big monied families. She was well-liked, divorced—ex actually died a year or two ago, so we're not looking at him—and she did not leave a good-looking corpse even though she died young. I've managed to keep the media away from this, but I don't know how much longer I can keep it under wraps." Hubie shoved himself to his feet. "Let me walk you downstairs to the front desk."

The squad room had begun to fill.

In the stairwell, Hubie put his hand on John's elbow, and brought him to a stop. He lowered his voice. "You still have a gun?"

John nodded.

A look of guilty relief swept over Valenzuela's round face. "Good."

The detective continued down the stairs. John followed. "I don't want Charlie out there, on this."

"I wouldn't do that to you, Ruby, you know that. There's not enough evidence to think of Valdor as a suspect yet."

"But if I can find a pattern . . ."

"Then I'll find him for questioning." They hit the

landing, and the noise and clamor of the front desk area reached them before they came out of the stairwell.

Hubie's cigar sagged for a moment at the sight of cameramen, well dressed reporters with mikes, and lighting technicians swarming the reception area. Someone shouted, "There's Valenzuela!"

Like a tidal wave, they surged forward. "Lieutenant! It is true Dinah Woolsey was found dead two days ago?"

"Tell us if this is a vampire cult that killed Dinah Woolsey."

"Lieutenant, do you have any suspects yet?"

Hubie put his big square bulk in front of John, muttering "Go back upstairs and out the back way."

Unnoticed, John backpedaled and then came to a dead halt as one blonde, determined reporter from the county news channel called out, "Valenzuela, can you comment on the rumor that local painter Charlotte Saunders, whose house and studio were gutted by fire this morning, has been painting intimate details about unsolved murders? That her work has been inspiring a serial killer?"

Valenzuela's lower jaw dropped. "Where in the hell did you pull out a rumor like that?"

Ashley Lowe lowered her mike and smiled faintly at the lieutenant. "My sources are confidential."

Someone to the back of the crowd snickered. "Probably the same call from the Finley family we all got . . . hoping for new leads on her abduction and assumed murder."

A reporter for the largest paper in the country called out, "Is it true you've brought Charlie in for questioning? If not, are you aware of her whereabouts now?"

That prompted a flurry of new shouts and questions.

Hubie coughed in shocked response. He put his shoulder to the crowd, his gruff voice hard to catch above the din. "Get out of here now, Ruby."

John sprinted up the stairwell, knowing that, no matter what he did now, Charlie was out there.

Chapter Thirty-One

He slept in the rental car. He had parked it down by the beach at Dana Point, in a small seaside area, relatively isolated and alone, watching the leaden waves of the Pacific roll in and out until even his frantic mind began to grow sleepy. Then he crawled in the back, curled up uncomfortably and cramped, and slept. He woke when the sunlight streaming in seared his face, and he looked up to see it was almost midday. He got out of the car, stiff and aching, and went to the concrete block bathroom, which stank and gritted under the soles of his shoes. The toilet flushed hesitantly. The water in the sink ran clear and cold. He splashed it and looked at himself in the mirror.

The face that stared back at him reminded him of a five-day gambling binge, trying to break an unlucky streak.

Valdor leaned on the cracked basin.

RETRIBUTION

He stared back. After long moments, he took out a comb and straightened his hair. Then began a careful if limited ordering of his shirt and jacket. The one-day growth of beard he could do nothing about, but it gave him a trendy Hollywood look. He rasped his fingers across his chin.

The chips were down. He had nothing to lose any more.

Valdor turned his collar down and smoothed it. Charlie Saunders would pay, one way or another.

Chapter Thirty-Two

It was one of those rare days in May, when the skies were interrupted by fluffy clouds crossing their shocking blue purity and the air remained crystal clear over the Laguna coastline. Mountains, in slate-blues and faint reddish-browns, framed the horizon view of the golf course, which he could faintly see. Over the balcony of his hilltop home lay the wild slopes of the canyon . . . the small villagelike environment below, in reality the clever shell of the Wood Chip Celebration, open-air booths with roofs and stages and platforms built into a labyrinth whimsically hugging the foot of the hill. In little more than a month, that village would burgeon with artists and their wares of everything imaginable, and at night, music from different local bands would drift up the hillside. But it was the other view which drew him, farther away, like a Shangri-la beckoning him with its cultivated tranquility.

RETRIBUTION

The greens on the course had just been clipped and prepared for the upcoming tournament, tee times were open and on time and the duffers had all gone to play somewhere else. He'd taken the day off and had already been out.

He'd even gotten a hole in one.

He sat, relaxed, on the patio, overlooking those verdant acres and listened to the ice cubes tinkle pleasantly in his glass as he sipped his Scotch . . . the finest one he had, not the social bottle. . . and thought about taking in a second round. He had time. Relatively speaking.

Yet the perfection of the day was something he wanted to savor a bit longer before trying to stretch it. He crossed his legs at the ankles as he put his feet up on the patio table and lay back even more comfortably in his chair.

The ice cubes had all but melted and the sippin' Scotch was less than half gone, and he was contemplating getting more ice and freshening up the Scotch when a shadow fell across him.

Laverman had not heard the approach . . . but he had left the sliding door open, and the marbled interior floors of his spacious home were not conducive to sound. He did not startle as the shadow instantly cooled the feel of the sun.

"A nice day," the visitor said.

"Yes," he agreed wholeheartedly without looking back to see who it was, for he knew the voice well.

"I went by the clubhouse first. I saw your hole in one posted. Congratulations."

Laverman beamed. "A beautiful shot that was. It felt good all the way through the swing. I could feel how right I hit it . . . one bounce and it rolled right in. Sweet." He downed the last of his Scotch in one swallow and felt the mellowness bloom inside him. He set the crystal glass down on the small table by his elbow.

"Shots like that are one in lifetime."

"Not quite," Laverman replied, "but close."

A lull came in the conversation, but it was not the comfortable lull between friends . . . it hung there, as though it knew it needed to be filled with something, and Laverman felt his first twinge of uneasiness.

The visitor finally filled that gap.

"You called me, George."

His heart gave him one of those squeezing, painful flutters that he was all too familiar with, in response.

"I know."

He watched the course. Saw a white egret float slowly over the brook that crossed the holes and land smoothly, then walk long-legged to a dot of white among the verdure. A golf ball? An egg, perhaps. He could not tell from where he sat.

After a moment, he said, "I thought of playing another nine holes."

"You can, if you wish." Pause. "After you've begun."

"Can I?" A genuine smile of delight split his weathered face. He ran his hands through his hair.

"Why not? If it's what you want to do. It might even be easier on Louise that way."

He nodded. He reached for the portable phone at his side and phoned the clubhouse. A few terse words and he was all set.

"They have room. I can tee off in twenty minutes. A perfect day," Laverman added in great satisfaction.

"Good."

The shadow slicing across him leaned forward slightly and dropped a couple of pills by the empty crystal glass.

"Take these just before you tee off."

Laverman looked at them without really looking at them. He uncrossed his legs, pulled his feet down, and sat up, leaning his elbow on his knees, peering at the capsules. "How . . . long?"

"You should be able to finish your nine."

"And if I've changed my mind. . . ."

"Laverman, we've talked about this before."

He took in deep breath. "I know."

"When was the last time you felt good enough to play?"

He did not answer. It had been days and days . . . weeks. He exhaled slowly.

"Days like today are rare, and will be rarer still. We've talked about this."

He let out a softer sigh. It lanced through his tired lungs and heart. It was a precursor of the downward spiral he'd fall into, a collapse from which no medicine could ultimately save him. "I know. I remember."

Laverman put out a fingertip and rolled the capsules around. He did not recognize them from anything he had been taking over the years. If he did not know better, he would almost think they had been personally manufactured for him. Perhaps they had. One of the capsules rolled away, off the table's edge, and onto the pavement. He just looked at it, caught up in his thoughts, and it was his companion who swiftly picked it up and deposited it where it belonged.

"You do not have to do this."

But he did. They had both spent many months discussing it, and they had come to the agreement. The pleasant haze of being pain free and the Scotch would dissipate soon. He gathered himself and stood. Days like this were rare indeed.

"Do you think I'm greedy?" Laverman asked.

"Of course not. We all want another day . . . and another, and another."

He picked up the capsules and dropped them into the pockets of his golfing pants. It was warmer now and he could change into shorts, but he did not feel like it. He was comfortable in his clothes, in his skin . . . it was only his decision that he felt uncomfortable about.

"No suffering?" he asked.

"No suffering. It will be quick and painless."

"Join me?"

"I'd like nothing better, but you know I can't. And I have to go to the Peppermill later. You'll be pleased to know, George, that Charlie is painting again."

"She is?" It did please him. It gave him faith in the overall continuity of things. "You'll be here for Louise."

"Tonight, of course."

He nodded. "Thank you, my friend." He walked off the patio to the side gate, where his golf cart waited, and the trail that led to the main clubhouse and the first tee.

He did not look back at his home, his friend, his life, as he went.

Wade watched him leave.

Normally, at these moments, he was alone.

But now he knew where he could go, an altar he could kneel at, one who could offer him comfort and understanding and even vision. Furthermore, he was expected.

He headed there.

Chapter Thirty-Three

He walked in the back gate of the Peppermill estate grounds. Janie's minivan was parked out front; otherwise the gallery seemed deserted. It would not be, Valdor mused, once the word of new paintings leaked out. His palms itched as if he already had the canvases in his hand. The number of them could be a problem if his Japanese buyer turned out not to be interested.

But he was not too worried about that. From the quickly scanned view he'd had, they all seemed to be interlocked, almost like animation cells, of a singular, catastrophic event. Whoever bought them would be most interested in keeping all of them together, to keep the story intact. His only worry would be shipping them out quickly, undiscovered, but he had connections for that. It would be a simple matter to take a razor and cut them from their plain stretch frames, roll them, and dispose of them appropriately.

RETRIBUTION

He, of course, would follow them out of the country. From there, he could handle the black market auctioning and pay his debts. All it would take was timing and planning. He had already called and made plane reservations.

Valdor found the back door open. He slipped inside with little worry that Janie would hear him. She would have her head buried in paperwork or catalogs, as usual, her thin, freckled face squeezed into a prune-shaped expression of concentration. He climbed the back stairs to the storage loft quietly, one wooden step at a time, listening to it creak softly under his weight, knowing that the whole building creaked and stirred and murmured, and that Janie would think nothing of it.

Upstairs, he found a shipment of paintings still cartoned, box cutters lying across their wrappings. Handy tools for almost any need, box cutters. With a smile, he took one and slipped it into his pocket.

Now all he needed was the patience to wait. He coiled up by a tiny window that looked down on the gallery, making himself comfortable on wooden crates holding the remnants of a ceramics exhibit, watching the floor below, peering into a labyrinth of art. There would come a moment, in a few hours, when Janie would close up the gallery and head down the street to a small corner tea shop, where she would sit and have a pot of stout English tea, and raisin scones, and perhaps a finger sandwich of some kind, and dream about going home to London on holiday. She was a creature of habit, Janie was, and Valdor knew he could count on that.

All he had to do was wait for his opportunity.

"I'm not letting you take my daughter anywhere. I have security on my grounds. No one will bother us there. This will blow over as soon as another news story comes down the road." Quentin Saunders put his shoulders back, stared angrily at John, and set his jaw. His rising voice attracted attention throughout the ICU. John could see nursing staff stop and peer at the room curiously.

"In the meantime, she'll be hounded."

"It was your meddling that set this off."

"I can't deny that. But what I did, I did to give Charlie peace of mind. She'll be safe with me. If I can connect Valdor to any of this—through the paintings—Hubie will be able to move in and pick him up for questioning. I have Jagger and Flint out in the car. If we hurry, we can get her out of here before the media find out she's at Sunset. The clock is ticking, Quentin. You're right, she'd be safer at your place . . . but sooner or later she's got to help me match those paintings to dates. The media is following a blood trail and they're not going to leave you alone if they think they have a story. You and I both know they're going to go for the throat." John faced Quentin down.

RETRIBUTION

Charlie had been bent over, fastening her brace. Her clothes reeked of smoke. She straightened. "Don't forget, Dr. Clarkson planned to meet me there, as well."

Mary took her husband's arm. "She'll be all right with John and the dog, Quentin. And if Wade can look at those paintings and get any understanding at all of the tumor . . ."

Quentin flinched as if to shake Mary off, then caught himself, and instead drew her in. He took the release papers from the hospital, folded them, and put them in his suit jacket, a gesture which seemed to reinforce him. "I blame you for this," he said to Rubidoux.

"After it's done and finished, and Valdor is in custody, I'll take all the blame you want. Right now, Charlie is all the matters."

The two men stared into each other's eyes. Then, abruptly, Quentin lowered his.

"Get the hell out of here."

John took Charlie's arm. "We're going out through emergency. Just stay with me, if you can."

She nodded and gave a slight, raspy cough. Mary gave her a hug and a kiss as they passed by.

John felt her leaning on him as he steered her through the hospital corridors. The sound of her breathing bothered him. He stopped once or twice to let her catch her breath.

"Are you all right?"

"My lungs feel like sandpaper, but they said that is normal, for a couple of weeks." Charlie entwined her arms around his. "You said you've got Jagger?"

"Waiting and anxious in the van." He rubbed her shoulder.

"Not as anxious as I am. Without him, I feel like my right arm has been cut off." She gave a slight shudder.

"What is it?"

"Just . . . just a chill." She chewed on the edge of her lower lip. "It's going to be rough, isn't it?"

"For a couple of days, yes. If there is any connection between your paintings and his activities, it might stay that way." He urged her into the elevator used only by staff.

"It doesn't matter. I have to do this. I have to know." She waited until the elevator door closed, shutting them away. "Don't leave me, John. I don't want to do this alone."

He drew her close. "I couldn't leave you now if I wanted to. Me and Jagger . . . we think you're the best thing this world has to offer."

That made her giggle. "Better than kibble?"

"Infinitely. A close run with a nice, juicy steak, though."

Charlie put her chin up, laughing. "I'm glad I understand my place in the scheme of things."

The ER was crowded with sick and mildly injured, who took little note of them as they wove their way through the sitting room and out the ambulance entrance.

John had his van parked there and handed her up to the front seat.

Jagger started chuffing and grumbling the minute he opened the door. He rattled the portable cage. Charlie put her hand back to its bars, tickling the dog's nose almost before she sat down. Flint raised his eye, looked at the scene with little curiosity, then dropped his wolfish face back to his paws.

As Ruby started the van, she let out a little cry. "Oh, John, his paws! He's hurt."

"Scraped up, he'll be fine. Running on asphalt will do that. His pads are tender, but he won't even notice it in another day or two."

She kept her fingers inside the cage, rubbing his silky ear, listening to the dog moan, half in complaint and half in contentment. "Makes you wonder, doesn't it?"

"How he got back?"

John pulled out of the lot and onto the service road, scanning for signs of the peculiar domed vans of the news units. To his relief, he saw none. "He's been that route with me a couple of times. They have senses we can hardly measure. I would have been more surprised if he hadn't made it back."

"Still." She rubbed the dog's knobby skull. "You're my good boy." Jagger's tail thwanged against the cage bars.

She noted John scanning the rearview mirror several times. "Even if we're free and clear . . . sooner or later, they'll come to the gallery. They'll want to look at the paintings themselves. I have to do this now, while we can."

He nodded.

They rode in comfortable silence to the gallery. Janie roused from her desk when Charlie limped in, Jagger's toenails clicking on the marble flooring. She pushed her fine, red hair away from her face and frowned in puzzlement. "Charlie! Are you all right?"

"I will be."

"How bad is it? Your father said it took out both your studios."

Charlie shuddered lightly. "I don't know yet, I haven't been back to look. He told me it was bad."

Janie hugged her lightly. "Oh, hon, I'm so sorry. If you need anything, tell me. You know I've kept duplicates of all your catalogs and such since I came aboard."

Charlie squeezed her back. "You're a peach, Janie."

The gallery manager blushed. "Hardly that." She frowned again as Charlie gave a hacking cough, then cleared her throat lightly. Janie swooped over her desk, rummaged around a drawer and brought up an unopened container of water.

"Sounds like you need this."

Charlie took the bottle gratefully. "Thanks. I need to look through the exhibit."

Janie smiled slightly. "They're all yours." She glance at John as he shifted his weight, feeling like a third wheel. She checked her watch. "How about if I take my teatime and give you some privacy?"

"That's not necessary—"

"You know I always eat lunch late. I've been working on that swap proposal with the Museum of Modern Art." Janie gathered up her purse. "Don't worry about the phones." She dialed in a code quickly to switch them over to voice mail. With a cheery wave, the thin woman ducked out the front door.

Charlie turned on her heel. Jagger flowed with her, close, happy to be in his harness, his own limp an uncanny echo of hers. She moved to the walls where her paintings had been hung. The latest were stood up at the far end, near the back, leaning up against one another.

John stood behind her as she moved from one to another, considering it. As she pointed, he took them down and stood them against the ladder used for hanging them.

Charlie took each in hand, examining her signature in the right corner, sometimes visible, sometimes half hidden by the framing. Then she turned the paintings over.

She shook her head. "The year, if we're lucky. Nothing closer than that."

"Do all artists do this?"

She smile ruefully at John. "We're an eccentric lot.

Most of us can remember our paintings by subject matter, and where we were in our life when we painted them, what moved us to paint them."

She pointed at a small painting, eight by ten, which showed a physician's caduceus, stark and bare, pared to an almost scalpel-sharp edge, against a blue-black background. "I painted that while I was waiting for surgery."

John picked up one of the paintings she'd examined, and turned it over. Faintly written in pencil on the wooden inner frame, almost hidden by the edges of the stapled down canvas, he could see V-11/86. "What is this?" He showed it to her.

Charlie frowned, studying it. Then she took it from him, and turned the canvas over. "One of my first big sales . . . I remember that."

"Could V be Valdor? Was he your agent then?"

She nodded. "This was the lead-off to a show he arranged for me. I remember, he'd sold everything almost before the first opening night. He bought champagne and Mom and Dad let me have a glass." Charlie wrinkled her nose in memory. "I didn't like it then."

He picked up another painting. Again, inconspicuously, penciled in was V and another date.

"Mom used to kid Valdor, telling him he sold the paintings before they were dry." She looked up at him, and their eyes met. "As good a dating system as any."

John pace down the wall. "Are either of them here?"

"I don't know." Charlie blushed faintly. "I haven't looked to see." She paused, then pointed.

"There is one," she said. "The abduction."

He stared at it for a moment, having seen only the magazine reproduction of it. In person, it was even more disturbing. Looking at the face, he recognized Linda Finley. Even more eerie, he could almost see her sister's and mother's faces in hers as well. He freed the ladder and put it in place to pull the painting down.

They held the painting between them, turned it over in concert, standing shoulder to shoulder. For a moment, he could not see any penciling. Then, very faintly, in the braced corner, he saw the marking.

V 12/88. Two months after Linda Finley disappeared.

"Thank God," Charlie said faintly. She let go of the painting, sagging abruptly against the ladder. She let out a sound that was half-cough, half-sob. He put the picture down and took her in his arms. "After the fact."

"Now," he told her, "all we have to do is try to understand what made you paint it in the first place."

There was a slight movement behind them. "Perhaps I can help with that."

John pivoted. Dr. Wade Clarkson smiled gently at

them. He had come in without their hearing, and stood at the entrance to the wings of Charlie's exhibit.

He took the picture up and looked at it for long moments, his large, capable hands holding the frame as if they knew instinctively its value was far greater than it appeared. Finally, he set the canvas down.

"Tell me," he said to Charlie, "about Midnight. Tell me everything you can."

Jagger pressed uneasily against Charlie's brace. His tail went down, his ears flattened. John watched him curiously.

Charlie swallowed. "When Midnight comes . . . it comes at night, usually. I can be asleep, and it wakes me. But it is like a great, dark cloud and it swallows me and all my senses and then it . . . fills me. It replaces my sight with its own, my hearing is drowned out by its voices. . . ."

"Voices," repeated Clarkson.

Jagger whined. Charlie seemed not to notice. "Yes. Voices. Midnight is never silent. It is loud, roaring . . . I try to listen . . . I can't always hear; it is too loud, too confused."

"Interesting." Clarkson leaned a hip to the wall. "When you can hear it, does it tell you what to paint?"

"No." She shuddered, the expression in her eyes hurt and vague. Jagger made a sharp sound, and bumped his nose against her leg. Charlie grew silent.

Clarkson said, "What else about Midnight?"

She did not answer.

"Charlie. Look at me. I want you to tell me if you see anything, do you get visions, feelings . . . ?"

She did not respond.

Clarkson frowned. He straightened. "Charlie." There was command in his voice, not unlike the command John used with his dogs to make them obey.

Jagger whined again, urgently. The dog's actions suddenly made him realize.

John put his hand on the doctor's sleeve. "I think we're going to see Midnight firsthand."

"She's in seizure, you mean." Clarkson stepped close, taking the pencil light from the inner pocket of his suit and checking her eye response. "How do you know?"

"The dog," Ruby told him, kneeling and petting Jagger to soothe him. "You do know there are service dogs trained to be aware of epileptic seizures. Somehow they can sense the onset."

"Charlie doesn't use a dog trained for that."

"No. It appears to be a talent he's worked on all by himself."

Clarkson stayed at Charlie's side. "She's not exhibiting classical epileptic symptoms, except for the long period of inattention. If she goes into grand mal, be prepared to catch her." He looked keenly at John. "Have you seen this before?"

"No." Ruby straightened. "But I know her."

Once again, the two looked into each other's eyes. John had the eerie feeling they had crossed paths before, but he could not place it.

Clarkson replaced his pencil light in his inner suit pocket. He avidly watched her expression, her eyes. "Are you with us, Charlie? Can you hear me?"

Charlie moved abruptly, her hands going to her head, grasping her thick, long hair and knotting it lightly at her neck, drawing it out of her way. Then she went to the back wall and lined up the unframed paintings, the new ones, side by side, almost identically to the way she'd had John line them up, although the order of the third to last and next to last were reversed. Still wordless, as if the two of them did not exist, she left the isolated area of her exhibit, going to the blank walls and the easel of the acrylics artist. She stepped back, sized up the white wallboard being prepped for the new hangings, her face neutral, bland, yet intense in concentration.

She turned and put a hand back, catching the rolling table the artist had his supplies stowed in and on, her fingers moving through the items, her attention still fixed on the blank wall. She sorted by touch, found what she wanted, a handful of marking pens, grasped them, and approached the wall. She put her left hand in front of her as though she could not quite see the wall, but must find it by touch. Once the palm of her hand rested on it solidly, she popped the lid from the marker. It bounced carelessly on the floor and rolled away without a single reaction from her.

Charlie took a deep breath and began to sketch. The marking pen ink flowed as she drew without hesitation, and John watched, having seen nothing like it before, though he was reminded of the single black ink drawings of Japanese brush paintings. She started high, arms above her head, and sketched downward till she was kneeling on the floor, finished, moved a panel over and began the process again. How she knew, without seeing, when the marker gave out on her, John could not have guessed, but she did, and popped another lid off, discarding the used marker without a look back.

Once or twice she paused, and put the side of her face to the wallboard, as if she could hear the surface tell her what it wished placed upon it. Out of the flowing lines, one of the panels she filled with a sketch of him, bare-waisted, blue-jeaned, shoeless, running with Jagger. Though she sketched impressionistically, with as little absolute detail as possible, there was no doubt in his mind it was him, and it made him flush a little to see it.

Clarkson looked at him briefly, then turned away, to watch Charlie, for she had literally painted herself into a corner. Faint rivulets of sweat ran down the front her shirt, and she was breathing hard, and John looked at his watch, realizing he had been almost in as much of a trance watching her . . . and nearly two hours had stolen by.

Clarkson said, "That's enough, Charlie, don't you think? You're done now."

She gave no sign of hearing, running her hands to the corner and across the adjoining wall which had already been hung with artwork . . . masks and collages, among other things, the objects d'art rattling under her touch.

She withdrew, then paced to the easel where a landscape-sized canvas sat. She reached into the drawer and began to fetch out tubes of acrylics, setting out primary colors and mixing others. With the same quickness she'd used on the wallboard, she began to sketch on the canvas, blocking out the basic picture she prepared to paint. She picked up an aluminum rod, set it diagonally across the canvas and rested her wrist on it as she drew out the detail.

The phone rang. It startled John. He looked at it and saw the second line button blinking. Whoever called knew the main line was going to the mailbox, and also knew the second number.

He bent over the desk and picked it up.

Quentin said tersely, "They've found Valdor's rental car less than a block from the gallery. Get out, and get out now."

John dropped the phone. "We have to go." He reached for Charlie. "Dr. Clarkson, somebody potentially very dangerous to Charlie is in the area."

RETRIBUTION

He touched her and something shocked him, like a jolt of static electricity, but sharper, and he let out a short cry at the same time as she did. For a moment, her eyes blinked, and he knew she saw him. He stopped dead when he saw the canvas sketching. . . .

The lights went out. Jagger yelped. John realized that Valdor was not only close, he was *there*. He heard the swoosh and had a forearm half up to protect himself when something cold and hard struck him hard enough to drop him to his knees.

Panting, he dragged himself to one side, and the second blow grazed him. Sharp pain sent him down face first, dazed but not out. In the moment or two it took him to get his senses back, everything had become silent.

The lights came flooding on. Janie stood in the doorway, her light, frizzy red hair drifting like a cloud about her startled face. "Oh, my God," she said in horror.

Federico Valdor lay spread-eagled on the floor, a box cutter buried in his throat, a pool of crimson gushing to frame his head and shoulders.

Of the good doctor and Charlie, there was no sign at all.

Chapter Thirty-Four

John held the bottle of refrigerator-cooled water to his head, wincing at its unyielding hardness but thankful for its chill, his other ear cradled to the phone.

"What do you mean . . . the doctor has her?"

"Quentin, Clarkson has her. I don't have time to explain now. If he stays in the area, where might he take her?"

"Why would he take her anywhere?"

"I don't know. But I do know Valdor was here . . . and he's dead. There was no way I could stop the massive blood loss. The doctor is gone, and so is Charlie. It could be self-defense or . . ." Ruby paused. The nagging image of that canvas stayed with him. The painting she had been about to do. That was missing also, as was Jagger.

Janie stood by the desk, dancing lightly, singing a nearly inaudible song to herself. She bent over to pick up the aluminum bar and held it lightly, looking at the flecks of blood and hair on it. "The mahl bar is ruined," she said absently.

Ruby looked at it. The contact with his head had been enough to bend it slightly.

"I'll be there in ten minutes," Quentin told him. "There's only one place I can think of he might go."

"And pray to God you're right."

Midnight left, as it always did, Charlie a remnant left behind, disoriented, stale, helpless. Jagger had his head on her knee, and raised it, nudging at her. She blinked, and pulled his warmth close to her. Her throat hurt, and as she took a deep breath, she realized she sat in the rear seat of a car.

She looked at the back of her physician's head. "Dr. Clarkson?"

He turned briefly. "Charlie, how are you?"

"I am . . ." she took a deep breath. "I am alone." She sat up, more alert. "Where's John?"

"There was some trouble at the gallery. He suggested I take you away for a bit while he settled it." Wade skillfully maneuvered the big car up the winding Laguna Road.

"Where?"

"The Lavermans. I'm sure you've been up here before."

"Once or twice." She felt uneasy. She looked at her hands. Small dots and lines decorated them. She examined them. They looked as though she had been using marking pens . . . quickly, without heed to being meticulous. She smelled her fingers, and the smell was unmistakable. What had she done?

They reached the crest of the hill. Wade pulled into a drive and got out. He opened the back door and urged both of them out. As she started to the front door, her hand on Jagger's harness, she saw the doctor lean back into the car and pull a canvas out.

She halted at the entryway to the house, the elaborate Chinese red carved door, for luck, Louise Laverman had always said. Wade carried the canvas so she could not see the face of it. "What is going on?"

"You were having a seizure. John got word that Valdor was in the neighborhood. He suggested I pack you out as soon as possible. Apparently Valdor's been stalking you." Wade got out a set of keys, hefted them, picked out a key, and opened up the Lavermans' front door. "George is in no shape to be hospitable this evening, nor is Louise, I'm afraid, but we can wait here until things shape up."

She followed him in. "What's wrong with George?"

"He died this afternoon. Keeled over on the seventh hole, I'm told. Louise is in the bedroom. I have her sedated. She took it very hard."

Charlie stumbled. Jagger groaned as she bumped him, forcing him to misstep on his sore pads. "He's dead?"

"Yes."

"I knew he'd been ill, but he still seemed so vigorous—" Charlie paused, the shock taking words away from her.

Wade Clarkson, however, did not seem to be concerned. He crossed the vast house until he reached the formal sitting room. Charlie trailed after him. The only two paintings of the trilogy Retribution sat on exhibition easels. She paused, looking at them.

Louise had brought them down for a showing at their anniversary dinner . . . a dinner which would now never take place because George had died.

The doctor began dragging the easels apart, setting one on either side of a Chippendale antique chair. He had the unframed canvas in his hand and set it on the seat of the chair, still turned about.

"What are you doing?"

He looked at her, and smiled.

"You did more than tell me about Midnight, you showed it to me yourself. I feel honored, Charlie, to have seen you at work."

A wrongness prickled at her, turning her cold. She gripped Jagger's harness. "Does John know where I am?"

"We really didn't have time to discuss that. He wanted me to bring you somewhere safe." Wade perched on the edge of another chair. "Do you realize what an extraordinary individual you are, Charlie?"

She listened, almost afraid to breathe.

"I knew it when I saw your paintings, of course, but I had no real idea of the breadth of your scope till you began painting again."

She decided she did not want to take credit for her art. "It's not me, you know it's not. It's that . . . thing . . . growing inside me."

Clarkson continued to smile, the professional, clinical smile that did not reach his deep blue eyes. "You have no growth, Charlie. The second reading came back clear, with the determination that the first reading had been a False Positive."

"A what? What are you talking about?"

"A False Positive is when an MRI gives an erroneous reading for a lesion or cancer growth. Our imaging equipment at the clinic is a little more powerful. It showed you as clear."

"I don't understand."

"You are not afflicted. You don't need my skills as a surgeon. But you need me, Charlie, and I need you. Look."

And he turned about the unfinished painting, set up between the two paintings of Retribution.

Staggered, Charlie backed into the wall, dropping Jagger's harness.

His artistic eye could not be faulted. If ever she had painted the third painting of the trilogy, this would have been it.

A rising angel, from ashes, its wings outflung . . .

those wings suggested in the paintings to either side of it, their feathered tips. . . .

There was more, of course. Hands being washed in what looked like blood from a bleeding heart.

And still more.

Clarkson stood. "You understand me, my skill, my work, better than anyone I have ever met except perhaps for Abby."

His words drew her shocked stare from the sketched out painting and she knew she looked into the eyes of a murderer. She recoiled and felt herself moving out onto the patio. He stood between her and the front door, blocking her, trapping her.

"What do you want from me?"

"What anyone wants from an artist. I want your vision, Charlie. I want that singular, gifted view you have of the world." Clarkson raised a hand. "I have been out there alone . . . for a long time now. I did not think I would ever find anyone who understood, until I saw your paintings." He brushed his hand over his dark hair, and his blue eyes looked at her with an expression of infinite gentleness. "Show me what you see. Paint for me. Find that divine spark and let me see it. Guide me."

She backed up another step. Jagger's low thundering growl began to rise slowly in his throat. "You kill people."

"I am a physician. I hold life in my hands every day. And there are times when you have to say to yourself, 'Should this life continue? To what lengths should it suffer and strive? Is it worthy of another's life so that it can go on?' And it begs judgment of me . . . anoints me so that I can save others . . . sometimes I have to take that sacrifice." He made a motion of washing his hands, a ritual ablution, as though cleansing and rinsing them through water, ending with his hands in front of him, elbows bent, fingers upward. "Those who died, deserved to. And they died so others could live. My hands . . ." He lifted them, observing them. "Blessed with the warmth of their sacrifice."

Charlie shuddered. She could see the crimson running down, like water, flowing over his hands and dripping to the patio. She felt her throat tighten. Jagger whined sharply.

He smiled at her. "It is a burden few could share. But you can look into a soul and tell me, be my beacon, show me who needs to die so that others may live."

She stepped back abruptly. Midnight pressed close to her; she could feel its suffocating presence, but it was not one voice. It was a multitude, crying to her, begging her.

Reveal the truth.

Bring us Retribution.

She understood at last what had afflicted her life. A haunting . . . come to her . . . an appeal for truth, for help beyond the ordinary borders of mortal life.

418

"I paint," she said shakily, "to give the murdered a voice. I see . . . so that they can speak." She reached down and with two quick jerks, ripped open the velcro straps on Jagger's harness, freeing him, pointed at Clarkson, and ordered, "Take him down!"

Jagger leaped, his body a golden flash. Wade moved aside, his hand sweeping down in a clubbing motion, brutal, unafraid. He struck. Jagger yelped and fell heavily to the patio, moved once, and lay still.

Charlie stood alone. He watched her carefully without seeming to note that she waited for him to make his next move.

"It would have been nice," he said, "to have shared the rest of the journey with you."

She knew then he was going to kill her as well.

Charlie looked at Jagger, who lay on the deck motionless, his tail flat and his eyes unmoving. Her throat tightened. She thought she saw his ribs lift slightly with a breath. Charlie closed her eyes. She dare not think the dog could save her now.

She gathered her strength to do whatever she had to do. A breeze came up the cliff, smelling of the ocean. It chilled her but she was already too cold to shiver. She took another swaying step.

He looked at her sharply. "What are you doing?"

"Nothing," Charlie said.

His hand twitched as if thinking of action on its own. Charlie took a half step backward as his attention flickered to the front of the house where head-lights slowly panned across the twilight.

"I won't let you suffer, Charlie." His voice lay across her, soothingly, a benediction.

She felt the low flagstone wall at the back of her legs. The edge of the stone cut roughly into her bare skin, but she knew the touch was gentle compared to what she must be facing.

The car headlights panned slowly away from the front of the house. She took a deep breath, realizing she had been holding it until the car moved away. He also took a deep breath. Then he ran his hand through his hair, brushing it out of his eyes.

Jagger suddenly jerked as if jolted awake. His sharp whine made them both jump and in that moment Wade took his eyes off her, and she knew she had but seconds to act.

Charlie threw herself over the balcony.

Chapter Thirty-Five

She hit with a thud that should have taken the breath out of her, but she did not feel it. Sage and mesquite and scrub brush bent under her as she scrambled to her feet, then half fell, half tumbled downslope. As purple shadows arched down the foothill, she slid and pitched toward the canyon below. Behind her, she heard a faint muffled curse and then a heavy thud as another body landed behind her.

Below, she could see the empty booths and labyrinth of the Wood Chip Celebration grounds. Beyond it, the main road through the canyon. As long shadows stabbed across the terrain, Charlie threw herself downward. Brush and thorn stabbed and tore at her. She pitched headlong, heedless, swimming through it, standing and running when she could before losing her balance again.

Once inside the labyrinth, he could never find her.

It was her only chance, if she did not break her neck getting there.

The slope grew steeper. She slid on her butt, hands tearing on mesquite. The crash and cursing of her pursuer sounded almost as loud as her ragged breath in her lungs.

Then, suddenly, the branches broke away under her, dropping her straight down.

Charlie fell heavily into the upper arm of the waterwheel. She lay stunned a moment, then rolled over with a groan. She'd reached the grounds. She pulled herself out of the wheel and, dangling by her fingertips, let go, falling a second time, to the deck and benched area surrounding the waterwheel. In a month or so, there would be a brook here, lazily turning the waterwheel, water endlessly circulating through the shady corner. Now the brook and pool were dry, cement being patched, its innards exposed like some great, beached animal.

Charlie skittered off the deck and hit the ground, wood chips flying from under her sneakers, her right leg aching in wicked protest. She breathed in great, painful gasps. Behind her, brush limbs crackled. She dove under the edge of the platform and began to crawl.

Underneath, the wood chips bit into the palms of her hands, drawing blood. Fine dust from past years rose, clogging her nose, her mouth, as she tried to breathe.

With her weak leg, and her raw lungs, she would not be able to run far. Footsteps drummed the deck above her.

"Charlie! Don't run from me, Charlie. I didn't mean to upset you."

She put the back of her hand to her mouth to keep her breathing from being heard, and kept crawling under the deck. Ahead of her she could see the refreshment area, the buildings intact, their signs faded, awaiting fresh painting for the summer season. Pepsi, Coca Cola, Iced Tea, Snow Cones, Chilled Wine. . . .

Spiderlike, she crept toward their facades.

Then she stopped, heart pounding, holding her breath. She could hear the footsteps above move away, head back in the other direction. Farther, farther.

Lungs bursting, Charlie exploded from under the deck, scrambling toward the refreshment stands. She rattled doors . . . locked, all locked, and he heard her, he came leaping back over the deck. She dove and rolled under a small bridge, and began crawling toward the exhibition booths.

Half the booths had been torn down. New exhibitors were coming in for the summer season, designing their own whimsical stands . . . their foundations bare and open.

Exposing Charlie.

Making it almost impossible to get to the front gate, and the road beyond, without being seen.

Twilight lowered, but not dark enough. A full moon overhead illuminated the grounds. She lay, and listened to him search for her, knowing that, inevitably, he would find her.

She reached down and carefully unfastened her leg brace. She slipped it off, then locked the knee hinges. Then she stood and began to limp her way to the gate.

He heard her. He came pounding up behind. She felt her breath sobbing in her lungs, her nose begin to run, her leg quiver as she hobbled, faster, faster. Then, like a great cat, he leaped.

She heard the split second, pivoted, both hands wrapped around her brace, and swung it at his face as hard as she could. The impact tore the brace from her hands.

He let out a scream of pain and fell limply to the ground.

Charlie gulped, hesitating, then backed up, turned, and began to run jaggedly to the gate again. Grateful tears started to stream down her face. She was free. She could see the lights on the road on the other side of the padlocked gate. She would have to climb it, but once beyond, there was help.

She wrapped her fingers around the top of the gate and pulled herself up, hooked her elbows, coughing, and tried to find the strength to hike her legs over.

Clarkson tackled her. He caught her waist with a savage noise, tearing at her shirt. He clawed at her, prying her away from the gate. Charlie tried to scream and could not gather the strength from her lungs. She clung desperately to the gatepost, her arms hugging it, his weight dragging her back, inch by inch.

He growled like a feral beast in anger.

She turned her head around, looking back, looking at her death, as her arms gave way and she slid back into his embrace.

Something growled back and lunged at him.

It struck his throat. It snarled and ripped him away from her, and Charlie crawled aside and watched as Jagger pulled the man to the ground, jaws on his neck, growling in unmistakable menace, and kept him there.

That was how John Ribidoux and her father found them.

Epilogue

Charlie picked up her art portfolio and suitcase, and stood at the edge of the great room of her parents' home. Quentin stayed on his feet, watching her. She had already said good-bye to her mother inside.

"You don't have to leave," he told her.

She shook her head. "Yes, I do."

"Your place isn't rebuilt yet."

"I need a studio."

"You're going to keep painting."

She smiled slightly. "I am more the brush than the artist, I think. Midnight is the painter. And, yes, I am going to keep painting."

"I'll build a studio here."

"Dad . . . you don't have to. It's all right. You don't have to worry about what I might, or might not paint."

He looked at her gravely. He looked old, older